Praise for Patricia Highsmith
and the *Ripley* novels

"Tom Ripley is one of the most interesting characters of world literature."
—Anthony Minghella

"Mesmerizing . . . a Ripley novel is not to be safely recommended to the weak-minded or impressionable." —*Washington Post Book World*

"The brilliance of Highsmith's conception of Tom Ripley was her ability to keep the heroic and demonic American dreamer in balance in the same protagonist—thus keeping us on his side well after his behavior becomes far more sociopathic than that of a con man like Gatsby."
—Frank Rich, *New York Times Magazine*

"The most sinister and strangely alluring quintet the crime-fiction genre has ever produced. . . . This young, charismatic American protagonist is, it turns out, a murderer, a gentleman of calm amorality. It's an unnerving characterization, and time and again Highsmith pulls it off, using all the singular tools of her trade." —Mark Harris, *Entertainment Weekly*

"Highsmith's subversive touch is in making the reader complicit with Ripley's cold logic." —*Daily Telegraph* (UK)

"[Highsmith] forces us to re-evaluate the lines between reason and madness, normal and abnormal, while goading us into sharing her treacherous hero's point of view." —Michiko Kakutani, *New York Times*

"[Tom Ripley] is as appalling a protagonist as any mystery writer has ever created." —*Newsday*

"Savage in the way of Rabelais or Swift."
—Joyce Carol (

T0026564

The Boy Who Followed Ripley

Patricia Highsmith

W. W. NORTON & COMPANY
NEW YORK LONDON

Published in Great Britain by Heinemann, London, in 1980
Published in the United States by Lippincott & Crowell, Publishers,
New York, in 1980

Manufacturing by LSC Harrisonburg
Production manager: Devon Zahn

Library of Congress Cataloging-in-Publication Data

Highsmith, Patricia, 1921–1995.
The boy who followed Ripley / Patricia Highsmith.
p. cm.
ISBN 978-0-393-33211-7 (pbk.)
1. Ripley, Tom (Fictitious character)—Fiction.
2. Serial murderers—Fiction. 3. Psychopaths—Fiction.
4. Criminals—Fiction. I. Title.
PS3558.I366B69 2008
813'.54—dc22

2008005021

W. W. Norton & Company, Inc.
500 Fifth Avenue, New York, N.Y. 10110
www.wwnorton.com

W. W. Norton & Company Ltd.
15 Carlisle Street, London W1D 3BS

5 6 7 8 9 0

To Monique Buffet

The Boy Who Followed Ripley

1

Tom crept forward as silently as possible on his parquet floor, crossed the threshold of his bathroom, and paused and listened.

Zz-zzz—zz-zzz—zz-zzz.

The industrious little beasts were at it again, though Tom could still smell the Rentokill he had painstakingly injected into their exit holes, or whatever they were, that afternoon. The sawing went on and on, as if his efforts had been for nothing. He glanced at a folded pink hand towel below one of the wooden shelves and saw—already—a minuscule heap of fine, tan sawdust.

"Shut *up!*" Tom said, and slammed the cabinet with the side of his fist.

They did shut up. Silence. Tom imagined the little bugheads with saws in their hands pausing, looking at each other with apprehension, but maybe nodding also as if to say, "We've had this before. It's the 'master' again, but he'll be gone in a minute." Tom had had it before too: if he walked into his bathroom with a normal tread, not even thinking of carpenter ants, he could sometimes detect their diligent buzz before they detected him, yet one more step of his, or the turning on of a tap would shut them up for a few minutes.

Heloise thought he took it too seriously. "It will be years before they make the cabinet *fall.*"

But Tom disliked the fact that he had been defeated by the ants, that they caused him to blow their dust off clean folded pajamas when he took a pair off a shelf, that his purchase and application of a French product called Xylophene (fancy name for kerosene), and his consulting two encyclopedias at the house had been futile. *Camponotus* gnaws galleries in wood and constructs its nest. See *Campodea*. Wingless, blind, but serpentine, fleeing light, lives under rocks. Tom couldn't imagine his pests serpentine, and they were not living under rocks. He had made a special trip to Fontainebleau for good old Rentokill yesterday. Yes, yesterday he'd launched his Blitzkrieg, second attack today, and he was still defeated. Difficult of course to fire Rentokill upward, as one had to do, because the holes were on the underside of the shelves.

The *zz-zz-zz* resumed, just as the music of *Swan Lake* from the gramophone below stairs swung gracefully into another gear too, an elegant waltz as if to mock him, as the insects were doing.

All right, give it up, Tom told himself, *for today anyway.* But he had wanted today and yesterday to be constructive: he had cleaned out his desk, thrown papers away, swept the greenhouse, written business letters, one an important one to Jeff Constant at Jeff's private address in London. Tom had been putting that letter off, but today he had written a letter which he asked Jeff to destroy at once: Tom advised absolutely no more pretended discoveries of Derwatt canvases or sketches, and Tom had asked rhetorically weren't the profits from the still flourishing art materials company and the art school in Perugia sufficient? The Buckmaster Gallery, specifically Jeff Constant, a professional photographer but now a part owner of the Buckmaster Gallery along with Edmund Banbury, journalist, had been toying with the idea of selling more of Bernard Tufts's failures, or not-so-good imitations of Derwatt's work. They had succeeded up to now in this, but Tom wanted it stopped for safety reasons.

Tom decided to take a walk, have a coffee at Georges' and change his thoughts. It was only half past 9 p.m. Heloise was in the living room, talking away with her friend Noëlle in French. Noëlle, a married woman who lived in Paris, was staying the night, but without her husband.

"Succès, chéri?" Heloise asked brightly, sitting up on the yellow sofa.

Tom had to laugh, a little wryly. "*Non!*" He went on in French. "I admit defeat. I am vanquished by carpenter ants!"

"A-a-aaaaah," Noëlle groaned sympathetically, then laughter bubbled out of her.

She was no doubt thinking about something else, dying to get back to her conversation with Heloise. Tom knew they were planning an Adventure Cruise in late September or early October together, maybe to the Antarctic, and they wanted Tom to come too. Noëlle's husband had already firmly declined: business reasons.

"I'm going to take a little walk. Back in half an hour or so. Need any cigarettes?" he asked both of them.

"Ah, oui!" said Heloise. She meant a pack of Marlboros.

"I stopped!" said Noëlle.

For at least the third time that Tom could remember. Tom nodded, and went out the front door.

Mme. Annette had not closed the front gates as yet. He would do it on his return, Tom thought. He turned left and walked toward the center of Villeperce. It was coolish, for mid-August. Roses bloomed in profusion in his neighbors' front gardens, visible behind wire fences. Daylight Saving Time made it lighter than normal, but Tom suddenly wished he had brought a flashlight for the walk home. There were no proper sidewalks on this road. Tom breathed deeply. Think of Scarlatti tomorrow, of the harpsichord instead of carpenter ants. Think of taking Heloise to America in late October, maybe. It would be her second trip. She had loved New York, and found San Francisco beautiful. And the blue Pacific.

Yellowish lights had come on in some of the small houses in the village. There was Georges' slanting red *tabac* talisman above the door, with a glow of light below it.

"Marie," Tom said with a nod as he walked in, greeting the proprietress who was just then slamming a beer down on the counter for a customer. This was a working-class bar, nearer to

Tom's house than the other bar in the village, and often more amusing.

"Monsieur Tome! Ca va?" Marie tossed her curly black hair with a trace of coquetry, and her big mouth, bright with lipstick, gave Tom a reckless smile. She was fifty-five if she was a day. "*Dis-donc!*" she yelled, plunging back into conversation with two male customers who were hunched over pastis at the counter. "That asshole—that *asshole!*" she shouted as if to gain an ear by this word which was bandied about many times a day in the establishment. With no attention from the roaring men who were now talking simultaneously she continued, "That *asshole* spreads himself like a whore who takes on too much work! He deserves what he got!"

Was she talking about Giscard, Tom wondered, or a local mason? "Café," Tom put in, when he got a split second of Marie's attention, "and a packet of Marlboros!" He knew Georges and Marie were pro-Chirac, the so-called Fascist.

"Eh, Marie!" Georges boomed in baritone from Tom's left, trying to quiet his wife down. Georges, a tub of a man with fat hands, was polishing stemmed glasses, putting them back daintily on the shelf to the right of the cash register. Behind Tom a noisy table football game was in progress: four adolescent boys whirled rods, and little lead men in lead shorts kicked a marble-sized ball as they spun backward and forward. Tom suddenly noticed, on his extreme left round the curve of the bar, a teenaged boy whom he had seen on the road near his house a few days ago. The boy had brown hair and wore a workman's jacket of the usual French blue, blue jeans too, as Tom recalled. When Tom had first seen him—Tom had been opening his gates one afternoon for an expected visitor—the boy had moved from his position under a big chestnut tree across the road and walked off, away from Villeperce. Had he been casing Belle Ombre, watching the family's habits? Another minor worry, Tom thought, like the carpenter ants. Think about something else. Tom stirred his coffee, sipped it, glanced at the boy again and found the boy looking at him. The boy at once lowered his eyes and picked up his beer glass.

"'Coutez, Monsieur Tome!" Marie was leaning over the counter toward Tom, and she jerked a thumb toward the boy. "Américain," she whispered loudly over the awful racket of the jukebox which had just started up. "Says he's over here to work this summer. Ha-ha-haah!" She laughed hoarsely, as if it were hilarious for an American to work, or maybe because she believed there wasn't any work to be had in France, hence the unemployment. "Want to meet him?"

"Merci, non. He works where?" Tom asked.

Marie shrugged, and picked up a cry for beer. "Oh, you know where to stick *that*!" Marie yelled merrily at another customer as she pulled the beer tap.

Tom was thinking about Heloise and the possible American tour. They ought to go up to New England this time. Boston. The fish market there, Independence Hall, Milk Street and Bread Street. It was Tom's native territory, even though he would hardly know it now, he supposed. Aunt Dottie, of the grudging $11.79 presents in the form of checks in the old days, had died, leaving him $10,000, but not her stuffy little house there, which Tom would have liked. Tom could at least show Heloise the house in which he had grown up, show it from the outside. Tom supposed that Aunt Dottie's sister's kids had inherited the house, since Aunt Dottie had no children of her own. Tom put seven francs down on the bar top for his coffee and cigarettes, glanced at the boy in the blue jacket again and saw him paying too. Tom put out his cigarette, called "'*Soir!*" to no one in particular and went out.

Now it was dark. Tom crossed the main road under the not very bright light of a street lamp, and entered the darker road on which his house sat a couple of hundred yards away. Tom's road was almost straight, two-lane and paved, and Tom knew it well, but was glad of the approach of a car whose lights enabled him to see the left side of the road on which he was walking. As soon as the car had passed, Tom became aware of quick but soft steps behind him, and turned.

A figure had a flashlight. Tom saw blue jeans and tennis shoes. The boy from the bar.

"Mr. Ripley!"

Tom tensed. "Yes?"

"Good evening." The boy stopped, fiddled with the flashlight. "B-Billy Rollins, my name is. Since I've got a flashlight—maybe I can walk you home?"

Tom vaguely saw a squarish face, dark eyes. He was shorter than Tom. His tone was polite. Was this going to be a mugging, or was he overanxious tonight? Tom had only a couple of ten-franc notes on him, but he didn't fancy a scuffle tonight either. "I'm all right, thanks. I live very nearby."

"I know. Well—I'm going the same way."

Tom cast an apprehensive glance at the darkness ahead, then walked on. "American?" he asked.

"Yes, sir." The boy was pointing his flashlight at a careful angle ahead, convenient for both of them, but his eyes were more on Tom than on the road.

Tom kept his distance from the boy, and his hands hung free for action. "You're on vacation?"

"In a way. Working a bit too. Gardener."

"Oh? Where?"

"In Moret. Private house."

Tom wished another car would approach, so he might get a better look at the boy's expression, because Tom sensed a tension that might be dangerous. "Where in Moret?"

"Chez Madame Jeanne Boutin, seventy-eight Rue de Paris," the boy replied promptly. "She has a fairly big garden. Fruit trees. But mainly I do weeding—mowing."

Tom clenched his fists nervously. "You sleep in Moret?"

"Yes. Madame Boutin has a little house in the garden. There's a bed and a sink there. Cold water, but it's all right in summer."

Now Tom was genuinely surprised. "Unusual for an American to choose the country instead of Paris. Where're you from?"

"New York."

"And how old are you?"

"Going on nineteen."

Tom would have thought younger. "You've got working papers?" Tom saw the boy smile for the first time. "No. Informal arrangement. Fifty francs a day, which is cheap, I know, so Madame Boutin lets me sleep there. She even invited me for lunch once. Of course I can buy bread and cheese and eat in the little house. Or in a café."

The boy wasn't from the gutter, Tom could tell from the way he spoke, and from the way he pronounced Mme. Boutin, he knew some French. "How long has this been going on?" Tom asked in French.

"Cinq, six jours," the boy replied. His eyes were still on Tom.

Tom was glad to see the big elm which slanted toward the road, which meant his house was some fifty paces farther. "What brought you to this part of France?"

"Oh—maybe the forest of Fontainebleau. I like to walk in the woods. And it's near Paris. I stayed in Paris a week—looking around."

Tom was walking more slowly. Why was the boy interested in him enough to know his house? "Let's cross."

The beige gravel of Belle Ombre's front court showed below the door light just a few yards away now. "How is it you knew where my house is?" Tom asked, and sensed the boy's embarrassment in the duck of his head, the twist of the torch's light. "I saw you on the road here—two or three days ago, wasn't it?"

"Yes," Billy replied in a deeper voice. "I'd seen your name in the newspapers—in the States. I thought I'd like to see where you lived, since I was near Villeperce."

In the newspapers when, Tom wondered, and why? Tom knew he had a dossier, however. "You left a bike in the village here?"

"No," said the boy.

"How're you getting back to Moret tonight?"

"Oh, I hitchhike. Or I walk."

Seven kilometers. Why did anyone who slept in Moret come seven kilometers to Villeperce after 9 p.m. with no transportation? Tom saw a faint glow of light to the left of the trees: Mme. Annette was still up, but in her own room. Tom's hand was on one of his iron gates, which were not quite closed. "You're welcome to come in for a beer, if you like."

The boy's dark brows frowned a little, he bit his underlip and looked up dismally at Belle Ombre's two front turrets, as if whether to come in were a big decision. "I—"

His hesitation puzzled Tom still more. "My car's right there. I can drive you to Moret." Indecision. Did the boy really work and sleep in Moret?

"All right. Thank you. I'll come in for a minute," the boy said.

They walked through the gates, and Tom closed them but did not lock them. The big key was in the lock on the inside. At night it was hidden at the foot of a rhododendron near the gate.

"My wife has a friend visiting tonight," Tom said, "but we can have a beer in the kitchen."

The front door was unlocked. One light was on in the living room, but Heloise and Noëlle had evidently gone upstairs. Often Noëlle sat up late talking with Heloise either in the guest room or in Heloise's room.

"Beer? Coffee?"

"What a nice place!" the boy said, looking around from where he stood. "Can you play the harpsichord?"

Tom smiled. "Taking lessons—twice a week. Let's go in the kitchen."

They went into the hall on the left. Tom put a light on in the kitchen, opened the fridge, and took out a six-pack of Heineken.

"Hungry?" Tom asked, seeing the remains of their roast beef on a platter under aluminum foil.

"No, sir. Thank you."

Back in the living room, the boy looked at the painting "Man in Chair" over the fireplace, then at the slightly smaller but genuine Derwatt called "The Red Chairs" on the wall near the French windows. The boy's glances had taken only seconds, but Tom had remarked them. Why the Derwatts and not the bigger Soutine, of striking reds and blues, which hung above the harpsichord?

Tom gestured toward his sofa.

"I can't sit there—in these Levi's. They're too dirty."

The sofa was covered in yellow satin. There were a couple of unupholstered straight chairs, but Tom said, "Let's go up to my room."

They climbed the curving stairway, Tom carrying the beer pack and the opener. Noëlle's room was open, a light on there, and Heloise's door slightly open, and from Heloise's room Tom heard voices, laughter. Tom went left toward his room, and put on the light.

"Take my chair. Wooden," Tom said, turning his desk chair, which had arms, toward the center of the room. He opened two bottles.

The boy's eyes lingered on the square Wellington chest, its surface and brass corners and countersunken drawer pulls now, as always, polished to perfection by Mme. Annette. The boy nodded with approval. He had a handsome face, a bit serious looking, a strong and beardless jaw. "It's a *nice* life you have, isn't it?"

The tone might have been mocking or wistful. Had the boy looked up his dossier and labeled him a crook? "Why not?" Tom handed him a beer bottle. "Forgot glasses, sorry."

"Would you mind if I washed my hands first?" the boy asked with earnest politeness.

"Certainly not. Right there." Tom put on his bathroom light.

The boy bent at the basin, scrubbing away for nearly a minute. He had not shut the door. He returned smiling. He had smooth lips, strong teeth, straight dark brown hair. "That's better. Hot water!" He smiled at his own hands, then picked up his beer. "What's that smell in there, turpentine? Do you paint?"

Tom laughed a little. "I do sometimes, but today I was attacking carpenter ants in the shelves there." Tom did *not* want to talk about carpenter ants. When the boy had sat down—Tom was seated on another wooden chair—Tom asked, "How long do you intend to stay in France?"

The boy appeared to think. "Maybe another month or so."

"Then you go back to college? Are you in college?"

"Not yet. I'm not sure I want to go to college. I'll have to decide." He shoved his fingers through his hair, pushing it toward the left side of his head. Some of his hair wanted to stand straight up on top. He seemed embarrassed by Tom's inspection, and took a gulp of beer.

Now Tom noticed a small spot, a mole, on the boy's right cheek. Tom said casually, "You're welcome to take a hot shower. No trouble at all."

"Oh, no, thanks very much. Maybe I look grubby. But really I *can* wash in cold water. I do. Anybody can." The full young lips attempted a smile. The boy set his beer bottle on the floor, and caught sight of something in the wastebasket by his chair. He looked more closely. "Auberge Réserve des Quatre Pattes," Billy read from a discarded envelope. "Now that's funny! You've been there?"

"No.— They send me mimeographed letters now and then, asking for donations. Why?"

"Because just this week I was walking in the woods somewhere—east of Moret on a dirt road, and I met a man and woman who asked me if I knew where this Auberge Réserve was, because it was supposed to be near Veneux les Sablons. These people said they'd been looking for it for a couple of hours. Said they'd sent money to it a couple of times and they wanted to see the place."

"They say in their bulletins they don't welcome visitors, because they make the animals nervous. They try to find homes by post—then they write success stories about how happy the dog or cat is in his new home." Tom smiled, recalling the sentimentality of some of the stories.

"You've sent them money?"

"Oh—thirty francs a couple of times."

"Where did you send it?"

"They have a Paris address. Post box, I think."

Billy smiled now. "Wouldn't it be funny if the place didn't *exist*?"

This possibility amused Tom too. "Yes. Just a charity racket. Why didn't that occur to me?" Tom opened two more beers.

"May I look at this?" asked Billy, meaning the envelope in the wastebasket.

"Why not?"

The boy fished out also the mimeographed pages that had come in the envelope. He glanced over them, and read out loud, ". . . 'adorable little creature who deserves the paradisical home that providence has found her.' That's a kitten. 'And now to our doorstep has strayed an extremely thin brown and white terrier—fox—who is in need of penicillin and other protective injections . . .' " The boy looked up at Tom. "I just wonder where their doorstep is? What if it's a *fraud*?" He pronounced fraud as if he relished the word. "If that place exists, I'm not too lazy to find it. I feel curious."

Tom watched him with interest. Billy—Rollins, was it?—had suddenly come alive.

"Post Restante Box two hundred eighty-seven, eighteenth arrondissement," the boy read. "I wonder which post office in the eighteenth? Can I keep this, since you seem to be throwing it away?"

The boy's zeal impressed Tom. And what had given him, at such an early age, an enthusiasm for exposing frauds? "Of course, keep it." Tom reseated himself. "You've been the victim of fraud yourself, perhaps?"

Billy laughed quickly, then looked as if he were reflecting on the past to see if he had been. "No, not really. Not out and out fraud."

Some kind of deception, perhaps, Tom thought, but decided not to pry further. "And wouldn't it be amusing," Tom said, "to send these people a letter signed with a phony name saying we're wise to you, making money on nonexistent animals, so prepare yourself for a visit from the police at your—post box."

"We shouldn't warn them, we should find out where they're based and crash in. Just suppose it's a couple of tough guys living in a fancy Paris apartment! We'd have to trail them—from the post box."

Just then Tom heard a knock at his door and got up.

Heloise stood in the hall, in pajamas and a pink seersucker robe. "Oh, you have someone with you, Tome! I thought the voices were your radio!"

"An American I just met in the village. Billy—" Tom turned, drawing Heloise by the hand. "My wife, Heloise."

"Billy Rollins. Enchanté, madame." Billy, on his feet made a small bow.

Tom continued in French. "Billy is working in Moret as a gardener. He is from New York.— A good gardener, Billy?" Tom smiled.

"My—intentions are good," Billy replied. He ducked his head, and again set his beer bottle carefully on the floor beside Tom's desk.

"I hope you have a pleasant sojourn in France," Heloise said lightly, but her quick eyes had looked the boy over. "I just came to say good night, Tome, and tomorrow morning—Noëlle and I go to the antique shop at Le Pavé du Roi, then to Fontainebleau for lunch at l'Aigle Noir. Want to join us for lunch?"

"I don't think so, thank you, dear. Enjoy yourselves. I'll see you both tomorrow morning before you leave, won't I?— Good night, sleep well." He kissed Heloise on the cheek. "I'll drive Billy home, so don't be alarmed if you hear me come in later. I'll lock the house when I go out."

Billy said he could catch a ride easily, he was sure, but Tom insisted on driving him. Tom wanted to see if the Moret house in the Rue de Paris existed.

In the car with Billy, Tom said, "Your family's in New York? What does your father do, if that's not an impertinent question."

"He's—in electronics. They make measuring equipment. For measuring all kinds of things electronically. He's one of the managers."

Tom sensed that Billy was lying. "You're on good terms with your family?"

"Oh, sure. They—"

"They write to you?"

"Oh, sure. They know where I am."

"And after France, where're you going? Home?"

A pause. "I might go to Italy. Not sure."

"Is this the right road? We turn here?"

"No, the other way," the boy said just in time. "But it's the right road, all right."

Then the boy indicated where Tom should stop, at a medium-sized, modest-looking house with windows all dark now, front garden bordered with a low white wall along the pavement, closed carriage gates to one side.

"My key," Billy said, fishing a rather long key from his inside jacket pocket. "I have to be quiet. I thank you very much, Mr. Ripley." He opened the car door.

"Tell me what you find out about the animal home."

The boy smiled. "Yes, sir."

Tom watched him walk to the dark gates, shine the torch on the lock, then turn the key. Billy passed through, waved at Tom, then closed the gates. As Tom backed to turn the car, he saw the number 78 plainly visible on its blue official metal plaque beside the main door. Odd, Tom thought. Why should the boy want a boring job like this, even for a short time, unless he was hiding from something? But Billy didn't look like a delinquent. The most

likely thing, Tom thought, was that Billy had had a quarrel with his
parents or suffered a disappointment with a girl, and had hopped
on an airplane to try to forget it. Tom had the feeling the boy had
plenty of money, and was in no need of garden work at fifty francs
a day.

2

Three days later, on a Friday, Tom and Heloise sat at the table
in the alcove off the living room, breakfasting and looking
over letters and newspapers that had arrived at 9:30. It was Tom's
second coffee, Mme. Annette having brought the first to him, along
with Heloise's tea, at eight or so. A storm was blowing up, or brew-
ing, creating an atmosphere of tension that had awakened Tom at
eight, before Mme. Annette's arrival. It was now ominously dark,
not a breeze stirred outside, and there were distant rumbles of
thunder.

"A postcard from the Cleggs!" Heloise exclaimed, discovering
it under letters and a magazine. "Norway! They're on their cruise.
Remember, Tome? Look! Isn't that beautiful?"

Tom looked up from his *International Herald Tribune*, and took
the postcard Heloise extended. It showed a white ship cruising up
a fjord between very green mountains, with a few cottages nestling
in a crease of the shore in the foreground. "Looks deep," Tom said,
for some reason suddenly thinking of drowning. He was afraid of
deep water, hated swimming or trying to, and often thought that
somehow his end might be watery.

"Read the postcard," Heloise said.

It was in English, signed by both Howard and Rosemary
Clegg, their English neighbors who had a house about five kilometers away. " 'Divinely restful cruise. We play Sibelius on the cassette to keep in the mood. Love from Rosemary. Wish you both

were here in the midnight sunshine with us—' " Tom paused as thunder cracked and rumbled like a determined dog. "We're going to get it today," Tom said. "I hope the dahlias stand up." He had staked them all, however.

Heloise reached for the card, which Tom handed back. "You're so nervous, Tome. We have had storms before. I am glad it comes now and not tonight at six. I have to go to Papa's, you know."

Tom knew. Chantilly. Heloise had a standing date with her parents for dinner on Friday nights, and usually she kept it. Sometimes Tom went and sometimes he didn't. He preferred not to go, because her parents were stuffy and they bored him, not to mention that they had never cared much for him. Tom found it interesting that Heloise always said she had to go to "Papa's" instead of to her "parents.'" Papa held the purse strings. Mama was considerably more generous by nature, but in case of a real crisis—if Tom stepped out of line in some way as had nearly happened in the Derwatt mess with Bernard and the American Murchison—Tom doubted if Mama would have much clout if Papa wanted to cut off Heloise's allowance. The proper running and upkeep of Belle Ombre depended on Heloise's allowance. Tom lit a cigarette, braced himself for the next shaft of lightning with a mixture of pleasure and anxiety, and thought of Jacques Plisson, Heloise's father, a plump, pompous man with the strings of destiny in his hands (purse strings) which he held like a twentieth-century charioteer. A pity money had such power, yet of course it had.

"Monsieur Tome, encore du café?" Mme. Annette stood suddenly at Tom's elbow with the silver pot that Tom noticed trembled ever so slightly.

"I'm all right, Madame Annette, but leave the pot, I may want some later."

"I'm going to check the windows," Mme. Annette said, setting the pot on a mat in the center of the table. "Such a darkness! This will be a storm!" Her blue eyes under the Norman lids met Tom's for an instant, then she bustled away toward the staircase. She had checked the windows once, Tom thought, maybe even closed some shutters, but to check them again pleased her. It pleased Tom too. He got up restlessly, went near the window, where there was a bit more light, and looked at the People column on the back page of the *Trib*. **Frank Sinatra** was making another final appearance, this time in a forthcoming film. Sixteen-year-old **Frank Pierson**, favorite son of the late super-food tycoon **John Pierson**, had taken off from the family home in Maine, and the family was anxious after nearly three weeks with no word from him. Frank had been extremely upset by his father's death in July.

Tom remembered a write-up of John Pierson's death. Even the *Sunday Times* of London had given it a few inches. John Pierson had been a wheelchair case, something like George Wallace of Alabama, and for the same reason—someone had attempted to assassinate him. He had been enormously wealthy, not quite as wealthy as Howard Hughes, but still with a fortune that went into hundreds of millions gained by his food products: gourmet, health, and diet foods. Tom had remembered the obituaries especially because it had not been determined whether he had committed suicide by pushing himself off a cliff on his estate or whether it had been an accident. John Pierson had been fond of watching the sunsets from a cliff, and had refused to have a handrail put up, because it would have spoiled the view.

Ka-a-*rack*!

Tom flinched from the French windows, and looked wide-eyed outside to see if his greenhouse's glass windows were still intact. Now the wind came, rattling something down the tiles of the roof, Tom hoped nothing more than a twig.

Heloise was reading a magazine, indifferent to the elements.

"Must get dressed," Tom said. "You haven't a lunch date, have you?"

"Non, chéri. I am not going out till five. You are always nervous about the wrong things. This house is very solid!"

Tom managed to nod, but it seemed natural to be nervous

with lightning striking all over the place. He took the *Trib* from the table and went upstairs, and showered and shaved, daydreaming. When was old Plisson going to die, die a natural death? Not that Tom and Heloise needed money, more money, not at all. But he was such a pain in the neck, classic, like the awful mother-in-law. Jacques Plisson was of course plumping for Chirac too. Dressed now, Tom opened the side window in his bedroom and got a gust of rain-filled wind in his face, which he breathed in because it was refreshing and exciting, but he closed the window at once. What a good smell, rain over dry land! Tom went to Heloise's bedroom, and saw that the windows were closed. They hissed with the rain now. Mme. Annette was just tucking the bedcover properly over the pillows on the double bed where he and Heloise had slept.

"All secure, Monsieur Tome," she said, patting a pillow, finished, straightening herself up. Her rather short, sturdy figure seemed charged with energy like that of a much younger person. She was in her late sixties, but she had many more years ahead of her, Tom thought, and the thought was comforting.

"I'm going to take a quick look at the garden," Tom said, and turned and left the room.

He ran down the stairs, out the front door and around to the back lawn. His dahlia stakes and their strings were still holding. The Crimson Sunbursts nodded their heads crazily, but they weren't going to be blown over, neither were the frizzy orange dahlias, Tom's favorites.

Lightning broke out in the slate-colored sky to the southwest, and Tom stood waiting for the thunder as the rain wet his face. It came with an arrogant, rending sound, hollow.

What if the boy he met the other night were Frank Pierson? Sixteen years old. That was certainly more like it than the nineteen the boy had told him. Maine, not New York. When old Pierson died, hadn't there been a picture of the whole family in the *IHT*? There had been a picture of the father, anyway, whose face Tom realized he couldn't at all remember. Or had that been in the *Sun-*

day Times? But the boy of three days ago he remembered better than he usually remembered people. The boy's face was rather brooding and serious, and he didn't smile easily. A firm mouth, and level dark eyebrows. And the mole on his right cheek, not large enough to show up in the average photograph, perhaps, but a mark. The boy had been not only polite, but cautious.

"Tome!— Come *in*!" That was Heloise, shouting from the French windows.

Tom ran toward her.

"Do you want to be hit by the lightning?"

Tom wiped his desert boots on the doormat. "I'm not wet! I was thinking of something else!"

"Of what? Dry your hair." She handed him a blue towel from the downstairs loo.

"Roger's coming this afternoon at three," Tom said, wiping his face. "Scarlatti for me. I must practice this morning and after lunch too."

Heloise smiled. In the rainlight, her blue-gray eyes showed lavender spokelike radiations from their pupils, which Tom adored. Had she chosen a lavender-colored dress especially for today, Tom wondered? Probably not, and it was merely a piece of aesthetic luck.

"I was just sitting down to practice myself," Heloise replied primly in English, "when I saw you standing on the lawn like an idiot." She went to the harpsichord and sat down, sat up straight and shook her hands—like a professional, Tom thought.

He went to the kitchen. Mme. Annette was clearing out the cabinet above the sideboard to the right of the sink. She had a dust-rag in her hand, and was wiping one spice jar after another from her perch of a three-legged wooden stool. It was too early for lunch preparations, and she had probably postponed her shopping in the village to this afternoon, because of the rainstorm.

"Just want to have a look at the old newspapers," Tom said, stooping near the threshold of the next hall, which led to Mme.

Annette's quarters on the right. The old newspapers were kept in a basket with a handle, the type of basket used for firewood.

"Something in particular, Monsieur Tome? May I help you?"

"Thank you.— I'll know in a minute. American newspapers I need. I think I can do it." Tom spoke absently as he riffled through July *IHT*s. Obituary page or the news, that was the question, but he had a recollection of the Pierson items being in an upper left column of a right-hand page, with a photograph. There were only ten or so *IHT*s to look at, the others having been discarded. Tom went up to his room. Here he found more *IHT*s, but none had the write-up of John Pierson.

Heloise's Bach Invention sounded quite good from Tom's room. Was he jealous? Tom wanted to laugh. Was his own Scarlatti not going to be as good (in the ears of Roger Lepetit, of course) as Heloise's Bach this afternoon? Now Tom did laugh, put his hands on his hips, and looked at the little heap of newspapers on the floor with disappointment. *Who's Who*, he thought, and crossed the hall to the other front, turreted room which was their library. Tom pulled the *Who's Who* down, and found no entry for John Pierson. He tried *Who's Who in America*, an older volume than the English, but still found nothing on John Pierson. Both his *Who's Who*s were about five years old. And John Pierson might have been the type to refuse permission for an entry.

Heloise's third performance of the Invention concluded with a delicately ringing Schlussakkord.

Was the boy called Billy going to look him up again? Tom thought he would.

Tom practiced his Scarlatti after lunch. He could now practice with concentration for thirty minutes or more without taking a break in the garden, which was progress from the original fifteen-minute session of months ago. Roger Lepetit (anything but petit, a tall plump young man, a French Schubert, Tom thought, spectacles and curly hair) said that gardening was ruinous for a pianist's or harpsichordist's hands, but Tom preferred to compromise: he didn't

want to give up gardening, but he could perhaps leave the wrench-
ing of milk-wort or whatever to their part-time gardener Henri.
After all, he was not aiming to become a concert harpsichordist. All
life was a compromise.

By 5:15, Roger Lepetit was saying, "This is legato here. You
must make an *effort* with the harpsichord to achieve a legato—"

The telephone rang.

Tom had been trying to achieve the correct tension, the correct degree of relaxation to do the simple piece properly. He now
took a deep breath and got up, excusing himself. Heloise was
upstairs, dressing to go off to her parents', having had her lesson.
Tom picked up the downstairs telephone.

Heloise had already answered upstairs, and was talking in
French. Tom recognized the voice of Billy, and interrupted.

"Mr. Ripley," Billy said. "I've been to Paris. You know—about
the Auberge thing. Interesting—it was." The boy sounded shy.

"You found out something?"

"A little and—since it might amuse you, I thought—if you
have a few minutes around seven tonight—"

"Tonight is fine," said Tom.

They hung up abruptly, before Tom had time to ask how the
boy would get here. Well, he had gotten here before. Tom flexed his
shoulders and went back to the harpsichord. He sat up straight. He
fancied his next rendition of the Scarlatti piccola sonata was better.

Roger Lepetit pronounced it fluent. High praise.

The rainstorm had exhausted itself by noon, and in late afternoon the garden shone bright and clean in unusually dustless sunlight. Heloise departed, saying she would be home by midnight or
before. It was a drive of an hour and a half to Chantilly. She and
her mother always talked after dinner, while her father retired no
later than 10:30.

"The American boy you met is coming tonight at seven," Tom
said. "Billy Rollins."

"Oh. Of the other night, yes."

"I'll offer him something to eat. He might be here when you get back."

It was of no importance, and Heloise did not reply. "Bye-bye, Tome!" she said, picking up her bouquet of long-stemmed Shasta daisies with a single red peony, almost their last. Providently she wore a raincoat over her skirt and blouse.

Tom was listening to the seven o'clock news, when the outside gate bell rang. Tom had told Mme. Annette he was expecting a caller at seven, and Tom intercepted her in the living room and said he would let his friend in himself.

Billy Rollins was walking across the graveled stretch between the gates, which had been open, and the front door. Now he wore gray flannel trousers, a shirt, and jacket. He carried something flat in a plastic bag under his arm.

"Evening, Mr. Ripley," he said, smiling.

"Evening. Come in. How did you get here—so punctually?"

"Taxi. Blowing it today," said the boy, wiping his shoes on the doormat. "This is for you."

Tom opened the plastic bag and pulled out a record of Schubert's Lieder sung by Fischer-Dieskau, a new recording of which Tom had recently heard. "Thank you very much. Just what I wanted, as they say. But I mean it, Billy."

The boy's clothes looked immaculate, in contrast to the other evening. Mme. Annette entered to ask what they wished. Tom introduced them.

"Sit down, Billy. A beer or something else?"

Billy sat down on the sofa. Mme. Annette went to fetch beer to be added to the bar cart's offerings.

"My wife went to visit her parents," Tom said. "It's a usual Friday evening date with her."

Tonight Mme. Annette was attempting Tom's gin and tonic, with a slice of lemon. The more work Mme. Annette had, the happier she was, and Tom had no complaint about the drinks she made for him.

"You had a harpsichord lesson today?" Billy had noticed the music books on the open harpsichord.

Tom said yes, Scarlatti, and for his wife a Bach Invention. "Much more fun than playing bridge in the afternoon." Tom was grateful that Billy did not suggest that he play something. "Now your Paris trip—our four-footed friends."

"Yes," said Billy, tilting his head back as if he were thinking carefully before beginning. "I spent Wednesday morning making sure the Auberge really didn't exist. I asked in a café, also at a garage which said they'd had a couple of people asking too—and I even asked the police in Veneux. They said they'd never heard of it, and they couldn't find it on a detailed map. Then I asked at a big hotel there, and *they'd* never heard of it."

Tom knew, the Hotel Grand Veneux, probably, a name which had always made Tom think of "the big venery," suggesting a huge letch of some kind. Tom winced at his own thoughts. "You were pretty busy Wednesday morning, it seems."

"Yes, and of course I worked Wednesday afternoon, because I do put in five or six hours a day for Madame Boutin." He took a gulp of beer from his glass. "Then Thursday yesterday I went to Paris, to the eighteenth arrondissement starting with Les Abbesses Metro stop. Then Place Pigalle. I went to their post offices and asked about box two hundred and eighty-seven. That was not information for the public, they said. I asked the name of the person who was collecting, you see." Billy smiled a little. "I was in my work clothes, and I said I wanted to give ten francs to an animal fund, and wasn't that box number an animal fund. You'd have thought *I* was a crook, the way they looked at me!"

"But do you think you asked at the right post office?"

"I couldn't tell, because all the post offices in the eighteenth— or four of them—refused to say if they *had* a box two eighty-seven. So I did the next best thing—the logical thing, I thought," Billy said, looking at Tom as if he expected him to guess what he had done.

THE BOY WHO FOLLOWED RIPLEY

Tom couldn't, at the moment. "What?"

"I bought some paper and a stamp, went to the next café, and wrote a letter to the Auberge saying, 'Dear Auberge et cetera, your mimeographed establishment does not exist. I am one of the many duped—*trompés*, you know—' "

Tom nodded appreciatively.

" '—and I have allied myself with other well-meaning friends of your charitable—*fraud*. Therefore be prepared for an invasion by the legal authorities.' " Billy sat forward, and there seemed to be a struggle going on in his face or mind, between amusement and righteous indignation. His cheeks had pinkened, he smiled and frowned at the same time. "I said their *post box* would be watched."

"Excellent," said Tom. "I hope they're squirming."

"I did hang around one promising post office, hoping.— I said to a girl behind the window, how often do they come to collect? She wouldn't tell me. That's typically French, of course. Not that she was trying to protect anybody necessarily."

Tom knew. "How is it you know so much about the French? And you speak a pretty good French too, don't you?"

"Oh—we had it in school, of course. Then—a couple of years ago I—my family spent a summer in France. Down south."

Tom had the feeling the boy had been brought several times to France, maybe starting at the early age of five. No one learned decent French in an ordinary American high school. Tom opened another Heineken at the bar cart and brought it to the coffee table. He had decided to plunge in. "Did you read about the death of the American John Pierson—about a month ago?"

Surprise showed in the boy's eyes for an instant, then he seemed to be trying to remember. "I think I heard something—somewhere."

Tom waited, then said, "One of the two boys in the family disappeared. The one called Frank. The family's worried."

"Oh?— I didn't know."

Had the boy's face gone paler? "It just occurred to me—he might be you," Tom said.

"Me?" The boy sat forward, beer glass in hand, and his eyes left Tom and fixed on the fireplace. "I wouldn't be working as a gardener, I think, if—"

Tom let some fifteen seconds pass. Nothing more came from the boy. "Shall we try your record? How did you know I liked Fischer-Dieskau? From the harpsichord?" Tom laughed. He switched on the hi-fi controls, which were on a shelf to the left of the fireplace.

The piano began, then Fischer-Dieskau's light baritone came in, singing in German. Tom felt instantly more alive, happier, then he smiled, thinking of an awful deep baritone he had happened to catch on his transistor only last evening, a groaning Englishman singing in English and making Tom think of a dying water buffalo, maybe lying in mud with its feet in the air, though the words had been about a dainty Cornish maiden he had loved and lost years ago, a good many years ago, judging from the maturity of the voice. Tom suddenly laughed out loud, and realized that he was unusually tense.

"What's funny?" asked the boy.

"I was thinking of a title I made up for a Lied. 'My soul has not been the same since Thursday afternoon, when on opening a book of Goethe's poems, I discovered an old laundry list.' It goes better in German. 'Seit Donnerstag nachmittag ist meine Seele nicht dieselbe, denn ich fand beim Durchblättern eines Bandes von Goethegedichten eine alte Wäscheliste.' "

The boy was laughing too—with the same kind of tension? He shook his head. "I don't understand many German words. But it's funny. Souls! Ha!"

The lovely music continued, and Tom lit a Gauloise and walked slowly about the living room, wondering how he should proceed. Really force it and ask to see the boy's passport, ask to see something—such as a letter addressed to him—by way of settling the matter?

At the end of a song, the boy said, "I don't think I want to listen to the whole side, if you don't mind."

"Of course not." Tom switched the machine off. He put the record back into its sleeve.

"You were asking me—about the man called Pierson."

"Yes."

"What if I were to say—"The boy's voice sank low, as if someone else in the room or maybe Mme. Annette in the kitchen might be listening. "—I'm his son who ran away?"

"Oh," Tom said calmly, "I would say that's your business. If you wanted to come to Europe—incognito—it's been done before."

The boy's face looked relieved, a corner of his mouth twitched. But he kept silent, rolling his half-full glass between his palms.

"Except that the family is worried, it seems," Tom said.

Mme. Annette came in. "Excuse me, Monsieur Tome, will there be—"

"Yes, I think so," said Tom, because Mme. Annette had been about to ask if there would be two for dinner. "You can stay for a bite, can't you, Billy?"

"Yes, I'd like to. Thank you."

Mme. Annette smiled at the boy, more with her eyes than her lips. She liked guests, liked making them happy. "About fifteen minutes, Monsieur Tome?"

When Mme. Annette left the living room, the boy squirmed to the edge of the sofa and asked, "Can we take a look at your garden before it gets dark?"

Tom stood up. They went out through the French windows, down the few steps to grass level. The sun was sinking in the left corner of the horizon, glowing orange and pink through the pine trees. Tom sensed that the boy wanted to get farther away from Mme. Annette's ears, but for the moment he was taken by the scenery.

"Now this has some quality—as a layout. Nice—but not too formal."

"I can't take credit for the design. It was here. I just try to maintain it."

The boy bent to look at some London Pride (not blooming now), and he knew it by name to Tom's surprise. Then he turned his attention to the greenhouse.

Here were multicolored leaves, blossoms, plants ready to be given away to friends, all in proper dampness and rich soil. The boy inhaled as if he loved it. Was this really the son of John Pierson, raised in luxury to take over the business reins—unless that was the older son's duty? Why didn't he talk now, in the privacy of the greenhouse? But the boy kept peering at pots, and touched one plant gently with a fingertip.

"Let's go back," Tom said, a bit impatient.

"Yes, sir." The boy straightened as if he had done something wrong, and followed Tom out.

What kind of school demanded "Yes, sir" these days? A military school?

They had dinner in the alcove off the living room. The main dish was chicken with dumplings, the dumplings laid on after the boy's telephone call this afternoon, at Tom's request. Tom had taught Mme. Annette how to make dumplings in the American style. The boy ate well and seemed to enjoy the Montrachet also. He asked polite questions about Heloise, where did her parents live, and what were they like? Tom restrained himself from giving his real opinion of the Plissons, especially the father.

"Does your—does Madame Annette speak English?"

Tom smiled. "She doesn't even say 'Good morning.' Doesn't like English, I think. Why?"

The boy moistened his lips and leaned forward. More than a meter of table still separated them. "What if I were to tell you that I am the—the person you were speaking of—Frank."

"Yes, you asked that before," Tom said, realizing that Frank was feeling what he had drunk. All to the good! "You're here—just to get away from home for a while?"

"Yes," Frank said in an earnest way. "You won't give me away, will you? I hope not." He was almost whispering, trying to look at Tom steadily, but his eyes swam a little.

"Certainly not. You can trust me. You probably had your own reasons—"

"*Yes*. I would like to be somebody else," the boy interrupted, "for maybe—" He stopped. "I was sorry to run off the way I did, but—but—"

Tom listened, sensing that Frank was coming out with only part of the truth, and might not come out with much more tonight. Tom felt grateful for the power of vino and its veritas. There was a limit to how much one could lie with it, at least someone as young as Frank Pierson. "Tell me about your family. Isn't there a John Junior?"

"Yes, Johnny." Frank twirled the stem of his wine glass. He was now staring at the middle of the table. "I took his passport. I stole it from his room. He's eighteen, nearly nineteen. I can forge his signature—or at least well enough to get by. I don't mean I ever tried it before—not at all till now." Frank paused, and swayed his head as if confused by many thoughts at the same time.

"Then what did you do after you ran away?"

"I took a plane to London, stayed there for—I think five days. Then I went to France. Paris."

"I see.— And you had enough money? You weren't forging traveler's checks?"

"Oh, no, I took some cash, two or three thousand. That was easy—from the house. I can open the safe, of course."

At this moment, Mme. Annette came in to remove some dishes and to serve the strawberry—fraises de bois—shortcake with whipped cream.

"And Johnny," Tom said to start the ball rolling again, when Mme. Annette was gone.

"Johnny's at Harvard. On vacation now, of course."

"And where's the house?"

Frank's eyes swam again, as if he were thinking, which house? "Maine. Kennebunkport.— That house?"

"The funeral was in Maine, was it? I seem to remember. You left from the Maine house?" Now Tom was surprised at the boy's apparent shock at the question.

"Kennebunkport, yes. We're usually there at this time of the year. The funeral was there—the cremation."

Do you think your father killed himself, Tom wanted to ask, but he thought the question was vulgar, would be only to satisfy his curiosity, so he did not put it. "And how is your mother?" Tom asked instead, as if he knew Frank's mother and was inquiring about her health.

"Oh, she's—she's rather pretty—even though she's forty something. Blonde."

"You get along well with her?"

"Yes, sure. She's more cheerful than—than my father was. She likes social life. And politics."

"Politics? What kind?"

"Republican." Here Frank smiled and looked at Tom.

"Your father's second wife, I think." Tom thought he remembered that from the obituary.

"Yes."

"And you told your mother where you are?"

"Well, no. I left a note saying I was going to New Orleans, because they know I like New Orleans. I've stayed before at the Hotel Monteleone—by myself. I had to walk to the bus stop from the house, otherwise Eugene—he's the driver—would've driven me to the railroad station and somehow—they might've known I wasn't going to New Orleans. I just wanted to get away on my own feet, so I did, and I got to Bangor, then New York, and caught a plane over.— May I?" Frank reached for a cigarette from a silver cup. "No doubt my family rang up the Monteleone, and found out I wasn't there, so this accounts for—I know, I read it in the *Trib* which I buy sometimes."

"How long after the funeral did you leave?"

Frank struggled for the exact answer. "A week—maybe eight days after."

"Now why don't you send your mother a cable and say you're okay and in France and want to stay a while longer? It's a bore to have to hide, isn't it?" But maybe the game amused Frank, Tom thought also.

"At the moment, I happen not to want—any contact with them. I'd like to be on my own. Free." He said it with determination.

Tom nodded. "At least now I know why your hair stands up. You used to part it on the left."

"I did."

Mme. Annette was bringing a tray of coffee to the living room. Frank and Tom got up, Tom glancing at his watch. It was not even ten as yet. Why had Frank Pierson decided that Tom Ripley would be sympathetic? Because Ripley had a shaky reputation, according to the newspaper files which the boy perhaps had seen? Had Frank done something wrong too? Killed his father, maybe, pushed him over the cliff?

"Ah-hem," Tom said for no reason, swinging a foot as he walked toward the coffee table. Disturbing thought, that. And was it the first time, even, that it had crossed his mind? Tom wasn't sure. Anyway, he would let the boy come out with that one, if and when he wished to. "*Coffee*," Tom said firmly.

"Maybe you want me to take off?" asked Frank, having seen Tom glance at his watch.

"No, no, I was thinking about Heloise. She said she'd be back before midnight, but it's a long time till midnight. Sit down." Tom fetched the brandy bottle from the bar cart. The more Frank talked tonight, the better, and Tom would see him home. "Cognac." Tom poured, and poured the same amount for himself, though he disliked cognac.

Frank looked at his own wristwatch. "I'll leave before your wife gets back."

Heloise, Tom supposed, was one more person who might discover Frank's identity. "Unfortunately, they're going to widen the
search, Frank. Don't they know already that you're in France?"

"I don't know."

"Sit down. They must know. The search might even get to a
small town like Moret, once they're finished with Paris."

"Not if I wear old clothes and have a job—and another name."

Kidnapping, Tom thought. That might come next, certainly
was a possibility. Tom didn't want to remind Frank of the Getty
boy's kidnapping, that fine-tooth-comb search that had still been
futile. The kidnappers had snipped off an ear lobe to prove that
they had the boy, and the three million dollars ransom had been
paid. Frank Pierson was hot property also. If crooks recognized him
(and they would be trying more than the general public), it would
be more profitable to kidnap him than to turn the attention of the
police to him. "Why," Tom asked, "did you take your brother's passport? Haven't you got a passport?"

"Yes. A new one." Frank had sat down, in the same corner of
the sofa as before. "I don't know. Maybe because he's older and I
felt safer. We look a little bit alike. Only he's blonder." Frank
winced as if with shame.

"You get along with Johnny? You like him?"

"Oh, pretty well. Sure." Frank looked at Tom.

That was a genuine answer, Tom felt. "Got along all right with
your father?"

Frank looked toward the fireplace. "It's hard to talk about
since—"

Tom let him struggle.

"First he wanted Johnny to take an interest in Pierson—the
company, I mean, then he wanted me to. Johnny can't make it into
Harvard Business School, or he doesn't want to. Johnny's interested
in *photography*." Frank said it as if it were something bizarre, and
gave Tom a glance. "So Dad then started on me. This was—oh,
more than a *year* ago. I kept saying I wasn't sure, because it's a very

big—business, you know, and why should I want to—dedicate my
life to it." There was a flash of wrath in Frank's brown eyes.

Tom waited.

"So—maybe no, we didn't get along so well—if I'm honest."
Frank picked up his coffee cup. He had not tasted the brandy, and
maybe didn't need it, because he was talking quite well.

The seconds passed, nothing more came from Frank, and out
of mercy, because Tom could see there was more pain to come,
Tom said, "I noticed you looking at the Derwatt." He nodded
toward "Man in Chair" over the fireplace. "Do you like it?— It's
my favorite."

"It's one I don't know. I know that one—from a catalogue."
Frank said with a glance over his left shoulder.

He meant "The Red Chairs," a genuine Derwatt, and Tom
knew at once which catalogue the boy had probably looked at, a
recent one from the Buckmaster Gallery. The gallery now made an
effort to keep the forgeries out of its catalogues.

"Were some really forged?" Frank asked.

"I don't know," Tom said, with his best effort at sincerity.
"Never was proven. No. I seem to remember Derwatt came to
London to verify—certain ones."

"Yes, I thought maybe you were there, because you know the
people at that gallery, don't you?" Now Frank perked up a bit. "My
father has a Derwatt, you know."

Tom was glad to veer slightly. "What one?"

"It's called 'The Rainbow.' Do you know it? Beige colors
below, and a rainbow mostly red above. All fuzzy and jagged. You
can't tell what city it is, Mexico or New York."

Tom knew. A Bernard Tufts forgery. "I know," Tom said, as if
with fond memory of a genuine. "Your father liked Derwatt?"

"Who doesn't? There's something warm about his stuff—
human, I mean, which you don't find in modern painting all the
time. I mean—if someone wants warmth. Francis Bacon is tough
and real, but so is *this*, even if it's just a couple of little girls." The

boy looked over his left shoulder at the two little girls in the red chairs, flaming red fire behind them, a picture that could certainly be called warm because of its subject matter, but Tom knew Frank meant a warmth of attitude on Derwatt's part, which showed in his repeated outlines of bodies and faces.

Tom felt a curiously personal affront, because apparently the boy did not prefer "Man in Chair," which showed an equal warmth on the part of the painter, though neither the man nor the chair was on fire. It was a phony, though. That was why Tom preferred it. At least Frank had not yet asked if it might be a phony, a question which if he put it would be based on something he had heard or read, Tom thought. "You evidently enjoy paintings."

Frank squirmed a very little. "I like Rembrandt a lot. Maybe you think that's funny. My father has one. He keeps it away in a *safe* somewhere. But I've seen it several times. Not very big." Frank cleared his throat and sat up. "But for pleasure—"

That was what painting was all about, Tom thought, regardless of Picasso saying that paintings were to make war.

"I like Vuillard and Bonnard. *They're* cozy. This modern stuff, abstracts— Maybe one day I'll understand it."

"So at least you had something in common with your father, you both liked paintings.— He took you to art exhibits?"

"Well, I went. I mean, I liked them, yes. Since I was about twelve, I remember. But my father was in a wheelchair since I was about five. Someone shot at him, you know?"

Tom nodded, realizing suddenly that John Pierson's condition would have made it a strange life for Frank's mother for the past eleven years.

"All business, charming business," Frank said cynically. "My father knew who was behind it, some other food company. Hired killer. But my father never tried to persecute—*prosecute*, because he knew he would only get more of the same. You know? That's the way things are in the States."

Tom could imagine. "Try your cognac." The boy picked it up, sipped, and winced. "Where's your mother now?"

"Maine, I suppose. Or maybe the New York apartment, I don't know."

Tom wanted to press the matter again, to see if Frank would say something new. "Call her up, Frank. You must know both numbers. The phone's right there." It was on a table near the front door. "I'll go upstairs so I won't hear anything you're saying." Tom stood up.

"I don't want them to know where I *am*." Frank looked with steadier eyes at Tom. "I would call up a girl, if I could, but I can't even let *her* know where I am."

"What girl?"

"Teresa."

"She lives in New York?"

"Yes."

"Why *don't* you ring her up? Isn't she worried? You don't have to tell her where you are. I'll still go upstairs—"

But Frank was shaking his head, slowly. "She might be able to tell it comes from France. I can't risk that."

Had he perhaps run away from the girl? "Did you tell Teresa you were going away?"

"I told her I was thinking of taking a short trip."

"Did you have a quarrel with her?"

"Oh, no. No." A quiet, happy amusement spread over Frank's face, a look of dreaming that Tom had not seen before. Then the boy looked at his wristwatch and stood up. "I'm sorry."

It was only eleven or so, but Tom knew Frank did not want Heloise to see him again. "Have you got a picture of Teresa?"

"Oh, yes!" Again happiness shone in his face as he reached into the inside pocket of his jacket for his billfold. "This one. My favorite. Even though it's only a Polaroid." He handed Tom a small square snapshot in a transparent envelope which just fit it.

Tom saw a brown-haired girl with lively eyes, a mischievous

smile with closed lips, eyes slightly narrowed. The hair was straight and shining, shortish, the face more full of fun than mischief, really, as if she had been snapped while dancing. "She has charm," Tom said.

Frank nodded, happy and wordless. "You don't mind driving me back? These shoes are comfortable but—"

Tom laughed. "Nothing easier." Frank wore Gucci shoes, black moccasin-style of crinkly leather, well-shined now. His brown and tan tweed jacket, a Harris tweed, had an interesting diamond pattern that Tom might have chosen for himself. "I'll see if madame is still awake and tell her I'm leaving and coming back. She sometimes gets disturbed by car sounds, but she *is* expecting Heloise. Use the downstairs loo, if you want." Tom gestured toward a narrow door in the front hall.

The boy went off to use it, and Tom walked through the kitchen to Mme. Annette's door. Her light was off, he saw from a look at the crack under the door. Tom scribbled a note on the desk where the telephone was: "Driving a friend home. Back by midnight probably. T." Tom left it on the third step of the stairs, where Heloise would be sure to see it.

3

Tom wanted to see Frank's "little house" tonight, and on the road he put the request casually. "Can I see where you're living? Or would that bother Madame Boutin?"

"Oh, she goes to bed around ten! Sure, you can see it."

They were just then entering Moret. Tom knew the route now, made the left turn into the Rue de Paris and slowed for number 78 on the left. There was a car parked near the Boutin house facing Tom. Since the street was empty of traffic, Tom pulled over to the left to park, his headlights lit the front of the parked car, and

Tom noticed that the license plate ended in 75, which indicated a car registered in Paris.

At the same time, the car's headlights came on at their brightest into Tom's windshield, and the Paris car backed quickly. Tom thought he saw two men in the front seats.

"What's that?" Frank asked, sounding a bit alarmed.

"Just what I was wondering." Tom watched the car back into the nearest turn on the left, then pull out and roll away at a good speed. "Paris car." Tom had stopped, but his lights were still on. "I'm going to park around the corner."

Tom did so, in the still darker and smaller road in which the Paris car had made its turn. Tom put out his lights, and locked three doors with the buttons after Frank had got out. "Maybe nothing to worry about," Tom said, but he felt a little worried, imagined that there might be one man, or two, lurking in Mme. Boutin's garden now. "A torch," Tom said, getting his from the glove compartment. He locked the driver's door, and they walked toward the Boutin house.

Frank took the long key from his inside jacket pocket, and opened the gates of the driveway or carriage entrance into the garden.

Tom tensed himself for a possible fistfight just inside the gates—which were only about nine feet high, not difficult to climb even with their spikes at the top. The front gate would have been even easier.

"Lock them again," Tom whispered as they both went through.

Frank did. Now Frank had the flashlight, and Tom followed him as he walked between grapevines and some trees that might have been apple toward a small house on the right. Mme. Boutin's house on the left was quite dark. Tom heard no sound at all, not even that of a neighbor's television. French villages could be deadly silent by midnight.

"Watch out," Frank whispered, indicating with the torch a cluster of three buckets that Tom should avoid. Frank pulled a

smaller key out, opened the door of the little house, switched on
the light, and handed Tom his torch back. "Simple, but it's home!"
Frank said gaily, closing the door behind him and Tom.

It was one not very big room with a single bed, a wooden table
painted white, on which lay a couple of paperback books, a French
newspaper, ballpoint pens, a mug of half-finished coffee. A workman's blue shirt hung over a straight chair. At one end of the room
was a sink and a small wood-burning stove, a wastebasket, a towel
rack. A brown leather suitcase, not new, rested on a high shelf, and
below the shelf a rod about a yard long served for clothes-hanging,
and Tom saw a couple of pairs of trousers, jeans, and a raincoat.

"Bed's more comfortable than this chair to sit on," said Frank.
"I can offer you Nescafé—made with cold water."

Tom smiled. "You don't have to offer me anything. I think
your place is quite—adequate." The walls looked freshly white-
washed, maybe by Frank. "And that's pretty," Tom said, noticing a
watercolor on a piece of white cardboard (the cardboard that came
at the bottom of writing paper tablets) propped against the wall on
Frank's bed table. The bedside table was a wooden crate on which
stood also a red rose with some wild flowers in a glass. The watercolor was of the gates they had just passed through, partly opened
in the picture. It was direct, bold, and not at all worked over.

"Yes, that. I found some kid's watercolors in the drawer of the
table here." Now the boy looked more sleepy than drunk.

"I shall be pushing off," Tom said, reaching for the doorknob.
"Phone me again when you feel like it." Tom had the door half
open, when he saw a light come on in Mme. Boutin's house about
twenty yards away straight ahead.

Frank saw it too. "Now what?" Frank said with irritation. "We
didn't make any noise."

Tom wanted to flee, but suddenly in the absolute silence he
heard her footsteps on what sounded like gravel and pretty near.
"I'm going to hide in the bushes," Tom whispered, and he moved
even as he spoke, out and to the left, where he knew there was
darkness either against the garden wall or under a tree.

The old lady was watching her footing with the aid of a feeble pencil-like flashlight. "*C'est Billy?*"

"Mais oui, madame!" Frank said.

Tom was crouched, with one hand on the ground, about six yards from Frank's little house. Mme. Boutin was saying that two men had arrived around ten o'clock, asking to see him.

"To see me? Who were they?" Frank said.

"They didn't say their names. They wanted to see my gardener, they said. Strangers to me! Bizarre to look for a gardener at ten o'clock, I thought!" Mme. Boutin sounded vexed and suspicious.

"It's not my fault," said Frank. "What did they look like?"

"Oh, I saw only one. Maybe thirty years old. He asked when you would be back. *I* didn't know!"

"I am sorry they disturbed you, madame. I am not looking for other work, I assure you."

"I trust not! I don't like such people ringing my doorbell at *night.*" Now her small, rather stooped figure was taking its leave. "I keep my two gates locked. But I came all the way to the front gate to speak to them."

"We should—forget it, Madame Boutin. I am sorry."

"Good night, Billy, and sleep well."

"And you too, madame!"

Tom waited, watching her progress back to the house. He heard Frank close his house door, then finally the turning of a lock in Mme. Boutin's house, the faint creak of a second key, then the firm clunk of a bolt that she slid home. Or was that even final? There were no more noises of closures, but still Tom waited. A light on the floor above the ground floor glowed dimly through clouded glass. Then that went out. Frank was evidently waiting for him to make the first move, which Tom thought intelligent of the boy. Tom crept from the bushes, approached the door of the little house, and tapped with his fingertips.

Frank opened the door partway, and Tom slipped in.

"I heard that," Tom whispered. "I think you'd better leave tonight. Now."

"*Do* you?" Frank looked startled. "I know you're right. I know, I know."

"Now—let's get going and pack up. You'll stay at my house tonight and worry about tomorrow tomorrow. This is your only suitcase?" Tom took it from the high shelf, and opened it on the bed.

They worked smoothly, Tom handing Frank things, trousers, shirts, sneakers, books, toothpaste, and toothbrush. Frank worked with his head down, and Tom felt he was on the brink of tears.

"Nothing to worry about if we evade those creeps tonight," Tom said softly, "and tomorrow we'll leave the nice old lady a note—maybe saying you phoned your family tonight and you have to get back to the States right away. Something like that. But we can't waste time with it now."

Frank pressed his raincoat down, and closed the suitcase.

Tom took his torch from the table. "Wait a sec, I want to see if they've come back."

Tom walked as noiselessly as possible over the mowed grass toward the gates. He was able to see only some three yards around him without the torch, and he didn't want to put the torch on. No car was in front of the Boutin house, anyway. Could they be waiting near his car around the corner? Nasty thought. The gates were now locked, so Tom couldn't go round the corner and see. He went back for Frank, and found him with suitcase in hand, ready to go. Frank left the key in the lock of the little house, its door locked, and they went on to the gates.

"Stay here for a minute," Tom said when Frank had unlocked the gates. "I want to look round the corner."

Frank lowered his suitcase, and nervously started to come with Tom, but Tom pushed him back, made sure the gate looked closed, and walked toward the corner. He felt rather safe, because the two men certainly weren't after him.

His own car was the only one that Tom could see. That was reassuring. People in this neighborhood had garages, and no cars were parked at the curbs. Tom only hoped that the two men had not taken notice of his license plates, because if they had, they might trace his name and address via the police on some made-up grounds of misdemeanor or affront. Tom walked back for Frank, who was still behind the gates. The boy came out when Tom beckoned.

"I don't know what to do with this key," Frank said.

"Drop it behind the gate," Tom whispered. Frank had locked the gate again. "We'll tell her in the note tomorrow."

They walked, Frank carrying his suitcase and Tom a small carry-all, round the corner, and got into the car, which seemed a haven to Tom as soon as they had closed its doors. Tom concentrated on getting out of the town, and by a different route. As far as he could see, he was not being followed. In the main part of town, across the old bridge with its four towers, very few streetlights were on, one bar was closing, only two or three cars moved, paying no attention to him. Tom took the big N 5, and made a right turn toward the tiny town of Obelique on a road that would take them finally to Villeperce.

"Don't be worried," Tom said. "I know where I'm going and I don't think anyone's following us."

Frank seemed sunk in his own thoughts.

The little world of Mme. Boutin was shattered, Tom thought, and the boy didn't know where he was now. "I'll have to tell Heloise you're staying the night," Tom said. "But you'll still be Billy Rollins to her. I'll tell her you want to do some gardening for us, and—" Tom looked into his car mirror again, but nothing was behind them. "I'll say you're looking for a part-time job. Don't worry." Tom glanced at Frank. The boy was staring through the windshield and biting his underlip.

They were home. Tom saw the gentle glow of Belle Ombre's front court light, which Heloise had left on for him, and he drove through the open gates into the garage at the right of the house. Tom saw that Heloise had parked the red Mercedes-Benz in the right-hand garage space. Tom got out, asked Frank to wait a moment, then he got the big key from under the rhododendrons and locked the front gates.

By then Frank was standing with suitcase and carryall beside the car. One living room light was on. Tom put on another light which lit the stairs, turned off the living room light, then went out and beckoned for Frank to follow him. They turned left at the top of the stairs, and Tom put on the light in the guest room. Heloise's door was closed.

"Make yourself comfortable," Tom said to Frank. "Closet's here—" He opened a cream-colored door. "Drawers there—and use my bathroom tonight, because the one here is Heloise's. I won't be asleep for another hour probably."

"Thank you." Frank had put his suitcase on the short oak bench at the foot of one of the twin beds.

Tom went into his room, put on the light and also the light in the bathroom. Then he couldn't resist going to his front window, whose curtains had been drawn by Mme. Annette, and peering out to see if any car was cruising past or parked. He saw nothing but darkness, except for the area of light under a street lamp to the left. Of course a lightless car could be parked out there, but Tom preferred to think none was.

Frank knocked on the partly open door, and came in in pajamas, toothbrush in hand, barefoot. Tom gestured toward the bathroom.

"All yours," Tom said, "and take your time." Tom smiled, watching the tired boy—shadows under his eyes now—walk into the bathroom and close the door. Tom got into pajamas. He would be interested to see what the *IHT* might have to say in the next days about the disappearance of Frank Pierson. Surely the search would be heating up. Tom went down the hall to Heloise's room, looked through the keyhole through which he could always see some light, if any light was on, though the key remained in the lock inside. No light.

Tom went back to his own room, and was in bed browsing in

a French grammar when Frank came out of the bathroom, smiling, with dampish hair.

"A hot shower! Wow!"

"Go and get some sleep. Sleep as late as you like."

Then Tom went to wash. He was thinking about the car in front of Mme. Boutin's. Whoever the two men had been, they had not wanted to risk a noisy fight, or even a meeting with Frank and another person. Still it boded no good. On the other hand, it might be petty curiosity: someone in Moret might have mentioned seeing a new boy, an American, who might be Frank Pierson, and the same person might have a Paris friend. The men hadn't asked for Frank, it seemed, just for Mme. Boutin's "gardener." Tom thought he would deliver Frank's note to Mme. Boutin tomorrow without the boy, and as quickly as possible.

4

A solitary bird—not a lark—awakened Tom with a six-note song. What bird was it? Its voice sounded questioning, almost timid, yet curious too, and full of vigor. This bird or one of its family often woke Tom in summer. Now with barely opened eyes he looked at his gray walls, darker gray shadows—which looked like a wash drawing. Tom liked it, the lump of brass-cornered chest, the darker lump of desk. He sighed, and snuggled deeper into his pillow for a final snooze.

Frank!

Tom suddenly remembered the boy was in the house, and came full awake. Seven thirty-five now by his watch. Tell Heloise that Frank was here—rather, Billy Rollins. Tom put on slippers and dressing gown, and went downstairs. It would be comforting to speak with Mme. Annette first, and he was ahead of her as to time for his coffee at eight. Guests never bothered Mme. Annette, and she never asked how long they were staying, except in regard to the next several meals.

The kettle had just begun to hum as Tom walked into the kitchen. "Bonjour, madame!" he called cheerily.

"Monsieur Tome! Vous avez bien dormi?"

"Excellently, thank you. We have a guest this morning, the young American you met last night—Billy Rollins. He is in the guest room and may be here for a few days. He likes to do gardening."

"Oh, yes? A *nice* young man!" Mme. Annette said with an air of approval. "And what time would he like his breakfast?— Your coffee, Monsieur Tome."

Tom's coffee had dripped, the kettle was for Heloise's tea. He watched Mme. Annette pour black coffee into a white cup. "Don't trouble yourself. I told him to sleep as late as he wished. He may come down. I can see about that." Heloise's tray was ready, and Mme. Annette picked it up. "I'll go up with you," said Tom, and followed her with his cup of coffee.

Tom waited until Mme. Annette had knocked and entered Heloise's room with the tray of tea, grapefruit, and toast, then went to the open door.

Heloise was awakening. "Ah, Tome, come in! I was so tired last night—"

"But at least you weren't late. I was home by midnight, I think. Listen, my dear, I asked the American boy to stay the night. He's going to do some gardening for us. He's in the guest room. Billy Rollins. You met him."

"Oh," said Heloise, and spooned some grapefruit into her mouth. She was not much surprised, but she asked, "Hasn't he a place to live? He has no money?"

Tom answered carefully. They were talking in English. "I'm sure he has some money, enough to put himself up somewhere, but he said last night he was not too happy with the place where he's staying, so I said come to our house for the night, and we fetched his things. He's a well brought up boy." Tom added, "Eighteen, likes gardening and seems to know quite a bit. If he wants to work for us for a while—there're cheap lodgings at the Jacobs'." The Jacobs were a couple in Villeperce who ran a bar-restaurant, with a three-room "hotel" on the floor above.

Munching into toast now, Heloise was more alert and said, "You are so impulsive, Tome. An American boy in our house—just like that! And suppose he is a thief? You ask him to stay the night—and how do you know he is there now?"

Tom lowered his head for a moment. "You are right. But this boy isn't one of the—hitchhiker types. You've—" At that moment, Tom heard a gentle buzz like that of his own travel clock's alarm. Heloise seemed not to have heard it, as she was not so near the hall. "I think he's set his alarm. See you in a while."

Tom went out, still carrying his coffee, closed Heloise's door, and rapped on Frank's door.

"Yes? Come in."

Tom found Frank sitting up on one elbow. On his night table was a travel clock much like Tom's own. "Morning."

"Good morning, sir." Frank pushed his hair back, and swung his legs over the edge of the bed.

Tom was amused. "Want to sleep some more?"

"No, I thought eight was a good time to get up."

"Coffee?"

"Yes, thank you. I can come down."

Tom said he preferred to bring him coffee, and went down to the kitchen. Mme. Annette had already prepared a tray of orange juice, toast, and the usual, and Tom started to pick it up, but Mme. Annette told him she had not poured the coffee as yet.

She poured coffee into the preheated silver pot on the tray. "Do you really want to take it up, Monsieur Tome? If the young man wishes an egg—"

"I think this will be perfect, Madame Annette." Tom went up. Frank tried the coffee and said, "Um-m!"

Tom replenished his own cup from the new pot, and sat down on a chair. He had put the tray on the writing table. "You must write that note to Madame Boutin this morning. Sooner the better, and I'll deliver it."

"Right." Frank was savoring his coffee, waking up. The hair on top of his head now stood straight up, as if in a wind.

"And where the gate key is. Just behind the gates."

The boy nodded.

Tom let him bite into some toast and marmalade. "Do you remember the date you left home?"

"July twenty-seventh."

It was now Saturday the nineteenth of August. "You were in London a few days and then—where did you stay in Paris?"

"Hôtel d'Angleterre, Rue Jacob."

Tom knew the hotel, but he had never stayed there. It was in the St-Germain-des-Près area. "Can I see the passport you've got now? Your brother's?"

Frank went at once to his suitcase, got the passport from the suitcase's top pocket, and handed it to Tom.

Tom opened it and turned it sideways to see a picture of a more blond young man, hair parted on the right, with thinner face, yet with some resemblance to Frank in eyes, brows, and mouth. How had he made it, however, Tom wondered. Luck, so far. This boy would be almost nineteen, five feet eleven, therefore a bit taller than Frank was at present. In French hotels it was no longer necessary to present a passport or card of identity. But the immigration bureaus of England and France must have been informed by now that Frank Pierson was missing, might have been sent a photograph of Frank. And wouldn't his brother have missed his passport by now?

"You may as well give up, you know," Tom said, trying a new tack. How are you going to go on in Europe like this? They'll stop you at any border. Maybe especially the French border."

The boy looked stunned, also affronted.

"I don't understand why you want to hide."

The boy's eyes shifted, but not with dishonesty. Frank seemed to be asking himself what he wanted to do. "I'd like to be *quiet*—just for a few more days."

Tom noticed a tremble in the boy's hand as he started to put the napkin back on the tray, then absently half folded it and dropped it. "Your mother must know by now that you took Johnny's passport, that yours is at home. They could easily trace you to France. It's going to be more unpleasant to be picked up by the police here than if you simply tell them now." Tom set his cup on Frank's tray. "I'll leave you so you can write that note to Madame Boutin. I told Heloise you're here. Got some paper you can write on?"

"Yes, sir."

Tom had been about to offer him some typewriter paper and a cheap envelope, because the notepaper in the guest room drawer had Belle Ombre's address on it. Tom went into his room, shaved with his battery razor, and put on old green corduroy trousers that he often wore when gardening. It was a lovely day, coolish and sunny. He did some watering in his greenhouse, thought about what he and Frank might do that morning, and put out his secateurs and fork. He was interested in the morning post, due in a few minutes. When Tom heard the familiar creak of the post van's handbrake, he walked toward his front gates.

He wanted to see if the *IHT* had an item anywhere in it about Frank Pierson, and he looked for this first, even though he saw a letter from Jeff Constant of London. Oddly, Jeff, a freelance photographer, was a better correspondent than Edmund Banbury, who hardly did anything else but manage the Buckmaster Gallery and spend most of his time there. Nothing in the news pages or in the People column about Frank Pierson. Tom suddenly thought of *France-Dimanche*, the old gossip rag of the weekend. Today was Saturday, and there would be a fresh edition. *France-Dimanche* was almost exclusively concerned with people's sexual activities, but

money came next in their interest. He opened Jeff's letter in the
living room.

Jeff didn't mention Derwatt's name, Tom saw from a glance at
the typewritten page. Jeff said he agreed with Tom that a stop
should be put, and had so informed the right people, after dis-
cussing it with Ed. Tom knew he meant by the right people a
young painter in London called Steuerman, who had been
attempting Derwatt forgeries for them—maybe five by now—but
whose work could not hold a candle to that of the dedicated
Bernard Tufts. Though Derwatt was presumed deceased by now, in
his little Mexican village whose name he had never disclosed, Jeff
and Ed had been keen for years now on "finding" old efforts of
Derwatt's, and trying to market them. Jeff went on: "This will cut
our intake considerably, but as you know, we've always listened to
your advice, Tom . . ." He ended by asking Tom to tear up his letter. Tom felt a bit relieved, and began to tear up Jeff's letter, slowly,
into little bits.

Frank came down with an envelope in his hand. He wore blue
jeans. "It's done. Could you take a look? I think it's all right."

He made Tom think of a schoolboy handing a paper to a
teacher. Tom noticed two small mistakes in the French, which he
thought normal. Frank had written that he had telephoned home,
and had to return at once because of an illness in the family. He
thanked Mme. Boutin for her kindness, and said that the gate key
was just inside the garden gates where he had dropped it.

"Quite okay, I think," Tom said. "I'll run over with it now. You
can look at the paper or go out in the garden. I'll be back in half
an hour."

"The paper," said Frank softly, with a wince that showed his
teeth.

"Nothing in that. I looked." Tom indicated the *IHT* on the
sofa.

"I'll go out in the garden."

"But not in front of the house, all right?"

Frank understood.

Tom went out and took the Mercedes, whose keys he had picked up from the hall table. The car was low on gasoline, and he would buy some on the way back. Tom drove as fast as the speed limit permitted. A pity the letter was in Frank's handwriting, but it would have been odd if he had written on a typewriter. Not unless the police knocked on Mme. Boutin's door would anyone be interested in Frank's handwriting, Tom hoped.

In Moret, Tom parked a hundred yards from the Boutin house, and went on foot. Unfortunately a woman was standing outside the front door gate, talking with Mme. Boutin, Tom supposed, though he couldn't see the latter. They might be talking about Billy's disappearance. Tom turned and walked the other way, slowly, for a couple of minutes. When he looked again, the woman who had been standing on the pavement was now walking toward him. Tom walked in the direction of the Boutin house, and did not glance at the woman as he passed her. Tom dropped the envelope into the slit marked LETTRES in the closed front gate, circled the block, and arrived back at his car. Then he headed for the center of town, toward the bridge over the Loing River, where he knew there was a newspaper shop.

Tom stopped and bought a *France-Dimanche*. It had red headlines as usual, but these were about Prince Charles's girlfriend, and the second headline about the catastrophic marriage of a Greek heiress. Tom crossed the bridge and bought gas, and opened the paper while the tank was filling. A full-face picture of Frank—left-side hair part, right cheek showing the little mole—made Tom start. It was a square, two-column item. AMERICAN MILLIONAIRE'S SON HIDES IN FRANCE, said the caption, and below the photograph: Frank Pierson. Have you seen him?

The item read:

Hardly a week after the death of multi-millionaire John J. Pierson, American food magnate, his younger son Frank, only 16, quit his luxurious home in Maine, USA, having taken his older brother John's passport. The sophisticated Frank is known for his independence, and was also extremely troubled by his father's death, said his beautiful mother Lily. The young Frank left a note saying he was going to New Orleans, Louisiana, for a few days. But the family and police found no evidence that he ever went there. The search has since led to London and now to France, according to authorities.

The fabulously wealthy family is desperate, and the older brother John may come to Europe with a private detective in an attempt to find Frank. "I can spot him better, because I know him," said John Pierson, Jr.

John Pierson, Sr., a wheelchair invalid since an attempt on his life eleven years ago, died on July 22 last, when he fell from a cliff on his Maine estate. Was he a suicide or was it an accident? The American authorities attributed his death to "accidental causes."

But—what is the mystery behind the boy's flight from home?

Tom paid the station attendant, and gave him a tip. He should tell Frank at once, show him the newspaper, Tom thought. It would surely jog the boy into making a move of some kind. Then he should get rid of the newspaper in case Heloise or Mme. Annette (more likely) looked at it.

It was 10:30 when Tom rolled through the gates of Belle Ombre, and into the shade of the garage. He folded the newspaper, stuck it under his arm, and walked around the house to the left, past Mme. Annette's door, which had prim pots of blossoming red geraniums, one on either side—a touch of pride, Tom thought, as she had bought them herself. He saw Frank at the far end of the garden, stooped and apparently pulling weeds. From the house, through the slightly opened French windows, he heard

Heloise virtuously practicing Bach. After one half hour, Tom knew, she would either put on a record of someone playing the same thing, or something to change her mood entirely, such as rock music.

"Bil-ly," Tom called gently, trying to fix in his mind that he must call him Billy and not Frank.

The boy stood up from the grass and smiled. "You delivered it? Did you see her?" he asked, just as gently, as if someone in the woods beyond might hear.

Tom was also wary of the woods behind the garden—after ten yards of scrubby underbrush the trees became thicker. Tom had once been buried there, for maybe a quarter of an hour. One couldn't see through the waist-high nettles, the wild and thorny blackberry vines three or four yards long that produced no fruit, not to mention the tall limes just beyond, so thick that their trunks could conceal a man who wished to hide behind one. Tom jerked his head, and the boy came closer to him. They moved toward the friendly structure of the greenhouse. "Something about you in the gossip rag," Tom said, opening the newspaper. He had turned his back on the house, whence Heloise's playing was still audible. "I thought you should see it."

Frank took the paper, and Tom saw his shock in the sudden twitch of his hands. "Damn," he said softly. He read it with his jaw clenched.

"Do you think your brother might come over?"

"I think it's—yes. But to say my family's 'desperate'—that's absurd."

Tom said lightly, "What if Johnny were to turn up here today and say, 'Well, here you are!' "

"Why should he turn up here?" asked Frank.

"Did you ever talk about me, mention me to your family? Or to Johnny?"

"No."

Tom was whispering now. "What about the Derwatt painting?

Weren't there conversations about that? Do you remember? A year or so ago?"

"I remember. My father mentioned it, because of what was in the newspapers. It wasn't particularly about *you*, not at all."

"But when you—you said you read about me—in the newspapers."

"In the Public Library in New York. That was just a few weeks ago."

He meant the newspaper archives. "You didn't mention me then to your family or to anybody?"

"Oh, *no*." Frank looked at Tom, then his eyes fixed on something behind Tom, and his anxious frown came back.

Tom turned around, and what should he see but the Old Bear Henri ambling toward them, looking big and tall as something out of a kid's fairy tale. "Our part-time gardener. Don't run and don't worry. Mess your hair up a little. And let it grow—for future use. Don't talk, just say 'Bonjour.' He'll quit at noon."

By this time the French giant was almost within hearing, and Henri's own booming voice, deep and loud, called out, "'Jour, Monsieur Reeply!"

"'Jour," Tom replied. "François," Tom said, gesturing toward Frank. "Cleaning out some weeds."

"Bonjour," Frank said. He had mussed his hair by scratching the top of his head, and now he assumed a slouch, and went off to where he had been pulling horsetail weeds and convolvulus at the back edge of the lawn.

Tom was pleased by Frank's performance. In his scruffy blue jacket, he might have been a local boy who had asked to do a couple of hours' work at the Ripley house, and God knew Henri couldn't be depended on, so Henri could hardly complain about competition. Henri could not tell the difference between Tuesday and Thursday, it seemed. Any day he set for himself was never the day he appeared. Henri didn't show surprise now at the sight of the boy, but kept his absentminded smile, visible in encircling brown mustache and untrimmed beard. He wore baggy blue work trousers, a checked lumberjack shirt and a pale blue-and-white striped cotton cap with a bill, like an American railwayman's cap. Henri had blue eyes. He gave the impression of being slightly fuzzy with drink always, but was never very drunk as far as Tom could see, and Tom thought perhaps that drink had done its damage at some period in the past. Henri was about forty. Tom paid him fifteen francs an hour, whatever he did, even if they just stood around and discussed potting soil or the methods of storing dahlia tubers over the winter.

Now Tom suggested that they make another attack on the hundred-meter-long back edge of the garden, where Frank was still working, but Frank was far on their left near the little road which went into the woods there. Tom handed Henri the secateurs, and himself took the fork and rake, a strong metal rake.

"Build a low stone wall here, and you won't have this trouble," Henri murmured cheerfully, taking the spade. He had made the remark many times before, and Tom did not mean to compound its boredom by repeating that he and his wife preferred the garden to appear to blend into the woods. Henri would have then told Tom that the woods were blending into the garden.

They both worked, and when Tom looked over his shoulder some fifteen minutes later, Frank was not in sight. Good, Tom thought. If Henri asked what had happened to the boy, Tom would say that he had probably drifted off, not really wanting to work. But Henri said nothing; all the better. Tom went into the kitchen via the service door. Mme. Annette was washing something at the sink.

"Madame Annette, a small request."

"Oui, Monsieur Tome!"

"The young man with us—he has just had an unhappy experience with his girlfriend from America. He was with a few young Americans in France. So he wants to stay quiet and with us for a few days, I think. It is best if you don't tell anyone in the village that Billy is staying with us. He doesn't want his friends to look him up here, you see?"

"Ah-h." Mme. Annette understood. Affairs of the heart were

personal, dramatic, wounding, and the boy was so young, her face seemed to say.

"You haven't mentioned Billy to anyone, have you?" Mme. Annette often visited Georges' bar-café for a cup of tea, sitting down at a little table, Tom knew. So did other housekeepers.

"Certainly not, monsieur."

"Good." Tom went out to the garden again.

It was nearly noon when Henri showed signs of slowing his already slow work, and remarked that it was warm. It was not warm, but Tom didn't mind stopping his raking. They went into the greenhouse, where Tom kept a reserve of six or more bottles of Heineken lager in a square cement recess in the floor which was for drainage. Tom hauled up two bottles and opened them with a rusty bottle opener.

The next few minutes passed vaguely for Tom, because he was thinking about Frank, wondering where he was. Henri kept up his murmuring about the meager crop of raspberries this summer, as he stalked about with his little beer bottle, bending to look at this and that plant on Tom's shelves. Henri wore old laced boots that came high above his ankles, thick mushy soles on them, the picture of comfort though not of chic. He had the biggest feet Tom could remember having seen on any man. Did Henri's feet really fill those boots? But judging from his hands, they might.

"*Non, trente*," Henri said. "Don't you remember the last time? You were short fifteen."

Tom didn't, but gave Henri thirty francs anyway rather than argue.

Then Henri pushed off, promising to return next Tuesday or Thursday. It was all the same to Tom. Henri was on "permanent retirement" or "repos," due to an injury on some job years ago. He had an easy, anxiety-free life, and in many ways was to be envied, Tom thought, as he watched his great figure stalk off and pass the beige turreted corner of Belle Ombre. Tom rinsed his hands at the greenhouse sink.

A few minutes later, Tom entered his house by the front door. A Brahms quartet was playing on the stereo in the living room, and perhaps Heloise was there. Tom went upstairs, looking for Frank. Frank's room door was closed, and Tom knocked on it.

"Come in?" said Frank's voice in the questioning tone Tom had heard before.

Tom went in and saw that Frank had packed his suitcase, removed sheets and blanket from his bed, and folded them neatly. He had also changed out of his work clothes. And he also saw that Frank was near breaking, or near tears, though the boy held himself straight. "Well," Tom said softly, and closed the door. "What's up?— Worried about Henri?" Tom knew it wasn't Henri, but he had to lead the boy to talk. The newspaper still poked from a back pocket of Tom's trousers.

"If it isn't Henri, it'll be somebody else," Frank said in a shaky but rather deep voice.

"Now what's wrong—up to now?" Johnny was coming, with a private detective, and the game might soon be up, Tom thought. But what game? "Why don't you want to go back home?"

"I killed my father," Frank said in a whisper. "Yes, I pushed him over that—" The boy gave up, his mouth seemed to crumple like that of an old man, and he lowered his head.

A murderer, Tom thought. And why? Tom had never seen such a gentle murderer. "Does Johnny know?"

Frank shook his head. "No. Nobody saw me." His brown eyes glistened with tears, but there were not enough tears to fall.

Tom understood, or was beginning to. The boy's conscience had driven him away. Or somebody's words. "Did anybody *say* anything? Your mother?"

"Not my mother. Susie—the housekeeper. But she didn't see me. She couldn't have. She was in the house. Anyway, she's shortsighted and the cliff isn't even visible from the house."

"She said something to you or somebody else?"

"Both. The police—didn't believe her. She's old. A little

cracked." Frank moved his head like someone under torture, and sought his suitcase on the floor. "I've told you—okay. You're the only person in the world I'd tell, and I don't care what you say. I mean, to the police or anyone. But I'd better take off."

"Come on now, take off to where?"

"I don't know."

Tom knew. He couldn't get out of France even with his brother's passport. He had nowhere to hide except in fields. "You're not going to be able to go anywhere outside of France and not far inside it. Look, Frank, we'll talk about this after lunch. We have all the—"

"Lunch?" Frank's tone sounded as if he were affronted by the word.

Tom advanced toward him. "I'm giving you orders now. It's lunchtime. You can't just disappear now, it'd look strange. Now you pull yourself together, eat a good lunch, and we'll talk afterward." Tom reached out to shake the boy's hand, but Frank edged back.

"I'll go while I can!"

Tom grabbed the boy's shoulder with his left hand, his throat with his right. "You will not. You will *not!*" Tom gave his throat a shake, then released him.

The boy's eyes were wide and thoroughly shocked. That was what Tom wanted. "Come on with me. Downstairs." Tom gestured, and the boy preceded him toward the door. Tom went into his own room for a minute to get rid of the *France-Dimanche*. For good measure, he stuck it in a back corner of his closet among shoes. He did not want Mme. Annette to find it even in the wastebasket.

5

Downstairs, Heloise was arranging orange and white gladioli— Tom knew she disliked them and that Mme. Annette must have cut them—in a tall vase on the coffee table. She looked up and smiled at Tom and Frank. To relax himself, Tom deliberately shrugged as if he were adjusting a jacket on his shoulders: he meant to be calm and cool.

"Nice morning?" Tom asked Heloise in English.

"Yes. I see that Henri decided to appear."

"Doing the minimum as usual. Billy's better." Tom motioned for Frank to follow him into the kitchen, whence Tom could smell—he thought—broiling lamb chops. "Madame Annette— excusez-nous. I would like a small aperitif before lunch."

She was indeed inspecting lamb chops in the over-the-stove grill. "But Monsieur Tome, you should have told me! Bonjour, monsieur!" she said to Frank.

Frank replied politely.

Tom went to the bar cart, which was now in the kitchen, and poured a scotch, not too big or too small, into a glass and poked it into Frank's hand. "Water?"

"A little."

Tom added some water from the sink tap, and handed the glass back to Frank. "This will loosen *you* up, not necessarily your tongue," Tom murmured. Tom made himself a gin and tonic without ice, though Mme. Annette wanted at once to get some out of the refrigerator. "Let's go back," Tom said to Frank, nodding toward the living room.

They went back, took their places at the table with their drinks, and Mme. Annette almost at once brought the first course of her homemade jellied consommé. Heloise chattered away about her Adventure Cruise for late September. Noëlle had rung her that morning with some more details.

"The Antarctic," said Heloise with joy. "We may need—oh— just imagine the kind of clothes! Two pairs of gloves at once!"

Longjohns, Tom was thinking. "Or do they turn on central heating somewhere at that price?"

"O-oh, Tome!" Heloise said with good humor.

She knew he didn't give a damn about the cost. Jacques Plisson was probably making Heloise a present of the trip, since he knew Tom was not going.

Frank asked how long the cruise would last, and how many people would be on the boat—this from Frank in French—and Tom found himself appreciative of the boy's upbringing, those old customs of writing thank-you letters three days after receiving a present, whether one liked the present or the aunt who had given it, or not. The average American boy aged sixteen would not have been able to keep such cool, Tom thought, under the circumstances. When Mme. Annette passed the lamb chop platter for the second helping—four remained on the platter and Heloise had eaten only one—Tom served Frank with a third chop.

Then the telephone rang.

"I'll get it," Tom said. "Excuse me." Odd to have a phone call in the sacred French lunch hour, and Tom was not expecting a call. "Hello," Tom said.

"Hello, Tom! It's Reeves."

"Hang on, would you?" Tom laid the telephone down on the table and said to Heloise, "Long distance. I'll take it upstairs so I don't shout." Tom ran up the stairs, lifted the telephone in his room, and told Reeves to hang on again. Tom went down and hung up the downstairs telephone. Meanwhile he was thinking that it was a piece of luck that Reeves had rung, because a new passport for Frank might well be in order, and Reeves was just the man for that. "Back again," said Tom. "What's new, my friend?"

"Oh, not too *much*," Reeves Minot said in his hoarse, naïve-sounding American voice. "Just a little—uh—well, that's why I'm calling. Can you put a friend up—for one night?"

Tom did not like the idea just now. "When?"

"Tomorrow night. His name is Eric Lanz. Coming from here. He can make it to Moret, so you won't have to pick him up at the airport, but—best if he doesn't stay at a hotel in Paris overnight."

Tom squeezed the telephone nervously. The man was carrying something, of course. Reeves was a fence, mainly. "Sure. Yes, sure," Tom said, thinking if he demurred, Reeves would not be so forthcoming when Tom put in his own request. "For one night only?"

"Yes, that's all. Then he's going to Paris. You'll see. Can't explain more."

"I'm to meet him at Moret? What does he look like?"

"He'll know you. He's in his late thirties, not very tall, black hair. Got the timetable here, Tom, and Eric can make the eight-nineteen tomorrow night. *Arrival* time, that is."

"Very—good," said Tom.

"You don't sound very keen. But it's sort of important, Tom, and I'd be—"

"Of course I'll do it, Reeves old boy! While you're here—on the line—I'm going to need an American passport. I'll send a photo to you express Monday and you ought to have it by Wednesday latest. I assume you're in Hamburg?"

"Sure, same place," said Reeves cozily, as if he were running a teashop, but Reeves's apartment house on the Alster—Reeves's apartment specifically—had been bombed once. "For yourself?" asked Reeves.

"No, someone younger. Not over twenty-one, Reeves, so not an old well-used passport. Can you do that?—You'll hear from me."

Tom hung up and went downstairs again. Raspberry ice had been served. "Sorry," Tom said. "Nothing important." He noticed that Frank looked better, that some color had returned to his face.

"Who was that?" Heloise asked.

Seldom did she ask him who rang, and Tom knew she mistrusted Reeves Minot, or at least didn't much like him, but Tom said, "Reeves from Hamburg."

"He's going to come here?"

"Oh, no, just wanted to say hello," Tom replied. "Want coffee, Billy?"

"No, thank you."

Heloise did not usually take coffee at lunch, and she didn't now. Tom said that Billy wanted to look at his *Jane's Fighting Ships* books, so the three left the table, and Tom and the boy went up to Tom's room.

"Damned annoying phone call," Tom said. "Friend of mine in

Hamburg wants me to put up a friend of his tomorrow night. Just for the night. I couldn't say no, because he's very helpful—Reeves."

Frank nodded. "Would you like me to go to a hotel or something—near here?—Or just *go*?"

Tom shook his head. He was lying on his bed, propped on an elbow. "I'll give him your room, you'll take mine—and I'll sleep in Heloise's room. So this room will remain closed and—I'll tell our guest we're fumigating the carpenter ants and the door can't be opened." Tom laughed. "Don't worry. I'm pretty sure he'll leave Monday morning. I've had overnight guests of Reeves's before."

Frank had sat down on the wooden chair that Tom used at his desk. "Is the fellow coming one of your—interesting friends?"

Tom smiled. "The fellow coming is a stranger." *Reeves* was one of his interesting friends. Maybe Frank had seen Reeves Minot's name in newspapers too. Tom wasn't going to ask. "Now," Tom said quietly, "your situation." Tom waited, noting the boy's uneasiness, the frown. Tom felt uneasy also, and deliberately pushed off his shoes and swung his feet up on the bed, pulled a pillow under his head. "By the way, I thought you did very well at lunch."

Frank glanced at Tom, but his expression did not change. "You asked me before," the boy said softly, "and I told you. You're the only person who knows."

"We shall keep it that way. Don't confess to anyone—ever. Now tell me—what time of day did you do it?"

"Around seven, eight." The boy's voice cracked. "My father always watched the sunset—nearly every evening in summer. I hadn't—"

Here there was a long pause.

"I absolutely had not planned to do it. I was not even very angry, not angry at all. Later—even the next day, I couldn't believe I'd *done* it—somehow."

"I believe you," Tom said.

"I didn't usually walk out with my father for those sunsets. In fact I think he liked to be alone there, but that day he asked me to

come with him. He'd just been talking with me about my doing
pretty well in school, and how Harvard Business School would
come soon and how easy it—well, the usual. He even tried to say
a nice word about Teresa, because he knew I—that I like her. But
up to then, *no*. He'd been stuffy about Teresa coming to the
house—twice only she was there—and saying it was stupid to be
in love at sixteen, get married early or something, even though I
never said a *word* about getting married, never even asked *Teresa*!
She'd laugh! Anyway, I suppose I suddenly had it that day. The
phoniness, the all-round phoniness, everywhere I looked."

Tom started to say something, and the boy nervously
interrupted.

"The two times Teresa did come to the Maine house, my
father was a bit rude to her. Unfriendly, you know? Just because
she's pretty, maybe, and my dad knows she's popular. Knew. You'd
have thought she was some girl I picked up off the streets! But
Teresa's *very* polite, she knows how to behave! And she didn't like
it—natch. She wasn't going to come to the house again, and she
more or less told me so."

"That must've been very tough for you."

"*Yes.*" Then Frank was silent for several seconds, looking at the
floor. He seemed stuck.

Tom supposed that Frank could visit at Teresa's house, or meet
her in New York now and then, but Tom didn't want to get side-
tracked from the essentials. "Who was at the house that day? The
housekeeper Susie. Your mother?"

"And my brother too. We were playing croquet, then Johnny
quit the game. Johnny had a date. He has a girlfriend whose family lives— Well, anyway my dad was on the front porch when
Johnny went off in his car, and Dad said good-bye to him. Johnny
had a lot of roses from the garden to give his girl, I remember,
and I remember thinking if it weren't for my dad's attitude, Teresa
could've been at the house that evening, *somehow*, and we
could've gone out somewhere. My dad won't even let me drive

yet, but I can drive. Johnny taught me on the dunes. My father always thought I'd have a wreck and kill myself, but fellows fifteen and younger in Louisiana or Texas, they're driving if they feel like it."

Tom knew. "Then what? After Johnny left. You'd been talking with your father—"

"I'd been listening to him—in the library downstairs. I wanted to escape, but he said. 'Come out with me, watch the sunset, it'll do you good.' I was in a lousy mood and I tried to hide it. I should've said. 'No, I'm going up to my room,' but I didn't. And then Susie—she's all right but a little in her second childhood, makes me nervous—she was around and made sure my dad got down the ramp in his wheelchair. There's a ramp from the back terrace down to garden level, made just for my father. But she needn't have bothered, because my dad can make it by himself. Then she went back in the house, and my father went on up the path—it's wide, flagstones—toward the woods and the cliff. And when we got there, he started talking again." Frank lowered his head, clenched his right fist and opened it. "Somehow after four or five minutes of it, I just couldn't stand it anymore."

Tom blinked, unable to look any longer at the boy who was looking at him now. "The cliff's steep there? Down to the sea?"

"It's pretty steep, but not straight down. But anyway—enough to—to kill someone, certainly. Rocks there."

"Lots of trees there?" Tom was still wondering who might have seen him. "Boats?"

"No boats, no. No harbor there, anyway. Trees, sure. Pines. Part of our land, but we let it grow wild up there, and just cut a path to the cliff."

"You couldn't've been seen from the house even with binoculars?"

"No, I know. Even in winter, if my father was on the cliff—it's not visible from the house." The boy gave a heavy sigh. "I thank you for listening to all this. Maybe I should write it out or try to—

somehow—to get it off my mind. It's terrible. I don't know how to analyze it. Sometimes I can't believe I did it. It's strange." Frank looked suddenly at the door, as if the existence of other people had just crossed his mind, but there had been no sound from the direction of the door.

Tom smiled a little. "Why not write it out? You could show it only to me—if you feel like it. Then we could destroy it."

"Yes," Frank said softly. "I remember—I had the feeling I couldn't look at his shoulders and the back of his head one second longer. I thought—I don't know *what* I thought, but I rushed forward and kicked the brake lever off and hit the forward button and I gave the chair a shove besides. Then it went forward, head over. Then I didn't look. I just heard a clatter."

Tom had an instant's sickish feeling, imagining it. Fingerprints on the wheelchair, Tom wondered? But they might have been expected, if Frank had accompanied his father to the cliff. "Did anyone talk about fingerprints on the chair?"

"No."

Fingerprints would have been looked for at once, Tom thought, if there had been any suspicion of foul play. "On that button you mentioned?"

"I think I hit it with the side of my fist."

"The motor must've been still running when they got to him."

"Yes, I think somebody said it was."

"Then what did you do—just afterward?"

"I didn't look down. I started walking back to the house. I felt suddenly very tired. It was strange. Then I started trotting toward the house, sort of to wake up. Nobody was on the lawn but Eugene—our driver, kind of butler too—he was in the big downstairs *dining room*, in fact, by himself, and I said, "My father just went over the cliff." Then Eugene told me to tell my mother and to ask her to call the hospital, and he ran out toward the cliff. My mother was with Tal in the upstairs living room watching TV, and I told her, and then Tal called the hospital."

"Who's Tal?"

"A New York friend of my mother's. Talmadge Stevens. He's a lawyer, but not one of my father's lawyers. Big fellow. He—" The boy stopped again.

Was Tal possibly his mother's lover? "Did Tal say anything to you? Ask any questions?"

"No," Frank said. "Well—I said my father sent the chair over himself. Tal didn't ask anything."

"So—the ambulance—and then I suppose the police came?"

"Yes. Both. It seemed like an hour before they got him up. Plus the wheelchair. They were using big spotlights. Then of course the journalists, but Mom and Tal got rid of them pretty fast. They're both good at that. Mom was furious at the journalists, but they were just the local journalists that night."

"And later—the journalists?"

"My mom had to see a couple of them. I spoke to one at least, had to."

"And you said what—exactly?"

"I said my father was near the edge. It seemed to me that he really did mean to send himself over." On the last word, Frank sounded as if he had no breath left. He got up from the chair and walked to the window, which was partly open. Frank turned. "I lied. I told you."

"Does your mother suspect you—at all?"

Frank shook his head. "I'd know if she did, and she doesn't. I'm considered rather—um—*serious*—if you know what I mean. Honest too." Frank smiled nervously. "Johnny was more rebellious at my age, they had to have tutors for him, he was so often running away from Groton, going to New York. Then he sobered up—a little. I don't mean he ever drank booze, but pot sometimes, sure. A little cocaine. He's better now. But I mean, I'm considered something like a Boy Scout by comparison. That's why Dad put the pressure on me, you see, to take an interest in his company, the Pierson *empire*!" Frank flung his arms out and laughed.

Tom saw that the boy was tired.

Frank wandered back to the chair, sat down, and tipped his head back with his eyes half shut. "You know what I sometimes think? That my father was so near to being dead anyway. Half dead in his chair and maybe going to die pretty soon. And I wonder if I think that just to excuse myself a little? Awful to think that!" Frank said with a gasp.

"Back to Susie for a minute. She thinks you sent the chair over and she said that to you?"

"Yes." Frank looked at Tom. "She even said she saw me from the house, so that's why no one believes her. You can't see the cliff from the house. But Susie was very upset when she said that. Sort of hysterical."

"Susie also talked to your mother?"

"Oh, sure, I know. My mother didn't believe her. My mother doesn't like Susie really. My father liked her, because she's very reliable—was—and she's been with us so many years, since Johnny and I were babies almost."

"She was your governess?"

"No, she was more the housekeeper. We always had separate—women as governess. Mostly English." Frank smiled. "Mother's helpers. We only got rid of the last one when I was about twelve."

"And Eugene? Did he say anything?"

"About me? No. Not a thing."

"Do you like him?"

Now Frank laughed a little. "He's all right. He's from London. Has a sense of humor. But whenever Eugene and I used to joke, my dad would say to me later that I shouldn't joke with the butler or the chauffeur. Eugene was both most of the time."

"Anyone else in the household? Other servants?"

"Not just now. Part-time people now and then. Vic the gardener, on vacation in July, maybe longer, so we have part-time fellows sometimes. My father always wanted the minimum of servants and secretaries around."

Tom was thinking that perhaps Lily and Tal were not so

unhappy at John Pierson's demise. What went on there? He got up and went to his desk. "Just in case you do feel like writing it all out," Tom said, handing the boy some twenty sheets of typewriter paper, "with a pen or on the typewriter. Anyway, they're both here." Tom's typewriter sat in the middle of his desk.

"Thank you." Frank stared at the sheets in his hand, musingly.

"You'd probably like to take a walk—but unfortunately you can't."

Frank stood up, paper in hand. "Just what I'd like to do."

"You could try the back road there," Tom said. "It's a one-lane; nobody ever on it but an occasional farmer. You know, beyond where we were working this morning." The boy knew, and moved toward the door. "And don't run," Tom said, because Frank looked charged with nervous energy. "Come back in half an hour, or I'll be worried. You've got a watch?"

"Oh, yes.— Two-thirty-two."

Tom checked his own, early by a minute. "If you want the typewriter later, just come in and get it."

The boy went to his room next door to deposit the paper, then went down the stairs. From a side window, Tom could see Frank crossing the lawn, plunging through a section of underbrush, jumping, tripping once and falling on his hands, then springing up as lithely as an acrobat. The boy turned to the right and became hidden by trees as he followed the narrow road.

A moment later, Tom found himself switching on his transistor. It was partly because he wanted to catch the French news at 3 p.m., partly because he felt a need to change the atmosphere after Frank's story. Amazing, in fact, that the boy hadn't broken down even more while telling it. Would that come, or wouldn't it? Or had it come in the night, perhaps nights before, when the boy was in London or alone at the house of Mme. Boutin, his mind in terror of an imagined judgment from somewhere? Or had the few seconds of tears, today before lunch, been enough? There were boys (and girls) aged ten or so in New York, who had witnessed

murder, murdered in gangs their contemporaries or strangers, but
Frank was hardly that type. Such guilt as Frank's would show itself
in some way, some time. Tom thought that every strong emotion
such as love, hatred, or jealousy eventually showed itself in some
gesture, and not always in the form of a clear illustration of that
emotion, not always what the person himself, or the public, might
have expected.

Restless, Tom went downstairs to speak with Mme. Annette,
who was engaged in the gruesome task of dropping a live lobster
into a huge pot of boiling water. She was just lifting it toward the
steam, the crustacean's limbs were stirring, and Tom recoiled at the
threshold, making a gesture to indicate that he would wait a
moment in the living room.

Mme. Annette gave him an understanding smile, because she
had seen such a reaction in him before.

Had Tom heard a hiss of protest from the lobster? Was Tom
even now, with some highly attuned part of his own auditory
nerve, hearing a cry of pain and outrage from the kitchen, a final
high-pitched shriek as the life went out? Where had the unfortunate creature spent the night, because Mme. Annette must have
bought it yesterday Friday from the mobile *poissonerie* van that
parked itself in Villeperce? This lobster was a big one, not like some
of the little creatures Tom had seen wriggling vainly, tied upside
down to the shelf bars in the fridge. When Tom heard the clunk of
the vessel's lid, he approached the kitchen again, head a little down.

"Ah, Madame Annette," he said. "Nothing important, just—"

"Oh, Monsieur Tome, you are always so worried about the
lobsters! Even the mussels, isn't it?" She laughed with real mirth. "I
tell my chums—*mes copines* Geneviève and Marie-Louise—"These
were other servants of local gentry, whom Mme. Annette encountered while marketing, and who sometimes visited one another on
good TV evenings, because they all had TV, and rotated their get-
togethers.

Tom admitted his weakness with a nod and a polite smile.

"Liver of yellow," Tom said in French, the phrase useless, he realized, because he had meant to translate either lily-livered or yellow-bellied. No matter. "Madame Annette, *another* guest tomorrow, but just for Sunday night till Monday morning. A gentleman. I'll bring him home around eight-thirty for dinner, and he'll have the young man's room, and I'll sleep in the room of my wife. Monsieur Billy will sleep in my room. I'll remind you tomorrow." But he knew he wouldn't need to remind her.

"Very good, Monsieur Tome. An American also?"

"No, he—European," Tom said with a shrug. He fancied he could smell the lobster, and he backed from the kitchen. "Merci, madame!"

Tom went back to his room, listened to the news at three on a French pop station, and heard nothing about Frank Pierson. When the news was over, Tom realized that a half hour had passed, just, since Frank's departure. Tom looked out his side window again. The woods at the corner of his garden showed no human figure. Tom waited, lit a cigarette, and went back to the window. Seven past three now.

Absolutely no reason to feel worried, Tom told himself. Ten minutes one way or the other. Whoever used that road? Sleepy-looking farmers leading or driving a horse and wagon, an old fellow driving a tractor now and then, headed for a field across the main road. Still, Tom was worried. Suppose someone had been watching, since Moret, and had trailed Frank to Belle Ombre? Tom had walked alone one night to Georges' and Marie's noisy café to take a coffee and see if any new character had appeared who showed curiosity even in him. Tom hadn't seen any new personage, and more important, the talkative Marie had asked nothing about a boy staying in his house. Tom had been slightly relieved.

At twenty past three, Tom went downstairs again. Where was Heloise? Tom went out by way of the French windows, and walked slowly across the lawn toward the little road. His eyes were on the grass, and he expected the boy to shout a "Hello!" at any moment.

Or did he? Tom picked up a stone from the grass and threw it awk-wardly with his left hand toward the woods. He kicked away a wild blackberry vine, and finally stepped onto the road. Now he could see at least thirty yards along the road, even if it was a bit over-grown, because the road was straight. Tom began walking, listening, but he heard only the innocent and absentminded tweets of spar-rows, and from somewhere a turtle dove.

He certainly didn't want to call Frank's name or even "Billy!" Tom stopped and listened again. Really nothing, no sound of a car motor, not even from behind him on the Belle Ombre road. Tom started trotting, thinking he'd better have a look at the end of the road—and what *was* the end? Tom thought it went on for a kilo-meter or so, and met another road more important, while all around were farm fields, corn for cattle, cabbages sometimes, mus-tard. Tom had by now begun to look for broken branches on either side of the lane, which might indicate a struggle, but he knew a wagon could have broken some just as well, and also he did not see anything unusual in the foliage. He walked again. He had by now come to the crossroad, a bigger road though still not paved, that ended what he thought of as the woods. Beyond lay cleared fields, belonging to farmers whose houses he could not see. Tom took a deep breath, and turned back. Had the boy possibly gone back to the house, got back, before Tom went out? Was he even now in his room? Tom leaned forward and again ran.

"Tom?" The voice had come from Tom's right.

Tom skidded in his desert boots and looked into the woods.

Frank came from behind a tree—or so it seemed to Tom, materializing suddenly from green leaves and brown tree trunks in gray trousers and beige sweater almost blending with the verdure in the spotty sunlight. He was alone.

Tom felt relief, like an ache. "What happened? You're okay?"

"Sure." The boy lowered his head and began to walk with Tom, back toward Belle Ombre.

Tom understood. The boy had deliberately hidden, to see if

Tom cared about finding him. Frank had wanted to see if he could trust him. Tom shoved his hands into his pockets and lifted his head. He felt the boy glance at him, shyly. "You *were* a bit late, later than you said you'd be."

The boy said nothing, and rammed his hands in his pockets, exactly like Tom.

6

Around 5 o'clock that same Saturday afternoon, Tom said to Heloise, "I don't feel like going to the Grais' tonight, dear. Is that so serious? *You* can go." They were invited for dinner and due around eight.

"Oh, Tome, why not? We can ask if they will have Billy. I'm sure they will say yes." Heloise looked up from the triangular table that she had bought that afternoon at an auction, and which she was now waxing. She knelt on the floor in blue jeans.

"It's not Billy," Tom said, though it was exactly Billy. "They always have a couple of other people—" Tom meant other people to amuse Heloise. "What does it matter? I'll phone them and make some excuse, if you like."

Heloise brushed back her blonde hair. "Antoine insulted you the last time. Is that it?"

Tom laughed. "Did he? If so, I forgot. He *can't* insult me, I'd just laugh." Antoine Grais, a hardworking architect of forty, diligent gardener at his country house, had a certain scorn for Tom's leisurely life, but his slightly insulting remarks bounced right off Tom, and Tom thought Heloise picked up fewer of them than Tom did. "Old Puritan," Tom added. "Belongs in America three hundred years ago. I just feel like staying home. I hear enough about Chirac from the locals." A right-winger, Antoine Grais, pretentious enough not to be caught dead with *France-Dimanche,* but just the type to sneak a look at someone else's in a bar-café. The last thing Tom wanted was Antoine to recognize Billy as Frank Pierson. Antoine and his wife Agnès, a little less straitlaced but not much, would never keep it quiet. "Want me to ring them, darling?" Tom asked.

"No, I shall just—arrive," said Heloise, going on with her waxing.

"Say I've got one of my awful friends visiting. Someone socially unacceptable," Tom said. He knew Antoine thought his social list suspect also. Who was it Antoine had once met by accident? Yes, the genius Bernard Tufts, who had often looked scruffy, and was sometimes too daydreamy to be polite.

"I think Billy is quite nice," said Heloise, "and I know you are not worried about Billy, you just don't like *les Grais*."

Tom was bored with this, and so nervous, because of Billy in the house, that he had to repress another remark about the Grais— that they *were* arch-bores. "They have a right to live—I suppose." Tom decided suddenly not to mention the man called Eric Lanz turning up tomorrow evening, though he had meant to tell Heloise now.

"But how do you really like the table? It's for my room, in that corner, the side where you sleep. Then my table there would look better between the *twin* beds in the guest room," Heloise said, admiring the shine now on the table top.

"I do like it—really," Tom said. "How much did you say?"

"Only four hundred francs. *Chêne*—and it's a Louis Quinze copy—a hundred years old itself. I bargained. Hard."

"You did well," said Tom, meaning it, because the table was handsome and looked sturdy enough to sit on, though no one ever would, and Heloise adored to think she had got a bargain, when often she hadn't. His mind was on other things.

Tom went back to his room, where he had set himself the boring task of spending one hour, by the clock, on his monthly income and expenses for his accountant. Rather, Heloise's father's accountant. This man, one Pierre Solway, kept Tom's and Heloise's accounts separate from the august Jacques Plisson accounts, of course, but Tom was glad enough to be relieved of the accountant's fee (paid by Jacques Plisson), and also to know that the accounts met Plisson's approval, because the old gentleman certainly found time to look them over. Heloise's income or allowance from her father was given her in cash, so was not liable for income tax on the Ripley bill. Tom's Derwatt company income—maybe ten thousand francs a month or close to two thousand dollars if the dollar was strong enough—came also under the table in the form of Swiss franc checks, this money being filtered almost entirely through Perugia, where the Derwatt Art Academy was, though some came from the Buckmaster Gallery sales too. Tom's ten percent of Derwatt profits derived also from Derwatt-labeled art supplies, from easels to erasers, but it was easier to smuggle money from northern Italy into Switzerland than to get it from London to Villeperce. Then there was the income from Dickie Greenleaf's bequest to Tom, which had risen to about eighteen hundred dollars a month from the original three or four hundred years ago. On this, curiously enough, Tom did pay full USA income tax, considerable because it was capital gains. Ironic and a bit fitting, Tom thought, because he had forged Dickie's will after Dickie's death, writing it on Dickie's own Hermes in Venice, and signing it with Dickie's forged signature.

But when you came down to it, Tom thought, as he thought every month, what was Belle Ombre apparently living on? Peanuts. After a fifteen-minute swat at listing expenditures, Tom's mind started to swim with ennui, and he stood up and smoked a cigarette.

Yes, well, why should he complain, he thought as he stared out his window. Tom declared some of the Derwatt company income, but not all of it, to the French, origin being labeled stocks in Derwatt Ltd. Tom now had his own stocks and a few U.S. Treasury Bonds, on which he had to declare the interest. His French Déclaration was for French-source income only (a bit for Heloise, not

him), while the Americans wanted to know his global income. Tom
was a French resident, though he still kept his American passport.
Tom had to make a separate worksheet for Pierre Solway in English, as Solway dealt also with the Ripleys' USA taxes. Mind-
boggling. Papers were the curse of the French populace, and even
the humblest citizen had to fill out a score of forms to acquire state
health insurance. Fond as Tom was of mathematics or plain arith-
metic, it bored him to copy postal expenses from last month's
record, and he stared down at the efficient-looking pale green
graph paper, income above, output below, and cursed it filthily.
One more swat, and he'd have filled out the hour and have it done.
This was for July, should have been done at the end of that month,
and now it was late August.

Tom was thinking of Frank, who was writing his account of
his father's last day. Now and again, Tom faintly heard his typewriter clicking. The boy had taken it into his room. Once Tom
heard an "Oof!" from Frank. Was he going through agony? There
were such long silences from the typewriter, that Tom wondered if
the boy were writing some of it in longhand.

Seizing his little batch of receipts—telephone, electricity, water
bill, car repair—Tom sat down for a final onslaught, determined to
finish. He did, and finally the worksheet and the receipts, but not
the canceled checks, because the French bank kept those, went into
a manila envelope to be kept in a bigger envelope with the other
monthly reports for Pierre Solway. Tom stuck the big envelope into
a lower left drawer of his desk, and stood up with a sense of joy and
virtue.

He stretched. And just at that moment one of Heloise's rock
'n' roll records started playing below stairs. Just what he needed!
This was a Lou Reed. Tom went into the bathroom and washed his
face in cold water. What time was it? Six fifty-five already! Tom
decided to tell Heloise about Eric now.

Frank just then came out of his room. "I heard the music," he
said to Tom in the hall. "Radio? No, it's the record, isn't it?"

"Heloise's," Tom said. "Come down."

The boy had changed from sweater to a shirt now, and the tails hung out of his trousers. He glided down the stairs with a happy smile, like one in a trance, Tom thought. The music had really struck a chord.

Heloise had it up loud, and was dancing by herself, with shoulder-shrugging movements, but she stopped shyly as Tom and the boy came down the steps, and she turned the music lower.

"Don't turn it down for me! It's nice," said Frank.

Tom could see that they were going to get on well in the music and dance department. "Finished the bloody accounts!" Tom announced loudly. "All dressed? You look nice!" Heloise wore a pale blue dress with a black patent leather belt, and high-heeled shoes.

"I telephoned Agnès. She said come early so we could talk," Heloise said.

Frank looked at Heloise with a new admiration. "You like this record?"

"Oh, yes!"

"I play it at home."

"Go ahead and dance," Tom said cheerfully, but he saw that Frank, at least, was a bit constrained at the moment. What a life for the boy, Tom thought, writing about murder minutes ago, and now plunged into rock. "Progress this afternoon?" Tom asked softly.

"Seven and a half pages. Some in my writing. I was switching."

Heloise, standing near the gramophone, had not heard the boy's words.

"Heloise," Tom said, "I'm picking up a friend of Reeves's tomorrow night. The friend stays the night only. Billy can take my room, so I'll be with you."

Heloise turned her pretty, made-up face toward Tom. "Who is coming?"

"Reeves said his name was Eric. I'll pick him up at Moret. We have no date for tomorrow evening, have we?"

She shook her head. "I think I will go now." She went to the telephone table, where she had left her handbag, and got a transparent raincoat from the front closet, as the weather looked uncertain.

Tom walked out with her to the Mercedes-Benz. "By the way, darling, don't mention to the Grais that anyone is staying with us. Don't say anything about an American boy. Say I'm expecting a phone call tonight. That's simple."

Her face lit with a sudden idea. "Are you maybe *hiding* Billy? To render Reeves a service?" She was talking through the open car window.

"No, dear. Reeves has never heard of Billy! Billy's just an American kid doing some gardening for us. But you know what a bourgeois snob Antoine is. 'Putting up a gardener in your guest room!'— Have a nice evening." Tom bent and kissed her cheek. "Promise?" Tom added.

He meant promise to say nothing about Billy, and he could see from her calm, amused smile and her nod that she did promise. She knew Tom did favors now and then for Reeves, some of which she had an inkling of, others of which she hadn't. Somehow his favors meant money earned, or acquired, anyway, and that was useful. Tom had opened the big gates for her, and he waved as she drove through and turned right.

By a quarter past nine that evening, Tom was lying on his bed with his shoes off, reading Frank's manuscript, or account. It went:

Saturday 22nd July had started like an ordinary day for me. Nothing unusual. The sun was shining and it was what everybody called a great day, meaning the weather. The day is doubly strange to me now, because I had no idea in the morning how it was going to end. I had no plans about anything. I remember Eugene asked me around three that afternoon if I wanted to play some tennis, since there were no visitors (guests) and he had some time. I

said no, don't know why I said no. I tried to phone
Teresa then, and her mother said she was out (Bar Harbor) and for the evening too and wouldn't be home till
maybe after midnight. I felt very jealous, wondering
whom she was with, even a lot of people or just one, it
would have been the same feeling. I decided I would go
to New York the next day no matter what, even if I
couldn't use our apartment which was closed for the
summer with drapes over the furniture and all. I would
telephone Teresa and persuade her to come to New
York, and we could either take a hotel room for several
days or she could stay with me in the New York apartment. I wanted to make a *move*, and NY seemed great to
suggest to her, to look forward to. I might have been in
New York already except for the fact that my father
wanted me to have "talks" with a guy called Bumpstead
or something that sounded like that, who was going to
be in Hyannisport for a couple of weeks vacationing.
This Bumpstead is a businessman of some kind about
30, my dad said, My dad thought 30 would be young
enough to convert me, I'm sure. To his way of life, business. This Bumpstead was due the next day. He didn't
come because of what happened.

(Here Frank had switched to a ballpoint pen.)

But I was trying to think of bigger things, of my whole
life, if I could. I was trying to sum my life up, as Maugham
says in a paperback I have called *The Summing Up*, but I am
not sure I could or that I got very far with it. I had been
reading some Somerset Maugham short stories (very
good), and they seemed to understand everything, in just
a few pages. I tried to think what is my life *for*, as if my life
of course had a meaning, which is not necessarily so. I

tried to think what I wanted from life, and all I could think of was Teresa, because I am so happy when I am with her, and she seems happy too, and I thought with the two of us together, we'd arrive at something called a meaning, or happiness, or going forward. I know I want to be happy and I think everyone should be happy and not confined by anything or anyone. By this I mean comfortable physically, and as to how they live. But

(Frank had crossed out the but and switched to the typewriter again.)

I remember after lunch my mother's friend Tal with us, my father as usual made some remark about having the grand-father clock in the downstairs hall repaired. It hasn't run for about a year, and Dad was always talking about getting it repaired, but he didn't trust any of the local places to do it and didn't want to send it to NY. It is an old clock from his family. I was bored at lunch. My mother and Tal managed to laugh a lot but they have their own jokes about people they know in NY.

After lunch I heard my father screaming on the telephone to Tokyo in the library. I switched off and waited in the hall. My father said he had something he wanted to say to me. Finally, this was to come and see him in the library around 6 p.m. I thought he could have told me that at lunch. I then went to my room, feeling angry. The others started playing croquet on the side lawn.

I detested my father, that I will admit, and I have heard that a lot of people detest their fathers. This does not mean that a person has to kill his father. I think I am unable as yet to realize what I did, and for this reason can walk around like a more or less ordinary human being, although I should not, and inside I feel different, uptight, and maybe

I will never get over it. This is why after I did it I decided
to look up T.R. who for some reason I felt very interested
in. This was partly because of the Derwatt picture mystery.
My family has a Derwatt, my father was interested a couple of years ago when some Derwatt paintings were suspected of being fakes or forgeries. I was around 14. Several
names mentioned in the newspapers, mainly English
names in London, Derwatt lived in Mexico, and I was
reading a lot of spy stuff then, and I got interested and
went to the big library in NY and looked up the records
of all those names in the newspaper files, the way detectives have to do in their work. T.R.'s entries seemed the
most interesting, American living in Europe, had lived in
Italy, something about a friend of his bequeathing him his
income when he died—so he must have liked T.R.—and
also something about a missing American called Murchison, in connection with the Derwatt mystery, the American disappearing after visiting T.R.'s house. I thought
T.R. might also have killed someone, just maybe, but that
anyway he did not look tough or like a stuffed shirt even,
because there were two pictures of him in the newspaper
items I saw. He was rather good looking and did not look
cruel. And whether he killed anybody seemed rather
unproven.

(Frank here picked up the pen again.)

I thought that day, not for the first time, why should I
join the old system, which had already killed the rats who
joined it? Or had killed and would kill a lot of them with
suicide, breakdowns, maybe simple insanity? Johnny had
already absolutely refused, and he was older than I and
therefore must know what he is doing, I thought. Why
shouldn't I follow Johnny instead of my father?

This is a confession, and I confess now to only one person T.R. that I killed my father. I sent his chair over that cliff. Sometimes I cannot believe that I did it and yet I know that I did it. I have read about cowards who do not want to face up to what they have done. I do not want to be like that. Sometimes I have a cruel thought: my father had lived long enough. He was cruel and cold to Johnny and me—most of the time. He could switch. Okay. But he tried to break us or change us. He had his life, with two wives, girls in the past, money galore, luxury. He was not able to walk for the last eleven years, because a "business enemy" tried to shoot him dead. How bad *is* what I did?

I am writing these lines to T.R. only, because he is the only person in the world I would tell these facts to. I know he does not detest me, because at this moment I am under his roof and he is giving me hospitality.

I want to be free and feel free. I just want to be free and be myself, whatever that is. I think T.R. is free in spirit, in his attitudes. He also seems kind and polite to people. I think I should stop here. Maybe it's enough.

Music is good, any kind of music, classic or whatever it is. Not to be in any kind of prison, that is good. Not to manipulate other people, that is good.

Frank Pierson

The signature was straight and clear, and underlined with what looked like an attempt at a dash. Tom suspected that the underlining was not usual for Frank.

Tom was touched, but he had hoped for a description of the very instant when Frank had sent his father over the cliff's edge. Was that hoping for too much? Had the boy blotted it out of his memory, or was he incapable of putting the instant of violence into words—which would require an analysis as well as a description of physical action? Probably, Tom thought, a healthy drive toward self-preservation was preventing Frank from going back in thought to that very moment. And Tom had to admit to himself that he would not care to analyze or relive the seven or eight murders he had committed, the worst undoubtedly having been the first, that of Dickie Greenleaf, beating that young man to death with the blade or the butt of an oar. There was always a curious secret, as well as a horror, about taking the life of another being. Maybe people didn't want to face it, because they simply couldn't understand it. It was so easy to kill someone, Tom supposed, if one were a hired killer, to dispose of some gang member or political enemy whom one didn't know. But Tom had known Dickie very well, and Frank had known his father. Hence the blackout, perhaps, or so Tom suspected. Anyway, Tom did not intend to pump the boy further.

But Tom knew the boy would be anxious to hear what Tom thought of his account, would probably want a word of praise for his honesty at least, and Tom felt the boy had really tried to be honest.

Frank was now in the living room. Tom had switched on the television for him after their dinner, but evidently Frank had been bored (very likely on a Saturday night), because he had put on the Lou Reed record again, though not so loudly as Heloise had played it. Tom went down, having left the boy's pages in his room.

The boy lay on the yellow sofa, his feet carefully over the edge so as not to soil the yellow satin, his hands behind his head, eyes closed. He had not even heard Tom come down the stairs. Or was he asleep?

"Billy?" Tom said, again trying to fix "Billy" in his mind for as long as he would need it, and how long would that be?

Frank sat up at once. "Yes, sir."

"I think what you wrote is very good—interesting as far as it goes."

"Do you?— What do you mean as far as it goes?"

"I was hoping—" Tom glanced toward the kitchen, but the light there was already off, Tom saw through the half open door. Tom had decided to stop, however. Why force his own thoughts into the mind of a sixteen-year-old? "Still, the moment when you did it, when you rushed forward toward the edge of the cliff—"

The boy shook his head quickly. "Amazing I didn't go over myself. I often think of that."

Tom could imagine, but it wasn't what he meant. He meant the realization that he had stopped the life of someone else. If the boy had so far escaped that mystery, or its puzzlement, then perhaps so much the better, because what could be accomplished by pondering it, even finally understanding it? Was it even possible?

Frank was waiting for a further word from Tom, but Tom had none.

"Did you ever kill a person?" the boy asked.

Tom moved nearer the sofa, a movement to relax himself, also to be farther from Mme. Annette's quarters. "Yes, I did."

"Even more than one?"

"To be honest, yes." The boy must have combed quite well through his dossier in the newspaper files of the New York Public Library, and used a bit of imagination too. Suspicion, rumors, nothing more, Tom knew, never an outright charge against him. Bernard Tufts's death over a mountainside near Salzburg oddly enough had been Tom's closest call in the direction of being accused, and Bernard—God rest his troubled soul—had been a suicide.

"I don't think what I did has sunk into me yet," Frank said in a voice barely audible. Now his left elbow rested on the sofa arm, a more relaxed attitude than that of a few minutes before, but he was far from relaxed. "Does it ever sink in?"

Tom shrugged. "Maybe we can't face it." The "we" had a special meaning for Tom then. He wasn't talking to a hired killer, and he had met a few.

"I hope you don't mind that I put this music on again. I used to play it with Teresa. She has it. We both have the record. So—"

The boy couldn't go on, but Tom understood, and he was glad to see that Frank's face looked more inclined to self-confidence, even inclined to a smile, rather than to the tears of a breakdown. *What about buzzing Teresa now,* Tom wanted to say, *and if you boomed the music up and told her you're okay and coming home?* But Tom had said this to Frank before and got nowhere. Tom pulled up one of the upholstered chairs. "You know—Frank, if no one suspects you, you have no reason to hide. Maybe now that you've written it out, you can go back home—soon. Don't you think?"

Frank's eyes met Tom's. "I just need to be *with* you for a few days. I'll work, you know? I don't want to be a drag in the house. But maybe you think I'm some kind of danger to you?"

"No." He was, slightly, but Tom couldn't have said how, exactly, except that the name Pierson was dangerous, because kidnappers would be interested. "I'm getting a new passport for you—by next week. Different name."

Frank smiled as if Tom had given him a surprise, a present. "You are? How?"

Tom again glanced unnecessarily toward the kitchen. "Let's go to Paris Monday for a new photograph. The passport will be done in—Hamburg." Tom was not used to betraying his Hamburg connection, Reeves Minot. "I ordered it today. That phone call at lunch. You'll have a different American name."

"Great!" said Frank.

The record moved into another song, a different, simpler rhythm. Tom watched the dream in the boy's face. Was he thinking of the new identity he would have, or of the pretty girl called Teresa? "Is Teresa in love with you too?" Tom asked.

Frank lifted his lip at one side, and it was not quite a smile. "She doesn't *say* so. She did say so once, weeks ago now. But there're a couple of other fellows—not that she likes them, but they're always hanging around. I know, because I told you, I think, her family has a house near Bar Harbor—also an apartment in New York. So I know. It's better not to make speeches about how *I* feel—to her or to anybody. But *she* knows."

"She's your only girlfriend?"

"Oh, yes." Frank smiled. "I can't imagine liking two girls at once. A little bit, maybe. But not really."

Tom left him to listen to the music.

Tom was upstairs in his room, in pajamas, reading Christopher Isherwood's *Christopher and His Kind*, when he heard a car turning in at Belle Ombre. Heloise. Tom glanced at his watch: five to midnight. Frank was still downstairs, playing records, in a trance of his own, Tom supposed, and he hoped a happy one. Tom heard the car give a *br-room* before the engine cut, and he realized that it was not Heloise. He leapt off the bed, grabbed his dressing gown and put it on as he went down the stairs. Tom opened the front door slightly and saw Antoine Grais' cream-colored Citroën on the graveled area in front of the steps. Heloise was getting out on the passenger side. Tom closed the door and turned the key.

Frank was on his feet in the living room, looking worried.

"Go upstairs," Tom said. "It's Heloise. She's come home with a visitor. Just go up and close your door."

The boy ran.

Tom was walking toward the door as Heloise tried the handle. Tom unlocked the door and Heloise entered, followed by Antoine who was smiling genially. Tom saw Antoine's eyes lift in the direction of the staircase. Had he heard something? "How *are* you, Antoine?" Tom asked.

"Tome, the strangest thing!" Heloise said in French. "The car wouldn't start just now, just wouldn't! So Antoine kindly brought me home. Come in, Antoine! Antoine thinks it's only—"

Antoine's baritone voice interrupted: "I think a bad connection of the battery. I looked. It needs a big wrench, a cleaning with a file. Simple. But I haven't got the big wrench. Ha-ha! And how are you, Tome?"

"Very well, thank you." They were by now in the living room where music still played. "May I offer you something, Antoine?" Tom asked. "Sit down."

"Ah, no more the harpsichord music," said Antoine, referring to the gramophone, and he seemed to be sniffing the air as if in hopes of picking up a scent of perfume. He had black and gray hair, and a stocky figure which swiveled now, on its toes.

"What's the matter with rock?" Tom asked. "My tastes are catholic, I hope." As Tom watched Antoine's eyes drift over the living room, looking for a clue as to what kind of person might have run up the stairs, possibly, Tom was reminded of the boring argument he and Antoine had got into over the pale blue rubber-tube-like structure called the Centre Pompidou, or Beaubourg. Tom detested it, Antoine defended it, saying it was "too new" for Tom's uneducated eye (that was the implication) to appreciate.

"You have a friend? I am sorry to disturb you," Antoine said. "Male or female?" This was meant to be funny, but had a nasty curiosity in it.

Tom could have hit him with pleasure, but only smiled, tight-lipped, and said, "Guess."

Heloise was in the kitchen during this, and appeared very soon with a small coffee for Antoine. "Here you are, Antoine dear. *Force* for the drive home."

The abstemious Antoine drank only a bit of wine at dinner.

"Sit down, Antoine," said Heloise.

"No, my dear, this is fine," said Antoine, sipping. "We saw the light in your room, you know, and the living room light on, so—I invited myself in."

Tom nodded politely, like a toy ducking bird. Was Antoine thinking that a girl or boy had fled at once to Tom's bedroom, and that Heloise connived at it? Tom folded his arms, and just then the record came to its end.

"Tome will take me to Moret tomorrow, Antoine," Heloise said. "We'll tell the garage mechanic and bring him to your house for the car. Marcel. Do you know him?"

"Very good, Heloise." Antoine set his coffee cup down, efficient as always, even at drinking hot coffee fast. "Now I must be off. Good night, Tome."

Antoine and Heloise exchanged French kisses at the door, smacks on the cheeks, one, two. Tom hated it. Not French kisses in the American sense, certainly, nothing sexy about them, just damned silly. Had Antoine been able to see Frank's legs dashing up the stairs? Tom didn't think so. "So Antoine thinks I might have a girlfriend!" Tom said with a chuckle after Heloise had closed the door.

"Of course he does not! But why are you hiding Billy?"

"I'm not hiding him, he's hiding himself. He's even a little shy with Henri, of all people. Anyway, darling, I'll take care of the Mercedes—Tuesday." It had to be Tuesday because tomorrow was Sunday, and Monday their usual garage was closed, as were most French garages, since they stayed open Saturday.

Heloise slipped out of her high-heeled shoes. Now she was barefoot.

"Nice evening? Any other people?" Tom put a record back in its sleeve.

"A couple from Fontainebleau, another architect—younger than Antoine."

Tom hardly listened. He was thinking of Frank's pages on his desk in the place where the typewriter usually sat. Heloise was now going up the stairs. She used his bathroom most of the time, now that the boy had the guest room. But Tom continued putting away records—only one more to go. Heloise was not inclined to pause and look at pages of any kind on his desk. Tom turned out the living room lights, locked the front door, and went upstairs. Heloise was in her own room undressing, Tom supposed. He took the boy's pages, put a paperclip on them, and stuck them in his top right drawer, then on second thought into a folder marked "Personal." The boy would have to get rid of those pages, regardless of their literary merit, Tom thought. Burn them. Tomorrow. With the boy's consent, of course.

7

On the following day, Sunday, Tom took Frank for an outing in the Fontainebleau woods, west of Fontainebleau where Frank had not been before, and to a section Tom knew where there were few or no hikers or tourists. Heloise had not wanted to come, and said she preferred to lie in the sun and read a novel that Agnès Grais had lent her. Heloise tanned amazingly well for a blonde. She never overdid her sunbathing, but sometimes her skin became a bit darker than her hair. Perhaps she had conveniently mixed genes, as her mother was blonde, and her father evidently brunette, because his hair, what was left of it, was a fringe of dark brown with an inner circle of gray, suggesting saintliness to Tom, though nothing was further from the truth.

Near noon, Tom and Frank were driving toward Larchant, a quiet village several kilometers west of Villeperce. The cathedral at Larchant had been half destroyed by fire a couple of times since the tenth century. The little private houses, all close together in cobble-stoned lanes, looked like illustrations from children's books, cottages almost too small for man and wife to live in, which made Tom think it might be interesting to live alone again. But when had he ever lived alone? With bloody Aunt Dottie—dotty about everything except money—from childhood, until he left her Boston establishment in his teens, then crummy apartments in Manhattan for brief periods, unless he shacked up with more affluent friends who had a spare bedroom or a living room sofa. And then Mongibello and Dickie Greenleaf when he had been twenty-six. And why should all that go through his head as he stood looking up at the cream-and-dust-colored interior of the Larchant cathedral?

The cathedral was empty but for them. Larchant attracted so few tourists, Tom was not afraid of Frank's being spotted. Tom would have been afraid of the château at Fontainebleau, for instance, with its international clientele, and probably Frank had already seen it. Tom didn't ask.

At an unattended counter by the door, Frank acquired some postcards of the cathedral, and dutifully dropped the correct sum into the slot in a wooden box, then seeing that his palm was still full of francs and centimes, Frank tipped his hand and dropped the lot in.

"Your family go to church?" Tom asked as they walked down a steep cobbled slope toward the car.

"Na-a-ah," Frank said. "My father always called the church a cultural lag and my mother's plain bored with it. She won't be pressured."

"Is your mother in love with Tal?"

Frank gave Tom a glance and laughed. "In love? My mother plays it cool. Maybe she *is*. But she'd never act silly, never show it. She was an actress, you know. I think she can act even in real life, I mean."

"Do you like Tal?"

Frank shrugged. "I suppose he's all right. I've seen worse. He's an outdoor type, very strong physically, considering he's a lawyer. I leave them alone, you know?"

Tom was still curious whether Frank's mother might marry Talmadge Stevens, but why should he be? Frank was more important, and Frank didn't care about his family's money, from what Tom could see, if his mother and Tal should for some reason, maybe even suspicion of patricide, decide to cut the boy off.

"Those pages you wrote," Tom said, "they ought to be destroyed, you know. Dangerous to keep, don't you think?"

The boy, watching his footing, seemed to hesitate. "Yes," he said firmly.

"If anyone found them, you couldn't say it's a short story, with all those names in it." Of course the boy could, Tom thought, but it would be a bit mad. "Or are you toying with the idea of confessing?" Tom asked, in a tone that implied that this would be total madness, out of the question.

"Oh, no. *No.*"

The strength of that negative pleased Tom. "Okay then. With

your permission I'll get rid of the pages this afternoon. Maybe you want to read them once more?" Tom was opening the car door.

The boy shook his head. "I don't think so. I read it over once."

After lunch at Belle Ombre Tom went out to the garden (because Heloise was practicing on the harpsichord in the living room where the fireplace was) with the pages folded twice in his hand. Frank was wielding the spade near the greenhouse, wearing his blue jeans, which Mme. Annette had washed in her machine for him and also ironed. Tom burned the pages in a back corner of the garden, near where the woods began.

Shortly before eight that evening, Tom drove to Moret to fetch Reeves's friend Eric Lanz from the railway station. Frank wanted to come with him for the ride, and to walk back, and insisted that he could get back to Belle Ombre on foot. Tom had reluctantly agreed. Tom had said to Heloise before leaving, "Billy's having dinner in his room tonight. He doesn't want to meet a stranger, and I don't want this friend of Reeves to meet him either." Heloise had said, "Oh? Why?" and Tom had replied, "Because he might try to engage Billy for some little job. I don't want the boy to get into trouble, even if he's paid well for it. You know Reeves and his chums." Indeed Heloise did, and Tom often had to say to her, "Reeves *is* useful—sometimes," which could and had meant that Reeves could do services that were sometimes much needed, such as providing new passports, acting as go-between, a safe house in Hamburg. Sometimes Heloise half understood what was going on, and the half that she did not know, she didn't want to know. All to the good. Her nosy father couldn't pump much out of her that way either.

At a clearing at the edge of the road, Tom pulled over and stopped the car. "Now let's compromise, Billy. You're three or four kilometers from Belle Ombre, a nice walk. I don't want to take you all the way to Moret."

"Right." The boy started to open the car door.

"And this. Just a sec." Tom pulled a flat box from his trousers pocket. It was pancake makeup that he had taken from Heloise's room. "I don't want that mole showing." He put a little of the paste on the boy's cheek and rubbed it smooth.

Frank grinned. "Makes me feel silly."

"Keep this. I don't think Heloise'll miss it, she's got so much other stuff. I'm going back one kilometer." Tom turned the car around. There was almost no traffic.

The boy said nothing.

"I want you to be home before I get back. I can't have you coming in the front door." Tom stopped the car only one kilometer from Belle Ombre. "Have a nice walk. Madame Annette's put your supper in my room—or she will. I told her you wanted to go to bed early. Stay in my room. All right, Billy?"

"Yes, sir." Now the boy smiled, and with a wave of his hand, walked away toward Belle Ombre.

Tom again turned the car and headed for Moret. He arrived just as the train from Paris was disgorging its passengers. Tom felt a bit awkward, because Eric Lanz knew what he looked like, and he didn't know Eric from Adam. Tom walked slowly toward the exit gate, where a scruffy little ticket-taker in a peaked cap bent over every passenger's ticket to see if it was valid for today, though Tom thought three-quarters of French passengers, being students, elderly, civil servants, war-damaged, traveled at half-fare anyway. No wonder the French railway was always crying bankruptcy. Tom lit a Gauloise and looked up at the sky.

"Miss-ter—"

Tom looked from the blue sky into the smiling face of a rather short, rosy-lipped man with black mustache, who wore a horrible checked jacket and a necktie of gaudy stripes. He had also round, black-rimmed spectacles. Tom waited, saying nothing. The man looked not at all German, but one never knew.

"Tom?"

"Tom, yes."

"Eric Lanz," he said with a short bow. "How do you do? And

thank you for meeting me." Eric was carrying two cases of brown plastic, both so small, they could be considered hand luggage on an airplane. "And greetings from Reeves!" Now his smile was broader as they walked toward Tom's car, whose position Tom had indicated with a gesture. Eric Lanz spoke with a German accent, though a slight one.

"Did you have a good trip?" Tom asked.

"Yes! And I always enjoy France!" Eric Lanz said, as if he were setting foot on a Côte d'Azur beach, or maybe walking into a splendid museum of French culture somewhere.

Tom felt in a thoroughly sour mood for some reason, but what did it matter? He would be polite, offer Eric dinner and bed and breakfast, and what else could Eric want? Eric declined to put his cases even in the back of the front seats of the Renault station wagon, but kept them at his own feet. Tom zoomed off toward home.

"Ah-h," said Eric, ripping off his mustache. "That's better. And these Groucho Marx things."

Off came his spectacles, Tom saw with a glance to his right.

"That Reeves! Too—much, as the English say. Two passports for something like *diss?*" Eric Lanz proceeded to effect the change in his passports from inside jacket pocket to something at the bottom and apparently in a bottom compartment of a shaving kit which he took from one of the awful plastic carryalls.

Now in his pocket he had a passport looking more like himself, Tom supposed. What was his real name? Was his hair really black? What else did he do besides odd jobs for Reeves? Safecracking? Jewelry thieving on the Côte d'Azur? Tom preferred not to ask. "You live in Hamburg?" Tom asked in German, by way of being polite and also practicing his German.

"*Nein!* West Berlin. Much more fun," said Eric, in English.

Maybe more remunerative too, Tom thought, if this chap was a runner for dope or illegal immigrants. What was the fellow carrying now? Only his shoes looked of quality, Tom noticed. "You

THE BOY WHO FOLLOWED RIPLEY

have an appointment with someone tomorrow?" Tom asked, again in German.

"Yes, in Paris. I shall be out of your ha-ar, as they say, by eight o'clock tomorrow morning, if that is agreeable to you. I am sorry, but it could not be arranged by Reeves that the—the man I am supposed to see would meet me at the airport. Because he is not here yet. Could not be."

They arrived at Villeperce. Since Eric Lanz seemed quite out-going, Tom ventured to ask:

"You're bringing him something? What—if I may be so rude?"

"Jewelry!" said Eric Lanz, almost giggling. "Ver-ry pretty. Pearls—which I know nobody these days cares about, but these are real ones. Also a necklace of *Smaragd*! Emeralds!"

Well, well, Tom thought, and said nothing.

"You like emeralds?"

"Frankly no." Tom particularly disliked emeralds, perhaps because Heloise, being blue-eyed, disliked green. Tom also thought he would not or did not care for women who would like emeralds or who wore green.

"I was thinking of showing them to you. I am very pleased that I have got here," Lanz said with an air of relief, as Tom drove through the open gates of Belle Ombre. "Now I can see your won-derful house which I have heard about from Reeves."

"Would you mind waiting here for a moment?"

"You have guests?" Eric Lanz looked on the alert.

"No-o." Tom pulled his handbrake. He had seen a light in the window of his own room, and he supposed Frank was there. Back in a sec." Tom leapt up the front steps and entered the living room.

Heloise lay face down on the yellow sofa, reading a book, with her bare feet over the sofa's arm. "By yourself?" she asked with surprise.

"No, no, Eric's outside. Billy's back?"

Heloise turned and sat up. "He is upstairs."

Tom went back to bring Eric Lanz in. He introduced the German to Heloise, then offered to show him to his room. Mme. Annette came into the living room then, and Tom said, "Monsieur Lanz, Madame Annette. Don't trouble, madame, I shall show our guest his room."

Upstairs, in the room which had just been Frank's and where there was no sign of Frank now, Tom asked, "Was that all right? I introduced you to my wife as Eric Lanz?"

"Ha-ha, my real name! Of course it's all right here." Eric set his plastic bags on the floor near the bed.

"Good," said Tom. "There's the bath. Come down soon and have a drink with us."

Had there been any need, Tom was thinking by ten that evening, for Eric Lanz to spend the night at his house? Lanz was taking the 9:11 a.m. train tomorrow from Moret to Paris, and he could get a taxi to Moret, he assured Tom, if Tom preferred. Tom was driving all the way to Paris tomorrow with Frank, but he wasn't going to tell Eric that.

Over coffee, Eric Lanz talked about Berlin, and Tom only half listened. Such fun! Lots of places open all night. All kinds of people, *individuals*, freewheeling, anything went. Not many tourists, just the mainly stuffy foreigners who came invited to attend one kind of conference or another. Excellent beer. Lanz was drinking a brand called Mützig, available at the Moret supermarket, and declared it better than Heineken. "But for me it's Pilsner-Urquell—*vom Fass!*" Eric Lanz seemed to admire Heloise and to be trying to put his best foot forward for her. Tom hoped Eric would not become inspired to haul out his gems tonight to show her. That would be funny! Showing a pretty woman his jewelry, then snatching it away again, because it wasn't his to bestow.

Now Eric was talking about possible industrial strikes in Germany which he said would be, if they came, the first since before Hitler. There was a certain fussiness about Eric, a neatness. He got up for a second time to admire the beige and black keyboard of the harpsichord. Heloise, bored to the point of nearly yawning, excused herself before coffee.

"I wish you a pleasant night's sleep, Monsieur Lanz," said Heloise with a smile, and went upstairs.

Eric Lanz was still gazing at her, as if he would have liked to make his night's sleep more pleasant by sharing her bed. He was on his feet, almost falling forward, and he made a second little bow. "*Madame!*"

"How is Reeves doing?" Tom asked casually. "Still in that flat!" Tom chuckled. Reeves and Gaby, the part-time housemaid, had not been in when the flat was bombed.

"Yes, and with the same maid! Gaby! She is a darling. Fearless! Well, she likes Reeves. He gives a little excitement to her life, you know?"

Tom shifted. "Could I see the jewels that you mentioned?" Tom thought he might as well improve his education.

"Why not?" Eric Lanz was on his feet again, giving what Tom hoped was a final glance at his empty coffee cup, his empty Drambuie glass.

They went up the stairs, into the guest room. The light showed under the door of Tom's room. He had told the boy to lock the door from the inside, and Tom thought Frank would have done this, because it was a bit dramatic. Now Eric had opened one of the pudgy plastic cases and he groped at its very bottom—maybe into a false bottom—and produced a purple velvet-like cloth which he spread on the bed. Within this cloth were the jewels.

The diamond and emerald necklace left Tom cold. He would not even have bought the thing, if he could have afforded it, not only not for Heloise, but not for anyone. There were also three or four rings, one a diamond of goodly size, another a separate emerald.

"And these two—sapphire," said Eric Lanz, relishing the word. "I won't tell you where these came from. But they are valuable indeed."

Had Elizabeth Taylor been robbed lately, Tom wondered.

Amazing, Tom thought, that people put value in such essentially
ugly objects—garish even—as this diamond and emerald necklace.
Tom would have preferred to own a Dürer etching or a Rembrandt. Perhaps his taste was improving. Would he have been
impressed by these jewels at the age of twenty-six, when he had
been with Dickie Greenleaf in Mongibello? Maybe, but strictly by
the monetary value of the objects. And that was bad enough. But
now he wasn't even impressed by that. He had improved. Tom
sighed, and said, "Very pretty. And no one took a look in your cases
at Charles de Gaulle?"

Eric laughed gently. "No one bothers with me. With my crazy
mustache, my boring?—yes, boring clothes, cheap and with no
taste, nobody pays any attention. They say passing customs is a
technique, an attitude. I have the right one, not too casual, but not
at all anxious. That's why Reeves likes me. To take things around
for him, I mean."

"Where are these going to end up?"

Eric was now refolding the purple cloth with the finery
inside. "I do not know. That is not my worry. I have a date tomorrow in Paris."

"Where?"

Now Eric smiled. "Very public place. St Germain area. But I
don't think I should tell you exactly where or exactly the time," he
said teasingly, and laughed.

Tom smiled also, not caring. It was almost as silly as the Italian
Count Bertolozzi affair. The Count had been an overnight guest at
Belle Ombre carrying, unbeknownst to the Count, microfilm in
his toothpaste tube. Tom had had to steal the toothpaste tube, he
recalled, on Reeves's request, from the bathroom which Eric Lanz
had now. "Have you a clock, or shall I ask Madame Annette to
awaken you, Eric?"

"Oh, I have a Wecker—a waker-clock, thank you. I should say
we take off a little after eight? I should like to avoid taking a taxi,
but if the hour is too early for you—"

"No problem," Tom interrupted pleasantly. "I'm very flexible as to hours. Sleep well, Eric." Tom went out, aware that Eric thought he had not sufficiently admired his jewels.

Tom realized that he had forgotten his pajamas, and he disliked sleeping nude. Nudity could come later in the night, if one wanted it, was Tom's feeling. With some hesitation, he rapped gently on the door of his room with his fingertips. A light was still visible under the door. "Tom," he whispered at the crack of the door, hearing the boy's light and probably barefoot tread.

Frank opened the door, smiling broadly.

Tom put a finger to his lips, went in, relocked the door, and whispered, "Pajamas, sorry." He got them from his bathroom, and also his house slippers.

"He's in there? What kind of fellow?" Frank asked, indicating the next room.

"Never mind that. He'll be gone tomorrow morning just after eight. You stay in this room till I get back from Moret. All right, Frank?" Tom noticed that the mole on the boy's right cheek was again visible, because Frank had washed or had a bath.

"Yes, sir," Frank said.

"Good night." Tom hesitated, then gave the boy a pat on his arm. "Glad you're home safe."

Frank smiled. "G'night, sir."

"Lock the door," Tom whispered, before he opened the door and went out. Tom paused long enough to hear the slide of the lock. Under the German's door a light showed, and Tom faintly heard running water in the bathroom, a melodious humming, and Tom recognized "Frag Nicht Warum Ich Weine"—a sweet, sentimental little waltz! Tom bent over with silent laughter.

Tom paused in front of Heloise's door, wondering suddenly if and when Johnny Pierson might turn up in France with a private detective to look for his brother. That was a nuisance, a little problem. When he and the boy went to the American Embassy area tomorrow—the neighborhood was convenient for passport photos—couldn't Johnny be making inquiries at the embassy about his brother? Why worry, since it hadn't happened yet, Tom told himself. And what if it did? Why should he guard Frank so zealously, just because Frank wanted to hide himself? Was he becoming as cloak-and-dagger as Reeves Minot? Tom tapped on Heloise's door.

"Come in," said Heloise.

THE NEXT MORNING, Tom drove Eric Lanz, still mustacheless, to Moret for the 9:11 train. Eric was in good spirits, talking about the farmland they were driving through, the inferior corn for cattle which people could be eating if it were better corn, the all-round subsidized inefficiency of the French farmer.

"Still—it is nice to be in France. I shall visit a couple of art exhibits today, since my rendezvous will be finished at—um—early."

Tom didn't care what time the rendezvous was, but he had thought to visit Beaubourg with Frank, as there was a major exhibit on now called "Paris-Berlin," and it would be a hell of a coincidence if Eric were there when he and the boy were, because Eric just might be aware of the disappearance of Frank Pierson. Funny, Tom thought, that so far no newspaper had suggested that Frank might have been kidnapped, though of course kidnappers usually announced their ransom demands pretty quickly. Evidently the family believed that Frank had run away on his own and was still on his own. It would be a splendid time for crooks to demand ransom money, claiming that they had the boy when they hadn't. Why not? Tom smiled at the idea.

"What is funny? I should think it is not very funny for you as an American," said Eric, trying to be light, but at his most Germanic. He had been talking about the falling dollar, and the inadequate policies of President Carter, as compared with the sagacious housekeeping of Helmut Schmidt's government.

"Sorry," Tom said, "I was thinking of Schmidt's or somebody's remark—'The financial affairs of America are now in the hands of rank amateurs.'"

"*Correct!*"

They were at the Moret station now, and Eric had no time to continue. Handshaking and many thanks.

"Have a good day!" Tom called.

"Same to you!" Eric Lanz smiled and was off, with his two plastic carryalls firmly in his hands.

Tom drove back to Villeperce, spotted the postman's yellow van in mid-village making its usual rounds, and knew that the post would be on time today at 9:30. But it reminded Tom of a little chore that would be easier to do here than in crowded Paris. He stopped outside the post office, and went in. That morning, with his first coffee, he had gone downstairs and written a note to Reeves. ". . . The boy is 16, 17, but *not* younger, 5 ft. 10 in., brown straight hair, born anywhere in USA. Send the thing to me soon as pos. express. Tell me what I'll owe you. Thanks in advance, in haste. E.L. here. All okay, it seems. Tom." In the Villeperce post office, Tom paid the extra nine francs for the red EXPRESS label, which the girl behind the grill pasted on the envelope for him. She started to take his letter, remarked that it wasn't sealed, and Tom told her that he had something else to put in it. Tom took the envelope home with him.

Frank was in the living room, dressed, finishing his breakfast.

Heloise was evidently still upstairs.

"Good morning. How are you?" Tom asked. "Sleep well?"

Frank had stood up, with his air of respect for Tom which made Tom a bit uneasy. The boy's face was sometimes radiant, almost as if he were looking at the girl Teresa with whom he was in love. "Yes, sir. You took your friend to Moret, Madame Annette told me."

"He's gone, yes. We'll take off in maybe twenty minutes. Okay?" Tom looked at the boy's tan polo-neck sweater, and supposed it would be all right for a passport photo. In the photograph in *France-Dimanche*, maybe his passport photograph, Frank wore a shirt and tie. All the better if Frank looked less formal. Tom went closer to the boy and said, "Keep the right-hand part in your hair, but loosen it as much as you can top and sides for the photograph today. I'll remind you again. Got a comb to take with you?"

Frank nodded. "Yes, sir."

"And that pancake?" The boy had covered the mole, Tom saw, but he had to keep it covered all day.

"Got it, yes." The boy touched his right back pocket.

Tom went upstairs and saw that Mme. Annette was changing the sheets in the room that had been Eric Lanz's, and thriftily replacing them with the same ones Frank had been sleeping on before. It reminded Tom of yesterday, when the boy had insisted that Mme. Annette not change Tom's sheets. Frank had seemed to prefer to sleep on them, and Mme. Annette had appeared to think this quite sensible.

"You and the young man will be back tonight, Monsieur Tome?"

"Yes, in time for dinner, I should think." Tom heard the post-man's van and his handbrake. From the closet in his room, Tom got an old blue blazer, which had always been a bit small for him. Tom didn't want the passport photograph to include Frank's interesting diamond-patterned tweed jacket, in case Frank elected to wear it today.

The row of shoes on the floor of his closet caught Tom's eye. All shined to perfection! All lined up like soldiers! He had never seen such a gleam on the Gucci loafers, such a deep glow in the cordovans. Even his patent leather evening slippers, with their silly grosgrain bows, had new highlights. Frank's work, Tom knew. Mme. Annette occasionally gave them a brushup, but nothing like this. Tom was impressed. Frank Pierson, heir to millions, pol-ishing his shoes! Tom closed his closet door and went down with the blazer.

The post looked uninteresting, two or three bank envelopes which Tom did not bother opening, a letter to Heloise whose envelope was addressed in her friend Noëlle's handwriting. Tom ripped the brown paper off the *International Herald-Tribune*. Frank was still in the living room, and Tom said, "Brought this for you to wear instead of that tweed. Old one of mine."

Frank put the jacket on carefully, and with obvious pleasure. The sleeves were a bit long, but the boy flexed his arms gently and said, "Just marvelous! Thank you."

"In fact, you can keep it."

Frank's smile widened. "*Thank* you—really. Excuse me, I'll be down in a minute." He ran upstairs.

Tom glanced over the *Trib*, and found a small item at the bottom of page two. PIERSON FAMILY SENDS DETECTIVE, said the modest headline. There was no photograph. Tom read:

> Mrs. Lily Pierson, widow of the late John J. Pierson, food manufacturing magnate, has sent a private detective to Europe to look for her missing son Frank, 16, who left their Maine home in late July and has been traced to London and Paris. Accompanying the detective is her older son John, 19, whose passport the younger brother took when he left his home. It is believed the search will begin in the Paris area. No kidnapping is suspected.

Tom felt an unease akin to embarrassment on reading this, yet what would happen if they ran smack into Frank's brother and the detective today? The family simply wanted to find the boy. Tom was not going to mention the item to Frank, and he would leave the *IHT* at home. Heloise gave the paper barely a glance, usually, but just might miss it if he took it with him and got rid of it. However, what were the French papers going to say about the private detective and the older brother? And would they oblige with a reprint of Frank's photograph?

Frank was ready. Tom went up to say good-bye to Heloise.

"You could have taken me," Heloise said.

The second sour note of the morning. It was unlike Heloise. She always had things to do. "I wish you'd said it last night." She was wearing pink-and-blue striped jeans, a sleeveless pink blouse. It didn't matter what someone as pretty as Heloise wore in Paris in August, but Tom didn't want Heloise to know that Frank was getting a passport photograph made. "We're going to Beaubourg, and you've already seen the show with Noëlle."

"What's the matter with this Billy?" she asked with a puzzled twitch of her blonde eyebrows.

"The matter?"

"He looks troubled about something. And he seems to adore you. Is he a *tapette*?"

That meant a homosexual. "Not that I can see. Do you think so?"

"How long does he want to stay with us? He's been here nearly a week, no?"

"I do know that he wants to go to a travel agency today. In Paris. He was talking about Rome. He'll be taking off this week." Tom smiled. "Bye-bye, darling. Back around seven."

When he left the house, Tom picked up the *IHT*, folded it, and jammed it into a back pocket.

8

Tom took the Renault, though he would have preferred the Mercedes. He reproached himself for not having asked Heloise if she needed a car today, because the Mercedes was still at the Grais'. Heloise would have said something, if she needed a car, Tom thought. Frank looked happy with his head back, and the wind blowing through the open window. Tom put on a cassette, Mendelssohn for a change.

"I always leave my car here. Parking's a bore in midtown." Tom had stopped at a garage near the Porte d'Orléans. "Back around— eighteen hours," Tom said in French to an attendant whom he

knew by sight. Tom had passed through the gate which mechani-
cally presented him with a ticket and his hour of arrival stamped
on it. Then he and Frank got a taxi. "Avenue Gabriel, if you please,"
Tom said to the driver. He did not want to get out right at the
embassy, and had forgotten the name of the street at a right angle
to Avenue Gabriel in which the photography place was. When they
were in the neighborhood, Tom intended to ask the driver to let
them out.

"This is the life, riding with you in a taxi in Paris!" Frank said,
still in his dream of—what? Freedom? The boy insisted on paying
the taxi. He took his wallet from the inside jacket pocket of Tom's
old blazer.

Tom wondered what else was in that wallet, in case the boy
was searched? Tom asked the driver to stop just off Avenue Gabriel
in the street he wanted. "There's the photo place," Tom said, indicating a small shingle hanging from a doorway twenty yards away.
"Called Marguerite or something. I don't want to go in with you.
That mole looks all right now, but don't touch it. Muss your hair.
Maybe put on a—slight smile. *Don't* look serious." Tom said this
because the boy did look serious most of the time. "They'll ask you
to sign your name. Sign Charles Johnson, for instance. They won't
ask for identity, I know, because I've recently been through this
with them. All right?"

"Okay. Yes, sir."

"I'll be here," Tom said, pointing to a bar-café across the street.
"Come out and join me, because they'll tell you you have an hour
to wait for the photos, but really it's about forty-five minutes."

Then Tom walked to Avenue Gabriel and went left toward
Concorde, where he knew there was a newsstand. He bought *Le
Monde, Figaro*, and *Ici Paris*, a gaudy scandal sheet, with blue, green,
red, and yellow on the front page. Tom saw at a quick glance as he
walked back toward the bar-café that *Ici Paris* had given a whole
page to Christina Onassis's surprising marriage to a Russian prole,
and another page to Princess Margaret's probably imaginary new

escort, an Italian banker slightly younger than she. All sex, as usual, who was doing it to whom, who might start doing it, and who had knocked it off with whom. When Tom had sat down and ordered a coffee, he took a look at every page of *Ici Paris*, and found nothing about Frank. No sex angle there, of course. On the penultimate page were a lot of advertisements, how to meet your true partner—"Life is short, so realize your dream now"—and ads with illustrations of various inflatable rubber dolls, ranging in price from fifty-nine francs to three hundred and ninety, the dolls said to be shippable in plain wrapper and to be capable of everything. How did one blow them up, Tom wondered. It would take all the breath out of a man to do it, and what would a man's housekeeper or his friends say, if they saw a bicycle pump and no bicycle in his apartment? Funnier, Tom thought, if a man just took the doll along to his garage with his car, and asked the attendant to blow her up for him. And if the man's housekeeper found the doll in bed and thought it was a corpse? Or opened a closet door and a doll fell out on her? A man could buy more than one doll, certainly, one his wife and two or three others his mistresses, and could lead quite a busy fantasy life that way.

His coffee had arrived, and Tom lit a Gauloise. He found nothing in *Le Monde*, nothing in *Figaro*. What if the French police had put a man *in* the photography place, a man who might be on the watch for Frank Pierson along with other wanted people? Wanted people often had to change their passports as well as their identification papers.

Frank came back, smiling. "They said an hour. Just like you told me."

"Just *as* you told me," said Tom. The mole was still covered, Tom saw, the boy's hair still standing up a little on top. "You signed another name?"

"In the book there, yes. Charles Johnson."

"Well, we can take a walk—for forty-five minutes," Tom said. "Unless you'd like a coffee here."

Frank had not yet sat down at the little table, and suddenly his body went rigid as he stared at something across the street. Tom looked also, but cars were just then passing. The boy sat down, averted his face, and rubbed a hand across his forehead nervously. "I just saw—"

Tom stood up now, looked on the pavement, the pavement across the street, and at that instant one of two men's figures turned to look back, and Tom recognized Johnny Pierson. Tom sat down again. "Well, well," Tom said, and glanced at the waiters behind the bar, who seemed to be paying no attention to them, so Tom at once got up and went to the doorway to look again. The detective (Tom assumed he was the detective) wore a gray summer suit and was bareheaded, with wavy reddish hair, a stocky build. Johnny was taller and blonder than Frank, wearing a waist-length, nearly white jacket. Tom wanted to see if they went into the passport photograph shop—which was not so labeled, it was just a place that sold cameras and took photographs for passports—and to Tom's relief, they walked past it. But they had probably made inquiries at the United States Embassy, which was just around the corner. "Well—" Tom said again, sitting down. "They didn't find out anything at the embassy, that's for sure. Nothing that *we* don't know, anyway."

The boy said nothing. His face was noticeably paler.

Tom took a five-franc piece from his pocket, ample for one cup of coffee, and motioned to the boy.

They went out and turned left, toward Concorde and the Rue de Rivoli. Tom looked at his watch, and saw that the photographs should be ready by a quarter past twelve. "Take it easy." Tom was not walking fast. "I'll go back to that shop on my own first, and see if they're possibly waiting there. But they just walked past it."

"They did?"

Tom smiled. "They did." Of course they could turn and go back, into the shop, if they had inquired of the embassy where people usually had photographs made. They might ask if a boy fitting Frank's description had come in recently, and so forth. But Tom was tired of fretting over things he couldn't do anything about. They gazed into windows in the Rue de Rivoli—silk scarves, miniature gondolas, swanky-looking shirts with French cuffs, postcards on racks out in front. Tom would have enjoyed looking into W. H. Smith's bookshop, but he steered Frank away, saying that the place was always full of Americans and English. Tom would have liked to think the cloak-and-dagger game amused the boy, but Frank's face looked stricken since he had seen his brother. Then it was time to walk back to the photography shop. Tom told Frank to walk slowly along the pavement, and to turn and go back to the arcades of the Rue de Rivoli in case he saw his brother and the detective again, and Tom would find him.

Tom walked to the shop and went in. An American-looking couple sat waiting on straight chairs and the same skinny, tall young man whom Tom remembered from a couple of months ago, the photographer himself, was offering the name-signing book to a new customer, an American girl. Then the young man disappeared with the girl behind a curtain, where Tom knew the studio was. Tom had pretended to be looking at cameras in a glass case, and now he went out. He told Frank that the coast was clear.

"I'll be on the street here," Tom said. "You've paid for the pictures, haven't you?" Tom knew the procedure, and the boy had paid thirty-five francs in advance. "Just take it easy, and I'll be here." Tom gave him an encouraging smile. "Slowly," Tom said, as the boy went off.

Frank obediently slowed his pace, and did not look back.

Tom walked not fast, but as if he might have a destination, to the end of the street. He was keeping an eye out for the return of Johnny and the detective, but he did not see them. When Tom reached the Avenue Gabriel end of the block, and turned, Frank was walking toward him from the shop. Frank crossed the street, pulled a small white envelope from his jacket pocket and handed it to Tom.

The pictures did look different from the one Tom had seen in

France-Dimanche, hair more mussed on top, the vague smile that Tom had suggested, the mole not visible, but still the eyes and brows were much the same. Under careful inspection, the two photographs would of course be seen to be of the same boy.

"As good as can be expected," Tom said. "Now let's get a taxi."

Frank had hoped for higher praise, Tom could see. They got a taxi by good luck before Concorde. Tom put one of the photographs into the envelope he had prepared for Reeves Minot. Tom sealed the envelope and felt relieved. He had asked the driver to go to Beaubourg, near which place there was bound to be a snack bar and a post box. Tom found both these things within yards of the bulbous exterior of the Centre Pompidou.

"Amazing, isn't it," Tom said, referring to the blue monstrosity of the museum's exterior. "I find it ugly—outside, anyway."

It looked like many long blue balloons inflated to near bursting point and wrapped around each other. There was definitely something like plumbing about it, but one hesitated to guess whether the ten-foot diameter balloons might contain water or air. Tom again thought of the inflated dolls for sexual purposes, and imagined one bursting under a man, which surely must happen occasionally. What a letdown! Tom bit his lip to stop his laughter. They had a mediocre steak with potato chips in a bar-café-tabac, outside which Tom had dropped his express letter into a yellow box. The collection time was at 16:00 hours.

At the "Paris-Berlin" show, Frank seemed most impressed by Emil Nolde's "Dance Before the Golden Calf," a violently prancing trio or quartet of vulgar ladies, one quite naked. "Golden calf. That's money, isn't it?" said Frank, looking dazed and glassy-eyed with what he had seen already.

"Money, yes," said Tom. It was not an exhibit to give one quietude, and Tom felt tense also because he thought he ought to look around now and then for Johnny Pierson and the detective. It was strange to try to take in artists' statements on German society of the 1920s, anti-Kaiser posters from World War I, Kirchner, portraits

by Otto Dix—plus his brilliant "Three Prostitutes on the Street"—
and at the same time to be worried about the possible appearance
of a pair of Americans who would put a sudden end to his pleasure. To hell with the Americans, Tom thought, and said to Frank,
"You keep an eye out for—you know, your brother. I'd like to
enjoy this." Tom spoke a bit severely, but the pictures that surrounded him were like music pouring into his ears in silence, or
into his eyes anyway. Tom took a deep breath. Ah, the Beckmanns!

"Does your brother," Tom asked, "like art exhibits?"

"Not as much as I do," was the reply, "but he does like them."

That was not very cheering. Now Frank was riveted by what
looked like a charcoal drawing of a room's interior with a window
at the back on the left, and a masculine figure standing in the foreground in an attitude of strain and confinement. The perspective of
the walls and floor suggested confinement. Not a brilliant drawing,
perhaps, but the conviction and intensity in the artist's mind was
plain. It was prison-like, whatever kind of room it was. Tom knew
why Frank was fixated.

Tom had to put his hand on the boy's shoulder to tear him
away.

"Sorry." Frank shook his head a little, and looked at the two
doors of the room in which they stood. "My dad used to take us
to exhibits. He always liked Impressionists. Mainly French. Snow-
storms in Paris streets. We have a Renoir at home—of that. Snow-
storm, I mean."

"So that's one thing nice about your father, he liked paintings.
And he could also afford to buy them."

"Well—at least. I mean, *paintings*—a few hundred thousand
dollars—" Frank said it as if it were nothing. "I notice you're always
trying to say something nice about my father," he added a bit
resentfully.

Was he? The exhibition was bringing out some emotion in
Frank. "De mortuis," Tom said, shrugging.

"He could buy Renoirs? Certainly." Frank flexed his arms as if he were getting ready to hit somebody, but he looked rather emptily straight ahead of him. "His market was the whole world, everybody. Well, everybody who could afford it. A lot of his stuff was luxury goods. 'More than half of America is too fat,' he used to say."

They were walking slowly back through a room where they had already been. One of the three or four miniature cinema shows was going on to their left, six or eight people sat on chairs looking at it, others stood. On the screen Russian tanks were attacking Hitler's army.

"I told you," Frank continued, "besides the ordinary and gourmet stuff, there's the same stuff with a low calorie count. It reminds me of what they say about gambling or prostitution—they make money out of other people's vices. You fatten them up, then make them thin, and start over again."

Tom smiled at the boy's intensity. What bitterness! Was he trying to justify himself in having killed his father? It was like a little steam being let out of a kettle, when the lid rises and falls again. How was Frank ever going to achieve the big justification, which would take away all his guilt? He might never find a total justification, but he had to find an attitude. Every mistake in life, Tom thought, had to be met by an attitude, either the right attitude or the wrong one, a constructive or self-destructive attitude. What was tragedy for one man was not for another, if he could assume the right attitude toward it. Frank felt guilt, which was why he had looked up Tom Ripley, and curiously Tom had never felt such guilt, never let it seriously trouble him. In this, Tom realized that he was odd. Most people would have experienced insomnia, bad dreams, especially after committing a murder such as that of Dickie Greenleaf, but Tom had not.

Frank clenched his hands suddenly—but he hadn't seen anything. The gesture was due to his own thoughts.

Tom took his arm. "Had enough? Let's go out this way." Tom steered him toward what he thought was an exit room, back through still another room, where Tom had a feeling of walking past one soldier after another—the pictures—as if they were an army of variously attired fighters, somehow armed to the teeth, even though some were in evening clothes. Tom felt in a curious way conquered, and he didn't like that. What caused it? Something besides the pictures, he was sure. He would have to send the boy away. The situation was getting a bit warm, emotional, worse.

Suddenly Tom laughed.

"What?" asked Frank, alert as ever to Tom, and he glanced around to see what might be funny.

"Never mind," Tom said. "I'm always thinking of crazy things." Tom had been thinking, if the detective and Johnny saw Tom Ripley with Frank, they might at first think Tom had kidnapped him, since Tom had such a bad reputation. That could still arise, Tom thought, if the detective even thought to discover his residence and learned that a boy had been staying at the Ripley's house. On the other hand, who in Villeperce knew that, besides Mme. Annette, and also Tom had not presented any ransom demand.

They took a taxi to the garage, and were back at Belle Ombre at a little after six. Heloise was upstairs, washing her hair, which would take another twenty minutes, Tom knew, with the dryer. All to the good, because he wanted to try once again with Frank. The boy had sat down in the living room and was looking at a French magazine.

"Why don't you ring up Teresa and tell her you're okay?" Tom asked in a cheerful voice. "You won't have to tell her *where* you are. She must know you're in France anyway."

At the name Teresa, the boy sat up a little. "I think you'd like to—you'd like me to get lost. I can understand that." Frank stood up.

"If you want to stay in Europe, you can. That's your affair. But it'll make you happier if you speak to Teresa and tell her you're all right. Won't it? Don't you think she's worried?"

"Maybe. I hope so."

"It's around noon in New York. She's in New York?—You dial nineteen, one, then two one two. I can go upstairs so I won't hear a word." Tom waved a hand toward the telephone, and walked toward the stairs. The boy was going to do it, Tom could tell. Tom went up to his room and closed the door.

Less than three minutes later, the boy knocked on Tom's door. He came in at Tom's word, and said, "She's out playing tennis." He announced this as if it were dreadful news.

Frank couldn't imagine Teresa so unconcerned about him that she would be out playing tennis, Tom supposed, and a further agony must be that she was playing tennis with a boy she liked more than she liked Frank. "You spoke to her mother?"

"No, the maid—Louise. I know her. She told me to call back in an hour. Louise said she was out with a few boys." Frank put the last phrase in miserable-sounding quotes.

"You said you were all right?"

"No," the boy said after an instant's reflection. "Why should I? I suppose I sounded all right."

"I'm afraid you can't call back from here," Tom said. "If the— if Louise mentions it, the family may want to get the call traced if you ring back. Anyway it's too likely for me to risk it. Post office in Fontainebleau is closed now, otherwise I'd drive you. I don't think you can reach Teresa tonight, Billy." Tom had hoped that the boy could reach Teresa tonight, and that she might have said something like, "Oh, Frank, you're okay! I miss you! When are you coming home?"

"I understand," the boy said.

"Billy," Tom said firmly, "you must make up your mind what you want to do. You're not suspected. You're not going to be accused. Susie doesn't seem to count for much or anything, because she didn't see anything. Just what are you afraid of? You have to come to terms with that."

Frank shifted and shoved his hands in his back pockets. "Of myself, I think. I already said that."

Tom knew. "If I weren't here, what would you do?"

The boy shrugged. "Maybe kill myself. Maybe be sleeping in

Piccadilly. You know the way they hang around the fountain there, the statue. I'd send Johnny's passport back to him, and then I don't know what I'd do—till somebody checked on me. Then I'd be sent home—" Another shrug. "And then I don't know. Maybe I wouldn't ever *confess*—" He emphasized the word, but spoke in a whisper. "But maybe I'd kill myself in a couple of weeks. Then there's Teresa. I admit I'm hung up—and if something goes wrong there—if something's already gone wrong—She can't *write* me, you know. So it's hell."

Tom didn't want to remark that Frank would probably be in love with seventeen more girls before he found the one he might finally marry.

WEDNESDAY JUST AFTER NOON, Tom was pleasantly surprised by a telephone call from Reeves. The object in question would be ready by late that night, and would be in Paris by tomorrow noonish. If Tom was in a hurry and wanted to pick it up himself, he could go to a certain Paris apartment, otherwise it could be sent from Paris to Tom by registered post. Tom preferred to pick it up. Reeves gave him an address, a name, third floor.

Tom asked for the telephone number there in case of need, and Reeves gave him this too. "Very fast work, Reeves, I thank you." It would have been quite all right, Tom thought, to have sent it registered from Hamburg, but the airplane delivery did save one day.

"And for this little job," said Reeves in his creaky, old man's voice, though he was not yet forty, "two thousand, if you don't mind, Tom. Dollars. Cheap at the price, because this wasn't easy, sort of a new one, you know. And I should think your friend can afford it, eh?" Reeves's tone was amused and friendly.

Tom understood. Reeves had recognized Frank Pierson. "Can't talk anymore here," said Tom. "I'll get it to you via the usual, Reeves." Tom meant via a request to his Swiss bank. "Are you going to be home in the next days?" Tom had no plans, but wanted to know this. Reeves could be wonderfully helpful.

"Yes, why? Thinking of coming?"

"No-o," said Tom cautiously, ever fearful that his line might be being tapped.

"You're staying put."

Tom supposed that Reeves knew he was sheltering Frank Pierson, if not under his own roof, then somewhere.

"What's all the trouble? Impossible to say, huh?"

"Impossible, yes, just now. I do thank you, Reeves."

They hung up. Tom walked to the French windows and saw Frank in his Levi's and darker blue workshirt plying the spade at the edge of a long bed of roses. He worked slowly and steadily, like a peasant who knew what he was doing, not like an amateur who would have knocked himself out in fifteen minutes of a fast attack on something. Strange, Tom thought. Maybe the work was some kind of penance in the boy's mind? Frank had been spending his time yesterday and today reading, listening to music, and doing chores such as car-washing and sweeping out Belle Ombre's cellar, which had involved shifting rather heavy racks of wine and putting them back in place. Frank had thought the tasks up himself.

Should they go to Venice, Tom wondered. A change of scene might shape the boy up, make him come to a decision, and Tom might be able to put him on a plane from Venice to New York, and return home himself. Or Hamburg? Same thing. But Tom didn't want to involve Reeves in the sheltering of Frank Pierson, and Tom in fact didn't care to involve himself much longer. Maybe with the new passport, Frank would find his courage and take off on his own, finish his personal adventure in his own style.

Thursday noon, Tom rang the Paris number in the Rue du Cirque, and a woman answered. They spoke in French.

"This is Tom here."

"Ah, oui. I think everything is in order. You are coming this afternoon?" She didn't sound like a maid, but like the woman of the house.

"Yes, if that is convenient. Around three-thirty?"

That would be all right.

Tom told Heloise that he was going to make a quick trip to Paris to talk with their bank manager, and would be back between 5 and 6 p.m. Tom was not in trouble with an overdraft, but one of the managers of Morgan Guarantee Trust did sometimes give him stock market advice, very general and minor, Tom considered, as Tom preferred to let his stocks ride rather than waste time in the dangerous game of playing the market. Anyway, Tom's excuse was good enough, because Heloise's mind was on her mother that afternoon. Her mother, a youthful fifty-odd and not inclined to illness, had had to go to hospital for an examination which might result in an operation for a tumor. Tom remarked that doctors always prepared people for the worst.

"She looks in the pink of health. Give her my good wishes when you speak with her," Tom said.

"Billy is going with you?"

"No, he's staying. He's got some little jobs he wants to do—for us."

In the Rue du Cirque, Tom was able to find a parking meter free, then he went to the house, an old well-kept edifice with the usual street door button to press, and then the door opened on a hall or foyer with a concierge's door and window, which Tom didn't bother with. He took the lift to the third floor, and rang the bell on the left marked Schuyler.

A tall woman with a lot of red hair opened the door slightly. "Tom."

"Ah, come in! This way, please." She led him toward a living room which was across a hall. "You have met before, I think."

In the living room stood Eric Lanz, smiling, hands on hips. There was a coffee tray on a low table in front of a sofa. Eric was standing. "Hello, Tom. Yes, me again. How are you?"

"Quite well, thanks. And you?" Tom was also smiling with surprise.

The redheaded woman had left them. There was a low drone of sewing machines from another room of the flat. What went on here, Tom wondered. Maybe another fence depot, as was Reeves's Hamburg apartment? With a couturière cover?

"And here we are," said Eric Lanz, opening a beige cardboard portfolio, which had strings to close it. He produced a white envelope from among other thicker envelopes.

Tom took the envelope, and glanced over his shoulder before he opened it. No one else had come into the room. The envelope was not sealed, and Tom wondered if Eric had already looked at the passport? Perhaps. Tom did not want to look at it in Eric's presence, but at the same time wanted to know if Hamburg had done a good job.

"I think you will be pleased," Eric said.

Frank's photograph had the official stamp which raised the surface, plus PHOTOGRAPH ATTACHED DEPARTMENT OF STATE PASSPORT AGENCY NEW YORK partly on and partly below it. BENJAMIN GUTHRIE ANDREWS was the name, born in New York, and height and weight and date of birth corresponded well enough to Frank's, though the date made him seventeen now. No matter. The job looked good to Tom, who had some experience, and maybe only a magnifying glass could detect that the raised stamp on the photograph might be a bit off from the stamp on the page—or was it? Tom couldn't tell. Inside of front page, full address was apparently that of parents in New York. The passport was some five months old, with a Heathrow entry stamp, then France, then Italy, where the unfortunate bearer must have been relieved of it. No current French entry, but unless a passport control officer's suspicions were aroused by Frank's appearance, no one was going to peer at entry and exit stamps, Tom knew. "Very good," Tom said finally.

"Nothing to do but sign it across the photograph."

"Do you happen to know if the name has been changed, or is the real Benjamin Andrews going to be looking for his passport?" Tom hadn't detected any sign of erasure in the typewritten name inside the front cover, and any previous signature

fragment had been neatly obliterated from beside the
photograph.

"It has been changed, the last name, Reeves told me.— Coffee?
This is finished, but I can ask the maid to make some." Eric Lanz
looked slimmer, even of better social class since Tom had seen him
three days ago, as if he were a miracle man who could effect a
transformation just by thinking about it. Now he wore the trousers
of a dark blue summer suit, a good white silk shirt, and the shoes
which Tom recognized. "Sit down, Tom."

"Thanks, I said I'd be home soon.— You travel a lot, it seems."

Eric laughed—rosy lips, white teeth. "Reeves always has work
for me. Berlin too. I am selling hi-fi gadgets this time," he said in a
lower tone and glanced at the door behind Tom. "*Supposed* to be.
Ha-ha!— When are you coming to Berlin?"

"No idea. No plans." Tom had put the passport back into its
envelope, and he gestured with it before sticking it into his inside
jacket pocket. "I've arranged to settle for this with Reeves."

"I know." Now Eric pulled a billfold from his blue jacket
which lay on the sofa. He extracted a card and handed it to Tom.
"If you are ever in Berlin, it would be a pleasure to see you, Tom."

Tom glanced at the card. Niebuhrstrasse. Tom didn't know
where that was, but it was in Berlin, with a telephone number.
"Thanks.— You've known Reeves a long time?"

"Oh—two, three years, ja." His rosy, neat mouth smiled again.
"Luck to you, Tom—and to your friend!" He moved to the door
with Tom to see him out. "Wiedersehen!" said Eric, softly but
clearly.

Tom went down to his car and drove homeward. Berlin, Tom
was thinking. Not for the presence of Eric Lanz at all, if he ever
was at home, but because Berlin was off the beaten tourist track.
Who wanted to visit Berlin, except perhaps scholars of the World
Wars, or as Eric had said, businessmen invited to conferences. If
Frank wanted to hide out a few days longer, Berlin might be an
idea for him. Venice—more attractive and beautiful, but also a place

where Johnny and the detective might spend a couple of days, looking. What Tom didn't want was that pair to knock on his own door in Villeperce.

9

"Benjamin. Ben. I like that name," Frank said, beaming now as he sat on the edge of his bed, gazing at his new passport.

"I hope it gives you courage," Tom said.

"I know this cost something. You can tell me how much, and if I can't—do it just now, I can do it later."

"Two thousand dollars. . . . Now you're free. Keep letting your hair grow. You've got to sign that passport across the photograph, you know." Tom made him try the entire name on a sheet of typewriter paper. The boy had rather quick and angular handwriting. Tom told him to round the capital B of Benjamin, and made him write the whole name out three or four more times.

At last the boy signed with one of Tom's black ballpoint pens. "How is this?"

Tom nodded. "All right. Remember when you sign anything else—take it easy so you'll round everything."

It was after dinner. Heloise had wanted to watch something on television, and Tom had asked the boy to come upstairs with him.

The boy looked at Tom and his eyelids blinked quickly. "Will you come with me, if I go somewhere? To another town, I mean? City?" He wet his lips. "I know it's been a pain having me—hiding me. If you'd come with me to another country, you could just leave me." Now he looked with sudden dismalness toward the window, and back at Tom. "It'd be so awful, somehow, leaving from here, *your* house. But I could, I suppose." He stood up straighter, as if to illustrate that he could stand on his own feet.

"Where're you thinking of going?"

"Venice. Rome, maybe. They're big enough to get lost in."

Tom smiled, thinking Italy was a hotbed of kidnappers. "Yugoslavia? Doesn't appeal to you?"

"Do you like Yugoslavia?"

"Yes," Tom said, but not in a tone that implied he would like to go there now. "Go to Yugoslavia. But I wouldn't advise Venice or Rome—if you want to stay free for a while. Berlin is another possibility. Off the tourist track."

"Berlin. I've never been there. Would you go to Berlin with me? Just for a few days?"

The idea was not unattractive, because Tom found Berlin interesting. "If you promise to go home after Berlin," Tom said quietly and firmly.

Frank's face was smiling again, as broadly as when he had received the new passport. "All right, I promise."

"Okay, we'll go to Berlin."

"Do you know Berlin?"

"I've been there—twice, I think." Tom suddenly felt picked up. Berlin would be all right for three or four days, fun in fact, and he would hold the boy to his promise to take off for home from there. Maybe it wouldn't be necessary to remind the boy of that promise.

"When shall we go?" Frank asked.

"The sooner the better. Maybe tomorrow. I'll see about plane tickets in Fontainebleau tomorrow morning."

"I've still got some money." Then the boy's expression changed. "Not much, I suppose, only about five hundred dollars' worth of francs."

"Never mind about money. We'll settle up later. I'll say good night. I want to go down and speak with Heloise.— Of course you can come downstairs again if you want to."

"Thanks, I think I'll write to Teresa." Frank looked happy.

"All right, but we'll post it from Düsseldorf tomorrow, not from here."

"Düsseldorf?"

"Planes to Berlin have to touch down somewhere inside Germany first, and I always aim for Düsseldorf instead of Frankfurt, because you don't change planes at Düsseldorf, just get out for a few minutes—passports. One other thing, most important, don't tell Teresa you're going to Berlin."

"All right."

"Because she might tell your mother, and I assume you want to be let alone in Berlin. The Düsseldorf postmark will let her know you're in Germany, but tell her you're—going to Vienna. How about that?"

"Yes—*sir*." Frank sounded like a newly promoted soldier, delighted to take orders.

Tom went downstairs. Heloise was lying on the sofa, watching a news program. "Look," she said. "*How* can they go on killing each other?"

A rhetorical question. Tom looked blankly at the television screen, which showed an apartment building blowing up, darts of red and yellow flame, an iron beam tumbling in the air. He supposed it was Lebanon. A few days ago it had been Heathrow, the aftermath of an attack on the Israeli airlines. Tomorrow the world, Tom thought. He was thinking that Heloise would have news of her mother tomorrow morning maybe by about ten, and Tom hoped the hospital tests would not mean surgery. Tom intended to go to Fontainebleau before ten, get the tickets, and tell Heloise that it was a most urgent job for Reeves Minot, which he had learned about by telephone during the night, something like that. There was no telephone in Heloise's room, and with her door closed, she could not hear the telephone in his room or in the living room downstairs. Awful news continued on the television set, and Tom postponed any kind of speech to Heloise.

Before he went to bed that night, Tom knocked on Frank's door and handed him some booklets on Berlin and a map.

"Might interest you. Tells you about the political situation and so forth."

By BREAKFAST TIME, Tom had altered his plans somewhat. He would use a Moret travel agency for the ticket—his own—and telephone the airport in regard to Frank's ticket. He told Heloise that Reeves had rung in the small hours and wanted him to come to Hamburg at once to lend both his presence and his advice on an art deal.

"I spoke with Billy this morning. He wants to come with me to Hamburg," Tom said, "and he'll be going back to America from there." Tom had told her that Billy had not made up his mind Monday in Paris where he wanted to go.

Heloise was visibly pleased that the boy would be going off with Tom, as Tom had thought she would be. "And you'll be coming back—when?"

"Oh—I'd say in three days. Maybe Sunday, Monday." Tom was dressed and having a second coffee and toast in the living room. "I'll take off in a few minutes to see about the tickets. And I hope the news is good, darling, by ten."

Heloise was supposed to ring a doctor at a Paris hospital at ten in regard to her mother. "Merci, chéri."

"I have a feeling there's nothing wrong with your mother." Tom meant that, because her mother looked very fit. Just then Tom saw that Henri the gardener had arrived—today being neither Tuesday nor Thursday but Friday—and was lazily filling big metal pitchers with rainwater from the tank by the greenhouse. "Henri's here. That's nice!"

"I know.— Tome, there's nothing dangerous about Hamburg, is there?"

"No, dear.— Reeves knows that I know about a Buckmaster sale that's a little like this one in Hamburg. A nice launching place for Billy too. I'll show him a bit of the city. I never do anything dangerous." Tom smiled, thinking of shoot-outs, which he consid-

ered he had never been in, but he also recalled an evening at Belle
Ombre, when a Mafia corpse or two had been lying on the marble floor right here in the living room, oozing blood, which Tom
had had to wipe up with Mme. Annette's sturdy gray floor rags.
Heloise hadn't seen that. Not a shoot-out, anyway. The Mafiosi had
had guns, but Tom had bashed one over the head with a piece of
firewood. Tom did not like to remember that.

Tom telephoned Roissy from his room, and learned that there
were seats available on an Air France flight taking off at 3:45 p.m.
that afternoon. He reserved a place for Benjamin Andrews, the
ticket to be picked up at the airport. He then drove to Moret and
bought his round-trip ticket in his own name. When he came
back, he informed Frank. They would leave the house around one
o'clock for Roissy.

Tom was glad that Heloise did not ask for Reeve's telephone
number in Hamburg. On some other occasion, Tom had certainly
given it to her, but maybe she had mislaid it. If she found it and
rang Reeves, it would be awkward, so Tom thought he should telephone Reeves once he got to Berlin, but somehow Tom didn't
want to do it now. Frank was packing. And Tom was casting an eye
over his house as if it were a ship he would soon abandon, although
the house was in good hands with Mme. Annette. Only three or
four days? That was nothing. Tom had thought of taking the
Renault and leaving it at the Roissy garage, but Heloise wanted to
drive them or at least accompany them in the Mercedes, which was
now running well. So Tom drove the Mercedes to Roissy–Charles
de Gaulle Airport, and thought how friendly and convenient Orly
airport had been a year or so ago, between Villeperce and Paris,
until they opened the north-of-Paris Roissy and routed everything
from there, even flights to London.

"Heloise—I thank you for putting me up so many days," Frank
said in French.

"A pleasure, Billy! And you have been a help to us—in the garden and in the house. I wish you luck!" She extended her hand

through the car's open window, and rather to Tom's surprise she kissed Frank on both cheeks as he bent toward her.

Frank grinned, embarrassed.

Heloise drove off, and Tom and Frank went into the terminus with their luggage. Heloise's affectionate good-bye reminded Tom that she had never asked him what he was paying the boy for his work. Nothing. Tom was sure the boy would not have accepted anything. Tom had given the boy five thousand francs this morning, the maximum one was allowed to take out of France, and Tom had the same amount himself, though he had not as yet ever been searched by the French on departure. If they should run out in Berlin, which was unlikely, Tom could wire for money from a bank in Zurich. Now he told Frank to go and buy his ticket at the Air France counter.

"Benjamin Andrews, flight seven-eight-nine," Tom reminded him, "and on the plane we won't sit together. Don't look at me. See you in Düsseldorf maybe, otherwise Berlin." He started for the luggage check-in, then found himself lingering to see if Frank was going to get his ticket without difficulty. One or two people were ahead of Frank, then the boy was at the counter, and Tom saw from the girl's scribbling and the money exchange that all was well.

Tom checked in his suitcase, then proceeded to one of the upward sloping escalators which eased him toward gate number six. These gates, called simply gates in England or anywhere else, were here absurdly labeled "Satellites," as if they were somehow detached from and whirling around the airport proper. Tom lit a cigarette in the last hall where one could smoke, and looked over his fellow passengers, nearly all men, one concealed behind a copy of the *Frankfurter Allgemeine* already. Tom was among the first to board. He did not look back to see if Frank had even come into the lounge. Tom settled himself in his smoking-section seat, half closed his eyes, and glanced at the passengers bumping up the aisle with attaché cases, but he did not see Frank.

At Düsseldorf, the passengers were told they could leave their hand luggage on board, but everyone had to get off. Here they were herded like sheep toward an unseen destination, but Tom had been here once before, and knew they were destined for nothing worse than a passport checking and stamping.

Then came a small waiting area to which they were also herded, and Tom saw Frank negotiating for a stamp for his letter to Teresa. Tom had forgotten to give the boy some of the German paper money and coins which Tom had in his pocket, left over from earlier trips, but the German woman was smiling now, apparently accepting Frank's French money, and the letter changed hands. Tom boarded the plane for Berlin.

Tom had said to Frank, "You'll love the Berlin-Tegel airport." Tom liked it, because it looked like an airport of human size: no frills, no escalators, triple levels, or eye-dazzling chromium, just a mostly yellowish-painted reception hall with a round bar-café counter in the center, and a single WC in evidence without a kilometer's walk to it. Near the circular refreshment counter Tom lingered with his suitcase, and gave Frank a nod when he saw him approaching, but Frank was evidently so dutifully obeying orders that he did not look at Tom, and Tom had to intercept him.

"Fancy seeing you here!" said Tom.

"Good afternoon, sir," said Frank, smiling.

The forty or so passengers who had debarked at Berlin seemed to have dwindled to less than a dozen now, which was another treat to the eye.

"I'll see about a hotel room," Tom said. "Wait here with the luggage." Tom went to a telephone booth a few yards away, looked up the number of the Hotel Franke in his business address book, and dialed it. Tom had once visited an acquaintance at this middle-category hotel, and had noted its address for possible future use. Yes, they had two rooms to offer, said the Hotel Franke, and Tom booked them under his name, and said he would be arriving in about half an hour. The few persons left in the homey-looking terminus appeared so innocuous to Tom that he risked a taxi together with the boy.

Their destination was the Albrecht-Achillesstrasse off the Kur-

fürstendamm. They rode at first through what seemed kilometers
of flat plains, past warehouses, fields and barns, then the city began
to show itself in a few very new-looking buildings, beige and
cream near-skyscrapers, a bit of chrome on aerial-like spires. They
were approaching from the north. Tom slowly and rather uncom-
fortably became aware of the pocketlike, islandlike entity called
West Berlin, surrounded by Soviet-controlled territory. Well, they
were within the Wall, and protected at least for the nonce by
French, American, and British soldiers. The one jagged, not new
edifice made Tom's heart leap, rather to his own surprise.

"That's the Gedächtniskirche!" Tom said to Frank with almost
proprietary pride. "Very important landmark. Bombed, as you see,
but they let it stand the way it was."

Frank was looking out the open window, rapt, almost as if it
were Venice, Tom thought, and in its way Berlin was just as unique.

The broken, reddish-brown tower of the Gedächtniskirche
passed by them on their left, then Tom said, "All this was flattened
around here—what you're looking at. That's why everything looks
so new now."

"*Ja*, and *kaputt* it was!" said the middle-aged driver in German.
"You are tourists? Just here for pleasure?"

"Yes," said Tom, pleased that the driver wanted to chat. "How's
the weather?"

"Yesterday rain—today like this."

It was overcast, but not raining. They sped along the Kurfürstendamm, and halted for a red light at Lehninplatz.

"Look how new all these shops are," Tom said to Frank. "I'm
really not mad about the Ku'damm." He remembered his first trip
to Berlin, alone, when he had walked up and down the long
straight Kurfürstendamm, vainly trying to sense an atmosphere
which one couldn't get from pretty shopwindows, chrome and
glass pavement booths that displayed porcelain and wristwatches
and handbags. Kreuzberg, the slummy old section of Berlin, now
so full of Turkish workers, had more personality.

The driver made a left turn into Albrecht-Achillesstrasse, past a corner pizzeria which Tom remembered, then past a supermarket, now closed, on the right. The Hotel Franke stood on the left around a little curve in the street. Tom paid the driver with some of his leftover marks, of which he had nearly six hundred.

They filled out little white cards that the receptionist gave them, and both consulted their passports for the correct numbers. Their rooms were on the same floor, but not adjacent. Tom had not wanted to go to the more elegant Hotel Palace near the Gedächtniskirche, because he had stayed there once before, and thought that for some reason they might remember him, and notice that he was with a teenaged boy not related to him. Just what anybody would make of that, even also at the Hotel Franke, Tom didn't care, but he thought a modest hotel like the Franke less apt to recognize Frank Pierson.

Tom hung up a pair of trousers, pulled the bedcover back, and tossed his pajamas onto the white, button-sheeted, feather-filled top item, which served both as blanket and sheet, a German institution that Tom knew of yore. From his window he had a thoroughly dull view of a grayish court, of another six-story cement building set at an angle, and a couple of distant treetops. Tom felt inexplicably happy suddenly, felt a sense of freedom, maybe illusory. He stuck his passport case with his French francs in it at the bottom of his suitcase, closed the suitcase lid, and went out and locked his door. He had told Frank he would pick him up in five minutes. Tom knocked on Frank's door.

"Tom?— Come in."

"Ben!" said Tom, smiling. "How are things?"

"Look at this crazy *bed*!"

They both suddenly laughed out loud. Frank had also pulled the bedcover back and laid his pajamas on the buttoned feather blanket.

"Let's go out and take a walk. Where're those two passports?" Tom made sure that the boy's new passport was out of sight, found

Johnny's passport in the suitcase, and put it in an envelope from the writing table drawer. This he stuck at the bottom of the boy's suitcase. "You don't want to whip out the wrong one." Tom wished they had burned Johnny's passport at Belle Ombre, since Johnny must have had to acquire a new one anyway.

They went out and could have taken the stairs, but Frank wanted to see the elevator again. He looked as happy as Tom felt. Why, Tom wondered.

"Press E. That's the Erdgeschoss."

They left their keys, went out, and turned right toward the Kurfürstendamm. Frank stared at everything, even at a dachshund being aired. Tom proposed a beer at the corner pizzeria. Here they bought chits and queued up at a counter for beer only, then carried their big mugs to the only partly free table, where two girls were eating pizzas. With a nod, they gave permission for Tom and the boy to sit down.

"Tomorrow we'll go to Charlottenburg," Tom said. "Museums there and a beautiful park too. Then there's the Tiergarten." And there was tonight. Lots of places to go to in Berlin at night. Tom looked at the boy's cheek and saw that the mole was covered. "Keep up the good work," Tom said, pointing to his own cheek.

By midnight or a little after, they were at Romy Haag's, and Frank was a bit drunk on three or four more beers. Frank had won a toy bear at a throwing-game stall outside a beerhall, and Tom was now carrying the little brown bear, the symbol of Berlin. Tom had been to Romy Haag's on his last visit to Berlin. It was a bar-disco, slightly touristy, and with a late show of transvestites.

"Why don't you dance?" Tom said to Frank. "Ask one of these to dance." Tom meant the two girls seated on stools at the bar with their drinks in front of them, but with their eyes on the dance floor over which a gray sphere kept turning. Spotted lights, shadows and white, played slowly over the walls. The rotating gray object, no bigger than a beachball and quite ugly *per se*, looked like a relic of the Thirties, evocative of pre-Hitler Berlin, and strangely fascinating to the eye.

Frank squirmed as if he hadn't the courage to approach the girls. He and Tom were standing at the bar.

"Not prostitutes," Tom added over the noise of the music.

Frank went off to the toilet near the door. When the boy came back, he walked past Tom and went on to the dance floor where Tom for a few minutes lost sight of him, and then saw him dancing with a blonde girl under the revolving sphere, along with a dozen other couples and maybe a few singles. Tom smiled. Frank was jumping up and down, having fun. The music was nonstop, but Frank came back after a couple of minutes, triumphant.

"I thought you'd think I was a coward if I didn't ask a girl to dance!" Frank said.

"Nice girls?"

"Oh, very! Pretty! Except that she was chewing gum. I said 'Guten Abend' and I even said 'Ich liebe dich' but I only know that from songs. I think she thought I was pissed. She laughed, anyway!"

He certainly was pissed, and Tom steadied him by one arm so he could slide a leg over a stool. "Don't drink the rest of that beer, if you don't want it."

A roll of drums heralded the floorshow. Three sturdy men pranced out in floor-length, ruffled dresses of pink, yellow, and white, in broad-brimmed flowered hats, and with huge plastic breasts entirely exposed and sporting red nipples. Enthusiastic applause! They sang something from Madame Butterfly, and then came several skits of which Tom understood barely half, but which the spectators seemed to appreciate.

"They are funny to look at!" Frank roared into Tom's ear.

The muscular trio wound up with "Das ist die Berliner Luft," flouncing their skirts and kicking high, as posies from the audience showered upon them.

Frank clapped and shouted "Bravo!— Bravi!" and nearly fell off his stool.

A few minutes later, Tom was walking arm in arm with the boy—mainly to keep Frank upright—along a darkish pavement, which however at half past two in the morning still had several pedestrians.

"What's *that*?" Frank asked, seeing a pair in strange costume approaching.

They seemed to be a man and woman, the man in harlequin tights and a hat with pointed brim fore and aft, while the woman resembled a walking playing card, and on closer inspection Tom saw that she was the ace of clubs. "Probably just come from a party," Tom said, "or going to one." Tom had noticed before in Berlin that people liked to change their clothing from one extreme to another, even disguise themselves. "It's a who-am-I game," Tom said. "The whole city's like this." Tom could have gone on. The city of Berlin was bizarre enough, artificial enough—at least in its political status—and so maybe its citizens attempted to outdo it sometimes in their dress and behavior. It was also a way for Berliners to say, "*We exist!*" But Tom was in no mood to get his thoughts together. He said only, "To think it's surrounded by these boring *Russians* with no sense of humor at all!"

"Hey, Tom, can we take a look at East Berlin? I'd love to see that!"

Tom clutched the little Berlin bear, and tried to think of any peril there for Frank, and couldn't. "Sure. They're more interested in taking a few DM off their visitors than in knowing who the visitors are.— There's a taxi! Let's get it!"

10

Tom telephoned Frank from his room the next morning at nine. How was Ben feeling?

"All right, thank you. I woke up just two minutes ago."

"I'll order breakfast for us in my room, so come over. Four fourteen. And lock your door when you go out."

Tom had checked around 3 a.m., when they had returned to the hotel, to see if his passports were still in his suitcase, and they had been.

Over breakfast, Tom suggested Charlottenburg, followed by East Berlin, and then the West Berlin zoo, if they had energy left. He gave the boy an item from the London *Sunday Times* by Frank Giles, which Tom had cut out and carefully kept, because it told a lot about Berlin in few words. "Is Berlin Split Forever?" was its title. Frank read it as he ate toast and marmalade, and Tom said it didn't matter if he got butter on the cutting, because he had had it so long.

"Only fifty miles from the Polish border!" said Frank in a tone of wonder. "And—ninety-three thousand Soviet troops within twenty miles of—the suburbs of Berlin." Then Frank looked at Tom and said, "Why're they so worried about Berlin? All this Wall stuff."

Tom was enjoying his coffee and did not want to embark upon a lecture. Maybe the reality would sink into Frank today. "The Wall goes all the way up and down Germany, not just Berlin. The Berlin Wall is talked about the most because it surrounds West Berlin, but the Wall goes down to Poland and Romania too. You'll see it—today. And maybe tomorrow we'll take a taxi out to the Glienicker-Brücke, where they exchange prisoners sometimes, West and East. I mean spies, really. They even divide the river there, you can see a wire above the surface dividing the river down the middle." At least some of it was sinking in. Tom thought, because the boy perused the article thoroughly. It explained the triple military occupation or control of Berlin by English, French, and American troops, which helped to explain (but not really to Tom, who always felt that something was just out of his grasp in regard to Berlin) why the German airline Lufthansa could not land at Berlin-Tegel airport. Berlin was artificial, something special, not even a part of West Germany, and perhaps it didn't even wish to be, since Berliners had always taken a pride in being Berliners.

"I'll get dressed and knock on your door in about ten minutes," Tom said, standing up. "Bring your passport, Ben. That's for the Wall." The boy was dressed, but Tom was still in pajamas.

They caught an old-fashioned streetcar from the Kurfürstendamm to Charlottenburg, and spent more than an hour in the museums of archaeology and paintings. Frank lingered over the models of activities of long ago in the Berlin area, copper mining by men in animal-pelt garments three thousand years before Christ. As at Beaubourg, Tom found himself watching out for anyone who might show an interest in Frank, but Tom saw only parents with chattering and curious children peering into cases. Berlin, so far, presented a mild and harmless scene.

Then another streetcar back to the Charlottenburg S-Bahn stop for the ride to the Friedrichstrasse stop and the Wall. Tom had his map. They were aboveground all the way, though this was now an underground or subway type of train, and Frank stared out the window at the passing apartment houses, mostly rather old and drab, which meant that they had not been bombed. Then the Wall, gray and ten feet high as promised, topped with barbed wire, sprayed with covering paint in spots by East German soldiers, Tom remembered, before President Carter's visit a couple of months ago, so that West German television could not send the anti-Soviet slogans painted on the Wall into the homes of East Berliners and of many East Germans who could get West German television programs on their sets. Tom and Frank waited in a room with some fifty other tourists and West Berliners, many laden with shopping bags, baskets of fruit, tinned hams, and what looked like boxes from clothing stores. These were mostly elderly people, probably visiting for the umpteenth time their siblings and cousins cut off by the Wall since 1961. Tom and Frank's seven-digit numbers were finally called out by a girl behind a grilled window, which meant that they could file through to another room with a long table manned by East German soldiers in gray-green uniforms. A girl returned their passports, and a few yards on they had to buy from a soldier six DM fifty pfennigs' worth of East German money, which came to more in East German marks. Tom had an aversion to touching it, and stuck it in an empty back pocket.

Now they were "free." Tom smiled at the thought as they began walking along the Friedrichstrasse, which continued here, beyond the Wall. Tom pointed out the still uncleaned palaces of the Prussian royal family. Why the hell didn't they clean them, Tom wondered, or plant some hedge boxes around them, if they wanted to make a good impression on the rest of the world?

Frank looked all around him, speechless for several minutes.

"Unter den Linden," Tom said, not in a merry tone. A sense of self-preservation made him try, however, for something cheering, so he took Frank by the arm and swung him into a street on the right. "Let's go this way."

They were back on a street—yes, Friedrichstrasse again now—where long stand-up counters projected from snack cafés halfway across the pavement, patrons stood spooning soup, eating sandwiches, drinking beer. Some of them looked like construction workers in plaster-dusty overalls, some were women and girls who might have been office workers.

"I might buy a ballpoint pen," said Frank. "It'd be fun to buy *something* here."

They approached a stationer's shop which had an empty newsstand in front, only to be greeted by a sign on the front door saying: CLOSED BECAUSE I FEEL LIKE CLOSING. Tom laughed, translating it for Frank.

"Bound to be another shop along here," said Tom as they walked on.

There was another, but it was also closed, and another handwritten sign said: CLOSED BECAUSE OF HANGOVER. Frank thought this hilarious.

"Maybe they do have a sense of humor, but otherwise it's just like what I read about it, sort of—drab, maybe."

Tom also felt a creeping depression that he remembered from his first trip to East Berlin. The people's clothes looked limp. This was Tom's second visit, and he would not have come if the boy hadn't wanted to see it. "Let's have some lunch, cheer ourselves up," Tom said, gesturing toward a restaurant.

This was a big, modest, efficient-looking restaurant, and some of the long tables bore white tablecloths. If they hadn't enough money on them, Tom thought, the cashier would be delighted to take DM. They sat down, and Frank studied the clientèle thoughtfully—a man in a dark suit with spectacles, eating by himself, and two plumpish girls chattering away over their coffee at a nearby table—as if he watched animals of a new species in a zoo. Tom was amused. These were "Russians" to Frank, he supposed, tinged with Communism.

"They're not all Communists, really," Tom said. "They're Germans."

"I know. But it's just the idea that they can't go and live in West Germany if they want to—can they?"

"That is correct," Tom said, "they can't."

Their food was arriving, and Tom waited until the blonde waitress, who had a friendly smile, had departed. "But the Russians say they built the Wall to keep the capitalists *out*. That's their pitch, anyway."

They went up to the top of the Alexanderplatz tower, pride of East Berlin, to take coffee and admire the view. Then both were seized by a desire to leave.

West Berlin, surrounded as it was, felt like the wide open spaces once they had quit the district of the Wall and were rattling along on the elevated train toward the Tiergarten. They had changed a few more ten-DM notes, and Frank was now pouring over his East Berlin coins.

"I might keep these as souvenirs—or send a couple to Teresa for fun."

"Not from here, please," Tom said. "Keep them till you get back home."

It was refreshing to see the lions strolling in apparent freedom in the Tiergarten, tigers lounging by their swimming pool, yawning in the faces of the public, though there was a moat between them and the visitors. The trumpeter swan, just as Tom and Frank walked by, lifted his long neck and trumpeted. They made their way slowly toward the aquarium. Here Frank fell in love with the Druckfisch.

"Unbelievable!" Frank's lips parted in astonishment, and he looked suddenly like a child of twelve. "Those eyelashes! Just like *makeup!*"

Tom laughed and stared at the little fish of brilliant blue, hardly six inches long, cruising at what could be called moderate speed, apparently in quest of nothing, except that its little round mouth kept opening and closing as if it were asking something. The lids of its oversized eyes were outlined in black, and above and below were what looked like long black lashes, gracefully curved, as if a cartoonist had drawn them on its blue scales with a grease pencil. It was one of the wonders of nature, Tom thought. He had seen the fish before. It astounded him again, and it pleased Tom that the Druckfisch evoked more admiration from Frank than the celebrated Picassofisch. The Picassofisch, equally smallish, bore a black zigzag on its yellow body, suggesting a Picasso brushstroke of his Cubist period, and a blue band across its head with several raised antennae—odd enough, surely, but somehow no match for the Druckfisch's eyelashes. Tom turned his eyes away from their watery world, and felt like a clumsy lump as he walked on, breathing air.

The crocodiles, in their heated and glass-enclosed quarters with a pedestrian bridge through, had a few slightly bleeding wounds on them, no doubt inflicted by their fellows. But just now they were all dozing, with fearful grins.

"Had enough?" Tom asked. "I wouldn't mind going to the Bahnhof."

They left the aquarium and walked a few streets to the railway

station, where Tom got some more German money with his
French francs. Frank changed some also.

"You know, Ben," Tom said as he pocketed his marks, "one
more day here, and you have to think about—home, maybe?" Tom
had cast an eye about the Bahnhof interior, meeting place for hus-
tlers, fences, gays, pimps, drug addicts, and God knew what. He
walked as he spoke, wanting to get out of the place, in case one of
the loitering people, for some reason, might be interested in him
and the boy.

"I might go to Rome," Frank said as they walked toward the
Ku'damm.

"Don't go to Rome. Save it for another time. You've been to
Rome, didn't you say?"

"Only twice when I was a little kid."

"Go home first. Get things straightened out. Also with Teresa.
You could still go to Rome this summer. It's only the twenty-sixth
of August."

Some thirty minutes later, when Tom was relaxing in his room
with the *Morgenpost* and *Der Abend*, Frank rang him from his room.

"I reserved a ticket to New York for Monday," Frank said.
"Takeoff eleven-forty-five Air France, then I switch to Lufthansa in
Düsseldorf."

"Very good—Ben." Tom felt relief.

"You might have to lend me a little money. I can buy the
ticket, but it'll leave me maybe a little short."

"No problem," Tom said patiently. Five thousand francs was
over a thousand dollars, and why should the boy need more if he
was going straight home? Was he so in the habit of carrying big
sums, he felt uncomfortable without a lot? Or had money, from
him, become a symbol of love to Frank?

That evening they went to a cinema, walked out before the
end, and since it was after eleven and they had had no dinner, Tom
steered them toward the Rheinische Winzerstuben, which was just
a few steps away. Half-drawn glasses of beer, at least eight, stood

lined up beside the beer taps, awaiting customers. The Germans took several minutes to draw a beer properly, a fact which Tom appreciated. Tom and Frank chose their food from a counter offering homemade soups, ham, roast beef and lamb, cabbage, fried or boiled potatoes, and half a dozen kinds of bread.

"It's true what you said about Teresa," Frank said when they had found a table. "I should get things clearer with her." Frank gulped, though he had not yet eaten a bite. "Maybe she likes me, maybe she doesn't. And I realize I'm not *old* enough. Five more years of school if I finish college. Good Christ!"

Frank seemed furious with the school system suddenly, but Tom knew his problem was uncertainty about the girl.

"She's different from other girls," the boy went on. "I can't describe it—in words. She's not silly. She's very sure of herself— that's what scares me sometimes, because I don't look as self-confident as she does. Maybe I'm *not.*— Maybe one day you'll meet her. I hope so."

"I hope so too.— Eat your meal while it's hot." Tom felt that he never would meet Teresa, but illusion, hope such as the boy was trying to hang onto now—what else kept people going? Ego, morale, energy, and what people so vaguely called the future— wasn't it for most people based on another person? So very few people could make it alone. And himself? Tom tried for a few seconds to imagine himself in Belle Ombre without Heloise. No one to talk to in the house except Mme. Annette, no one to switch on the gramophone and fill the house suddenly with rock music or sometimes Ralph Kirkpatrick on the harpsichord. Even though Tom kept from Heloise so much of his life, his illegal and potentially dangerous activities which could put an end to Belle Ombre if discovered, she had become a part of his existence, almost of his flesh, as they said in the marriage vows. They didn't often make love, didn't always when Tom shared her bed, which was hardly half the time, but when they did, Heloise was warm and passionate. The infrequency of their making love didn't seem to bother her at all.

Curious, since she was only twenty-seven, or was it twenty-eight? But convenient too, for him. He couldn't have borne a woman who made demands several times a week: that really would have turned him off, maybe at once and permanently.

Tom summoned his courage and asked in a tone both light and polite, "May I ask if you've been to bed with Teresa?"

Frank glanced up from his plate with a quick and shaky smile. "Once. I— Well, of course it was wonderful. Maybe too wonderful."

Tom waited.

"You're the only person I would tell this to," Frank continued in a lower voice. "I didn't do very well. I think I was too excited. She was excited too, but nothing happened—really. It was at her family's apartment in New York. Everybody was out, we had all the doors locked.— And she laughed." Frank looked at Tom as if he had made a statement of fact, not one that hurt him, even, just a fact.

"Laughed at you?" Tom asked, trying to assume an attitude of only mild interest. He lit a Roth-Händle, the German equivalent of a Gauloise.

"*At* me, I dunno. Maybe. I felt awful. Embarrassed. I was ready to make love to her and then I couldn't finish. You know?"

Tom could imagine. "Laughed *with* you, maybe."

"I *tried* to laugh.— Don't ever tell anybody, will you?"

"No. Who would I tell, anyway?"

"Other guys at school, they're always boasting. I think half the time they're lying. I know they are. Pete—one year older—I like him a lot, but I know he doesn't always tell the truth. About girls, I mean. Sure, it's easy, I think, if you *don't* like a girl so much. You know? Maybe. Then you just think about yourself and being tough and making it and everything's fine. But—I've been in love with Teresa for *months*. Seven months now. Since the night I met her."

Tom was trying to compose a question: had Teresa other boyfriends with whom she might be going to bed? Tom didn't get

the question out before a loud introductory chord rang out over
the beerhall's clatter and chatter.

Something was happening on the far wall opposite them. Tom
had seen the show once before. Lights had come on there, and the
rumbustious overture to *Der Freischütz* boomed out from a rather
rusty gramophone somewhere. From the wall, a flat tableau of
spooky houses made of cutout silhouettes projected a few
inches—an owl perched in a tree, the moon shone, lightning
flashed, and a real rain of water drops slanted down from the right.
There was also thunder, which sounded like big pieces of tin
being shaken backstage. A few people got up from their tables for
a better view.

"That's *mad*!" Frank said, grinning. "Let's go look!"

"You go," said Tom, and the boy went. Tom wanted to stay
seated to assess Frank from a distance, to see if anyone paid attention to him.

Frank, in Tom's blue blazer and his own brown corduroy
trousers—a bit short, the trousers, and the boy must have grown
since he bought them—watched the tableau-almost-vivant with
his hands on his hips. No one that Tom could see paid the boy any
attention.

The music ended with crashes of cymbals, the lights went off,
the raindrops trickled out, and people returned to their seats.

"What a great idea!" Frank said, ambling back, looking relaxed.
"The rain falls in a little gutter in front, you know?— Can I get
you another beer?" Frank was eager to be of service.

It was nearly one when Tom asked a taxi driver to take them
to a bar called the Glad Hand. Tom didn't know what street it was
on. He had heard of it from someone, maybe even Reeves.

"Maybe you mean the Glad Ass," said the driver in German,
smiling, though the name of the bar remained in English.

"Whatever you say," said Tom. He knew the Berliners changed
the names of their bars when they spoke about them among
themselves.

This bar had no sign at all outside it, just a lighted list of beverage and snack prices behind glass on the outside wall by the door, but booming disco was audible from within. Tom pushed the brown door open, and a tall, ghostlike figure pushed Tom back in a playful way.

"No, no, you can't come in *here!*" said the figure, then grabbed Tom by his sweater front and pulled him in.

"You're looking *charming!*" Tom shouted at the figure that had pulled him in—over six feet tall in a sloppy muslin gown that swept the floor, his face a mask of pink and white paste.

Tom made sure that Frank was in tow as he forged toward the bar, which looked impossible to get to because of the crowd—entirely men and boys, all yelling at each other. There seemed to be two big rooms for dancing, maybe even three. Frank was much stared at and greeted as he endeavored to follow Tom. "*What the hell?*" Tom said to him, with a cheerful shrug, meaning he didn't think he would ever make it to the bar to order beer or anything else. There were tables against the walls, but these were taken and more than taken with fellows standing and talking to the ones seated.

"*Hoppla!*" roared another figure in drag into Tom's ears, and Tom realized, almost with a twinge of shame, that it was perhaps because he looked straight. A miracle they didn't throw him out, and maybe he had Frank to thank for being in. This led to a happier thought: Tom himself was an object of envy for having a nice-looking boy of sixteen in his company. Tom could in fact see that now, and it made him smile.

A leather figure was asking Frank to dance.

"*Go ahead!*" Tom shouted to Frank.

Frank looked for an instant bewildered, scared, then seemed to collect himself, and he went off with the leather chap.

". . . my cousin in *Dallas!*" an American voice was shouting to someone on Tom's left, and Tom moved away from that.

"Dallas-Fort *Vort!*" said his German companion.

"Naw, that's the fuckin' *airport*! I mean Dallas! *Friday* the bar's called. Gay bar! Boys and girls!"

Tom turned his back to them, somehow got a hand on the bar edge, and managed to order two beers. The three barmen or barmaids wore beaten up blue jeans but also wigs, rouge, ruffled blouses, and very gay lipsticky smiles. No one looked drunk, but everyone seemed wildly happy. Tom clung with one hand to the bar, and stood on tiptoe to look for Frank. He saw the boy dancing with even more abandon than with the girl in Romy Haag's. Another fellow seemed to be joining them, though Tom couldn't be certain. Now an Adonis-like statue, bigger than life and painted gold, descended from the ceiling and rotated horizontally over the dance floor, while from above colored balloons floated down, twisting, rising, stirred by the activity below. One of the balloons said MOTHERFUCKER in Gothic black letters, others sported drawings and words Tom couldn't make out from where he was.

Frank was coming back, pressing his way through to Tom. "Look! Lost a button, sorry. Couldn't find it on the dance floor and I got knocked down trying to look for it." He meant the middle button on the blazer.

"No importance! Your beer!" Tom said, handing the boy a tall, tapering glass.

Frank drank through the foam. "They're having such a good time—" he yelled, "*and no girls!*"

"Why'd you come *back*?"

"The other two got in an argument—a little bit! The first guy—he said something I didn't understand."

"Never mind," said Tom, quite able to imagine. "You should've asked him to say it in *English*!"

"He did and I *still* didn't understand!"

Frank was being eyed by a couple of men behind Tom. Frank was trying to tell Tom it was a very special night, somebody's birthday, hence the balloons. The loudness of the music almost prevented talking. Talking of course was unnecessary, as customers could see one another's wares, and either walk out together or exchange addresses. Frank said he didn't feel like dancing again, so they left after their one beer.

SUNDAY MORNING TOM AWAKENED just after ten, and rang down to ask if breakfast was still available. It was. Then he rang the boy's room. No answer. Was Frank taking a morning walk? Tom shrugged. Had he made himself shrug? Had it been involuntary? What if the boy ran into trouble on the street, got spoken to by some alert policeman? "May I ask your name? May I see your passport or identification?" Was there an umbilical cord between him and Frank? No. Or if so, cut it, Tom thought. It was going to be cut tomorrow, anyway, when the boy took the plane for New York. Tom hurled a wadded cigarette package at the wastebasket, missed, and had to go and pick it up.

Tom heard a gentle tapping on his door, with fingertips, the way he himself knocked.

"Frank."

Tom opened the door.

Frank had a transparent green plastic bag of fruit. "Went for a walk. They said you'd ordered breakfast, so I knew you were up. I asked them in German. How about that?"

Just before noon, they were standing at a Schnell-Imbiss wagon in Kreuzberg, both with tinned beers, Frank with a *Bulette* or bunless hamburger, cold but cooked meat that one could hold in one's fingers and dip into mustard. A Turk standing with beer and a frankfurter next to them wore the last word in casual summer gear: no top at all, hairy abdomen bulging over short green shorts not only worn out but eaten nearly to pieces perhaps by a dog. His dirty feet were in sandals. Frank looked this chap up and down with an unfazed eye, and said:

"I think Berlin is quite big. Not cramped at all."

That gave Tom an idea for the afternoon's activities: Grunewald, the big forest. But first perhaps the Glienicker-Brücke.

"I'll never forget this day—my last day with you," Frank said. "And I don't know when I'll see you again."

The words of a lover, Tom thought, and would Frank's family—his mother in particular—be overjoyed if Tom looked up Frank on his next trip to America in October of this year? Tom doubted that. Did his mother know anything about the suspicion of forgery in regard to Derwatt paintings? Very likely, since Frank's father had talked about it, maybe at the dinner table. Would his name ring a sour bell with Frank's mother? Tom did not want to ask.

They had a late lunch at an outdoor table on a height overlooking the Pflauen-Insel in the Wannsee, a blue lake below. Pebbles and earth underfoot now, leaves shading them, a portly and friendly waiter. Sauerbraten with potato dumplings, red cabbage, and beers. They were in the southwest area of West Berlin.

"Gosh, it's marvelous, isn't it? Germany," Frank said.

"Really? Nicer than France?"

"The people seem friendlier here."

Tom felt the same way about Germany, but Berlin seemed a funny place to say it in. That morning they had driven past a long section of the Wall, unguarded by visible soldiers, but of the same ten-foot height as at Friedrichstrasse, and the attack dogs on sliding leashes behind the Wall had barked at the mere sound of their taxi. The driver had been delighted to make the tour, and had talked a blue streak. Beyond the Wall, out of sight and behind the dogs even, lay a strip of minefield "Fifty meters wide!" their driver had said in German, and beyond that a nine-foot-deep anti-vehicle trench, and yet beyond that a strip of land plowed so as to reveal footprints. "Such trouble they take!" Frank had said. And Tom, inspired, had replied, "They call themselves revolutionaries, but they happen to be the most backward just now. They say every country needs a revolution, but why some groups still ally themselves with *Moscow*—" He had tried to say it in German to the driver. "Oh, Moscow just has the military now, to show force here and there. Ideas, no," the driver had said, resigned, or with an air of resignation. At the Glienicker-Brücke,

Tom had translated for Frank the statement written in German on a big placard:

Those who gave this bridge the name Bridge of Unity built the Wall also, laid barbed wire, created death-strips, and so hinder unity.

Tom translated it thus, but the boy wanted it in the German original, and Tom copied it out for him. The driver, Hermann, had been so friendly, Tom had asked him if he would like some lunch, and then he could take them on somewhere else. Hermann had agreed to the lunch, but politely suggested that he eat by himself at another table.

"Grunewald," Tom said to Hermann after he had settled their bills. "Can you do that? Then you can get rid of us, because we want to walk around a little."

"Absolutely! Okay!" said Hermann, hauling himself up from his chair, looking as if he had taken on a couple of kilos with his lunch. It was a warmish day, and he wore a short-sleeved white shirt.

Now it was nearly a four-mile drive generally northward. Tom had his map of Berlin on his lap to show Frank where they were. They crossed the Wannsee bridge and turned north, went through a lot of wooded areas that held clusters of small houses. At last Grunewald where, Tom had told Frank, the troops of France, England, and America often did their tank exercises and fired guns for practice. War Games.

"Can you let us off at the Trümmerberg, Hermann?" Tom asked.

"*Trümmerberg, ja, neben dem Teufelsberg,*" he replied.

Hermann did this, his taxi climbed a slope, then the Trümmerberg, a mountain made from the rubble of war ruins, covered with earth, rose still higher. Tom gave Hermann his tariff and an extra twenty DM.

"*Danke schön und schönen Tag!*"

A small boy stood a little way up the mountain, maneuvering a toy airplane by electronic control. There was a curving groove down the side of the Trümmerberg for skiing and tobogganing.

"They ski here in winter," Tom said to Frank. "Fun, isn't it?" Tom didn't know really what was fun about it just now—with no snow—but he felt euphoric. It was fantastic to see vast woods on one side and the city of Berlin, low and remote in the distance, on the other. Unpaved lanes led into Grunewald, a wild-looking forest, something like twelve miles square, Tom judged from his map, and that this forest could lie within the city limits of Berlin struck Tom as amazing, or as a kind of blessing, since the whole of West Berlin was hemmed in, including, of course, Grunewald itself.

"Let's go this way," Tom said.

They took one of the lanes into the woods, and after a couple of minutes the trees closed over them, shutting out much of the sunlight. A boy and girl picnicked a few yards away on a blanket spread on pine needles. Frank looked at them dreamily, maybe with envy. Tom picked up a small pinecone, blew on it, and stuck it into his trousers pocket.

"Aren't the birches great! I love birches!" Frank said.

Speckled birches stood everywhere, of all sizes, among pine trees and the occasional oak.

"Somewhere—there's the sector for the military. Barbed wire fences around it, red warning signs, I remember." But Tom was feeling vague, not like talking, about anything. He sensed a sadness in the boy.

Around this time tomorrow Frank would be flying westward toward New York. And what would he be going back to? A girl he was not quite sure of, and a mother who had once asked him if he had killed his father—and had seemed to believe him when he had said no. And would anything in America have changed? New evidence come up against Frank? Maybe. Tom couldn't guess how, but he supposed there was a possibility of new evidence. Had Frank really killed his father, or was it a fantasy of Frank's? It was not the first time Tom had wondered about that. Was it because the sunlit woods were so beautiful, the day so pleasant, that he didn't want to believe the boy had killed anyone? Tom noticed a big fallen tree on their left. Tom motioned toward it, and the boy followed him.

Tom leaned against the tree, which he now saw had been felled, lit a cigarette, and glanced at his watch: thirteen minutes to four. Tom felt like turning back toward the Trümmerberg, where he knew there were a few cars and a chance of a taxi. It would be easy to get lost if they wandered farther. "Cigarette?" Tom asked. Last evening the boy had smoked one.

"No thanks. Excuse me a minute. Got to pee."

Tom pushed himself from the tree as the boy walked past him. "I'll be around here." He gestured toward the lane they had just come from. Tom was thinking that he could go back to Paris tomorrow afternoon, unless he decided to look up Eric Lanz, and perhaps spend the evening with him. That might be amusing, to see what kind of apartment Eric had here in Berlin, what kind of life he led. It would also give him time to buy Heloise a present, something nice from the Ku'damm, a handbag, for instance. Tom glanced to his right, thinking he had heard something, maybe voices. He looked for the boy. "Ben?" he called. Tom went back a few paces. "Hey, Ben, are you lost? This way!" Tom walked back to the tree they had been leaning against. "*Ben!*" Did he hear a crackling of underbrush far ahead in the woods, or was it the wind?

Frank was playing a trick again, Tom supposed, as he had on the little road near Belle Ombre. Waiting for Tom to find him. Tom didn't fancy walking through the scruff, the bushes that would tear his trousers cuffs. He knew the boy was within hearing, so he yelled, "Okay, Ben! Stop the kidding! Let's go!"

Silence.

Tom swallowed, with sudden difficulty. What was he worried about? Tom wasn't quite sure.

Suddenly Tom broke into a run for the area ahead of him and slightly on his left, where he thought he had heard some rustling of branches. "*Ben!*"

No answer, and Tom plunged on—paused only once to look back into empty, dense forest—then ran again. "*Ben?*"

Abruptly he came to a dirt road and took it, going still left. The road soon bent to the right. Should he keep going or turn back? Tom was curious enough to keep going, trotting now, at the same time deciding that if he didn't see the boy in another thirty yards, he would turn back and try the woods again. Was the boy running away again? That would be too stupid, Tom thought, for Frank to do, and where would he get without his passport which was at the hotel? Or had Frank been nabbed?

Ahead of him, on a lower level than the road and in a small clearing, Tom suddenly had that answer before him: a dark blue car faced Tom with both its front doors open. The driver at that moment started the engine with a zoom, and banged his door shut. Another man ran from behind the car, started to jump into the passenger's seat, but saw Tom and stopped with one hand on the door, while his other hand reached for something inside his jacket.

They had Frank, Tom was sure. Tom advanced. "What the hell are you—"

Tom found himself looking at a black pistol pointed straight at him, perhaps five yards away. The man held the gun with both hands. Then the man slipped into the car, closed the door, and the car backed. B-RW-778 the registration plate read. The driver was blondish, the man who had jumped in was a heavy fellow with straight black hair and a mustache. And they had seen him clearly, Tom realized.

The car moved away, not even going very fast now. Tom could have sprinted after it, but for what? To get a bullet in his stomach? What would a little thing like the death of Tom Ripley matter compared to a boy worth a few million dollars? Was Frank in the trunk in back, gagged? Or hit over the head and unconscious? Hadn't there been one more man, a third, in the back seat? Tom thought so.

This went through his head before the car, an Audi, rolled quite out of sight around the next curve in the woods.

Tom had a ballpoint pen, but finding no paper, pulled out his pack of Roth-Händle cigarettes, took off the cellophane, and wrote on the pink package the car's license number while it was still in his head. They might abandon the car or change its plates, knowing he had had a glimpse, Tom thought. Or the car might have been stolen for this job.

There was also the uncomfortable possibility that they had recognized him as Tom Ripley. Maybe they had been following him and Frank since yesterday or so. Would it be useful for them to eliminate him? Fifty-fifty, Tom thought. He really couldn't think clearly at the moment, and his hand had shaken when he wrote the license number. Of course he had heard voices in the woods! The kidnappers might have approached Frank with some harmless-sounding question.

Best for him not to stay one more day in Berlin. Tom plunged into the unpleasantly thick woods again, taking a shortcut to the path, because he was afraid the kidnappers might decide to come back along the road and have a shot at him.

11

Tom made his way back along the lane he had walked with Frank to the Trümmerberg, where he had an irritating wait of nearly twenty minutes for a taxi, and then one came only by accident as most visitors to Grunewald came in their own cars. Tom asked the driver to go to the Hotel Franke, Albrecht-Achillesstrasse.

Wouldn't it be great, as Frank often said, if the boy were back in his hotel room, having played another trick, and if the people Tom had seen with the car and the gun had been up to some different mischief? But such wasn't the case. Frank's key hung on its hook at the hotel desk, as did Tom's.

Tom took his key and went to his room, locked his door nervously on the inside, sat on his bed, and reached for the telephone directory. The police department's numbers should be in the front, he thought, and so they were. He dialed the "emergency" number, and put the cigarette packet with the car number before him.

"I think I have seen a kidnapping," Tom said. Then he answered the man's questions. When? Where?

"Your name, please?"

"I do not wish to give my name. I took the license number of the car." Tom proceeded to give it, and the color of the car, dark blue, an Audi.

"Who was the victim? Do you know the victim?"

"No," Tom said. "A boy—he looked sixteen, seventeen. One of the men had a gun. May I telephone you again in a couple of hours to ask what you have found out?" Tom was going to phone, whatever the man said.

The man said "yes," and with a brusque thank you hung up.

Tom had said the kidnapping took place about 4 p.m. in Grunewald not far from the Trümmerberg. It was now nearly half past five. He should get in touch with Frank's mother, he thought, warn her that she might be presented with a ransom demand, though what good it would do to warn her, he didn't know. Now that the Pierson detective had a real job to do, he was in Paris, and Tom didn't know how to reach him. Mrs. Lily Pierson, however, would know.

Tom went down to the hotel desk, and asked for the key to Herr Andrews's room. "My friend is out and he needs something."

The key was handed to Tom without question.

Tom went up and entered Frank's room. The bed was made, the room tidy. Tom glanced at the writing table for an address book, then thought of Johnny's passport in Frank's suitcase. Johnny's address in the United States was a Park Avenue address in New York. His mother would probably be in Kennebunkport now, but the New York address was better than nothing, and Tom took note of it, and replaced the passport in the suitcase. Then in the pocket of the suitcase lid he found a little brown address book and opened it eagerly. Under Pierson there was only a Florida address and telephone number, the entry headed Pierson Sunfish. Tough luck. Most people, Tom supposed, didn't write down their own addresses, because they knew them by heart, but with as many houses as the Piersons must have, Tom had had hopes.

Tom thought it best after all to go down to the desk for what he wanted—post offices being closed today, Sunday. But first he went back to his own room, dropped Frank's key on his bed, took his sweater off, and wet a towel. He washed his face and his body down to his trousers tops, put his sweater back on, and tried to assume an air of calm. He realized that he was thoroughly shattered by the boy's—rape, in the sense that he had been snatched away. Tom had never felt thus shaken by something that he himself had done, because in such cases in the past, he had been in control of things. Now he was anything but in control. He went out of his room and locked it, and took the stairs down.

At the hotel desk, he printed on some notepaper: John Pierson, Kennebunkport, Maine (Bangor). Tom thought Bangor was the closest big town, and might be able to provide the Kennebunkport number. "Could you ask information in Bangor, Maine, to give me the Pierson telephone number?" Tom asked the man behind the desk, who looked at what Tom had written and said, "Yes, right away," and went at once to a girl on Tom's right who sat at a switchboard.

The man came back to Tom and said, "Maybe two, three minutes. Do you wish to speak to a certain person?"

"No. First I'd like just to get the number, please." Tom lingered in the lobby, wondering if the girl would succeed, if the American operator was going to say the number was unlisted and could not be given out?

"Herr Ripley, we have the number," said the desk man, who had a paper in his hand.

Tom smiled. He copied it on another piece of paper. "Can you ring this? And I'll take it in my room. Please don't give my name. Just Berlin calling."

"Very good, sir."

Back in his room, Tom had hardly a minute's wait before his telephone rang.

"This is Kennebunkport, May-yun," said a female voice. "Am I speaking to Berlin, Germany?"

The Hotel Franke operator confirmed this.

"Go ahead, please," said Maine.

"Good morning, Pierson residence," said an Englishman's voice.

"Hello," said Tom. "May I speak with Mrs. Pierson, please?"

"May I ask who's speaking?"

"This is in regard to her son Frank." The formality at the other end gave Tom the cool that he needed.

"One moment, please."

It was more than a moment that Tom had to wait, but at least it seemed that Frank's mother was home. Tom heard a woman's voice, a man's also, as Lily Pierson perhaps approached the telephone accompanied by the butler whose name was Eugene, as Tom recalled.

"Hel-*lo-o*," came the high-pitched voice.

"Hello.— Mrs. Pierson, can you tell me at what hotel your son Johnny and your private detective are staying? In Paris?"

"Why are you asking that? You're an American?"

"Yes," Tom said.

"May I ask your name?" She sounded cautious and frightened.

"That's of no importance. It's more important that—"

"Do you know where Frank *is*? He's with *you*?"

"No, he is not with me. I would simply like to know how to reach your private detective in Paris. I'd like to know what hotel they're in."

"But I don't know why you want to know that." Her voice was becoming shriller. "Are you holding my son somewhere?"

"No, indeed, Mrs. Pierson. I can find out where your detective is, I think, by telephoning the French police. So can't you tell me now and save me the trouble? It's no secret, is it, where they're staying in Paris?"

Slight hesitation. "They're at the Hôtel Lutetia. But I'd like to know *why* you want to know."

Tom had what he wanted. What he did not want was the police of Berlin to be alerted by Mrs. Pierson or by her detective. "Because I may have seen him in Paris," Tom said, "but I'm not sure. Thank you, Mrs. Pierson."

"Seen him where in Paris?"

Tom wanted to hang up. "In the American Drugstore, St. Germain-des-Prés. I've just come from Paris. Good-bye, Mrs. Pierson." Tom put the telephone down.

He began to pack. The Hotel Franke seemed suddenly a very unsafe place. The duet or trio who had Frank might well have followed him and Frank to the hotel at some time since Friday evening, and might think nothing of firing a shot at him as he left the hotel, or even of coming up to his room to do it. Tom picked up the telephone and told the desk that he would be leaving in a few minutes, and could they make up his bill and also the bill for Herr Andrews? Then Tom closed his suitcase, and went to Frank's room with its key. He had thought a moment ago of ringing Eric Lanz. Eric might be willing to put him up, but if Eric couldn't, then any hotel in Berlin was safer than this one. Tom packed Frank's things, shoes from the floor, toothpaste and toothbrush from the bathroom, the Berlin bear, closed the suitcase, and went out with it, leaving the key in the lock. He took the suitcase to his own room, found Eric's card in his jacket pocket still, and dialed the number.

A German voice, deeper than Eric's, answered, and asked who was calling.

"Tom Ripley. I'm in Berlin."

"Ach, Tom *Ripley*! Einen Moment, bitte! Eric ist im Bad!"

Tom smiled. Eric home and having a bath! After a few seconds, Eric came on.

"Hello, Tom! Welcome to Berlin! When can we see each other?"

"Now—if possible," Tom said as calmly as he could. "Are you busy?"

"No-o. Where are you?"

Tom told him. "I'm about to check out of the hotel."

"We can fetch you! Have you got some time?" Eric asked gaily. "Peter! Albrecht-Achillesstrasse, easy for us . . ." His voice faded away in German, then came back. "Tom! We shall see you in less than ten minutes!"

Tom put the telephone down, much comforted.

The desk man had not sounded surprised at Tom's request for the bills, but might think it odd that he was leaving with the boy's suitcase. Tom was prepared to say that Herr Andrews was waiting at the air terminus. Tom paid the two bills, plus the extra for his telephone calls, and no questions were asked. Fine. He might have been one of Frank's kidnappers, Tom thought, or in cahoots with them, simply taking away Frank's belongings.

"Have a good trip!" said the desk man, smiling.

"Thank you!" Then Tom saw Eric walking into the lobby.

"Hello, Tom!" said Eric, beaming. His dark hair looked still damp from his bath. "You are finished?" he asked with a glance at the desk. "I'll take one suitcase, shall I?— By yourself?"

There was a bellhop, but he was lingering near another man who had three suitcases.

"Yes, just now. My friend's waiting at the Flughafen," Tom said in case the desk man or anyone else might be able to hear them.

Eric had Frank's suitcase. "Come! Peter's car is just here to the right. Mine's at the garage till tomorrow. Temporarily *kaputt*. Ha!"

A pale green Opel sat at the curb not far away, and Eric introduced Tom to Peter Schubler, or so the name sounded, a tall slender man of about thirty, with a lantern jaw and black hair cut quite short as if from a fresh haircut. The luggage went easily on the backseat and floor. Eric insisted that Tom sit in front with Peter.

"Where is your friend? Really at the airport?" Eric leaned forward with interest as Peter started the car.

Eric didn't know who his friend was, though he might suspect he was Frank Pierson, recipient of the passport Eric had brought for Tom to Paris. "No," Tom said. "Tell you later. Can we possibly go to your house now, Eric, or is it awkward for you?" Tom spoke in English, not knowing if Peter understood.

"But of course! Yes, we go *home*, Peter!— Peter was going home anyway. We thought you might have a little time free."

Tom was looking on either side of the street, as he had on coming out of the hotel, at the people on the pavement, even at cars parked at the curbs, but by the time they arrived at the Kurfürstendamm, Tom was feeling easier.

"You're with the boy?" Eric asked in English. "Where is he?"

"Taking a walk. I can reach him later," Tom said casually, and suddenly felt sick and awful. He lowered his window all the way.

"My house is your house, as the Spanish say," said Eric, pulling out a key-ring inside the front door of an old but refurbished apartment house. They were in Niebuhrstrasse, parallel with the Ku'damm.

The three of them rode up with the suitcases in a roomy elevator, and Eric opened another door. More words of welcome from Eric, and with Peter's help Tom set the suitcases in a corner of the living room. It was a bachelor's flat with no frills, substantial old furniture, and only a highly polished silver coffeepot flashed a bit of glitter from a sideboard. There were several nineteenth-century German landscapes and woodland paintings on the walls, which Tom recognized as valuable, but such paintings bored Tom to a degree.

"Excuse us a minute, Peter. Take a beer, if you like," said Eric.

The taciturn Peter nodded, picked up a newspaper, and prepared to sit on a large black sofa under a lamp.

Eric beckoned Tom into an adjacent bedroom and closed the door. "Now what's the matter?"

They did not sit down. Tom told his story quickly, including his telephone conversation with Lily Pierson. "It occurred to me that the kidnappers might like to get rid of me. It's possible that they recognized me in Grunewald. Or they can get it out of the boy. So I'd be more than grateful, Eric, if you can put me up tonight."

"Tonight? Two nights! More! What a happening, *mein Gott!* And now—the ransom request, I suppose? To the mother?"

"I suppose." Tom drew on a cigarette, and shrugged.

"I doubt if they will try to get the boy *out* of West Berlin, you know. Too difficult. Every car searched thoroughly at the East borders."

Tom could imagine. "I'd like to make two phone calls tonight, one to the police to ask if they found out anything about that Audi in Grunewald, and one to the hotel to ask if Frank possibly turned up. It occurred to me that the kidnappers might get cold feet and let the boy go. But I—"

"But?"

"I shall not give your phone number or address to anybody. That's not necessary."

"Thank you, not to the police anyway. Important."

"I could even ring from outside, if you'd prefer."

"My telephone!" Eric waved a hand. "Your calls are innocent compared to what goes on here! Often in code, I will admit! Go ahead, Tom, and ask Peter to do it for you!" Eric sounded sure of himself. "For the moment, Peter is my chauffeur, secretary, bodyguard—all! Come out and have a drink!" He pulled Tom's arm.

"You trust Peter."

Eric whispered. "Peter escaped from East Berlin. The second attempt he made it. I should say, they threw him out. The first attempt, they threw him in prison, where he made himself such a nuisance, they couldn't stand him. Peter—he looks *mild und leise,* but he has—um—guts."

They went into the living room where Eric poured whiskeys, and Peter went at once to the kitchen to fetch ice. It was almost eight now.

"I shall ask Peter to ring the Hotel Franke and ask if there has been a message from— What was his name?"

"Benjamin Andrews."

"Ah, yes." Eric looked Tom up and down. "You are nervous, Tom. Sit down."

Peter pressed ice from a black rubber tray into a silver bucket. Tom soon had a scotch in his hand. Eric turned to Peter and related the story in rapid German.

"*Wa-as?*" Peter said, astounded, and he gave Tom a respectful look, as if he suddenly realized that Tom had been through a bit of hell that day.

". . . the emergency department," Eric was saying to Peter in German. "And the number of the car, you said. You didn't tell them your name, I suppose."

"Certainly not." Tom copied out the number from the Roth-Haendle packet more legibly on some paper by Eric's telephone, and added "dark blue Audi."

"Maybe early to get news on the car," said Eric. "Maybe they will abandon it, if it is stolen. That gets us nothing, unless the police will take fingerprints."

"Ring the hotel first, Peter," Tom said. He got the number from his hotel bill. "The less they hear my voice there, the better, somehow. Can you ask if there is a message from Herr Andrews?"

"Andrews," Peter repeated, and dialed the number.

"Or any message for Herr Ripley."

Peter nodded, and put those questions to the Hotel Franke. After a few seconds, Peter said, "Okay. Thank you." To Tom he said, "No messages."

"Thank you, Peter. Now could you try the police about the

car?" Tom looked in Eric's telephone directory, and made sure the emergency number was the same one he had dialed, and pointed it out to Peter. "This one."

Peter dialed, spoke to someone for a couple of minutes, with long pauses, and finally hung up. "They have not found such a car," Peter said.

"We can try again later—both places," Eric said.

Peter went into the kitchen, and Tom heard a rattle of plates, the fridge door closing. Peter seemed quite familiar with the house.

"Frank Pierson," said Eric with his neat little smile, oblivious of Peter who was coming in with a tray. "Didn't his father die not so long ago? *Yes.* I read that."

"Yes," Tom said.

"Suicide, wasn't it?"

"So it seems."

Peter was setting the table. He had brought out a cold roast beef, tomatoes, and a bowl of sliced fresh pineapple which gave out an aroma of kirsch. They pulled up chairs and sat down at a long table.

"You spoke with the mother. Are you supposed to speak with the detective in Paris?" Eric poked red meat into his mouth, and followed it with a sip of red wine.

Eric's casualness annoyed Tom slightly. This was merely a little crooked situation, and Eric was willing to help Tom a bit, because Tom was a friend of Reeves Minot. Eric had never even met Frank. "I don't have to speak with Paris, no," Tom said, meaning that he didn't have to appoint himself as go-between. "As I said, the mother doesn't know my name."

Peter was listening carefully, maybe understanding everything.

"But I hope that detective doesn't put the Berlin police onto this—after Mrs. Pierson gets a ransom demand. Police don't always help in a case like this."

"No, not if you want the boy back alive," Eric said.

Tom was wondering if the American detective was going to

come to Berlin? The boy would very likely be released in Berlin, since it was so difficult to get him out to anywhere else. And where would the kidnappers want the money deposited? That was anybody's guess, Tom thought.

"What are you worried about now?" asked Eric.

"Not worried," Tom said, smiling. "I was thinking that Mrs. Pierson might tell her detective to beware of an American in Berlin who is either playing tricks or is in cahoots with the kidnappers. I told her—"

"Cahoots?"

"Working with them. I told her I thought I'd seen Frank in Paris, you know. Unfortunately she knows I rang from Berlin, because the Hotel Franke operator said it."

"Tom, you worry too much. But maybe that is why you are successful."

Successful? Was he?

Peter said something to Eric in German so fast that Tom missed it.

Eric laughed, and when he had swallowed his food, he said to Tom, "Peter hates kidnappers. He says they pretend to be leftists, all that political *Scheiss*, when all they want is money, just like any other crooks."

"I think I would like to ring the Hôtel Lutetia tonight to see if they have news," Tom said. "The kidnappers may have phoned Mrs. Pierson. I can hardly imagine them sending her a telegram or an express letter."

"No," said Eric, pouring more wine for everybody.

"By now the Paris detective might know where the money's to be delivered and where the boy's to be released and all that."

"Is he going to tell *you* all that?" Eric asked, reseating himself.

Tom smiled again. "Maybe not. But I'll still pick up something, I imagine. By the way, Eric, I'll be responsible for my telephone bill." Tom was envisaging more calls.

"What an idea! Very English, friends and guests paying telephone bills. Not in my house—which is *your* house. What time is it? Would it help if I telephoned the Lutetia instead of you, Tom?" Eric looked at his wristwatch and spoke before Tom could answer. "Just about ten now, same time in Paris. Let us give the detective time to finish his Fr-rench dinner—at the Piersons' expense. Ha-ha!"

Eric switched on his television, while Peter made the coffee. There was a news program after a few minutes. Eric had to answer his telephone twice, and the second time spoke in rather awful Italian. Then Eric and Peter listened to a political figure who spoke for several minutes, and they chuckled throughout and made comments to each other. Tom was not interested enough to try to follow what the man on the screen was saying.

Around eleven, Eric proposed ringing the Hôtel Lutetia. Tom had refrained from mentioning it, lest Eric call him nervous again.

"I think I have the number right here." Eric consulted a black leather address book. "Ja, here we are—" He began to dial.

Tom was standing by. "Ask for John Pierson, would you, Eric? Because I don't know the detective's name."

"Don't they know your name by now?" Eric asked. "Wouldn't the boy have said—" Eric pointed to the little round receiver at the back of his telephone.

Tom picked it up and put it to his ear.

"Hello. May I speak to John Pierson, if you please?" Eric said in French, and gave a satisfied nod to Tom as the operator promised to connect him.

"Hello?" said a young American voice, much like Frank's.

"Hello. I am ringing to ask if you have news of your brother."

"Who are you?" asked Johnny, and there were sounds of his being spoken to by another male voice.

"Hello?" said a deeper voice.

"I am calling to ask for news about Frank. Is he all right? Have you had news?"

"May I ask your name? Where are you calling from?"

Tom nodded at Eric's questioning glance.

"Berlin," said Eric. "What is the message for Mrs. Pierson?" Eric asked with almost bored matter-of-factness.

"Why should I tell *you*, if you don't identify yourself," replied the detective.

Peter was leaning against the sideboard, listening.

Tom motioned for Eric to pass the telephone to him, and Tom handed Eric the little receiver. "Hello, this is Tom Ripley."

"Oh!— Yes. Was it you who spoke with Mrs. Pierson?"

"Yes, it was. I would like to know if the boy is all right, and what the arrangements are."

"We don't know if the boy is all right," the detective replied frigidly.

"They've asked for a ransom?"

"Y-yes-s." It came out as if the detective had reflected that he had nothing to lose by disclosing this.

"Money to be delivered in Berlin?"

"I don't know why you're interested, Mr. Ripley."

"Because I'm a friend of Frank's."

The detective refrained from comment.

"Frank can tell you that—when you speak with him," Tom said.

"We haven't spoken with him."

"But they'll let him speak to prove they've got him—won't they? Anyway, Mr.— May I ask your name?"

"Yes-s. Thurlow. Ralph. How did you know that the boy was kidnapped?"

Tom couldn't answer or didn't want to. "Have you informed the Berlin police?"

"No, they don't want us to do that."

"Any idea where they are in Berlin?" Tom asked.

"No." Thurlow sounded discouraged.

Not easy to have a call traced without police cooperation, Tom supposed. "What kind of proof are they going to give you?"

"They said he'd speak to us—maybe later tonight. Said he'd had some sleeping pills.— Can you give me your telephone number there?"

"Sorry, I can't. But I can reach you. 'Night, Mr. Thurlow." Tom put the telephone down as Thurlow was saying something else.

Eric looked at Tom brightly, as if the conversation had been a success, and put back the receiver.

"Yes, well, I've learned something," Tom said. "The boy *has* been kidnapped and I wasn't—mistaken."

"What's the next step?" asked Eric.

Tom poured still more coffee for himself from the silver pot. "I want to stay in Berlin till something happens. Till I know Frank is safe."

12

Peter left then, promising Eric to visit the garage tomorrow morning and see that Eric's car was delivered in front of his apartment house. "Tom Ripley—good success!" Peter said to Tom, and his handshake was firm.

"Isn't he wonderful?" Eric said after he had closed his apartment door. "I helped Peter get out of the East, and he has never forgotten it. He is an accountant by profession. He could get a job here. He had one for a while. But just now he does so much work for me, he doesn't need a job. He is very good also with my income tax forms." Eric chuckled.

Tom was listening, but thinking also that he would ring Paris again tonight, maybe at two or three in the morning, to find out if Thurlow had spoken with Frank. Sleeping pills, of course. That was to be expected.

Eric produced a cigar box, but Tom declined. "You were right not to give my telephone number to that detective. He might give it to the kidnappers! Lots of detectives are boobs—wanting to get all the information they can, and to hell with anybody else. *Boobs!*— I love American slang."

Tom refrained from saying that boobs had another meaning too. "Must send you a book of it.— Zurich, Basel, which," Tom mused, enjoying being able to muse out loud in the presence of Eric, because usually he had to keep his thoughts to himself.

"You think that's where the money will change hands?"

"Don't you think it's likely? Unless the kidnappers want it in marks in Berlin for their anti-establishment activities or something. But Switzerland's always safer—I'd think."

"How much do you think they'll ask?" Eric drew gently on his cigar.

"One, two million dollars? Thurlow might know the sum already. Maybe he's leaving for Switzerland tomorrow."

"Why are you so interested in this kidnapping event—if I may ask you, Tom?"

"Oh. Well—I'm interested in the boy's safety." Tom walked around the room with his hands in his pockets. "He's an odd boy, considering his family's so wealthy. He has a fear of money or a hatred of it.— Do you know he shined every pair of shoes I possess? These, for instance." Tom lifted his right foot. The shine still remained on the loafer, despite the plunge through Grunewald. Tom thought of Frank's murder of his father. Tom was sympathetic because of *that.* But to Eric, Tom added only, "He's in love with a girl in New York. She hasn't been able to write to him while he's been in Europe, because he couldn't give her an address. He wanted to be incognito for a while. So he's on tenterhooks— uncertain, I mean, whether the girl still cares for him. He's only sixteen. You know how it is." But had Eric ever been in love? It was hard for Tom to imagine. There was something strongly selfish and self-preserving about Eric.

Eric was nodding thoughtfully. "He was in your house when I was. I knew there was somebody there. I thought—maybe a girl— or a—"

Tom laughed. "A girl I was hiding from my wife?"

"Why did he run away from home?"

"Oh—boys do. Maybe upset about his father's death. Maybe his girlfriend too. He wanted to hide for a few days—to be quiet. He worked in the garden at my house."

"Did he do something illegal in America?" Eric sounded almost prudish.

"Not that I know of. But for a while he didn't want to be Frank Pierson, so I got him another passport."

"And you brought him to Berlin."

Tom took a deep breath. "I thought I could persuade him to go home from here, which I did. He has a plane ticket reserved for tomorrow, back to New York."

"Tomorrow," Eric repeated, without any emotion.

Why should Eric have any emotion, Tom thought. Tom looked at the buttons of Eric's silk shirt, which were strained by the bulge of his abdomen. The buttons looked the way Tom felt. "I'd like to ring Thurlow again tonight. Maybe quite late. Two or three in the morning. I hope it won't disturb you, Eric?"

"Certainly not, Tom. The telephone is here at your disposal."

"Maybe I should ask you where I'm to sleep. Here, maybe?" Tom meant the big horsehair sofa.

"Ach, I'm glad you said that! You do look tired, Tom. On this sofa, yes, but it is a *bed* sofa. Watch!" Eric removed a pink pillow from the sofa. "It looks like an antique, maybe, but it is the latest thing. One button—" Eric pressed something, and out zoomed the seat, the back fell flat, and it was the size of a double bed. "Look!"

"Marvelous," said Tom.

Eric fetched blankets and sheets from somewhere, and Tom helped him. A blanket first to fill in the indentations caused by the sofa's buttons, then the sheets. "Yes, time you turned in. Turn in, turn out, over, on, off, turn against and turn up. Really I think sometimes that English is just as—movable as German," said Eric, plumping pillows now.

Tom, taking off his sweater, realized that he was going to sleep

like a top tonight, but he didn't want to get into an etymological
discussion about sleeping like a top, in case Eric was interested in
the phrase, so Tom said nothing, and dragged his pajamas from the
bottom of his suitcase. He was thinking that the kidnappers might
have forced Frank to reveal his name. Would Mrs. Pierson trust him
to deliver the ransom money? Tom realized that he dearly wanted
a swat of some kind at the kidnappers. Maybe that was foolhardy,
quite mad, because just now he felt vaguely angry and much too
tired to be logical.

"The bathroom is yours, Tom," said Eric. "I shall say good
night, so I don't disturb you any more. Do you want me to set my
Wecker for you at two, maybe, so you can telephone?"

"I think I'll make it—wake up," Tom replied. "Thank you—
very much, Eric."

"Oh, while I think of it, one little question. Do you say 'waken
somebody, wake somebody, or—awaken somebody'?"

Tom shook his head. "I don't think the English know."

Then Tom took a shower and went to bed, trying to fix in his
mind the hour of 3 a.m., so he would wake up, exactly one hour
and twenty minutes from now. Was it worth it to risk getting kidnapped himself, or worse shot dead, to deliver the ransom money,
when anyone else could do it? The kidnappers might appoint their
own man. Who? Might the kidnappers insist that Tom Ripley
deliver it? Quite possible. If the kidnappers managed to seize him,
they could get some more money, and Tom tried to imagine
Heloise getting his ransom money together—how much, a quarter
of a million?—and asking her father— Good Lord, no! Here Tom
had to laugh into his pillow. Would Jacques Plisson cough up
money for son-in-law Tom Ripley? Not bloody likely! A quarter
of a million would certainly take all the investments he and Heloise
had, and maybe even Belle Ombre would have to be sold.
Unthinkable!

And maybe none of what he was thinking about would come
to pass.

Tom awakened from an anxiety dream in which he had been trying to drive a car up an impossibly steep road, more vertical than any hill of San Francisco, and the car had been about to topple over backward before it reached the top. His forehead and chest were sleek with perspiration. But it was one minute to three, just right.

He dialed the Lutetia number from Eric's address book, where Eric had written also the dial code for Paris. Tom asked for Monsieur Ralph Thurlow.

"Hello.— Yes—Mr. Ripley. Thurlow here."

"What's the news? Have you spoken with the boy?"

"Yes, we spoke with him about an hour ago. Says he's not hurt. Sounded very sleepy." And Thurlow sounded tired.

"And the arrangements?"

"They haven't set the place. They—"

Tom waited. He supposed Thurlow was hesitant about mentioning money, and maybe Thurlow had had a tough day at the Hôtel Lutetia. "But they told you what they wanted?"

"Yes, that will be coming from Zurich tomorrow—I mean today. Mrs. Pierson is having it telexed to three Berlin banks. They want three banks. And Mrs. Pierson thinks it's safer too."

Maybe the sum was so big, Mrs. Pierson wanted to draw as little attention to it as possible, Tom thought. "You're coming to Berlin?"

"I haven't arranged that as yet."

"Who's picking it up at the banks?"

"I don't know. They want to know if the money's in Berlin—first. And they're going to tell me later where it's to be delivered."

"To be delivered in Berlin, you think."

"I would think. I don't know."

"The police are not in on this—listening to your phone?"

"No, indeed," said Thurlow. "That's the way we want it."

"What's the sum?"

"Two million. USA. In German marks."

"Do you expect a bank messenger to handle it all?" The idea made Tom smile.

"They—they sound as if they're arguing among themselves," Thurlow's American voice droned on. "About place and time. One man talks to me—German accent."

"Shall I call you again around nine this morning? Won't the money be here by then?"

"I should think so."

"Mr. Thurlow, I'm willing to pick up the money and take it to wherever they want it. Might be faster, in view of—" Tom stopped. "Don't mention my name to them, please."

"The boy told them your name, said you were his friend, and said that to his mother too."

"Very well, but if they ask about me, say you haven't heard a word from me, and since I live in France, I may have gone home. Please say the same thing to Mrs. Pierson, as I assume they're phoning her."

"They're mainly phoning *me*. They just let the boy talk with her once."

"You might ask Mrs. Pierson to tell her Swiss bank or the Berlin banks that I'm to pick the money up—if Mrs. Pierson is agreeable to that."

"I'll see about that," said Thurlow.

"I'll ring you in a few hours. And I'm delighted that the boy's okay—or that he's not suffering anything worse than sleepiness at the moment."

"That's right, let's *hope*!"

Then Tom hung up and went back to bed. Eric's quiet bustling in the kitchen awakened him, the clink of a kettle, the buzz of an electric coffee grinder, comforting sounds. It was twelve minutes to nine, Monday 28th August. Tom went into the kitchen to tell Eric the results of his 3 a.m. telephone call.

"Two million dollars!" said Eric. "Just what you have guessed, is it not?"

That seemed to be more interesting to Eric than the fact that Frank was alive and well enough to talk to his mother. Tom let it go, and drank his coffee.

Tom dressed, then managed to put his bed into the form of a sofa again, and he folded his sheets neatly, thinking he might need them tonight. When the living room looked tidy again, Tom glanced at his watch, thinking of Thurlow, and then out of curiosity went to the long Schiller section of Eric's bookcase, and pulled out *Die Räuber*. It really was an individual, leather-bound book. Tom had suspected that the row of Schiller's complete works was a façade concealing a safe or a secret compartment perhaps in the books themselves.

Tom picked up the telephone, dialed the Lutetia number, and asked for Monsieur Ralph Thurlow.

Thurlow answered. "Yes, Mr. Ripley, hello. I have the banks' names now, three of them." Thurlow sounded considerably more awake and cheerful.

"The money's arrived here?"

"Yes, and Mrs. Pierson is willing for you to pick it up today—as soon as you can, in fact. She's told Zurich that this is a transfer with her approval and Zurich has done the same with the Berlin banks. The banks seem to have odd hours there for opening, but that doesn't matter. You should phone each bank and tell them when you'll arrive and they'll—uh—"

"I understand." Tom knew, some banks didn't open until half past three, others closed at one. "So—the banks—"

Thurlow interrupted. "The people who—are phoning me, they'll phone me later today to make sure the money's been collected, and then they'll set a place where it's to be left."

"I see. You didn't mention my name to them?"

"Certainly not. I just said it will be picked up, it will be delivered."

"Good. Now the banks, if you will." Tom had a ballpoint pen and proceeded to write. The first was the ADCA Bank at Europa-

Center, which was to have a million and a half DM. The second the Berliner Disconto Bank with the same sum. The third the Berliner Commerz Bank with "not quite" a million DM. "Thank you," Tom said as he finished writing. "I'll try to collect this in the next couple of hours and ring you back around noon—with luck."

"I'll be here."

"By the way, did our friends say they were with any group?"

"Group?"

"Or gang? Sometimes they give themselves names and are pleased to tell them. You know, like the Red Saviors."

Ralph Thurlow chuckled nervously. "No, they didn't."

"Do you think they're phoning from a private apartment?"

"No, mainly not. Maybe when the boy spoke with his mother. *She* seemed to think so. But this morning they were dropping coins somewhere. They phoned around eight to ask if the money got to Berlin. We've been at this all night."

When Tom hung up, he heard the click of Eric's typewriter in Eric's bedroom, and Tom didn't want to interrupt him. He lit a cigarette, and thought he should ring Heloise, since he had promised to be home today or tomorrow, but now he did not want to take the time. And where might he be at this time tomorrow?

Tom imagined Frank confined in a room somewhere in Berlin, maybe not tied with ropes, but under surveillance day and night. Frank was the kind of boy who would make a dash to escape, who might even jump out of a window if the ground were not too far away, and the kidnappers might have realized that. Tom also knew that the anti-establishment people, the groups who kidnapped, had friends among the public who would give them shelter. Reeves had spoken with Tom about this not long ago on the telephone. The situation was complex, because the revolutionaries, the gangs, claimed to be part of the political left-wing movement, although they were rejected by its majority. These gangs seemed directionless to Tom, except for their obvious efforts to create an atmosphere of disturbance, provoking the authorities to crack down and show their presumably true, that was to say fascist, colors. The kidnapping and murder of Hanns-Martin Schleyer, who had been decried by some as an old Nazi and representative of management and factory owners, had unfortunately inspired a witchhunt by the authorities against intellectuals, artists, and liberals. And right-wingers, seizing the moment, insisted that the police were still not cracking down hard enough. Nothing in Germany was black or white and simple, Tom thought. Were Frank's captors "terrorists" or even political in any way? Were they going to drag out negotiations, publicize them? Tom hoped not, because he simply couldn't afford any more publicity.

Eric came into the living room, and Tom told him about the banks.

"What sums!" Eric looked for a moment stunned, then blinked his eyes. "Peter and I could help you this morning, Tom. Those banks are mostly on the Ku'damm. We could go in my car or Peter's car. Peter keeps a gun in his car, but I do not. Certainly not allowed here."

"I thought your car was on the blink."

"On the blink?"

"Kaputt," Tom said.

"Oh, just till this morning. Peter said he would try to get it here by ten, I remember. Nine-thirty-five now. For safety, you know, Tom, we should all go together this morning, don't you think so?" Eric looked at his most cautious, about to approach the telephone.

Tom nodded. "We collect the money and bring it here—with your permission, Eric."

"Ye-es—of course." Eric glanced at his walls as if he might find them stripped in a few hours. "I'll give Peter a call."

Peter's line did not answer.

"He is maybe seeing about my car," Eric said. "If he buzzes me from downstairs—soon—I shall ask him if he can come with us this morning. And where does the money go later, Tom?"

Tom smiled. "I hope to find that out by noon. By the way, Eric, I think I'll need a suitcase for this morning's haul, don't you think so? Could I borrow one from you, perhaps, instead of emptying mine or Frank's?"

Eric was at once obliging, went to his bedroom, and came back with a medium-sized brown pigskin suitcase, not new or expensive looking, and perhaps just the right size, though Tom had no idea of the bulk of nearly four thousand banknotes of a thousand DM each.

"Thank you, Eric. If Peter can't come with us, we can do this by taxi, I should think. First I've got to ring those banks. Now."

"I shall ring them for you, Tom. The ADCA Bank, didn't you say?"

Tom put his list by Eric's telephone, and consulted the directory for the number of the ADCA Bank. While Eric dialed the ADCA Bank, Tom wrote down the numbers of the other two banks. Eric did it calmly and smoothly: he asked for the Herr Direktor, and said he was telephoning in regard to collecting some money being held in the name of Thomas Ripley. This took several minutes, during which time Tom pocketed his passport for identification, and listened. Eric was not able to speak with each manager personally, but all three banks confirmed that money was being held. Eric said that Herr Ripley would arrive in the next hour.

During the last telephone call, Eric's doorbell rang, and Eric motioned for Tom to press the release button in the kitchen. Tom pressed the speaker button and asked, "Who is it?"

"Peter here. The car of Eric is downstairs."

"Just a minute, Peter," Tom said. "Here's Eric."

Eric took over the speaker, and Tom left the kitchen.

Tom heard Eric asking if Peter had some time this morning for a "very important couple of errands." Then Eric came into the living room and said, "Peter has time, and he says also my car is downstairs. Isn't he marvelous?"

Tom nodded, and pocketed his list of banks. "Yes."

Eric put on a jacket. "Let us go."

Tom picked up the empty suitcase, Eric double-locked his door, and they went down Eric's stairs.

Peter was sitting in his car at the curb, and Eric's Mercedes was parked not far from Eric's doorway. Eric got into Peter's passenger seat, and motioned for Tom to get into the backseat.

"I have to explain this behind closed doors," Eric said to Peter. Then he said in German that Tom had to call at three banks now to collect some money for the kidnappers' ransom, and would Peter drive them, or should they all go in his, Eric's, car?

Peter glanced at Tom with a smile. "My car, all right."

"You have your gun, Peter?" Eric asked, laughing a little. "I hope we shall not need it!"

"Right here, *ja,*" said Peter, pointing to his glove box, and he smiled as if it would be an absurdity to use it under these circumstances, when Tom's collecting of the money had been authorized.

They decided at once on the ADCA Bank at Europa-Center first, since the other two banks were on the Ku'damm and on the way back to Eric's apartment house. They were able to park quite near the ADCA Bank, because there was a curved parking area in front of the Hotel Palace meant for patrons of the hotel and for taxis coming and going. This bank was open. Tom went alone to the bank doors, and he did not take the suitcase with him.

Tom gave his name to the receptionist, and said in English that the manager was expecting him. The girl spoke into a telephone, then indicated a door at the rear on Tom's left. It was opened by a blue-eyed man in his fifties, with gray hair, straight posture, and a pleasant smile. A man carrying a few briefcases, who had been in the room, departed almost at once, giving Tom no special look, which made Tom feel easier.

"Mr Ripley? Good morning," the man said in English. "Would you like to sit down?"

"Good morning, sir." Tom did not at once take the leather

armchair that was offered, but took his passport from his pocket. "May I? My passport."

Standing behind his desk, the Herr Direktor or manager put on his spectacles and looked at the passport carefully, compared the photograph with Tom's face, then sat down and made a note on a pad. "Thank you." He handed the passport back to Tom, and pressed a button on his desk. "Fred? Alles in Ordnung.— Ja, bitte." The man folded his hands and looked at Tom with still smiling but slightly puzzled eyes. Then the same man Tom had seen before came in, bearing two large tan envelopes. The door closed behind him automatically with a deep click, and Tom felt it was extremely locked.

"Would you care to count the money?" asked the Herr Direktor.

"I'm sure I should take a look," Tom said politely, as if accepting a canapé at a party, but he had no desire to count all that. He opened the two manila envelopes, which had been closed with rubber bands, and saw that they contained bundles of DM held by brown paper strips. Tom saw what looked like at least twenty little bundles in one envelope, and both envelopes seemed of equal weight. The notes were all of one thousand DM each.

"One million five hundred thousand DM," said the Herr Direktor. "One hundred such notes in each band."

Tom was riffling through the end of one bundle, which looked to be a hundred. Tom nodded, wondering if the bank had noted serial numbers, but he did not want to ask. Let the kidnappers worry. The kidnappers must have said nothing about denomination either, or Thurlow surely would have told him. "I shall believe you."

The two Germans smiled, and the man who had brought the envelope left the room.

"And the receipt," said the Herr Direktor.

Tom signed a receipt for one million five hundred thousand DM, and the manager initialed it, kept the carbon, and handed Tom the top paper. Tom was on his feet, and extended his hand. "Thank you."

"Have a nice stay in Berlin," the Herr Direktor said, as he shook Tom's hand.

"Thank you." The man's words had sounded as if he thought Tom might be intending to have a spree on the money he was taking away. Tom tucked the thick envelopes under his arm.

The manager looked amused. Was he thinking of a joke he would tell at lunch, or was he going to tell a story about an American picking up nearly a million dollars in marks and walking out with it under his arm? "Would you like an escort to where you are going?"

"No, thanks," said Tom.

Tom walked through the bank without looking at anyone. Eric sat in Peter's car, and Peter stood smoking a cigarette with one hand in his trousers pocket, his face turned up to the sunlight.

"Alles gut gegangen?" asked Peter, seeing the envelope.

"Fine," Tom said. In the backseat, he opened the suitcase, stuck the envelopes in, and zipped it closed. Tom noticed that Eric was glancing about at people on the pavement as they moved off. Tom did not. Tom deliberately yawned, leaned back, and watched Peter make a left turn that brought them into the Kurfürstendamm.

The next two banks were rather near to each other on the broad avenue, which was neatly bordered by its young trees. All chromium and sparkling glass shop fronts again. The edifices Tom wanted were also brand-new and had their names in broad letters above their windows, which were perhaps bulletproof. Peter had stopped in front of one bank at a corner, where there was no parking meter free, but Eric said he would be outside somewhere on the pavement to tell Tom where the car was, when Tom came out.

This transaction went as the first: the receptionist, a manager, Tom's passport for identification, and then the money and the receipt for the same sum as that of the ADCA Bank. This time the money was in a single larger envelope. Again Tom was asked if he

wished to count it, and Tom declined. Would he like a bank guard
to accompany him to his destination?

"No, thank you," Tom said.

"Shall I seal the envelope—for safety?"

Tom glanced into the big envelope, and saw bundles of DM
with paper wrappers around their middles, similar to the bundles
he already had. Tom handed over the envelope, and the manager
sealed it with some broad tan tape which he pulled from a gadget
on his desk.

Now Eric was on the pavement, looking as if he expected a
friend to come from right or left, anywhere but from the bank
door. Eric gestured toward the right. Peter was double-parked. Eric
and Tom got in, Tom in the back again, and he deposited this envelope in the suitcase.

Tom collected some six hundred thousand DM from the third
bank, and walked out with a green envelope, and again found Eric
on the pavement. Peter was around a corner to the right.

Bang! The closing of the car door was a pleasure. Tom sank
back, the green envelope on his lap. Peter was driving toward Eric's
apartment, Tom knew from his next turn. Peter and Eric
exchanged pleasantries, which Tom did not try to follow. Something about bank robbers. Laughter. Tom stuck the final envelope
into the suitcase.

In Eric's apartment the good humor continued, Peter and Eric
chuckling over the suitcase which Peter had insisted on carrying,
because he was the chauffeur. Peter set the suitcase against the wall
by the sideboard, on the opposite side of the room from the apartment door.

"No, no, in my closet where it always is!" said Eric. "It looks
just like a couple of others there."

Peter did as he was told.

A quarter to noon. Tom was thinking of ringing Thurlow. Eric
put on a record of Victoria de los Angeles, which he said he always
played when he felt euphoric. Eric looked in a good humor, but
more nervous than euphoric, Tom thought.

"Maybe I'll meet Frank tonight," Eric said to Tom. "I hope so! He can stay here, have my bed. I'll sleep on the floor. Frank will be my guest of honor!"

Tom only smiled. "I'll have to ask you to turn the music down a little while I try Thurlow again."

"With pleasure, Tom!" Eric did so.

Peter had come in with a tray of cold beers, and Tom took one, put it by the telephone, and dialed.

Thurlow's line was engaged, and Tom told the hotel operator he would wait. It was a short wait before Thurlow came on.

"Everything is in order here," Tom said, trying to sound calm.

"You've got it?" asked Thurlow.

"Yes. And you've got the place?"

"Yes, I have. It's in the northern part of Berlin, they said. Lub— I can spell it for you. L–u–two dots–b–a–r–s. Got that?— And the streets—"

Tom was writing, and motioned for Eric to pick up the little receiver at the back of the telephone, which Eric did quickly.

Thurlow gave a street name, then spelled it: Zabel-Krüger-Damm, which he said crossed a street called Alt-Lübars. "The first street runs east and west, Alt-Lübars goes north when it intersects there. *You* keep going north on Alt-Lübars onto a little dirt road— so it sounds like—which hasn't got any name. About a hundred meters or yards on, you'll see a shed on the left side of the road. Got that so far?"

"Yes, thanks." Tom had, and Eric gave him a reassuring nod, as if to say the streets were not so difficult to find as Tom might think.

Thurlow continued, "You're to leave the—the sum in a box or a sack at four o'clock in the morning. That is tonight, you understand."

"Yes," said Tom.

"Set it behind the shed and leave. One messenger, they said."

"And what about the boy?"

"They'll call me once they get the money. Can you phone me after four in the morning to tell me if all went well?"

"Yes, of course, sure."

"And very good luck to you, Tom."

Tom put the telephone down.

"Lübars!" Eric put his little receiver back. He turned to Peter. "Lübars, Peter, at four o'clock in the morning! That is an old farm district, Tom, north. Up by the Wall. Not many people living there. The Wall borders Lübars on the north. Have you got a map, Peter?"

"Ja-a. I was there once, I think, maybe twice—driving around." Peter spoke in German. "I can take Tom tonight. One must have a car there."

Tom was grateful. He trusted Peter's driving and Peter's nerve, and Peter had a gun in his car.

Peter and Eric produced some lunch, a bottle of wine.

"I have a date this afternoon in Kreuzberg," Eric said to Tom. "Come with me. Change your thoughts, as the French say. Takes just about an hour, maybe less. Then I have to meet Max later tonight. Come with me too!"

"Max?" Tom asked.

"Max and Rollo. Friends of mine." Eric was eating.

Peter's rather pale face smiled at Tom, and he lifted his eyebrows slightly. Peter looked calm and sure of himself.

Tom could not eat much, and barely listened to Eric's and Peter's jocular conversation about an anti-dog-dropping campaign now being waged in Berlin in imitation of New York's campaign, which involved little scoops and paper bags being carried by dog owners. The Berlin sanitation department intended now to build *Hundetoiletten*, dog WCs big enough for German shepherds to enter, which Peter remarked might inspire the dogs to start using their owner's houses, if they couldn't tell the difference.

13

Eric and Tom drove off in Eric's car for the Kreuzberg area of Berlin, which Eric said was less than fifteen minutes away. Peter had departed, promising to come to Eric's apartment around 1 a.m. Tom had said to Peter that he would be grateful if they could get an early start for the Lübars rendezvous. Even Peter admitted that the driving, plus the finding of the place might take an hour.

Eric stopped in a dismal-looking street of reddish-brown, old four- or five-story apartment houses near a corner bar with an open front door. A couple of kids—the word urchins sprang to Tom's mind—rushed up and begged pfennigs from them, and Eric fished in his pocket, saying if he didn't give them some coins, they might do something to his car, though the boy looked only about eight years old, and the girl perhaps ten, with lipstick messily applied to her lips and rouge on her cheeks. She wore a pavement-length gown which looked as if it had been fashioned from a brownish-red and pinned-together window curtain to create something like a dress. Tom erased his first idea, that the girl was playing with her mother's makeup and wardrobe: there was something more sinister going on here. The little boy had a thick mop of black hair which had been whacked in places by way of a haircut, and his dark eyes were glazed or maybe simply elusive. His projecting underlip seemed to indicate a fixed contempt for all the world around him. The boy had pocketed the money that Eric had given the girl.

"Boy's a Turk," said Eric, locking his car, keeping his voice low. Eric gestured toward a doorway they were supposed to enter. "They can't read, you know? Puzzles everyone. They speak Turkish and German fluently, but can't read *anything!*"

"And the girl? She looks German." The little girl was blonde. The strange juvenile pair were watching them still, standing by Eric's car.

"Oh, German, yes. Child prostitute. He's her pimp—or he is trying to be."

A buzz released the door and they went in. They climbed three flights of badly lit stairs. The hall windows were dirty, and let in almost no light. Eric knocked on a dark brown door, its paint scarred as if from kicks and blows. When clumping footsteps approached, Eric said, "Eric" at the door crack.

The door was unlocked, a tall, broad man beckoned them in, talking in mumbled German in a deep voice. Another Turk, Tom saw, with a swarthiness of face that not even dark-haired Germans ever achieved. Tom walked into a terrible smell of what he thought was stewing lamb mingled with cabbage. Worse, they were promptly ushered into the kitchen whence the smell originated. A couple of small children played on the linoleum floor, and an old woman with a tiny-looking head and fuzzy, thin gray hair stood at the stove, stirring a pot nervously. The grandmother, Tom supposed, and maybe German, as she didn't look Turkish, but he couldn't really tell. Eric and the burly man sat down at a round table to which Tom was urged also, and Tom sat down reluctantly, yet he meant to enjoy the conversation if he could. Just what was Eric doing here? Eric's slangy German, and the Turk's hash of it made it difficult indeed for Tom to understand anything. They were talking numbers. "Fifteen . . . twenty-three" and prices, "Four hundred marks . . ." Fifteen what? Then Tom remembered that Eric had said the Turk did some work as go-between for the Berlin lawyers who issued papers to Pakistanis and East Indians, permitting them to remain in West Berlin.

"I don't like this nasty little work," Eric had said, "but if I don't cooperate to some extent, as go-between of papers myself, Haki won't do jobs for me that are more important than his smelly immigrants." Yes, that was it. Some of the immigrants, illiterate even in their own language, and unskilled, simply took the underground from East Berlin to West Berlin, and were met by Haki, who steered them to the right lawyers. Then they could go on relief, at

West Berlin expense, while their claims to be "political refugees" were investigated, a process that might take years.

Haki was either a full-time crook or on unemployment too—maybe both—otherwise what was he doing home at this hour? He looked no more than thirty-five, and strong as an ox. His trousers, which he had long ago outgrown as to belly, were now held together at the waist by a piece of string that bridged the gap. A few fly buttons showed, unfastened.

An awful white-lightning-type of homemade vodka (Tom was told) was brought forth by Haki, or would Tom prefer beer? Tom did prefer beer, after sampling the vodka. The beer arrived in a big half-empty bottle, flat and tepid. Haki went off to fetch something from another room.

"Haki is a construction worker," Eric explained to Tom, "but on leave because of some injury—at work. Not to mention that he enjoys the—*Arbeitslosenunterstützung*—the—"

Tom nodded. Unemployment benefits. Haki was lumbering back with a dirty shoebox. His tread made the floor shake. He opened the shoebox, and produced a brown-paper-wrapped parcel the size of a man's fist. Eric shook the parcel and it rattled. Like pearls? Drug pellets? Eric pulled out his wallet and gave Haki a hundred-mark note.

"Only a tip," said Eric to Tom. "Are you bored? We'll leave in a minute."

"*Inna minnit!*" repeated the grubby little girl on the floor, staring.

It gave Tom a small jolt. How much of all this were the kids understanding? The old woman, stirring the pot like a *Macbeth* witch, or maybe an inmate of an insane asylum, also stared at Tom. She appeared to tremble slightly, as if she might have a disease of the nerves.

"Where's the wife?" Tom murmured to Eric. "The mother of these kids?"

"Oh, she's working. German—from East Berlin. Sad type but

she works. Well—" Eric spoke softly, and gestured with his smooth fingers as if to say he could not speak further just now.

Tom was delighted when Eric got to his feet. They had been there half an hour, and it seemed to Tom much longer. Good-byes, and suddenly Tom and Eric were on the pavement, where the sunlight fell cleanly on their faces. The little parcel bulged Eric's jacket pocket. Eric looked around before he opened his car door. They drove off. Tom was curious about what was in the package, but thought it might be rude to ask.

"It is funny—about his wife, as you called her. East Berlin prostitute, and she was smuggled over in something like a jeep by American soldiers! And here her life was a little *better*—as a prostitute, but she is a drug addict too. She manages to hold some kind of a job, maybe cleaning public toilets, I don't know. Do you know—American soldiers cannot afford West Berlin prostitutes now, because the dollar has sunk so low, so they have to go to East Berlin for them? The Communists are furious, because they are not supposed to have any prostitutes—officially."

Tom smiled, mildly amused, and tried to shift himself into another gear in order to get through the hours ahead. What kind of people were the kidnappers? Young amateurs? Reasonably clever professionals? A girl with them? So useful to make an innocent impression on the public sometimes, a girl. And maybe all they wanted was money, as Eric had said, and they had no intention of harming Frank or anyone else physically.

Back at Eric's flat, Tom dialed Belle Ombre. It had the same dial code as Paris. The telephone rang six, seven times, and Tom imagined Heloise perhaps in Paris, having had an impulse to go to an afternoon film with Noëlle, and Mme. Annette sitting over a tea or a cold soda pop in Marie's and Georges' café, exchanging the latest gossip with another *femme de ménage* of Villeperce. Then on the ninth ring, Mme. Annette said:

"'Allo?"

"Madame Annette, c'est Tome ici! How is everything at home?"

THE BOY WHO FOLLOWED RIPLEY

"Très bien, Monsieur Tome! When are you returning home?"

Tom smiled, relieved. "Wednesday, probably, not sure. Don't worry. Is Madame Heloise there?"

She was, but Mme. Annette had to summon her from upstairs.

"Tome!" Heloise came to the telephone so quickly, Tom knew she had picked it up in his room. "Where are you? Hamburg?"

"N-no, moving about a little. Did I wake you up from a nap?"

"I was soaking my finger in something Madame Annette made for me, so I thought I would let her answer."

"Soaking your finger?"

"A vasistas in the greenhouse fell on it yesterday when I was watering. It is swollen, but Madame Annette does not think the nail will fall off."

Tom gave a sympathetic sigh. She meant one of the windows that propped up in the greenhouse. "Let *Henri* take care of the greenhouse!"

"Ah, Henri!— The boy is still with you?"

"Yes," Tom said, wondering if someone had rung Belle Ombre and asked about Frank. "Flying home tomorrow maybe. Heloise," Tom said quickly before she could put a word in, "if anybody telephones and asks where I am, say I've gone out for a walk in Villeperce. That I'm home—just gone out. Any long distance caller—tell him that."

"*Why* is this?"

"Because I very soon will be home taking a walk, Wednesday, I think. I'm moving around here—in Germany—so nobody can reach me just now anyway."

That went down reasonably well.

"I kiss you," were Tom's last words.

Tom felt very much better. Sometimes, he admitted to himself, he felt like a married man, solid, loved, or whatever one was supposed to feel. Even though he had just lied, a little bit, to his wife. It wasn't a lie for the usual reasons anyway.

Around eleven that evening, Tom was in a gayer place than

Kreuzberg, a men's bar considerably more chic than the one he had gone to with Frank. This one had a glass-enclosed stairway going up to the toilets, and patrons stood on the stairs making contacts, or trying to, with other patrons below.

"Amusing, eh?" said Eric, who was waiting for someone. They stood at the bar, there being no tables free. The place was of course a disco as well. "Easier to—" Here Eric was jostled by someone behind him.

Tom supposed Eric had been going to say it was easier to pass things in a place like this than even on a street corner, because all the customers, except those who were dancing, were either engrossed in shouted conversation or staring with their minds on pickups and not contraband goods. Tom had to admire one boy in drag, with a long black stole—or what was it—of feathers partly around his neck and partly hanging, one end of which he wafted gently as he strolled about. Few women went to such trouble to look their best.

Eric's contact arrived, a tallish young man in black leather, hands jammed into the pockets of a short leather jacket. "This is *Max*!" Eric yelled to Tom.

Eric didn't say Tom's name. Just as well, Tom thought. The package, which Eric had wrapped in gift paper with a blue ribbon, changed hands and went into Max's leather jacket front, which he zipped up again. Max's hair was cut very short, and his nails were painted in shocking pink.

"No time to take this away," Max said to Tom in English with a German accent. "Busy all day. You like it?" He grinned mockingly, meaning did Tom like his nails.

"Drink, Max? Dornkaat?" Eric shouted at him over the throbbing music. "Or a *vodka*?"

Max's expression suddenly changed. He had seen something in a far corner. "Thanks, I think I must fuck off." He nodded in the direction Tom had seen him look, and dropped his eyes with embarrassment. "Guy over there I don't want to see just now.

Painful. I am sorry, Eric. G'night." He gave Tom a nod, turned and went out the door.

"*Guter Junge!*" Eric shouted at Tom, nodding toward the door where Max had disappeared. "*Good* boy! Gay but just as reliable as Peter! Max's friend is called *Rollo*! You may meet him!" Eric put a hand on Tom's forearm, and pressed him to have one more drink—anything—maybe a beer? Best if they didn't leave right away, Eric conveyed.

Tom consented to a beer and paid the barman in advance. "I love this crazy fantasy here!" Tom said to Eric. He meant the occasional figure in drag, the makeup, the mock flirtations, and the laughter and good humor everywhere. It gave Tom a lift, as *A Midsummer Night's Dream* overture always gave him a lift before he went into battle. Fantasy! Courage was all imaginary, anyway, a matter of a mental state. A sense of reality did not help when one was faced with a gun barrel or a knife. Tom was now noticing, not for the first time, Eric's furtive or at least anxiously observant glances over his shoulder. Eric wasn't looking for an old or a new acquaintance among the men and boys. Or was he? No, Tom thought. Eric was a businessman, taking care of his apparently widely scattered business. Looking over his shoulder had become a habit with Eric.

"Ever have any trouble with the police here, Eric?" Tom asked, close to Eric's ear. "I mean this kind of bar?"

But still Eric hadn't heard him, thanks to a crash of cymbals in the music just now, a quivering climax of some kind that went on for several seconds before the deep heartbeat set in again, seeming to hit the walls as if they were drumheads. On the dance floor, male figures hopped up and down and twirled as if in a trance. Tom gave it up, shook his head, and picked up his fresh beer. He wasn't going to yell the word "police" at the top of his lungs.

14

Berlin, the city's lights, dwindled behind them, and Peter and Tom drove on through semi-rural, rather boring little communities, where nearly all the café lights were off now. Their direction was north. Eric had decided to stay at home, which was just as well, because Tom couldn't imagine what good he could have done by coming, and if the kidnappers saw a third man in Peter's car, they might suspect a police officer.

"Now—this is the beginning of Lübars," Peter said after some forty minutes of driving. "Now I go to the correct street and we shall have a look." He sat up straight, as if he had an important job to do. He had drawn a little sketch, which he had shown Tom in Eric's flat, and which now lay above his dashboard. "I think I have taken an unright road. *Verdammt!* But it does not matter, as we have plenty of time. It is only thirty-five minutes past three." Peter took a small flashlight from the shelf over his dashboard, and focused it on his sketch. "I know what I did. I must turn."

As Peter turned, his headlights illuminated a dark field of cabbages or lettuce in rows, buttoning the earth down with their neat green dots. Tom readjusted the thick suitcase between his feet and knees. The night was pleasantly cool, and there seemed to be no moon.

"Sure—this is the Zabel-Krüger-Damm again and I should go left up here. They go to bed so early here—get up early too!— Alt-Lübars, yes." Peter made a careful left turn. "Up here to the right should be the village green," Peter said softly in German, "according to my little map at home. Church and so on. And do you see those lights ahead?" His voice took on a rise of tension that Tom had not heard before. "That is the Wall."

Tom saw a fuzzy, whitish-yellow glow ahead, low and long, a bit lower than the road level, the searchlights on the other side of the Wall. The road sloped a little downward. Tom looked around for other cars, another car, but all was black except for a couple of per-haps obligatory streetlights in the direction of what Peter had called the village green. Now Peter's car barely crept. The kidnap-pers, as far as Tom could see, had not arrived as yet.

"This little road is not for cars, which is why I am going so slowly. Now we should soon see the—*Lagerhalle* on the left. There, maybe?"

The shed. Tom saw it, a low structure, longer than it was high, and it appeared to be open on the side facing the road. Tom could vaguely see a few structures that might be horse paddocks in a field to the right. Peter stopped by the shed.

"Go ahead. Put the suitcase behind the shed. Then we'll back out," said Peter in German. "I cannot turn here." Peter had dimmed his lights.

Tom was ready to get out. "You go ahead and back. I'll stay. I'll make it back to Berlin, don't worry."

"What do you mean, 'stay'?"

"Stay. I have a sudden inspiration."

"Do you want to *meet* that gang?" Peter's hands twisted on the steering wheel. "*Fight* them? Don't be crazy, Tom!"

Tom said in English, "I know you have a gun. Can I borrow it?"

"Sure, sure, but I can wait for you too—if—" Peter looked puzzled, pushed the knob of his glove compartment, and took a black gun from under a cloth. "It is loaded. Six shots. Safety here."

Tom took the gun. It was smallish and did not weigh much, but looked lethal enough. "Thank you." Tom put it in the right side pocket of his jacket, then peered at his watch. Three-forty-three. He saw Peter glance nervously at the clock in the dashboard, which was one minute fast.

"Look, Tom. You see that little hill of land over there?" Peter pointed behind them and to the right, toward the village green. "Where the church is. I shall wait for you there. With my lights out." Peter said it like a command, as if he had compromised enough by letting Tom take his gun.

"Don't wait. There's even a bus running all night on this Krüger-Damm, you told me." Tom opened the door and took the suitcase out.

"I just mentioned the bus, I didn't mean for you to *take* it!" Peter whispered. "Don't shoot at them! They will only shoot back and kill you!"

Tom closed Peter's door as softly as he could, and headed for the shed.

"This!" Peter whispered through his window. He was handing Tom his small flashlight.

"Thanks, my friend!" The torch was certainly a help, because the ground was rough. Tom felt he had left Peter bereft—of gun and torch. Tom clicked off the little torch when he was behind the back corner of the shed, and lifted his arm to Peter in a sign of farewell, whether Peter could see him or not. Peter backed, slowly and straight, on the dirt road that Peter surely could not see well if at all with his parking lights. Tom saw Peter's car reach Alt-Lübars, then turn slowly to Tom's left, headed for the village green. Peter was going to wait.

Now there was a faint, but very faint sign of dawn coming, though Lübars' sparse streetlights remained on. Peter's car was not in sight. Tom heard distant dog barks, and realized with a slight chill that they were the barks of the East German attack dogs beyond the Wall. The dogs did not sound excited. A breeze blew from the Wall's direction, and perhaps he had heard merely a bit of dog conversation as the animals slid along their wires. Tom turned his eyes from the eerie glow of the Wall's searchlights, and concentrated on listening.

He listened for the sound of a car motor. Surely the collector of the money wouldn't come via the field behind him?

Tom had set the suitcase against the wooden back of the shed, and he shoved it gently even closer with his foot. He took Peter's gun from his jacket pocket, pushed the safety off, and stuck it back in his pocket. Silence. It was so silent, Tom felt he could have heard the breathing of any person who might be in the shed, on the other side of the boards. Tom felt of the wooden planks with his fingertips. There were a few chinks in the rough wood.

He had to pee, and it reminded him of Frank in Grunewald, but he went ahead and relieved himself anyway, while he could. And what did he want? Why was he staying here? To get a look at the kidnappers again? In this darkness? To scare them off and save the money? Certainly not. To save Frank? His staying was not necessarily a help in that direction, maybe just the opposite. Tom realized that he hated the kidnappers, and that he would relish a blow back at them. He also knew this was illogical, since he would probably be outnumbered. Yet here he was, vulnerable, an easy target for a bullet, and it would be an easy getaway for the kidnappers too, most likely.

Tom straightened up at the sound of a car's motor from the Alt-Lübars direction. Or was it Peter departing? The car purred forward, however, Tom could see its dim parking lights. Very slowly the car entered the unpaved road on which the shed stood, and lumbered on, swaying with the lane's irregularities. The car stopped about ten yards to Tom's right. The car looked to be dark red, but Tom was not sure. Tom was now pressed against the back of the shed, and peering around the back corner, because the car's lights did not reach the shed.

The left side back door of the car opened, and one figure got out. The car's lights went off, and the man who had got out switched on a torch. He looked sturdy and not tall, and he walked on with assurance, but slowed when he left the road and stepped onto the field. Then he paused, and waved a hand at his chums in the car, as if to say that all looked well so far.

How many were in the car, Tom wondered? One? Two? Maybe there were two others, since the man had got out of a backseat.

The man approached the shed slowly, torch in his left hand, and his right hand moved to his trousers pocket and pulled out what might have been a gun. He came on to Tom's right, toward the back of the shed.

Tom picked up the suitcase and gripped its handle, and as the man rounded the corner, Tom swung the suitcase and caught him on the left side of his head with it. The impact made not a loud thud but a solid one, and there was a second bump as the man's head hit the back of the shed. Tom brought the suitcase down once more, aiming at the left side of the man's head as he was falling. The paleness of the shirt collar above what might have been a black sweater guided Tom as he brought the butt of Peter's gun down on the man's left temple. Now the man was not stirring, nor had he cried out. The torch beamed to Tom's left on the ground. Tom gripped Peter's gun in a firing position and pointed it upward.

"*Got* the *swine!*" Tom yelled hysterically, or maybe, "*Gott*, das Schwein!" and at the same time he fired two shots into the air.

Tom yelled again, shouted another phrase of nonsense, maybe a curse, and kicked the shed's back. He realized that his voice had gone shrill, that he was yelling at nothing.

Behind the Wall the dogs yelped, excited by the shots.

The click of a car's door closing startled Tom as if he had been shot himself. He looked around the shed's corner just in time to see a man in the driver's seat draw his leg in. The interior light had been on for a moment. This door then closed, and without parking lights, the car moved backwards to Tom's right, and the parking lights came on. The car backed to the left in Alt-Lübars, then went off at faster speed toward the bigger avenue.

The kidnappers were abandoning their chum. They could of course afford to abandon him and even the money just now, because they still had Frank Pierson. They had probably thought it a police trick, with no money on the scene. Tom breathed through his mouth, as if he had been in a fight. He pushed the safety onto Peter's gun, stuck it in his right trouser pocket, picked up the fallen torch and shone it for a couple of seconds on the man on the ground. His left temple looked all blood, was perhaps crushed, and

to Tom he looked indeed like the Grunewald Italian type, though
now his mustache was gone. Search his pockets? With the torch still
on, Tom felt quickly in the one back pocket of the man's black
trousers, found nothing, then with difficulty reached into the left
front pocket, which yielded a box of matches, a couple of coins,
and a key which looked like a house key. Tom pocketed the key
quickly and almost absently, and avoided looking at the red splotch
of the man's temple and face, which was making him feel faint, or
so he thought. The right front pocket felt flat and empty. Tom
took the man's gun from the ground near his hand, stuck it into a
corner of the suitcase, and zipped the suitcase shut again. He
rubbed the torch against his trousers, cut it off, and dropped it on
the ground.

Then Tom made his way to the road without putting on Peter's
small torch—tripping once badly—and walked toward Alt-Lübars,
backed by the yelps of attack dogs. Tom didn't as yet see anyone
who had ventured out of his house to investigate the shots, so he
dared to put on the little torch for a second or two at a time, so he
could see his footing. Once at Alt-Lübars, he didn't need the torch
as the road was smoother. Tom did not look to the left, where Peter
might still be, because he did not want to run into an inhabitant of
the village who might just be coming out his door.

Behind him somewhere, a window opened, a voice cried
something.

Tom did not look back.

What had the voice said? "Who is there?" or "Who is that?"

The dog's barks had faded out, and Tom wet his lips as he
rounded the corner to the right into Zabel-Krüger-Damm. The
suitcase suddenly seemed weightless. Here cars were parked, a couple of cars even zoomed past. Dawn was definitely rising, and as if
to confirm him half the streetlights went out. In the distance, not
more than a hundred yards away, Tom saw what he thought was a
bus-stop sign. Peter had mentioned a number 20 bus going to
Tegel. That was the airport area, in the direction of Berlin at any

rate. Tom dared to lift the suitcase and to glance at its corners for the red or pink of blood. He could hardly be sure in the dim light, and what was earth or mud might have looked the same as blood, but he saw nothing to be concerned about. He made himself walk at a moderate pace, as if he had somewhere to go, but was not in a hurry. There were only two other people on the pavement now, both men, one elderly and a bit stooped. They seemed to pay him no attention.

How often did the buses run? Tom paused by the bus stop, and looked back. A car appeared, full lights on, and passed Tom.

"Äpfel, Äpfel!" That was from a small boy who came running and fell against the elderly man, who nearly embraced him.

Tom watched. Where had the little boy come from? Why was he crying "Apples!" when he had none in his hands? The elderly man took the boy's hand, and they walked on, away from Berlin.

Here came the yellowish lights of what looked like a bus. Tom saw 20 TEGEL on its lighted front. When Tom paid for his ticket, he noticed that a couple of knuckles of his left hand were dark red with blood. How had that happened? Tom took a seat in the nearly empty bus, suitcase between his feet, stuck his left hand in his jacket pocket, and avoided looking at the other passengers. Tom gazed out the window on his left, at the encouragingly increasing houses, cars, people. It was now light enough to see the colors of cars. What had happened to Peter? Tom hoped he had fled at the sound of the gunshots.

How soon would the body be found? In an hour, by some curious dog, the dog maybe in the company of a farmer? The body would not be visible from the road. Tom felt reasonably sure it was a body, not an unconscious man. Tom sighed, almost gasped, shook his head, and stared at the brown pigskin suitcase between his knees which contained two million dollars in paper. He leaned back and relaxed. Tegel must be the terminal stop, he thought, and he could almost afford to sleep. But he didn't sleep, only rested his head against the window.

The bus arrived at Tegel, which seemed a U-Bahn station rather than the air terminus. Tom was interested in a taxi, and after a few seconds, he found the taxi rank. He asked a driver if he could go to Niebuhrstrasse. Tom did not give the number, and told the driver he would know the house once he got to the street. Tom settled back and lit a cigarette. His knuckles were scraped, nothing serious there, and it was his own blood at least. Wouldn't the kidnappers try again, ring up Paris and make another date? Or would they be so scared or rattled now, they would turn Frank loose? The last idea seemed amateurish to Tom, but how professional were these kidnappers?

Tom got out somewhere in Niebuhrstrasse, paid and tipped the driver, and walked in the direction of Eric's apartment house. He had the two keys on a ring which Eric had given him, and he opened the front door with one, and took the lift. At Eric's door Tom knocked, and gave the bell one short push. It was now nearly half past six.

Tom heard footsteps, then Eric's voice asked in German:

"Who is there?"

"Tom."

"A-ah!" A chain rattled, a couple of bolts slid.

"Back again!" Tom whispered cheerfully, and set the suitcase down in Eric's hall, near where it became the living room.

"Tom, why did you make Peter *leave?* Peter is so worried, he telephoned twice!— And you brought the suitcase back!" Eric smiled and shook his head, as if at a silly economy.

Tom took off his jacket. The August sunlight was starting to blaze beyond Eric's window.

"Two shots, Peter told me. Now what happened?— Sit down, Tom! Would you like a coffee? Or a drink?"

"A drink first, I think. Could you manage a gin and tonic?"

Eric could, and while he was making it, Tom went to the bathroom and washed his hands with warm water and soap.

"How did you get back? Peter said you took his gun."

"I still have his gun." Now Tom was standing with a Gauloise in one hand and his drink in the other. "I took a bus and a taxi. The money's still there." Tom nodded toward the suitcase. "That's why I brought your suitcase back."

"Still there?" Peter's pink lips parted. "Who fired the shots?"

"I did. But only in the air." Tom's voice had gone hoarse. He sat down. "I hit one with your suitcase. The Italian type, I think. I think he's dead."

Eric nodded. "Peter saw him."

"Did he?"

"Yes. I must put on something, Tom, I feel silly." Eric, in pajamas, hurried into his bedroom, and came back tying the belt of his black silk dressing gown. "Peter waited, he said, maybe ten minutes, and then he went back to look, thinking you might be dead or wounded. He saw a man lying behind the shed."

"True," Tom said.

"So you just— Why didn't you go back to Peter who was waiting at the church?"

Waiting at the church! Tom laughed, and stretched his legs out in front of him. "I don't know. Maybe I was scared. I didn't think. I didn't even look toward the church." Tom sipped more of his glass, and said, "Coffee, yes, please, Eric, and then a little sleep."

On his last words, the telephone rang.

"That certainly is Peter again." Eric went to his telephone. "Just come back!" Eric said. "No, he is all right, not hurt.— He took a bus and a taxi!" Then Eric laughed at something Peter was saying. "I shall tell Tom, yes. Very funny.— Yes, at least we are all safe.— Here! Can you believe it?" Eric put the telephone against his chest, still smiling broadly. "Peter cannot believe the money is back *here*! Peter wants to talk to you."

Tom got up. "Hello, Peter . . . Yes, I am okay. My infinite thanks to you, Peter, you did well." Tom said that in German. "No, I did not shoot the man."

"I could not see well in the dark—with no light," Peter said. "I only saw he was not you. So I went away."

He was brave to go back, Tom thought. "I've still got your gun and your torch."

Peter chuckled. "Let us both get some sleep."

Eric made coffee for Tom—Tom knew it was not going to disturb his sleep in the least—and then together they opened the horsehair sofa and spread the sheets and blanket.

Tom carried the brown suitcase to the window, and looked at it for signs of blood. He saw none, but he took, with Eric's permission, a floor rag from the kitchen, moistened it at the sink, and went over the exterior of the suitcase with it, then rinsed the rag out and hung it on a rod to dry.

"You know," Eric said to Tom, "a man approached Peter as he was walking away from that little road, and said, 'Did you hear the shots?' and Peter said yes, that was why he had walked onto the road. Then the man asked what Peter was doing there, since Peter was a stranger and Peter said, "Oh, I am only with my girlfriend by the church!' "

Tom was not in a mood to laugh. He washed in a perfunctory way in the bathroom, and pulled on his pajamas. He was thinking that if the kidnappers released Frank, they would not necessarily inform Thurlow. Frank might know and probably did know that his brother and Thurlow were at the Hôtel Lutetia in Paris, and Frank might make his way there on his own, if he were freed. Or—the kidnappers might simply kill the boy with an overdose and leave his body in some Berlin apartment which they would abandon.

"What are you thinking about, Tom? Let us both go back to bed for a little while. A long while. Sleep as late as you like! My housekeeper does not come tomorrow. And I have locked and chained the door."

"I'm thinking I have to ring Thurlow in Paris, because I said I would."

Eric nodded. "Yes—what *is* going to happen now? Go ahead and do it, Tom."

Tom went in his pajamas and loafers to the telephone, and dialed.

"How many were there?" Eric asked. "Could you see?"

"Not really. In the car? Three maybe." Two now, Tom thought. He turned off the lamp by Eric's telephone. There was light enough from the window.

"*Hello!*" Thurlow said. "What happened there?"

Thurlow had heard from them, Tom could tell. "Can't say on the telephone. Are they willing to make another date?"

"Ye-es, I'm pretty sure, but they're sounding scared—nervous, I mean, and a little threatening. They said if there were any police—"

"No police. There won't be any police. Tell them we're willing to make another date, would you?" Tom suddenly had an idea as to a meeting place. "I think they still want the money. Make them prove the boy's still alive, would you? Then I'll call you back later today when I've had a little sleep."

"Where *is* the money now?"

"Safe with me." Tom put the telephone down.

Eric stood with Tom's empty coffee cup, listening.

Tom lit a final cigarette. "Asking about the money," he said to Eric, smiling. "I'm betting they still want the money. Much nicer than killing the boy and having a corpse on their hands."

"Ja, sure it is.— I took the suitcase back into my bedroom. Did you notice?"

Tom hadn't.

"Good night, Tom. Sleep long!"

Tom glanced at the chain on the door, then said, "Good night, Eric."

15

"Eric, I'd like to borrow some drag—for tonight probably. Do you think your friend Max would be kind enough to lend me some?"

"Drag?" Eric gave a mystified smile. "Drag for what? A party?"

Now Tom laughed. They were breakfasting, or Tom was, at a quarter past one in the afternoon. Tom sat in pajamas and dressing gown on Eric's smaller sofa. "Not a party, but I have an idea. Might work, and anyway it would be fun. I thought I'd try to make a date with the kidnappers at the Hump tonight. And maybe Max can even come with me." Der Hump was the name of the gay bar with the glass stairway.

"You will deliver the money at the Hump in *drag*?"

"No, no money. Just drag. Can you reach Max now?"

Eric stood up. "Max may be working. Rollo is more likely. He sleeps till noon usually. They live together. I shall try—yes." Eric dialed a number which he had not needed to look up. After a few seconds, he said, "Hello, Rollo! How are you? . . . Is Max there? . . . So. Listen," he went on in German, "my friend Tom would like— Well, Max has met him. Tom is staying with me. Tom would like some drag for tonight . . . *Ja!* A long dress—" Eric glanced at Tom and nodded. "Ja, a wig certainly, makeup—shoes." Eric looked at Tom's loafers and said, "Max's maybe, yours are *too* big, ha-ha! . . . At the Hump maybe! . . . Ha-ha! Oh, I am sure you can come if you want to."

"Some kind of *handbag*," Tom whispered.

"Oh, and a handbag," said Eric. "I don't know. Fun, I suppose." Eric chuckled. "You think so? Good, I'll tell Tom. Wieder-sehen, Rollo." Eric hung up and said, "Rollo thinks Max can arrive tonight around ten—here, I mean. Max is working in a beauty parlor till nine, and Rollo goes out at six to do a window-dressing job until ten, but he says he will leave a note for Max to find."

"Thank you, Eric." Tom felt cheered, even though nothing was as yet arranged.

"Again I have a date at three this afternoon," Eric said. "Not Kreuzberg. Want to come?"

This time Tom didn't. "No, thanks, Eric. I think I might take a little walk—buy a present for Heloise, maybe. And I must ring Paris again. I shall owe you a thousand dollars for your phone bill."

"Ha-ha!— To leave money for phone bills! No. We are all friends, Tom." Eric went off to his bedroom.

His words lingered in Tom's ears as he lit a Roth-Händle. They were friends, and so was Reeves a friend of theirs. They used one another's telephones, houses, lives sometimes, and somehow it all evened out. Tom could, however, send Eric an American slang dictionary, at least.

Once more, Tom dialed the Lutetia.

"Hel-lo, I am glad to hear from you," said Thurlow, sounding as if he were chewing something. "Yes," he said in answer to Tom's question, "they phoned around noon today, this time with what sounded like fire engines in the background. Anyway they would like another definite—place and time and they've set it up. It's a restaurant—I'll give you the address—and you're simply to leave a *package* to be picked—"

"I have a place to suggest," Tom interrupted. "A bar called the Hump. That's H-u-m-p, just the way it sounds. In— Just a minute." Tom put his hand over the telephone and called, "Eric!— Sorry to bother you. What is the street of Der Hump?"

"Winterfeldtstrasse!" said Eric promptly.

"Winterfeldtstrasse," Tom said to Thurlow. "Oh, never mind the number, let them find it . . . Oh, yes, just an ordinary bar, but a pretty big one. I'm sure the taxi drivers will know it . . . Around midnight. Between eleven and midnight, let's say. They are to ask for Joey, and Joey will have what they want."

"That will be *you*?" Thurlow asked in an interested tone.

"Well—not sure. But Joey will be there. I assume you've heard that the boy is still all right?"

"Only their word. We didn't speak with him. With fire engines in the background, they must've been calling from the street."

"Thank you, Mr. Thurlow. I expect success tonight," Tom said in a firm tone, firmer than he felt. Tom plunged on. "Once they've got the money, I trust they'll acknowledge it and tell you where the boy's to be released. Can you ask them to do that? I suppose they'll ring you again before tonight to confirm a date?"

"I *hope* so. They gave me orders to tell *you*. About that restaurant, I mean— So you'll call me back when, Mr. Ripley?"

"I can't say an exact time just now. But I'll call back, yes." Tom hung up, vaguely dissatisfied, wishing he could be sure the people who had Frank would ring Thurlow again today.

Eric walked in from the hall with a purposeful air, licking an envelope. "Success? What is the news there?"

Eric's lack of anxiety gave Tom a bit of cool. They were both going to quit the apartment in a few minutes and leave two million dollars in it, unguarded. "I made a date for between eleven and twelve tonight at the Hump. The kidnappers are supposed to ask for Joey."

"And you are not taking the money?"

"No."

"And then what?"

"I shall plan things as I go along. Has Max got a car?"

"No—they haven't." Eric adjusted his dark blue jacket on his shoulders, and looked at Tom, smiling. "I shall see you to a taxi in your drag tonight."

"Want to come?"

"Not sure." Eric wagged his head. "Tom, make yourself at home. But double-lock the door if you go out—please."

"Definitely. I shall."

"Would you like to see where the suitcase is—in my closet?"

Tom smiled. "No."

"Bye-bye, dear Tom. Back by six, I think I am."

A few minutes later, Tom also went out, double-locking the door as Eric had requested.

Niebuhrstrasse looked peaceful and ordinary to Tom, no figure anywhere that appeared to be loitering or paying attention to him. Tom walked left into Leibnizstrasse, and left again when he reached the Kurfürstendamm. Here were the shops, the book-and-record stores, the four-wheeled snack wagons on the pavement, life, people—a small boy running with a big cardboard box, a girl trying to scrape chewing gum from the heel of her boot without having to touch it. Tom smiled. He bought a *Morgenpost*, and took a brief look at it, not expecting and not finding anything that had to do with a kidnapping.

Tom stopped in front of a shop window full of good attaché cases, handbags, and wallets. He went in and bought a dark-blue suede handbag with a shoulder strap. Heloise would like it, he thought. Two hundred and thirty-five DM. And maybe he had bought it as a guarantee that he would get back home and be able to present it to her. That was a bit illogical. He bought a couple of packets of Roth-Händle at a Schnell-Imbiss wagon. Convenient, Tom thought, that they sold cigarettes and matches as well as food and beer. Did he want a beer? No. He strolled back toward Eric's.

Tom held Eric's front door open for a woman coming out with an empty shopping trolley. She thanked him, but barely glanced at him.

He did not like going into Eric's silent apartment, wondered for an instant if someone might be hiding in Eric's bedroom. Absurd. But he went into the bedroom—which was quiet and neat with the bed made—and looked into the closet. The brown suitcase stood at the back, behind a larger suitcase, and in front of the larger suitcase was a row of shoes. Tom lifted the brown suitcase, and felt its familiar weight.

In the living room, Tom found himself staring at one of Eric's woodland paintings—hating it—of an antlered stag with terrified and bloodshot eyes under dark-blue storm clouds. Were dogs pursuing the stag? If so, Tom didn't see any. He looked in vain for a rifle barrel poking from anywhere in the picture. Maybe the stag had hated the painter.

The telephone rang, and Tom jumped almost off his feet. It had sounded unusually loud. Could the kidnappers have got Eric's number? Of course not. Should he answer it? Put on a different voice? Tom picked up the telephone and spoke in his usual voice.

"Hello?"

"Hello, Tom. This is Peter," Peter said calmly.

Tom smiled. "Hello, Peter. Eric's not here, back around six, he said."

"Not important. You are okay? Slept?"

"Yes, thank you.— Are you free tonight, Peter? Say from ten-thirty or eleven for a little bit?"

"Ja-a. I have only to see a cousin for dinner. What is happening tonight?"

"I am visiting Der Hump, maybe with Max. Again I am requesting your taxi service, but tonight should be safer. Well," Tom added hastily, "I hope it will be safer, but that would be my problem, not yours."

Peter said he could come to Eric's between ten-thirty and eleven.

MAX LAID OUT his drag offerings in Eric's living room like a salesman displaying something which would probably interest the customer, though this was the only outfit Max had brought. "This is my best one," Max said in German, clumping around the living room in his boots and black leather gear, spreading the long gown to best advantage against himself.

Tom was relieved to see that it had long sleeves. The gown was pink and white and transparent, with a triple row of ruffles at the hem. "Terrific," said Tom. "*Very* pretty," he added.

"And this, of course." From his red canvas carryall, Max pulled a white slip or petticoat that looked as long as the dress. "Put the dress on first, it will inspire me for the makeup," Max said with a smile.

Tom lost no time, took off his dressing gown under which he wore shorts, pulled on the slip, and followed it with the dress. This caused a problem with the tights, which looked like a wraith of beige and which Max said he had to sit down to put on properly, but finally Max said, "What the hell?" if the shoes felt all right without the tights, because the dress came nearly to the floor. Max was as tall as Tom. The gown had no belt but fell loose.

Then Tom sat down before a rectangular looking glass that
Eric had fetched from his bedroom. Max had spread his parapher-
nalia on Eric's sideboard, and now he got to work on Tom's face.
Eric watched all this with folded arms and silent amusement. Max
slapped heavy white cream on Tom's eyebrows and spread it, humming as he worked.

"Never mind this," said Max. "I'll get the eyebrows back. Just
what you need."

"Music!" said Eric. "We need *Carmen!*"

"No, we *don't* need Carmen!" Tom said, hating the idea of *Carmen*, mainly because it wasn't funny enough, or he wasn't in the
mood for Bizet. The transformation in Tom's lips amazed him. His
upper lip had become thinner, the under lip fuller. He would
hardly have recognized himself!

"Now the wig," Max murmured in German, shaking out the
auburn, rather frightening thing that had been lying on a corner of
Eric's sideboard. It had dangling curls that Max proceeded to comb
out delicately.

"Sing something," Tom said. "Do you know that song about
the slick little girl?"

"Ach!— The things you do to your *face*— *Make*up!" Max was
off, singing, doing a fine imitation of Lou Reed. "Rouge and col-
oring, incense and ice . . ." Max swayed with his work.

It reminded Tom of Frank, of Heloise, of Belle Ombre.

"Open *your* ice!" Max sang to him, concentrating on Tom's
eyes now. Max paused for a look at Tom, then a look into the
mirror.

"Are you free tonight, Max?" Tom asked in German.

Max laughed, adjusting the wig, viewing his product. "Are you
serious?" Max had a broad, generous mouth, now spread in a smile,
and Tom thought that Max blushed. "I keep my hair very short, so
these wigs fit better, but really it is silly to be so fussy. *I* think this
looks nice."

"Yes." Tom gazed into the mirror as if at another person, but without much interest at the moment. "*Ernsthaft*, Max. Have you got an hour to spend with me at the bar? At the Hump tonight? Around midnight or even earlier? Bring Rollo. Be my guests. Just for an hour or so, eh?"

"Am I left out?" Eric asked in German.

"Oh, up to you, Eric."

Now Max was helping Tom into the high-heeled patent leather pumps, which were rather full of cracks.

"Secondhand from a thrift shop in Kreuzberg," Max said, "but they don't torture my feet like a lot of these high heels. Look! They fit!"

Tom sat down again before the mirror, and felt in a fantasy world as Max created a beauty spot on his left cheek with one masterly black dot.

The doorbell rang, and Eric went into his kitchen.

"You really want Rollo and me to join you at the Hump tonight?" Max asked.

"You can't expect me to sit there or stand there all by myself like a wallflower, can you, Max? I'll need you both. Eric isn't the right type." Tom was practicing a lighter voice.

"All this just for fun?" Max asked, touching Tom's auburn curls again.

"Just for fun. I think I'll stand up an imaginary date. He won't know me when he walks in, anyway."

Max laughed.

"Tom!" Eric said, walking back into the living room.

Don't call me Tom, Tom felt like saying.

Eric stared, speechless for a moment, into the mirror which reflected Tom's transformed face. "P-Peter's downstairs, says he cannot park so easily, so maybe you can come down?"

"Oh, indeed," said Tom. Coolly, Tom picked up his handbag, a largish thing of red leather and black patent leather which crisscrossed in a basket pattern. Coolly too, he reached in a pocket of his jacket that hung in Eric's front closet, and took the key that he had found on the Italian type, and from the back right corner of the closet floor picked up the gun that belonged to Peter. Eric and Max were chatting, looking at Tom's attire, and neither of them noticed his putting the gun into his handbag. Tom had his back to them. "Ready, Max? Who's escorting me down?"

Max did. Max had been a bit late in getting to Eric's, and he said Rollo might already be at the Hump, but Max wanted to dash home first to "partly" change his clothes, because he had been working all day in the shirt he was wearing.

Peter's cigarette nearly fell from his mouth. He was sitting in his car.

"Tom," Tom said. "Hello, Peter."

Peter and Max apparently knew each other. Max told Tom that he lived so near, it was better for him to run home on foot, since the Hump was in the other direction. He would see Tom in a few minutes. Peter and Tom drove off toward Winterfeldtstrasse.

"Now what is all this? For fun?" Peter asked, a bit tense.

Had Tom detected a slight coolness in Peter? "Not entirely." Tom realized that he could have rung Thurlow back, and hadn't, to find out if the kidnappers would keep the date tonight. "While we have a minute—you went back to that *shed*, Peter."

Peter shrugged or squirmed. "I went on foot, yes, not wanting to make noise with the car motor. Very dark without a light."

"I can imagine."

"I thought maybe you were dead there—wounded maybe, which would have been worse. Then I saw the man there on the ground—not you. So I went away. You did not shoot him?"

"I hit him with the suitcase." Tom swallowed. He did not feel like saying that he had also bashed his temple with Peter's gun butt. "I think the kidnappers thought I was more numerous than I was. I fired your gun twice in the air and yelled. But I think the fellow on the ground there was dead."

Peter chuckled, perhaps nervously, but it made Tom feel better. "I didn't stay long enough to find out. Didn't see the papers tonight—and I wasn't watching the news tonight either."

Tom said nothing. For the moment, he was in the clear, Tom thought, and he had to think about the present. Did he dare ask Peter to wait again, outside the Hump? Peter could be extremely useful tonight.

"And they drove away," Peter said. "I saw their car going away, and then I waited for you—more than five minutes, I think."

"That was when I walked back to that avenue—the Krüger-Damm and caught the bus. I didn't even look toward the church. My fault, Peter."

Peter turned a corner. "All that money in Eric's house now!—And what will they do to the boy if they don't get it?"

"Oh, I think they would rather have the money than the boy." They had now entered the street where the bar was, and Tom was watching for the pink neon sign which said *Der Hump* in script with a horizontal underlining on the side of a building, but he didn't yet see it. Tom had to enlighten Peter about the possible events of tonight, and Tom with difficulty tried to get started. His drag, at that moment, made him feel silly and vulnerable, and he lifted nervously the black and red handbag on his lap: it was heavyish because of Peter's gun. "I've got your gun with me. Four bullets left."

"Now? You have the gun?" Peter asked in German, and glanced at Tom's handbag.

"Yes. I made a date with the kidnappers tonight—and maybe just one of them will turn up, I don't know—at the Hump—between eleven and midnight. So, Peter, if you're willing to wait for me— It's eleven now and a little after. I'm going to ignore them inside, and then I hope to be able to follow them. I think they may come in a car, but I'm not sure of that. If they haven't a car, I'll do what I can on foot by way of following them."

"O-oo-oh," said Peter dubiously.

Was Peter thinking of his high-heeled shoes, Tom wondered? "If they don't show up at all, at least it's fun tonight and nobody gets hurt." Tom had just seen the pink *Der Hump* sign, not nearly as large as he had remembered it. Now Peter was trying to park.

"There's a place!" Tom said, having spotted a gap in a line of cars parked on the right side of the street.

Peter was taking it.

"Are you willing to wait nearly an hour? Maybe more?"

"Sure, sure," Peter said, parking.

Tom explained: if the kidnappers kept this date, they were going to ask for "Joey," ask the barman or a waiter, and when Joey did not appear after a while, they would leave, and then Tom wanted to follow them. "I doubt if they'll wait till closing time at dawn. They'll know it's a trick by midnight or a little after. But if you have to pee, you had better go somewhere now."

Peter's long jaw dropped slightly and he laughed. "No, I am okay. You are alone there? By yourself?"

"Do I look so delicate? Max is coming. Probably Rollo too. Bye-bye, Peter. See you here later. If it gets to be quarter past twelve, I'll come out and speak with you."

Tom looked at Der Hump's door. One masculine figure came out, two others slipped in, and the beat of the disco music came louder through the opened door. BOOM-PAH . . . BOOM-PAH . . . BOOM-PAH . . . like a heartbeat, not fast, not too slow either, but strong. A little phony too, Tom thought, artificial, electronic, not exactly human. Tom knew what Peter was thinking.

"You think this is intelligent to do?" Peter asked in German.

"I want to find out where the boy is." Tom took up his hand-bag. "If you don't want to wait, Peter, I don't blame you. I can try to get a taxi in time to follow them."

"I'll wait." Peter smiled, tense. "If you have trouble—I'm here."

Tom got out and crossed the street. The evening breeze made him feel naked, and he glanced down to make sure he wasn't, that his skirt hadn't blown up. His ankle turned as he stepped onto the curb, and he warned himself to take it easy. Tom touched his wig nervously, and with slightly parted lips pulled open the door of Der Hump. The disco pulse engulfed him, created echoing vibrations in his eardrums. Tom moved—under the gaze of at least ten cus-

tomers, many of whom smiled at him—toward the bar. The air
smelled of pot.

Again there was no room at the bar, but it was amazing how
four or five men stepped aside so Tom could finally touch the
round, shiny chromium rim of the bar.

"And who are you?" asked a young man in Levi's so worn out,
they revealed the absence of any underwear.

"Mabel," Tom said, and fluttered his eyelashes. Coolly he
opened his handbag, in order to get at the loose marks and change
at the bottom for a drink. Tom suddenly realized he had not
thought of nail polish, and neither had Max. The hell with it. It
seemed masculine to dump coins on the counter in the English
manner, so Tom didn't.

Men and boys on the dance floor twisted and jumped to the
din of pounding rock, as if the floor were exploding or undulat-
ing beneath them. Figures hovered, gazed, drifted up the glass-
enclosed stairway which led to the loos, and as Tom watched, one
figure fell down the stairs, was righted by two other men, and
walked on down apparently undamaged. There were at least ten
other figures in long-dress drag, Tom noticed, but now Tom was
looking around for Max. With infinite slowness, Tom extracted a
cigarette from his handbag and lit it, in no hurry to catch the eye
of a barman and order a drink, for the nonce. It was now a quarter past eleven, and Tom looked around—especially at the bar
where it would be logical for someone to ask a barman about a
Joey—but so far Tom did not see anyone who could by any stretch
of the imagination be called straight, and he assumed the kidnappers were.

And here came Max in a Western white shirt with pearl buttons, black leather trousers, and boots still, from the back part of the
establishment where most of the dancing was going on. He was
followed by a tall figure in a long dress that seemed made of beige
tissue paper, and with crew-cut hair that had slender yellow rib-
bons somehow tied in it above both ears.

"*Good* evening," Max said, smiling. "Rollo." He gestured to the tissue paper figure.

"Mabel," said Tom, smiling merrily.

Rollo's thin red lips turned up at the corners. Otherwise his face was a floury white. His blue-gray eyes seemed to glitter like cut diamonds. "You wait a friend?" asked Rollo. He was carrying a long black cigarette holder without a cigarette.

Was Rollo kidding or not? "Ja-a," said Tom, letting his eyes roll again over what he could see of the fellows against the walls in the tables department. Tom could hardly imagine one of the kidnappers or even two of them dancing, but perhaps anything was possible.

"What to *drink*?" Rollo asked Tom.

"I shall do it. Beer, Tom?" Max asked.

Beer seemed unladylike, but Tom at once thought this absurd, was about to say yes, when he noticed an espresso machine behind the bar. "*Kaffee, bitte!*" Tom took some of the loose coins from the bottom of his handbag and put them on the counter. He had not brought his wallet.

Max and Rollo wanted Dornkaats.

Tom maneuvered himself so that he could face the door, lean against the bar, and chat with Max and Rollo who were now facing him. Chatting was a bit difficult in the noise. Every few seconds, a male figure or two came in the door, and fewer seemed to depart.

"Who are you standing up?" Max shouted into Tom's ear. "Do you *see* him?"

"Not yet!" Just then Tom noticed a young man with dark hair in the very corner or end of the bar which curved to Tom's right and stopped against the wall. This one could be straight. He looked in his late twenties, wore a tan canvas-like jacket, and he held a cigarette in his left hand which rested on the bar. He was drinking beer, and he kept looking around, slowly and alertly, glancing at the door too. But many other people were also looking at the door, so

Tom didn't know what to think. Sooner or later the man Tom wanted would ask the barman—possibly for a second time, if he had already done it once—if he knew or saw or had a message from someone called Joey.

"*Dance?*" said Rollo, bending politely toward Tom, because Rollo was even taller.

"Why not?" He and Rollo forged their way to the dance floor.

Within seconds, Tom had to remove his high-heeled shoes, which Rollo gallantly took and began to clap together over his head like castanets. Whirling skirts, everybody laughing, but not at them, and in fact no one paid any attention to him and Rollo. *DEW-IT . . . DEW-IT . . . DEW-IT . . .* Or the words might have been *CHEW IT* or *PEE WIT* or *BLEW IT*, it didn't matter. The floor felt good under Tom's bare feet. Now and then he put his hand on the top of his head to straighten his wig, and once Rollo did it for him. Rollo had had the good sense to wear flat sandals, Tom noticed. Tom felt exhilarated and stronger, as if he were having a workout in a gym. No wonder Berliners liked disguises! One could feel free, and in a sense like *oneself* in a disguise.

"Shall we go back to the bar?" Tom knew it was 11:40 at least, and he wanted to have another look.

Tom didn't put his shoes back on till he got to the bar, where his unfinished coffee still stood. Max had been guarding his handbag. Tom resumed his place from which he could watch the door. The man Tom had noticed was no longer at the end of the bar, and Tom glanced around, looking for a tan jacket among the men milling around the tables, or those standing and staring at the dance floor or the stairway. Then Tom saw him just a couple of yards behind him at the bar, nearly concealed by the customers between, trying to catch the attention of a barman. Max started to yell something at Tom, and Tom silenced him with a wave of a finger, and watched the man through his nearly closed false eyelashes.

The barman leaned forward—he wore a curly blond wig— and shook his head.

The tan-jacketed man was still speaking, and Tom stood on
tiptoe to try to see his lips. Was he saying "Joey"? It looked like it,
and now came a nod of the barman's head, a nod that might mean,
"I'll tell you if he turns up." Then the man in the tan jacket slowly
made his way through standing groups and solitary figures toward
the wall opposite the bar. Here he spoke with a blondish man in a
bright blue open-necked shirt who was leaning against the wall.
The blue shirt said nothing in reply to whatever the other man had
said to him.

"What were you saying?" Tom asked Max.

"*That* your friend?" Max asked, grinning, nodding toward the
tan jacket.

Tom shrugged. He pushed his pinkish ruffled sleeve back, and
saw that it was eleven minutes to midnight. Tom finished his coffee. He leaned toward Max and said, "I *may* have to leave in a
minute. Not sure. So I'd better say good night and *thank* you,
Max—in case I have to run—like Cinderella!"

"You want a taxi?" Max asked, puzzled, polite.

Tom shook his head. "Another Dornkaat?" Tom signaled for
two by pointing at Max's glass, holding up two fingers, then put
out two ten-mark notes over Max's protest. At the same time, Tom
was watching the tan-jacketed man make his way back to the bar,
aiming for the same place by the wall, which was now occupied
by a man and a boy, deep in conversation. Then the tan jacket
seemed to give up the bar idea, and moved nearer the door. Tom
saw him lift an arm to get the eye of a barman who happened to
be near the end of the bar just then. The barman shook his head at
once, and then Tom knew that the man in the tan jacket was the
one looking for Joey. Or Tom felt sure enough of it. The man
looked at his wristwatch, then at the door. Three teenaged boys
came in, all in Levi's, all eyes, all swinging empty hands. The man
in the tan jacket looked in the direction of the blue shirt, and gave
a movement of his head in the direction of the door. The tan jacket
went out.

"Good night, Max," Tom said, picking up his handbag. "Lovely to meet you, Rollo!"

Rollo gave a bow.

Tom saw the blue shirt moving toward the door, and let him go out first. Then in an unhurried manner, Tom made his way to the door and out. Tom saw both men on the pavement to his right, the tan jacket waiting as the blue shirt walked toward him. Tom went left, toward Peter's car, which was headed in the wrong direction, Tom realized. Some more fellows were entering the Hump, and one whistled at Tom, and the others chuckled.

Peter had his head back, but snapped to attention when Tom tapped his half-closed window.

"Me *again*!" said Tom, and went round the car and got in. "You'll have to turn. I just saw them. On this street. Two men."

Peter was already turning. The street was darkish, full of parked cars, but there was no traffic just now.

"Go slow, they're on foot," Tom said. "Pretend you're looking for a parking place."

Tom saw them walking, not looking behind them, and apparently engaged in conversation. Then they stopped at a parked car, and at a gesture from Tom, Peter slowed still more. A car was behind Peter's but had room to pass, and it did. "I'd like to follow them without being noticed," Tom said. "Give it a try, Peter. If they suspect we're following them, they'll give us a bum steer or zoom off somewhere—one or the other." Tom tried to put bum steer into German, but Peter seemed to understand well enough.

Some fifteen yards in front of them, the car pulled out, and turned smartly left into the next cross-street. Peter followed, and they saw the car turn right into a busier street. Two cars then got between them, but Tom kept the men's car in view, and at its next left turn saw in the headlights of another car that the car's color was maroon.

"The car's dark red. That's the car!"

"You know it?"

"It's the car that was in Lübars."

They followed, for what seemed to Tom five minutes but was perhaps half that, through two more turns, Tom navigating all the way, until Tom saw the car slow at a parking place on the left side of a street full of four- or six-story dwellings, whose windows looked mostly unlighted now.

"Can you stop here and back a bit," Tom said quickly.

Tom wanted to try to see which house they went into. And then, if possible, see if a light came on on a certain floor. These were again the dreary middle-class or lower middle-class apartment buildings which had escaped the bombs of World War II. Thanks to the tan jacket, Tom was able to make out a fuzzy shadow, lighter than the background, which mounted some steps at one of the front doors. He saw the light jacket disappear into the house.

"Go ahead about three meters—please, Peter."

As Peter inched ahead, Tom saw a third floor light grow brighter, and a second floor light grow dim to nonexistence. A minuterie system? Hall lights? A third floor light to the left then came on more strongly. A second floor light on the right remained bright and unchanged. Tom groped in the bottom of his handbag, where coins and paper money lay disorganized, and found the key he had taken from the pocket of the Italian type.

"Right, Peter, you can drop me here," Tom said.

"You want me to wait?" Peter whispered. "What are you going to do?"

"Not sure." Peter's car now stood on the right side of the street close to a row of parked cars, not annoying anyone. Peter might have been able to stay here fifteen minutes, but Tom did not know how long he would be, and he did not want to endanger Peter's life, in case a couple of them stormed out of the house shooting at him, and Peter tried to pick him up. Tom knew he sometimes imagined the worst, the absurdest. Did the key he had work the front door, the apartment door, or neither? Tom envisaged himself pressing half a dozen buttons downstairs until some innocent soul, not the kidnappers, let him into the building. "I'll just try to scare them," Tom said, tapping his fingertips on the door handle.

"You don't want me to telephone the police? Now or in five minutes?"

"No." Tom was going to get the boy or not, accomplish something or not, before the police could get here, and if the police arrived in time or too late, Tom's name would be dragged in by them, and that he did not want. "The police don't know anything about this, and I want it that way." Tom opened the car door. "Don't wait, and slam the car door when you're farther away." He half-closed the door after himself, so that it made only a faint click.

A woman in a light-colored dress passed Tom on the pavement, gave Tom a rather startled glance, and walked on.

Peter's car slid onward into darkness, into safety, and Tom heard its door slam. Tom concentrated on getting up the few front steps in his high heels, holding his long skirt a few inches above step level, so he wouldn't trip.

Inside the first front door, there was a panel of at least ten buttons, most marked with unclear names and not all with apartment numbers indicated. Discouraging, Tom thought, as he might have dared ring 2A or 2B, if he had seen it. That had been a second floor light by European counting, third floor by American. Tom tried the Yale lock type of key which he had in his hand. It worked in the lock. Tom felt a shock of surprise. Perhaps each of the gang carried such a housekey, and there was always someone in the apartment to open the apartment door? Which apartment now? Tom pressed the minute-light button, and saw an uninviting brown stairway of unpolished wood, and two closed doors, one on either side of where he stood.

He dropped the key into his handbag, and felt for the gun. He pushed the safety to an off position, left the gun in the handbag, and began climbing the stairs, again holding up his skirt in front. As Tom approached the next floor, a door closed, a man appeared in the hall, and another minute-light came on when the man pressed a wall button. Tom was confronted by a thick, middle-aged man in trousers and sports shirt, who wished to descend the stairs, and who stepped aside less out of politeness than as if alarmed by the sight of Tom.

Tom supposed the man might think he was a prostitute making a call, or some such, rather than a man in drag, and kept on climbing and turned to go to the next floor.

"Do you live here?" asked the old gent in German.

"Jawohl," Tom replied softly, but with conviction.

"Strange goings on here," the man murmured to himself, and went on down the stairs.

Tom climbed another flight. The stairs creaked a little. He saw lights under two doors, left and right. There seemed to be two other flats at the rear, doors anyway. The apartment Tom was interested in would be on the left, but Tom listened briefly at the door on the right, heard what he thought was a television voice, then went to the left-hand door. He heard a very low hum of voices, at least two voices. Tom pulled Peter's gun out. He had pressed the minute-light on this floor, and it had perhaps thirty seconds of light left. The door appeared to have a single lock, but it looked strong enough. What the hell to do next? Tom was not sure, but he knew his best ploy was to surprise them, get them off balance.

Tom pointed his gun at the lock, just as the light went out. Then Tom knocked loudly on the door with the knuckles of his left hand, causing his handbag to slide down to his left elbow.

There was a sudden silence behind the door. Then after a few seconds, a man's voice asked in German, "Who is it?"

"*Polizei!*" Tom yelled in a firm, no-nonsense voice. "*O-pen!*" he added in German.

Tom heard a scurrying, a scrape of chair legs, which however sounded not yet panicky. He again heard low voices. "*Polizei, öffnet!*" he said, and banged on the door with the side of his fist. "*Ihr seid umringt!*"

Were they even now getting out via some window? Tom took

the precaution of stepping to the right of the door, in case they
fired through the door, but his left hand rested on the door lock,
just under the knob, so he knew where it was.

The minute-light went out.

Then Tom stepped in front of the door and set the muzzle of
the gun at the crack between metal and wood and fired. The gun
bounced back in his hand, but he kept his grip on it, and at the
same time he gave the door a push with his shoulder. The door did
not yield completely: it appeared to have a chain, Tom wasn't sure.
Tom yelled again, "*Open!*" in a voice that might terrorize even the
people on the same floor behind their closed doors, and Tom
hoped they stayed there, but now one door opened slightly behind
him, Tom saw from a glance over his shoulder. Tom didn't care
about the door behind him. He heard someone opening the door
in front of him. They might be giving up, Tom thought.

The young blond man in the blue shirt had opened the door,
the light from behind him fell on Tom. The man started with surprise, and reached for his back pocket. Tom had his gun pointed at
the blue shirt front. Tom took a step into the room.

"Surrounded!" Tom repeated in German. "Get out over the
roof! You are not going to get out the door *below*!— Where is the
boy? Is he here?"

The man in the tan jacket—open-mouthed in the middle of
the room—made an impatient gesture, and said something to a
third man, a sturdy type with brown hair, shirtsleeves rolled up. The
blue shirt had kicked the shattered door shut—it would not shut
and hung partly open—and then had run into a room on Tom's
left, where the front window would be. There was a big oval table
in the room where Tom stood. Someone had turned out a ceiling
light, which left one standing lamp's light on.

All was confusion for a few seconds, and Tom even thought of
fleeing while he could. *They* might flee and plug him on the way.
Had he made a mistake in not having Peter get the police, complete with sirens below? Tom yelled suddenly in English:

"Get out while you *can*!"

The blue shirt, after quick words with the man in shirtsleeves, handed his gun to the tan jacket, and went into a room on Tom's right. Tom at once heard a thud from there, as if a suitcase had fallen.

Tom was afraid to look for the boy, as long as he had his own gun focused on the man in the tan jacket—for what Tom's gun was worth, because the tan jacket also had a gun in his hand. Tom heard a voice behind him ask in German:

"What's going on *here*?"

Tom glanced behind him. That had come from a curious neighbor in the hall—so it seemed—a man in house slippers and with wide-eyed fear in his face, ready to duck back into his apartment.

"Get away from here!" yelled the man in the tan jacket.

The shirtsleeved man, who had been in the front room, hurried into the room where Tom was, and Tom was aware of the neighbor fading away behind him.

"Okay, *shnell*!" said the shirtsleeved man, grabbing a jacket that had been over a chair by the oval table. He put the jacket on, and his free hand for an instant pointed upward. He ran across the room toward the door on Tom's right, and collided with the man in the blue shirt who was coming through the door with a suitcase.

Had they really seen something on the street, Tom wondered, cops already, due to the shot he had fired? Not likely! Past him now ran the man in the blue shirt with the suitcase, and then the man in the tan jacket. They were taking the stairs to the roof, Tom saw, and either the roof door was open by prearrangement, or they had the key. Tom knew there were no fire escapes in such houses, only central courts for fire engines, and roof exits. The man in the ordinary jacket now dashed past Tom, carrying what looked like a brown briefcase. He went up the stairs, slipping, recovering. He had run into Tom in his dash and nearly knocked him down. Tom now closed the door as well as he could. A big splinter of old wood made closing impossible.

Tom went into the room on the right. He still held Peter's gun pointed forward, as if at an enemy.

This room was a kitchen. On the floor lay Frank with a towel tied to cover his mouth, hands behind his back, ankles tied, on a blanket. But the boy moved, rubbed his face against the blanket as if in an effort to get the towel off.

"He-ey, *Frank!*" Tom knelt by the boy and pushed the tied dish towel down over Frank's chin to his neck.

The boy drooled, bleary with drugs or sleeping pills, Tom supposed, unable to focus his eyes.

"F'God's sake!" Tom murmured, and looked around for a knife. He found one in a drawer of the kitchen table, but it felt so dull to his thumb, he seized a breadknife from the drainboard. There were a couple of empty Coca-Cola tins on the drainboard. "Have you loose in a minute, Frank," Tom said, and began sawing away at the rope around Frank's wrists. The rope was strong and half an inch in diameter, but the knot looked much too tight to try to untie. During this sawing, Tom listened for another entry at the apartment door.

The boy spat, or tried to, onto the blanket. Tom slapped him nervously on the cheek.

"Wake up! It's *Tom!* We're leaving in a minute!" Tom wished there were time for him to make some instant coffee, even with cool water from the sink, but Tom did not dare take the time even to look for instant coffee. He attacked the ankle ropes now, sawed half the wrong loop first, and cursed. Finally he got the rope off, and hauled the boy up. "Can you walk, Frank?" Tom had lost one high-heeled pump, and he kicked off the other. Better to be barefoot under the circumstances.

"T-to-um?" said the boy, looking one hundred percent drunk.

"Here we go, boy!" Tom swung one of Frank's arms around his neck, and they started in the direction of the apartment door, Tom hoping that some movement might wake the boy up a little. As they struggled toward the door, Tom looked around in the carpetless living room for anything the men might have left, a notebook,

a scrap of paper, but he saw nothing like that. Evidently they had
been neat and efficient, with all their gear gathered in one place.
Tom saw only what looked like a dirty shirt that had been dropped
in a corner. He saw that he had still, somehow, the handbag on his
left arm, and remembered sticking the gun back into it, and shov-
ing the handbag on his arm, before lifting Frank. In the hall, three
neighbors confronted him, two men and one woman, astounded,
scared.

"*Alles geht gut!*" Tom said, realizing that he sounded mad and
shrill, and the three did fall back slightly as Tom made for the stairs.

"Is that a woman?" one of the men asked.

"We have telephoned the *police!*" the woman said menacingly.

"All is in order!" Tom replied. It sounded so good in German.

"*Drugged* the boy is!" said one of the men. "Who *are* these
animals?"

But Tom and Frank continued down the stairs, Tom support-
ing nearly all of the boy's weight, and suddenly they were out the
front door—having passed only two slightly opened apartment
doors with curious eyes peering out. Tom nearly fell going down
the stone front steps, as there was no wall to lean against.

"*Sacred holy spirits!*" This came from one of a pair of young
men walking on the pavement, and they laughed loudly. "May we
help you, *gnädige Frau?*" This with exaggerated politeness.

"Yes, thank you, we need a taxi," Tom replied in German.

"That we can easily see! Ha-ha! A taxi, *meine Dame!* At once!"

"Never did a lady need a taxi *more!*" the other contributed.

With the aid of these two, Tom and Frank got to the next corner without much difficulty, the two young men guffawing at
Tom's bare feet, and asking such questions as, "What have you two
been *doing?*" But the two stood by, and one of the young men went
out into the street and energetically tried to hail a taxi. Tom
glanced up at a street signpost and saw that the street he had just
walked through, where the kidnappers' apartment was, was called
Binger Strasse. Tom now heard police sirens. But a taxi had been

found! It slid up. Tom got into the taxi first and pulled the boy after him, much helped by the cheerful young men.

"Happy trip!" one yelled, closing the door.

"Niebuhrstrasse, bitte," Tom said to the driver, who gave Tom a look somewhat longer than necessary, then put his meter on and started off.

Tom opened a window. "Breathe," he said to Frank, and squeezed his hand to try to waken him further, not giving a damn what the driver thought. Tom snatched off his wig.

"Good party?" asked the driver, looking straight ahead.

"Oo-oh, ja," Tom groaned, as if it had been a hell of a good party.

Niebuhrstrasse, thank God! Tom began groping for money. Out came a ten-mark note at once, ample as the fare was only seven. The driver wanted to give him change, but Tom told him he could keep it. Now Frank seemed slightly more awake, though still weak-kneed. Tom held his arm firmly and pressed Eric's bell. This time he had not Eric's keys with him, but Tom thought surely Eric would be in, because of the money in his apartment, and then the blessed buzzer sounded, and Tom pushed the door open.

Peter came, lanky and swift, down the stairs. "Tom!" he whispered. Then "Oh—oh—*oh!*" at the sight of the boy.

Frank was now trying to hold his head up, and it wobbled as if his neck were broken. Tom felt like laughing—from nerves and hysteria—and bit his underlip as he and Peter got the boy into the elevator.

Eric had his door open slightly, and opened it wider when he saw them. "Mein Gott!" said Eric.

Tom still had the wig in his hand. He dropped this and the handbag on Eric's floor, and he and Peter got Frank seated on the horsehair sofa. Peter went off for a wet towel, Eric to fetch a cup of coffee.

"I don't know *what* they've been giving him," Tom said. "And I've lost Max's shoes—"

Peter smiled nervously, and stared at the boy as Tom wiped his face. Eric was ready with the coffee.

"Cool but good for you—coffee," Eric said to Frank in a gentle voice. "My name is Eric. Friend of Tom's. Don't be afraid." Eric said over his shoulder to Peter, "Mein Gott, is he *out*!"

But Tom could see that the boy was looking better, sipping a bit of the coffee, though still in no condition to hold the cup for himself.

"Hunger?" Peter asked the boy.

"No, no, he might choke," said Eric. "This coffee has sugar in it. Good for him."

Frank smiled at all of them, like a drunken child, and smiled especially at Tom. Tom, dry in the mouth, had taken a cold Pilsner Urquell from Eric's fridge.

"What happened, Tom?" Eric asked. "You went *in* their *house*? Peter said so."

"I shot the lock off. But nobody was hurt. They scared—got scared." Tom felt suddenly exhausted. "Dying for a wash," he murmured, and went off to the bathroom. He showered under hot water, then cool. His dressing gown hung luckily on the back of the bathroom door. Tom folded his gown and slip neatly to return to Max.

When Tom went back to the living room, Frank was eating a bit of something Peter was holding for him: buttered bread.

"Ulrich—is one," said Frank. "And Bobo . . ." Something else he said was unintelligible.

"I asked him their names!" Peter said to Tom.

"Tomorrow!" said Eric. "He'll remember tomorrow."

Tom went to see if the chain was on Eric's door, and it was.

Peter was smiling at Tom, looking happy. "It's marvelous!— Where did they go to? They ran out?"

"I think they took to the roofs," Tom said.

"Three of them." Peter spoke in a tone of awe. "Maybe your drag scared them."

Tom smiled, too tired to talk. Or he might have been able to talk about anything else but what he had just been through. Tom laughed suddenly. "You should've been at the Hump tonight, Eric!"

"I must go," said Peter, hovering, not really wanting to go.

"Oh, your gun, Peter, and the torch, while I think of it!" Tom got the gun from the handbag, the torch from the closet. "Many, many thanks! Three shots fired, three shots left.'"

Peter pocketed his gun, smiling. "Good night, sleep well," he said in a soft voice, and went out.

Eric said good night to him, and replaced the chain on the door. "Now let's get this bed open, don't you think so, Tom?"

"Yes. Come on, Frank old boy." Tom smiled at the sight of Frank sitting with an elbow on an arm of the sofa, viewing them with a silly smile and half-open eyes, like a sleepy spectator in a theater. Tom hauled the boy up and sat him in an armchair.

Then he and Eric got the sofa undone, the sheets on.

"Frank can sleep with me," Tom said. "Neither of us is going to know *where* we are." Tom started undressing Frank, who gave him some cooperation but not much. Then Tom fetched a big glass of water. He meant to encourage Frank to drink all he could.

"Tom, should you not telephone Paris?" Eric asked. "To say the boy is all right? Just suppose that gang tries something else with Paris!"

Eric was right, but the thought of ringing Paris bored him. "I'll do it." He got Frank onto his back in bed, and pulled the sheet up to his neck, and also drew a light blanket over him. Then he dialed the Hôtel Lutetia, whose number he had to make an effort to recall, but he got it right.

Eric lingered.

And Thurlow answered sleepily.

"Hello, this is Tom. Everything is all right here . . . Yes, that's what I mean . . . Quite all right, but sleepy. Tranquilizers . . . I don't care to go into details tonight . . . No, I'll explain that later. It's untouched . . . *Yes* . . . Not before noon, Mr. Thurlow, we are very tired here." Tom hung up as Thurlow was saying something else. "Asking also about the money," Tom said to Eric, and laughed.

Eric laughed too. "The suitcase is in my bedroom closet!— Good night, Tom."

16

For the second time in Eric's apartment, Tom awakened to the cozy hum of the coffee grinder. This morning he was happier. Frank lay facedown, asleep, and breathing. Tom had yielded to an impulse to check if he was breathing by looking at his ribs. Tom put on his dressing gown and went in to see Eric.

"Now tell me more about last night," Eric said. "One shot—"

"Yes, Eric. Only one. At the door lock."

Eric was putting various kinds of bread, rolls, and jams on a tray—extra festive in Frank's honor, perhaps. "We'll let the boy sleep, of course. Isn't he a nice-looking boy!"

Tom smiled. "You think so? Yes. Rather handsome and unaware of it. That's always attractive."

They sat on Eric's smaller sofa in the living room, which had a coffee table in front of it. Tom narrated the evening's events, even to Max and Rollo standing by him in the Hump, and said that the two who had been looking for Joey finally left, disappointed.

"They sound amateurish—to let you follow them," Eric said.

"Evidently. They looked young, in their twenties."

"And the neighbors there in Binger Strasse. Did they recognize the boy, do you think?'

"Doubt it." He and Eric were keeping their voices low, though Frank showed no sign of waking. "What can the neighbors do now? They should be more familiar with the kidnappers' faces, since they were going in and out of the house. One of them said she'd called the police. I think she did. Anyway the police'll surely look the apartment over, get a lot of fingerprints if they take the trouble. But do the neighbors know what was going *on?*— The police will find Max's pumps there. That'll throw them off!" Tom was feeling much better with Eric's strong coffee. "I'd like to get the boy out of Berlin as soon as possible—and get myself out too. I'd like to take off for Paris this afternoon, but I don't think the boy's up to it."

Eric looked at the bed, then back at Tom. "I shall miss you," he said, sighing. "Berlin can be dull. Maybe you don't think so."

"Really?— There is one chore today, Eric, returning the money to the banks here. Can't we get messengers for that? Maybe one messenger can do it all? I certainly don't want to do it."

"I'm sure, yes. We shall telephone." Eric suddenly bubbled with laughter and looked rather Chinese in his shiny black dressing gown. "I am thinking of all that money here, and that *boob* in Paris is there doing nothing!"

"No, he is collecting his fee," said Tom.

"Imagine," Eric went on, "the boob in drag! I bet he could not have done it! I wish I had been at the Hump last night. I would have taken Polaroids of you with Max and Rollo!"

"Please return Max's drag with my thanks. Oh—and I must get that Italian's gun out of that suitcase. No need for the bank messenger to see that. May I?" Tom motioned toward Eric's bedroom.

"Of course! Back of my closet. You will find it."

Tom got the suitcase from the depths of Eric's closet, carried it into the living room, and unzipped its top. The longish muzzle of the gun pointed right at him, because its handle had fallen between a manila envelope and the side of the suitcase.

"Something missing?" Eric said.

"No, no." Tom took the gun out carefully, and made sure the safety was on. "I'll make someone a present of this. I doubt if I could fly out of Berlin with it. Would you like it, Eric?"

"Ach, the gun of yesterday! Most welcome, Tom. Not easy to get here, guns, even flick-knives beyond a certain length. Very strict regulations here."

"House present," Tom said, handing the gun to Eric.

"I do thank you, Tom." Eric disappeared with it into his bedroom.

Now Frank stirred, and lay on his back. "I s-no-*no*." He said it in a reasoning tone of voice.

Tom watched the boy's frown tighten.

"To g'up, you said, I dunno so—*stop!*" The boy arched his back.

Tom shook his shoulder. "Hello, it's Tom. You're okay, Frank."

Frank opened his eyes, frowned again, and pushed himself nearly to a sitting position. "Wow!" He shook his head, and smiled fuzzily. "Tom."

"Coffee." Tom poured a cup for him.

Frank looked all around him, at walls and ceiling. "I— How did we get here?"

Tom didn't answer. He brought the coffee and held it while the boy had a sip.

"Is this a hotel room?"

"No, Eric Lanz's house.— Remember the man you had to hide from at my house? A week or so ago?"

"Yes. . . . Sure."

"His apartment. Have some more coffee. Got a headache?"

"No. . . . Is this Berlin?"

"Yes. Apartment house. Third floor. . . . I think we ought to leave Berlin today if you feel up to it. Maybe this afternoon. Back to Paris." Tom brought a plate of bread and butter and jam. "What were they giving you there? Sleeping pills? Injections?'

"Pills. They put them in cokes—made me drink it. In the car they gave me a needle—in my thigh." Frank spoke slowly.

In Grunewald. That sounded a little more professional. The boy was able to take a bite of toast and chew it, Tom was glad to see. "They feed you anything?"

Frank tried to shrug. "I threw up a couple of times. And they—w-would not let me go to the john often enough.— Think I wet my trousers—awful! My clothes—" The boy looked around, frowning, as if these unmentionable items might be in sight. "*That I—*"

"No importance, Frank, really." Eric was coming back, and Tom said, "Eric, meet Frank. He's a bit more awake now."

Frank was covered to the waist by the sheet, but he pulled the sheet higher. His eyelids still sagged. "Good morning, sir."

"I am delighted to meet you," said Eric. "You are feeling better?"

"Yes, thank you." Frank was now looking at the horsehair edge of his bed, which the sheet did not cover, in apparent wonderment. "Your house—Tom told me. Thank you."

Tom went into Eric's bedroom, where Frank's brown suitcase was, and took Frank's pajamas from it. He brought them in to Frank and tossed them on the bed. "So you can walk around," Tom said. "Your suitcase is here, Frank, so nothing's lost.— I'd love to take him for a walk in the fresh air, but I don't think it's advisable," Tom said to Eric. "The next thing really is to ring up one of those banks. The ADCA Bank or the Disconto. The Disconto sounds bigger, doesn't it?"

"Banks?" asked Frank, pulling pajama pants on under the sheet. "Ransom money?" But his voice was still sleepy, and he sounded unconcerned.

"Your money," said Tom. "What do you think you're worth, Frank? Guess." Tom was trying to wake the boy up by talking to him. Now he looked in his wallet for the three receipts he had, which would also have the telephone numbers of the banks.

"Ransom money— Who has it?" Frank asked.

"I have it. It's going back to your family. Tell you about that later, not now."

"I know there was a date," Frank said, drawing on his pajama jacket. "One was talking in English on the phone. Then they went out—once—all except one." Frank's speech was still slow, but he sounded sure of his statements.

Eric reached for a black cigarette from a silver bowl on his coffee table.

"You know—" Frank's eyes began to swim again. "I was always
in the kitchen there—but I think that's right."

Tom poured more coffee for Frank. "Drink that."

Eric was now on the telephone, asking to speak with the Herr
Direktor. Tom heard him give his own address in regard to money
collected yesterday by Thomas Ripley. Eric also mentioned the two
other banks. Tom felt relieved. Eric was handling it well.

"A messenger will come before noon," Eric said to Tom. "They
have got the Swiss account number and they can telex it back."

"Excellent. I thank you, Eric." Tom watched Frank crawl out
of bed.

Frank looked at the open suitcase on the floor with the fat
manila envelopes inside. "Is that it?"

"Yes." Tom took some clothes and started for the bathroom to
dress. Glancing behind him, he saw Frank edging around the suitcase as if it were a poisonous snake. Under the shower, Tom
remembered that he had promised to ring Thurlow around noon.
Maybe Frank would also like to talk with his brother.

When Tom came back to the living room, he told Frank that
he had to ring Paris, and that he had rung last night and the detective Thurlow knew he was safe. Frank showed little interest in
Paris. "Wouldn't you like to talk with Johnny?"

"Well, Johnny—yes." Frank was still barefoot, and walking
around, which Tom thought was good for him.

Tom dialed the Lutetia number. He got Thurlow, and said,
"Yes, the boy's right here. Would you like to speak with him?"

Frank frowned and shook his head, but Tom pressed the telephone on him.

"Give him some proof," Tom said, smiling. Tom whispered,
"Do *not* mention Eric's name."

"Hello? . . . Yes, I'm fine . . . Yes, sure, Berlin . . . *Tom*," Frank
said. "Tom got me last night . . . I don't know, really . . . Yes, it's *here*."

Eric pointed to the little receiver for Tom's use, but Tom didn't want to listen in.

"I'm sure not," Frank said. "Why should Tom want any of it, it's going—" Longish listening now on Frank's part. "How do you expect me to talk about something like that over the phone?" Frank said with some irritation. "I don't know, I just don't know . . . Okay, fine." Then Frank's expression softened, and he said, "Hi, Johnny . . . Sure, I'm okay, I just said so . . . Oh, I dunno, I just woke up. But quit worrying. I haven't got even a broken bone or anything!" Now a long speech from Johnny, and Frank squirmed. "Okay, okay, but— What do you mean?" Now the boy frowned. "Not in a hurry!" he said mockingly. "What you really mean—you really mean she's not coming and doesn't—doesn't care."

Tom could hear Johnny's easy chuckle as he spoke from Paris.

"Well, at least she *telephoned*." Frank's face looked paler. "All right, all right, I see," he said impatiently.

From where he stood, Tom heard Thurlow's voice come on, and then Tom picked up the little receiver.

". . . when you're coming *here*. Something holding you there?— You there, Frank?"

"Why should I go to Paris?" Frank asked.

"Because your mother wants you home. We want you—safe."

"I *am* safe."

"Is—Tom Ripley trying to persuade you to stay on there?"

"Nobody is persuading me," said Frank, shaping every word.

"I'd like to speak with Mr. Ripley, if he's there, Frank."

Frank grimly handed the telephone to Tom. "That f——" He didn't get the second word out. Suddenly Frank had become an ordinary American boy, furious.

"Tom Ripley," said Tom. He watched Frank walk into the hall, maybe in quest of the bathroom, which he found on the right.

"Mr. Ripley, as you can understand, we want the boy safe and back in America, that's why I'm here. Can you tell us—I'm most grateful for what you've done, but I have to tell his mother a few facts, namely when the boy will be coming home. Or should I come to Berlin and get him?"

"No-o, I'll consult with Frank. He's just been held under unpleasant conditions for the last couple of days, you know. He's been given a lot of tranquilizers."

"But he sounds pretty much all right."

"He's not hurt."

"And as for the German marks, Frank said—"

"Those will be returned to the bank or the banks today, Mr. Thurlow." Tom laughed a little. "Fine subject in case your phone is being tapped."

"Why should it be tapped?"

"Oh, because of your profession," Tom said, as if his profession might be anything bizarre, even call girl.

"Mrs. Pierson was glad to hear that the marks are safe. But I can't just stay here in Paris while you or Frank or both of you make up your minds when Frank comes home.— You can probably understand that, Mr. Ripley."

"Well—there are worse cities than Paris," Tom said in a pleasant tone. "Could I perhaps speak with Johnny?"

"Yes.— Johnny?"

Johnny came on. "We're very glad about Frank! Can't tell you!" Johnny sounded open and friendly, with an accent like Frank's but a deeper voice. "Have the police got the gang or whoever it was?"

"No, no police involved." Tom heard Thurlow trying to shush Johnny on the subject of police, or so it seemed.

"You mean, you got Frank all by yourself?"

"No—with a little help from my friends."

"My mother's *so* happy! She was—uh—"

Dubious about him, Tom knew. "Johnny, you said something to Frank about somebody phoning? From America?"

"Teresa. She was going to come over, but now she's not. I'm sure she's not, now that Frank's okay, but—I know she's sort of tied up with someone else, so I know she won't. She didn't say it to me, but I happen to know the fellow, I introduced them and—he told me before I left America."

Now Tom understood. "You told Frank that?"

"I thought the sooner he knew it the better. I know he's pretty hung up. I didn't tell him who the fellow was. I just said I know Teresa's got another interest."

In that Tom saw a world of difference between Johnny and Frank. Easy come, easy go with Johnny, evidently. "I see." Tom didn't even feel like saying, what a pity you had to spill it just now. "Well, Johnny, I'll sign off." Tom heard faintly Thurlow asking to be put on again, or Tom thought so. "Bye-bye," Tom said, and hung up. "*Asses—both* of them!" Tom shouted.

But no one heard him. Frank was flat out asleep again on the bed, and Eric was somewhere else in the apartment.

The bank messenger might arrive at any minute.

When Eric came into the living room, Tom said, "How about lunch at Kempinski? Are you free for lunch, Eric?" Tom had a desire to see Frank eat a steak or a big portion of Wiener schnitzl and get some color back in his face.

"I am, yes." Eric was dressed now.

The doorbell rang. The bank messenger.

Eric pressed his release button in the kitchen.

Tom shook Frank's shoulder. "Frank, old boy—up! Take my dressing gown." Tom snatched it from his suitcase. "Go into Eric's bedroom, because we have to see someone here for a couple of minutes."

Frank did as Tom told him. Tom spread the blanket over the sheets, so the bed would look a bit neater.

The bank messenger, a short, bulky man in a business suit, was accompanied by a taller guard of some kind in uniform. The messenger presented his credentials, and said he had a car waiting downstairs with a driver, but he was in no hurry. He carried two big briefcases. Tom didn't feel like looking at the credentials, so

Eric examined them. Tom did watch the first few seconds of the counting. One envelope had been sealed and still was. The paper-banded bundles of DM had not been touched in the other envelopes, but it would have been possible to slip a thousand-mark note from any or several of the bundles. Eric watched.

"Can I leave this to you, Eric?" Tom asked.

"*Aber sicherlich*, Tom! But you must sign something, you know?" Eric and the messenger were standing at the sideboard, envelopes separated, money stacks separated.

"Back in a couple of minutes." Tom went off to speak with Frank.

Frank was in Eric's bedroom, barefoot, holding a damp towel against his forehead. "I felt faint for a minute just now. Funny—"

"We're going out to lunch soon. We'll have a good lunch and cheer up, all right, Frank?— Want a cool shower?"

"Sure."

Tom went into the bathroom and adjusted the shower for him. "Don't slip," Tom said.

"What're they doing in there?"

"Counting dough. I'll bring you some clothes." Tom went back into the living room, found a pair of blue cotton trousers in Frank's suitcase, a polo-neck sweater, and he took a pair of his own shorts, not finding any of Frank's. Tom knocked on the bathroom door which was not quite closed.

The boy was drying himself with a big towel.

"How do you feel about Paris? Want to go back today? Tonight?"

"No."

Tom noticed that the boy's eyes were shiny with tears under a very determined and grown-up frown. "I know what Johnny said to you—about Teresa."

"Well, that's not everything," Frank said, hurled the towel at the side of the tub, and at once picked it up and hung it properly on a rod. He took the shorts Tom was holding out to him and turned his back as he put them on. "I don't want to go back just yet, I just don't!" Frank's eyes flashed with anger as he looked back at Tom.

Tom knew: it would be two defeats, the loss of Teresa, and being recaptured. Maybe after lunch, Tom thought, Frank would calm down, see things differently. However, Tom knew that Teresa *was* everything.

"Tom!" Eric called.

Tom had to sign. Tom did look over the receipt. The three banks were listed, the sums due each. The bank messenger was now on Eric's telephone, and Tom heard him say a couple of times that things were in *Ordnung*. Tom signed. The name Pierson still did not appear, only the Swiss Bank Corporation number. Much handshaking upon leaving, and Eric accompanied the two men to the elevator.

Frank came into the living room, dressed but for shoes, and Eric returned, beaming with relief, wiping his forehead with a pocket handkerchief.

"My apartment deserves—a *Gedenktafel!* How do you call it?"

"A plaque?" said Tom. "As I was saying, lunch at Kempinski. Do we have to make a reservation?"

"It would be wiser. I shall do it. Three." Eric went to his telephone.

"Unless we can reach Max and Rollo. It'd be nice to invite them. Or are they—working?"

"Oh!" Eric chuckled. "Rollo's hardly awake by now. He likes to stay up very late, till seven or eight in the morning. Then Max is freelance—a hairdresser when certain places need him. I never can reach them except sometimes around six in the evening."

He would send them a present from France, Tom thought, maybe a couple of interesting wigs, when he got their address from Eric. Eric was now making the reservation for a quarter to one.

They went in Eric's car. Tom had applied a flesh-colored salve—for cuts and abrasions, the tube said—from Eric's medicine cabinet to Frank's famous cheek mole. Somewhere Frank had lost Heloise's pancake from his back pocket, which did not surprise Tom.

"I want you to eat, my friend," Tom said to Frank at the table, starting to read the huge à la carte menu. "I know you like smoked salmon."

"Ah, I shall have my favorite!" said Eric. "There is a liver dish here, Tom—out of this world!"

The restaurant had high ceilings, gilt and green scrolls on its white walls, elegant tablecloths, and uniformed waiters who put on a grand air. A grill—another part of the restaurant—served people who were not quite properly attired, Tom had noticed while they were waiting to be shown to their table. This had meant a pair of men in blue jeans, though with neat enough sweaters and jackets, who had been told in German, somehow politely, that the grill was *that* way.

Frank did eat, aided by a couple of Tom's jokes, dredged up, because he didn't feel like telling jokes. He knew Frank was under a black cloud of Teresa, and he wondered if Frank suspected or knew definitely who Teresa's new interest was? Tom could not possibly ask. Tom knew only that Frank had begun that painful process known as turning loose, turning loose emotionally of a moral support, of a mad ideal, of what had been to him embodied, and still was, in the only girl in the world.

"Chocolate cake, Frank?" Tom suggested, and refilled Frank's glass of white wine. It was their second bottle.

"That is good here and so is the strudel," Eric said. "Tom, a meal to remember!" Eric wiped his lips carefully. "A morning to remember too, no? Ha-ha?"

They were in one of the little alcoves against the restaurant wall, nothing so primitive as a booth, rather a romantic curve giving semi-privacy, yet enabling them to see what they wished of the other patrons. Tom had seen no one paying attention to them. And Tom suddenly realized, pleasantly, that Frank would be leaving Berlin under his false passport as Benjamin Andrews. The passport was in Frank's suitcase at Eric's.

"When shall I next see you, Tom?" Eric asked.

Tom lit a Roth-Händle. "Next time you have a little thing for Belle Ombre? And I don't mean a house present."

Eric chuckled, pink with food and wine now. "That reminds me, I have a three o'clock date. Excuse me for this rudeness." He looked at his wristwatch. "Only a quarter past two. I am fine."

"We can take a taxi back. Leave you free."

"No, no, it is on the way, my house. Easy." Eric poked with his tongue at something in a tooth, and looked speculatively at Frank.

Frank had eaten nearly all of his chocolate cake, and was pensively turning the stem of his wine glass.

Eric lifted his eyebrows at Tom. Tom said nothing. Tom got the bill and paid. They walked the one street to Eric's car in bright sunlight. Tom smiled and patted Frank impulsively on the back. But what could he say? He wanted to say, "Isn't this better than the floor of a kitchen?" But Tom couldn't. Eric was the type to come out with it, but Eric didn't. Tom would have liked a longer walk, but he did not feel a hundred percent safe, or unnoticed, walking with Frank Pierson, so they both got into Eric's car. Tom had Eric's housekeys, and Eric dropped them off at a corner.

Tom approached Eric's house carefully, on the watch for loiterers, but saw none. The downstairs hall was empty. The boy was silent.

In the apartment, Tom took off his jacket and opened the window for fresh air. "About Paris," Tom began.

Frank suddenly plunged his face into his hands. He was seated on the small sofa by the coffee table, elbows on his spread knees.

"Never mind," Tom said, embarrassed for the boy. "Get it out." Tom knew it wouldn't last long.

After a few seconds, the boy snatched his hands down, stood up and said, "Sorry." He stuffed his hands in his pockets.

Tom strolled into the bathroom, and brushed his teeth for a good two minutes. Then he went back into the living room with a calm air. "You don't want to go to Paris, I know.— What about Hamburg?"

"Anywhere!" Frank's eyes had the intensity of madness or hysteria.

Tom looked down at the floor and blinked. "You don't just say "anywhere" like a madman, Frank.— I know—I understand about Teresa. It's a—" what was the right word? "—a letdown."

Frank stood stiff as a statue, as if defying Tom to say more. *Still you'll have to face your family at some point,* Tom thought of saying. But wouldn't that be unsympathetic, just now? Wouldn't it be a good idea to see Reeves? Have a change of atmosphere? Tom needed it, anyway. "I find Berlin a bit claustrophobic. I feel like seeing Reeves in Hamburg. Didn't I mention him in France? Friend of mine." Tom made an effort to sound cheerful.

The boy looked more alert, polite again. "Yes, I think you did. You said he was a friend of Eric's."

"True. I'm—" Tom hesitated, looking at the boy who, with hands still in pockets, stared back at him. Tom could easily put the boy on a plane to Paris—insist—and say good-bye to him. But Tom had the feeling the boy would lose himself again, in Paris, as soon as he got off the plane. He wouldn't go to the Hôtel Lutetia. "I'll try Reeves," Tom said, and moved toward the telephone. Just then it rang. Tom decided to answer it.

"Hello, Tom, this is Max."

"Max! How are you? I have your wig and your drag here—safe!"

"I wanted to telephone this morning and I was—stuck, ja? Not home was I. Then by Eric an hour ago nobody was home. So last night? The boy?"

"He's here. He's okay."

"You got him? You are not hurt, nobody is hurt?"

"Nobody." Tom blinked away a sudden vision of the Italian type with the smashed head on the ground in Lübars.

"Rollo thought last night you looked wonderful. I was almost jealous. Ha!— Is Eric there? I have a message."

"Not here because he has a three o'clock date. Can I take a message?"

Max said no, he would call back.

Tom then consulted the telephone book for the Hamburg code, and dialed Reeves's number.

"'Allo?" said a female voice.

This was Reeves's *Putzfrau* and part-time housekeeper, Tom supposed, a figure more portly than Mme. Annette, but equally dedicated. "Hello—Gaby?"

"Ja-a?"

"This is Tom Ripley. How are you, Gaby?— Is Herr Minot there?"

"*Nein, aber er*—I *hear* something," she went on in German. "One minute." A pause, then Gaby came back and said, "He comes in just now!"

"Hello, *Tom!*" said Reeves, breathless.

"I'm in Berlin."

"*Berlin!* Can you come and see me? What're you doing in Berlin?" Reeves's voice sounded gravelly and naïve as usual.

"Can't say now, but I was thinking of coming to see you— even tonight, if that's all right with you."

"Of course, Tom. You've always got priority and I'm not even busy tonight."

"I have a friend with me, an American. Could you possibly put us up for one night?" Tom knew Reeves had a guest room.

"Even two nights. When're you arriving? Got your plane tickets?"

"No, but I'll try for this evening. Seven, eight, or nine. If you're in I won't ring you again, just turn up. I'll ring you if I can't make it. Okay?"

"Okay and I'm *very* pleased!"

Tom turned to Frank, smiling. "That's settled. Reeves is glad to have us."

Frank was sitting on the smaller sofa, smoking a cigarette, unusual for him. The boy stood up, and he seemed suddenly as tall as Tom. Had he grown in the last few days? That was possible. "I'm sorry I was in the dumps today. I'll pull out."

"Oh, sure you'll pull out." The boy was trying to be polite. Maybe that was why he looked taller.

"I'm glad about Hamburg. I don't want to see that detective in Paris. Good *Christ!*" Frank whispered the last, but with venom. "Why don't they both go home now?"

"Because they want to be sure you're coming home," Tom said patiently.

Tom then telephoned Air France. He made two reservations for a takeoff at 7:20 p.m. for Hamburg. Tom gave their names, Ripley and Andrews.

Eric arrived while Tom was on the telephone, and Tom told him their plans. "Ah, Reeves! A nice idea!" Eric glanced at Frank, who was folding something away in his suitcase, and motioned for Tom to come into his bedroom.

"Max rang up," Tom said as he followed Eric. "Said he'd ring you back."

"Thank you, Tom.— Now this." Eric closed his bedroom door, pulled a newspaper from under his arm, and showed the front page to Tom. "I thought you should see this," Eric said with one of his twitching smiles, more full of nerves than amusement. "No clues, it seems—now."

The front page of *Der Abend* had a two-column photograph of the Lübars shed with the Italian type just as Tom had seen him last, prone, head turned slightly to the left, and the left temple a darkened mass of blood, some of which had run down the face. Tom read quickly the five-line comment below. An as yet unidentified man wearing clothing made in Italy, underwear made in Germany, had been found dead early Wednesday in Lübars, his temple crushed by blows of a blunt instrument. Police were trying to identify him, and were making inquiries among residents of the region to find out if they had heard any disturbances.

"You understand it all?" asked Eric.

"Yes." Tom had fired two shots into the air. Surely a resident was going to remark hearing two shots, even if the man had not been killed by a bullet. Some neighbor might describe a stranger with a suitcase. "I don't like to look at this." Tom folded the newspaper and put it on a writing table. He glanced at his watch.

"I can drive you to Tegel. Plenty of time," said Eric. "The boy really doesn't want to go home, does he?"

"No, and he had some bad news today about a girl he likes in America. The brother told him that she has a new boyfriend. So there's that. If he were twenty, it might be easier for him." Or would it? Frank's murder of his father was keeping him from going back home too.

17

As the plane began its descent to Hamburg, Frank waked from a doze and caught between his knees a newspaper that had nearly slipped to the floor. Frank looked out of the window on his side, but they were still too high for anything but clouds to be visible.

Tom finished a cigarette covertly. The stewardesses bustled up and down the aisle, collecting last glasses and trays. Tom saw Frank lift the German newspaper from his lap and look at the picture of the dead man in Lübars. To Frank it would be just another newspaper photograph. Tom had not told Frank that his date with the kidnappers had been in Lübars, he had simply said that he stood the kidnappers up. "Then you followed them?" Frank had asked. Tom had said no, he had got on their trail via the gay bar and the message passed to the kidnappers by Thurlow to ask for Joey there. Frank had been amused, full of awe at Tom's daring—maybe his courage too, Tom liked to think—in crashing in on the kidnappers single-handed. Tom had found nothing in this newspaper about any of the three kidnappers having been caught in the vicinity of Binger Strasse or anywhere else. Of course no one but Tom knew them as kidnappers. They might have criminal records and no fixed addresses, but that was about it.

Their passports were rather quickly glanced at and handed back, then they got their luggage and took a taxi.

Tom pointed out landmarks to Frank, what he could see in the gathering darkness, a church spire that he remembered, the first of the many filled-in canals, or "fleets," which had little bridges over them, then the Alsters. They got out in the upward sloping driveway leading to Reeves's white apartment house, a large, formerly private house which had been partitioned to make several apartments. It was Tom's second or third visit to Reeves. Tom pressed a button downstairs, and Reeves at once let him in after Tom said his name into the speaker. Tom and Frank went up in the elevator, and Reeves was waiting outside his apartment door.

"Tom!" Reeves kept his voice low, because of at least one other apartment on the same floor. "Come in, both of you!"

"This is—Ben," said Tom, introducing Frank. "Reeves Minot."

Reeves said "How do you do" to Frank, and closed his door behind them. As ever, Reeves's flat struck Tom as spacious and immaculately clean. Its white walls bore Impressionist and more recent paintings, nearly all in frames. Rows of low bookcases, containing mostly art books, bordered the walls. There were a couple of tall rubber plants and philodendrons. The two big windows on the Aussenalster's water had their yellow curtains drawn now. A table was set for three. Tom saw that the pinkish Derwatt (genuine) of a woman apparently dying in bed still hung over the fireplace.

"Changed the frame of that, didn't you?" asked Tom.

Reeves laughed. "How observant you are, Tom! Frame got damaged somehow. Fell in that bombing, I think, and cracked. I prefer this beige frame. The other frame was too white. Look now, put your suitcases in here," Reeves said, showing Tom to the guest room. "I hope they didn't give you anything to eat on the plane, because I have something for us. But now we must have a glass of cold wine or something and talk!"

Tom and Frank set their suitcases in the guest room, which had a three-quarter bed with its side against the front wall. Jonathan Trevanny had slept here, Tom remembered.

"What did you say your friend's name was?" Reeves asked softly, but he did not bother to be out of the boy's hearing as he and Tom went back into the living room.

Tom knew from Reeves's smile that Reeves knew who the boy was. Tom nodded. "Talk to you later. It was not—" Tom felt awkward, but why did he have to hide anything from Reeves? Frank was in a far corner of the living room now, looking at a painting. "It was not in the papers, but the boy was just kidnapped in Berlin."

"*Ree-eally?*" Reeves paused with the corkscrew in one hand, a wine bottle in the other. He had an unpleasant pink scar down his right cheek almost to the corner of his mouth. Now with his mouth open in surprise, the scar looked even longer.

"Last Sunday night," Tom said. "In Grunewald. You know, the big woods there."

"Yes, I do. Kidnapped how?"

"I was with him, but we were separated for a couple of minutes and— Sit down, Frank. You're among friends."

"Yes, sit down," Reeves said in his hoarse-sounding voice, and drew the cork.

Frank's eyes caught Tom's, the boy nodded his head as if to indicate that Tom could tell the truth if he wished. "Frank was released just last night. The men holding him gave him sedatives and I think he's still a bit drowsy." Tom said.

"No, I hardly notice it now," Frank said politely and firmly. He got up from the sofa he had just sat down on, and went to look more closely at the Derwatt over the fireplace. Frank shoved his hands in his back pockets and glanced at Tom with a quick smile. "Good, yes, Tom?"

"Isn't it?" said Tom with satisfaction. He loved the dusty pink-ness of it, suggesting an old lady's bedcover, or maybe her nightdress. The background was murky brown and dark gray. Was she dying or simply tired and bored with life? But the title was "Dying Woman."

"Woman or a man here?" Frank asked.

Tom had just been thinking that Edmund Banbury or Jeff Constant at the Buckmaster Gallery had probably given the picture its title—often Derwatt hadn't bothered with titles—and one could not really tell if the figure was male or female.

" 'Dying Woman,' it's called," Reeves said to Frank. "You like Derwatt?" he asked in a tone of pleased surprise.

"Frank says his father has one at home—in the States. One or two, Frank?" Tom asked.

"One. 'The Rainbow.' "

"Ah-hah," said Reeves, as if he could see it before his eyes.

Frank drifted away toward a David Hockney.

"You delivered a ransom?" Reeves asked Tom.

Tom shook his head. "No, had it and didn't deliver it."

"How much?" Reeves smiled as he poured wine.

"Two million American."

"Well, well.— And now what?" Reeves nodded toward the boy who had his back to them.

"Oh, he's going back home. I thought if we could, Reeves, we'd stay tomorrow night also with you, and leave Friday for Paris. I don't want the boy to be recognized in a hotel, and another day's rest would do him good."

"Certainly, Tom. No problem." Reeves frowned. "I don't quite understand. The police are still looking for him?"

Tom shrugged nervously. "They were *before* the kidnapping, and I'm assuming the detective in Paris has notified at least the French police that the boy's been found." Tom explained that there had been no police anywhere informed of the kidnapping.

"You're supposed to take him where?"

"To the detective in Paris. He's employed by the family. Frank's brother Johnny is there with the detective too.— Thank you, Reeves." Tom took his glass.

Reeves carried another glass to Frank. Then Reeves went into his kitchen, and Tom followed him. From his refrigerator, Reeves produced a platter of sliced ham, cole slaw, and a variety of sliced sausages and pickles. Reeves said it was Gaby's production. Gaby lived in the building with some other people who employed her, and she had insisted on coming in at seven this evening after her late shopping to "arrange" what she had bought for Reeves's guests. "I'm lucky, she likes me," Reeves said. "Finds my place more interesting than where she sleeps—in spite of that damned bomb here. Well, she happened to be out at the time it hit."

The three sat down at the table, and talked of other things than Frank, but it was still of Berlin. How was Eric Lanz? Who were his friends? Had he a girlfriend? A laugh from Reeves along with the question. Had Reeves a girlfriend, Tom wondered. Were Reeves and Eric so lukewarm, girls and women just didn't matter? It was nice to have a wife, Tom thought, as the wine began to warm him. Heloise had once said to him that she liked him, or had she said she loved him, because he let her be herself, and gave her room to breathe. Tom had been gratified by her remark, though he had never thought about giving Heloise Lebensraum.

Reeves was watching Frank. And Frank was looking extremely sleepy.

They got Frank to bed by a little after eleven. Frank took the guest room bed.

Then with another bottle of Piesporter Goldtröpfchen, Reeves and Tom installed themselves on the living room sofa, and Tom narrated the events of the last days, even the first days, when Frank Pierson, working as part-time gardener, had looked him up in Villeperce. Reeves laughed at the drag bit in Berlin, and wanted every detail. Then something dawned on Reeves, and he said:

"That Berlin picture then—in the papers today. They said Lübars, I remember." Reeves leapt up to look for his newspaper, and found it on a bookshelf.

"That's it," Tom said. "I saw it in Berlin." Tom felt sickish for a moment, and set his wineglass down. "The Italian type that I mentioned." Tom had told Reeves that he had only knocked the man out.

"No one saw you? You're sure? Getting away?"

"No.— Shall we wait for tomorrow's news?"

"The boy knows?"

"I didn't tell him. Don't mention Lübars to him.— Reeves, old pal, could I trouble you for some coffee?"

Tom went with Reeves into the kitchen, not wanting to sit by himself. It was not pleasant, the realization that he had killed a man, even though the Italian type was not the first. He saw Reeves glance at him. There was one thing he had not told Reeves, and was not going to tell him, which was that Frank had killed his father. Tom took a little comfort from the fact that though Reeves had read about Pierson Senior's death, and the question of suicide or accident, which had not been answered, Reeves had not thought to ask Tom if someone could have murdered Pierson Senior by pushing him over the cliff.

"What was it made the boy run away?" Reeves asked. "Upset by his father's death?— Or maybe the girl? Her name's Teresa, you said?"

"No, I think the Teresa situation was all right when he left. He was writing to her from my house. It's only yesterday that he heard she has a new boyfriend."

Reeves chuckled in an avuncular way. "The world is full of girls, even pretty ones. Certainly Hamburg is! Shall we try to distract him—take him to a club? You know?"

Tom said as lightly as he could, "He's only sixteen. It's hit him pretty hard.— The brother's a bit thick-skinned, or he wouldn't have blurted it out as he did—now."

"You expect to meet the brother? And the detective?" Reeves laughed as if at the word "detective," as he might laugh at anybody whose job it was presumably to try to track down crime in the world.

"I rather hope not," Tom said, "but I may have to put the boy right in their charge, because he's not keen to go home." Tom was standing in the kitchen with his coffee. "I'm getting sleepy, even though your coffee tastes great. I'm going to have another cup."

"Won't bother your sleep?" Reeves asked hoarsely, but with the concern of a mother or a nurse.

"Not in my state. Tomorrow I'll take Frank around Hamburg. One of those boat rides around the Alster, you know? I'll try to cheer him up. Can you meet us for lunch, Reeves?"

"Thanks, Tom, but I have a date tomorrow. I can give you a key. I'll do it now."

Tom walked out of the kitchen with his cup. "How's business been?" Tom meant the fence business, and a little bit of legitimate talent-scouting among German painters, and some art-dealing, the latter activities being Reeves's front, at least.

"Oh—" Reeves put a ring of keys into Tom's hand, then cast an eye around his living room walls. "That Hockney's—on loan, I might say. Really it's stolen. It's from Munich. I put it on the wall because I like it. After all, I'm very careful about the people I let *in* here. The Hockney's being collected very soon."

Tom smiled. It struck him that Reeves led a delightful life in a most pleasant city. Something was always happening. Reeves never worried, he always bungled through even the very awkward moments, once for instance when he had been beaten up and tossed unconscious out of a moving car. Reeves hadn't suffered even a broken nose on that occasion, which had been in France, Tom remembered.

When Tom crept into bed that night, Frank didn't stir. The boy was facedown with his arms around his pillow. Tom felt safe, safer than in Berlin. Reeves's flat had been bombed, maybe burgled, but it felt as snug as a little castle. He might ask Reeves what kind of protection he had, besides perhaps a burglar alarm. Did he have to pay off anybody? Had Reeves ever asked the police for extra protection, because of the valuable pictures he sometimes dealt with?

Not very likely, Tom thought. But maybe it would be rude to inquire into Reeves's safety measures.

A gentle knock awakened Tom, and he opened his eyes and realized where he was. "*Herein?*"

Gaby came in, heavy and shy, talking in German, carrying a tray of coffee and rolls. "Herr Tom . . . we are so glad to see you again after such a long time! How long has it been? . . ." She spoke softly because of Frank, still asleep. Gaby was in her fifties, with black straight hair done in a bun behind her head. Her cheeks were rather blotchily pink.

"I am so glad to be here, Gaby. And how have you been?—You can put it here, that is fine." Tom meant on his lap. The tray had legs.

"Herr Reeves has gone out, but he says you have the keys." She looked, smiling, at the sleeping boy. "There is still more coffee in the kitchen." Gaby spoke stolidly, giving the facts, and only her dark eyes showed liveliness and a childlike curiosity. "I am here another hour—not quite—in case you want something."

"Thank you, Gaby." Tom wakened himself further with coffee and a cigarette, then went off to take a shower and shave.

When he came back into the guest room, he saw Frank standing with one bare foot on the sill of the window which he had opened. Tom had the feeling the boy was about to jump. "Frank?" The boy hadn't heard him come in.

"Great view, isn't it?" said Frank, both feet on the floor now.

Had the boy shuddered, or had Tom imagined it? Tom moved to the window and looked out at excursion boats plowing toward the left on the Alster's blue water, at a half dozen little sailboats scooting about, at people strolling on the quay beside the water. Bright pennants flew everywhere, and the sun shone. It was like a Dufy, only German, Tom thought. "You weren't thinking of jumping out just now, were you?" Tom asked as if he were joking. "Only a few stories here. Not very satisfying."

"Jumping?" Frank shook his head quickly, and took a step back from Tom, as if he were shy about standing so close to him. "Certainly not. . . . Okay if I wash?"

"Go ahead. Reeves is out, but Gaby's here, the housekeeper. Just say 'Guten Morgen' to her. She's very friendly." Tom watched the boy take his trousers and go across the hall. He thought perhaps he had been wrong to be anxious. Frank had a purposeful air this morning, as if the pills had worn off.

By mid-morning, they were at St Pauli. They had taken a look at the sex-shop windows in the Reeperbahn, at the garish fronts of the nonstop blue-film cinemas, at shop windows with astounding underwear for all sexes. Rock music poured from somewhere, and even at this hour there were customers browsing and buying. Tom found himself blinking, maybe with amazement, maybe at the glaring colors that seemed circus-like in the clear sunlight. Tom realized that he had a prudish side, maybe due to his childhood in Boston, Massachusetts. Frank looked cool, but then he would make an effort to look cool, confronted by dildoes and vibrators with price tags.

"Place must be hopping at night," Frank remarked.

"Doing all right now," Tom said, seeing two girls approaching them with intent. "Let's hop a streetcar—or a taxi. Let's go to the zoo, that's always fun."

Frank laughed. "The zoo again!"

"Well, I like zoos. Wait till you see this zoo." Tom saw a taxi.

The two girls, one of whom looked in her teens and rather attractively unmade-up, seemed to think the taxi might be for all four of them, but Tom waved them away with a polite smile and shook his head.

Tom bought a newspaper at the kiosk in front of the Tierpark entrance, and took a minute to glance at it. He went through it a second time, looking now for a small item that might have to do with the kidnappers in Berlin, or Frank Pierson. His second search was not thorough, but he didn't see anything. This was *Die Welt*.

"No news," Tom said to Frank, "is good news. Let's go."

Tom bought tickets which came in orange-colored perforated strips. These enabled them to ride the toylike trains that traveled all over the Carl Hagenbeck Tierpark. Frank looked enchanted, and Tom was pleased. The little train had perhaps fifteen carriages; one stepped aboard from the ground without opening a side door, and the train had no roof. They rolled along almost noiselessly past adventure playgrounds where kids hung from rubber tires that slid along cables from a height, or crawled in and out of two-story plastic constructions with holes, tunnels, and slopes. They passed lions and elephants with, apparently, no barrier between them and the human race. In the bird section, they detrained, bought beer and peanuts at a stand, then got aboard another passing train.

Then a taxi to a big restaurant on the harbor which Tom remembered from a previous trip. Its walls were glass, and one could look down at the port where tankers, white cruise liners, and barges lay moored, being loaded and unloaded, while water poured from their automatic pumps. Seagulls cruised, and occasionally dived.

"We go to Paris tomorrow," Tom said after they had begun their meal. "How about that?"

Frank at once looked on guard, but Tom could see him collecting himself. It was either Paris tomorrow, Tom thought, or the boy would blow up in another day and insist on striking out somewhere from Hamburg on his own. "I don't like to tell people what they should do. But you've got to face your family at some point, haven't you?" Tom glanced to right and left, but he was speaking softly, the wall of glass was just to his left, and the nearest table was more than a yard away behind Frank. "You can't hop one plane after another for months to come, can you?— Eat your *Bauernfrühstück.*"

The boy fell to again, more slowly. He had been amused by "Farmer's Breakfast" on the menu and ordered it: fish, home-fried potatoes, bacon, onions, all mixed on a king-sized platter. "You'll be coming to Paris too tomorrow?"

"Sure, since I'm going home."

After lunch, they walked, crossed a Venice-like inlet of water bordered by beautiful old peak-roofed houses. Then on the pavement of a commercial street, Frank said, "I want to change some money. Can I go in here for a minute?"

He meant a bank. "Okay." Tom went into the bank with him and waited while the boy stood on a short queue and made a transaction at the window marked "Foreign Exchange." Frank hadn't his Benjamin Andrews passport with him, as far as Tom knew, but he wouldn't need it if he was changing French francs into marks. Tom did not try to see. Tom had put some other kind of cream on Frank's mole that morning. Why was he always thinking about that damned mole? What if anybody *did* recognize Frank now? Frank came back smiling, pushing marks into his billfold.

They walked on to the museum of Völkerkunde und Vorge-schichte, where Tom had been once before. Here were table models of fire bomb implosions that had flattened much of the Hamburg dock area in World War II: nine-inch-high warehouses on fire, sculpted yellow and blue flames. Frank poured over a model of ship-raising, the little ship three inches long resting on sand and under what appeared to be meters of sea. As usual, after an hour of this, including oil paintings of Hamburg Burgermeisters signing this and commemorating that, all in dress of the Benjamin Franklin period, Tom was rubbing his eyes and longing for a cigarette.

Minutes later, in an avenue of shops and pushcarts of flowers and fruit, Frank said, "Will you wait for me? Five minutes?"

"Where're you going?"

"I'll be back. By this tree." Frank pointed to a plane tree near the curb beside them.

"But I'd like to know where you're going," Tom said.

"Trust me."

"All right." Tom turned away, walked slowly several paces on, doubting the boy, and at the same time reminding himself that he couldn't play nursemaid to Frank Pierson forever. Yes, if the boy disappeared—and how much money had he cashed at the bank, how much had he left in French or American?—Tom would take Frank's suitcase to Paris and deliver it to the Lutetia. Had Frank possibly taken his passport with him this morning? Tom turned back and walked toward the plane tree, which he recognized from others only because of an elderly gentleman sitting on a chair and reading a newspaper under it. The boy was not there, and more than five minutes had passed.

Then Frank reappeared through a trickle of pedestrians, smiling, carrying a big red-and-white plastic bag. "Thanks," Frank said.

Tom was relieved. "Bought something?"

"Yep. Show you later."

Next, the Jungfernstieg. Tom remembered the name of the street or promenade, because Reeves had once told him it was where the pretty girls of Hamburg strolled in the old days. The sightseeing boats set off for round-the-Alsters cruises from a quay at right angles to the Jungfernstieg, and Tom and Frank boarded one.

"My last day of freedom!" Frank said on the boat. The wind blew his brown hair back and whipped his trousers against his legs.

Neither wanted to sit down, but they were not in anyone's way, hanging onto a corner of the superstructure. A jolly man in a white cap spoke through a megaphone, explaining the sights they were passing, the big hotels on sloping green lawns overlooking the water, where he assured everyone the tariff was "among the highest in the world." Tom was amused. The boy's eyes had focused on some distant point, maybe on a seagull, maybe on Teresa, Tom didn't know.

When they got back to Reeves's at just after six, Reeves was not home, but he had left a message in the middle of the neatly made bed in the guest room: "Back at seven or before. R." Tom was glad Reeves was still out, because he wanted to speak with Frank alone.

"You remember what I told you at Belle Ombre—in regard to your father," Tom said.

Frank looked puzzled for an instant, then said, "I think I remember everything you ever said to me."

They were in the living room, Tom standing near the window, the boy sitting on the sofa.

"I said, never tell anyone what you did. Don't confess. Don't entertain for a minute the idea of confessing."

Frank looked from Tom to the floor.

"Well—are you thinking about telling someone? Your brother?" Tom threw it out in the hope of eliciting something.

"No, I'm not."

The boy's voice was firm and deep enough, but Tom was not sure he could believe him. He wished he could take the boy by the shoulders and shake some sense into him. Did he dare? No. And what was he afraid of, Tom wondered—failure to shake any sense into the boy? "This you ought to know. Where is it?" Tom went to the little heap of newspapers at one end of the sofa and found yesterday's. He opened it to the front page on which was the picture of the dead man in Lübars. "I saw you looking at this yesterday on the plane. This—this man I killed in Lübars, north Berlin."

"*You?*" Frank's voice rose an octave with astonishment.

"You never asked me where the meeting place was for the ransom. Never mind. I hit him over the head. As you can see."

Frank blinked and looked at Tom. "Why didn't you tell me before? Sure, I recognize this fellow now. He was the Italian in the apartment there!"

Tom lit a cigarette. "I tell you this because—" Because, why? Tom had to pause to collect his words. There was no comparison, really, between pushing one's father off a cliff, and bashing the skull of a kidnapper who was walking toward you with a loaded gun. But both involved the taking of a life. "The fact that I killed this man— It's not going to change my life. Granted he was probably a criminal himself. Granted he wasn't the first man I ever killed. I don't think I have to tell you that."

Frank was looking at him with wonder. "Did you ever kill a woman?"

Tom laughed. That was just what he had needed, a laugh. Tom was aware of relief also, because Frank had not asked him about Dickie Greenleaf, the one murder Tom felt a bit of guilt about. "Never—a woman. Never had to," Tom added, and thought at once of the joke about the Englishman who told a friend he had had to bury his wife, simply because she was dead. "Situation never arose. A woman. Surely not on your mind, Frank. . . . Who?"

Now Frank smiled. "Oh, no one! Gosh!"

"Good. The only reason I bring this up—" Tom was again at a loss, but plunged on. "It—I mean the—" He gestured toward the newspaper. "The act shouldn't be devastating—to the rest of your life. There's no reason to collapse." Did the boy, could he, know the meaning of collapse at his age? To collapse from a sense of total failure? But many adolescents did collapse, even committed suicide, because they had met a problem they couldn't cope with, sometimes just schoolwork.

Frank was brushing the knuckles of his right fist against the sharp corner of Reeves's coffee table. Was the top made of glass? It was black and white, but not marble. Frank's gesture made Tom nervous.

"Do you understand what I mean? You either let some event ruin your life or not. The decision is yours.— You're lucky, Frank, in your case the decision *is* yours, because no one is accusing you."

"I know."

And Tom knew that part—how much?—of the boy's mind was on the apparently lost love, Teresa. That was a sickness Tom felt unable to deal with, quite another subject than murder. Tom said nervously, "Don't hit your knuckles against that table, will you, because it won't solve anything. You'll only get to Paris with bleeding knuckles. *Don't be silly!*"

The boy had made a downward swipe at the table, but not quite hit it. Tom tried to relax, and looked away.

"I wouldn't be that stupid, don't worry, don't worry." Frank stood up and pushed his hands into his pockets, walked to a window, then turned to Tom. "The plane tickets for tomorrow. Shall I do it? I can make the reservations in English, can't I?"

"I'm sure. Go ahead."

"Lufthansa," said Frank, picking up the telephone directory. "What time, around ten tomorrow morning?"

"Even earlier." Tom felt much relieved. Frank seemed to be standing on his feet at last, or if he wasn't quite, he was trying.

Reeves came in as Frank was fixing the time for tomorrow: 9:15 takeoff. Frank gave the names, Ripley and Andrews.

"Did you have a nice day?" Reeves asked.

"Very fine, thanks," Tom said.

"Hello, Frank. Got to wash my hands," Reeves said in his croaky voice, at the same time displaying his palms, which were visibly gray. "Handling pictures today. Not a dirty—"

"A real day's work, Reeves?" said Tom. "I admire your hands!"

Reeves cleared his hoarse throat in vain, and began again. "I was about to say not a dirty day's work, but a day's *dirty* work. Did you make yourself a drink, Tom?" Reeves went off to his bathroom.

"Would you like to go out for dinner, Reeves?" Tom asked, following him. "It's our last night."

"I really don't, if you don't mind. Always something here, you know. Gaby sees to that. I think she made a casserole or something."

Reeves never liked restaurants, Tom remembered. Reeves probably kept a low profile on the Hamburg scene.

"Tom." Frank beckoned Tom into the guest room, and pulled a box out of the red and white plastic bag. "For you."

"For me?— Thank you, Frank."

"You haven't opened it yet."

Tom untied some blue and red ribbon, then opened the white box, which had a lot of white tissue paper inside. He found something reddish, shiny, golden, pulled it out, and it became a dressing gown with a belt of the same dark-red silk, with black tassels. The red material was flecked with gold in the form of arrowheads. "Really pretty," said Tom. "Very handsome." Tom took his jacket off. "Shall I try it on?" he asked, trying it on. It fitted perfectly, or would with pajamas underneath instead of his sweater and trousers. Tom glanced at the sleeve length and said, "Perfect."

Frank ducked his head, and swung away from Tom.

Tom took the dressing gown off carefully and laid it across the bed. It made a fine and impressive rustle. The color was maroon, the same as the kidnappers' car in Berlin, a color Tom didn't like, but if he made himself think of it as Dubonnet, maybe he could forget that car.

18

On the plane going to Paris, Tom noticed that Frank's hair had grown so long, it was falling partly over his cheek where the mole was. Frank had not had a haircut since the middle of August, which was the time Tom had advised Frank to let it grow. Between noon and one o'clock, he would be delivering Frank to Thurlow and Johnny Pierson at the Lutetia. Tom had reminded Frank, last evening at Reeves's, that he ought to see about getting a genuine passport, unless Thurlow had had the wit to bring his passport or ask his mother to send it from Maine.

"You see this?" Frank asked, showing Tom a page in a glossy little magazine donated by the airline. "That's where we were."

Tom read a small item about Romy Haag and its transvestite show. "I bet they haven't got the Hump there! That magazine's for tourists." Tom laughed, and stretched his legs as far as the seat in front of him permitted. Airplanes were getting increasingly uncomfortable. He could travel first class, though probably with a sense of guilt about spending so much extra when the inter-European rates were already inflated, and moreover Tom would

have felt embarrassed at being seen in first class. Why? He always
had a desire to step on the toes of people in the roomy first class
when he boarded an airplane and had to pass through their more
luxurious quarters, where champagne corks started to pop before
takeoff.

This time, not looking forward to the encounter at the Lutetia, Tom proposed the train from the airport to the Gare du Nord,
and a taxi from there. At the Gare du Nord they queued for a taxi,
the queue kept in order by no less than three policemen in white
spats and with guns on their hips, and then they rode toward the
Hôtel Lutetia. Frank, tense and silent, stared out the window. Was
he planning his stance, Tom wondered, and what would it be? A
don't-touch-me attitude toward Thurlow? An awkward explanation to brother Johnny? A defiance even? Was Frank going to insist
on staying in Europe?

"I think you'll like my brother all right," Frank said nervously.

Tom nodded. He wanted Frank to get home safely, resume his
life, which was bound to mean school again, face what he had to
face, and learn to live with it. Kids of sixteen, at least from Frank's
kind of family, could not leave home and expect to cope, as a boy
from the slums might, or a boy from such a wretched home that
the street might be better. They slid up in front of the Lutetia.

"I have francs," Frank said.

Tom let him pay. A doorman carried their two suitcases in, but
once inside the rather pretentious lobby, Tom said to the doorman,
"I'm not staying in the hotel, so could you check mine for half an
hour or so?"

Frank wanted his checked too, and a bellhop returned and gave
them two tickets, which Tom pocketed. Frank came back from the
desk, and reported that Thurlow and his brother were out, but due
back in less than an hour.

Amazing to find them out, Tom thought, and looked at his
watch. It was 12:07. "Maybe they're out for lunch? I'm going to
the next bar-café and ring home. Want to come?"

"Sure!" said Frank, and led the way to the door. On the pavement, he hung his head as he walked.

"Stand up straight," Tom said.

Frank did so at once.

"Order me a coffee, Frank?" Tom said as they went into a bar-tabac. Tom went down some winding stairs to the *toilettes-téléphones*. He put two francs into the telephone slot, not wanting to be cut off for being a few seconds late with his money, and dialed Belle Ombre. Mme. Annette answered.

"Ah-h!" She sounded as if she were fainting at the sound of his voice.

"I'm in Paris. All goes well?"

"Ah, oui! But Madame is not here at the moment. She went out to lunch with a friend."

A female friend, Tom noticed. "Tell her I'll be home this afternoon, maybe around—oh, by four, I hope. By six-thirty anyway," he added, remembering the gap between trains from a little past 2 p.m. until 5 p.m. something at Gare de Lyon.

"You do not wish Madame Heloise to fetch you in Paris?"

Tom didn't. He went back to Frank and his coffee.

Frank, with a hardly touched Coca-Cola in front of him at the bar, spat out chewing gum into an empty and crushed cigarette packet that he took from a big ashtray. "Sorry. I hate chewing gum. Don't know why I bought it. Or this." He pushed the Coca-Cola away.

Tom watched the boy drift toward the jukebox near the door. The box was now playing something, an American song sung in French.

Frank came back. "Is everything all right at home?"

"I think so, thanks." Tom pulled some coins from his pocket.

"This is paid for."

They went out. Again the boy's head sank, and Tom said nothing.

Ralph Thurlow, at any rate, was in. Tom had let Frank ask at the desk. They rode up in a decorated lift that suggested to Tom a bad performance of Wagner. Was Thurlow going to be cool, self-important? That at least would be amusing.

Frank knocked on the door of 620, and the door opened at once. Thurlow beckoned the boy in enthusiastically and without a word, then saw Tom. Thurlow's smile remained. Frank made a gracious gesture, ushering Tom in. No one said a word until the door was closed. Thurlow wore a shirt with sleeves rolled up and no tie. He was a chunky man in his late thirties, perhaps, with rippling short-cut reddish hair and a rather tough face.

"My friend Tom Ripley," Frank said.

"How'd you do, Mr. Ripley?— Please sit down," said Thurlow.

There was plenty of space, and chairs and sofas, but Tom did not at once sit down. A door to the right was closed, a door to the left by the windows open, and Thurlow went to it and called to Johnny, saying to Frank and Tom that he thought Johnny was taking a shower. There were newspapers and a briefcase on a table, and more newspapers on the floor, a transistor radio, a tape recorder. This was not a bedroom but a sitting room between two bedrooms, Tom supposed.

Johnny came in, tall and smiling, in a fresh pink shirt he had not yet stuffed into his trousers. He had straight brown hair lighter than Frank's, and his face was more narrow than Frank's. "*Franky!*" He swung his brother's right hand and almost embraced him. "How *are* yuh?"

Or so it sounded to Tom. How are yuh. Tom felt that he had entered America, just by stepping into room 620. Tom was introduced to Johnny and they shook hands. Johnny looked like a straightforward, happy, and easygoing boy, even younger than nineteen, which Tom knew he was.

Then down to business, which Tom let Thurlow stumble on with. Thurlow first assured Tom, with thanks from Mrs. Pierson, that the marks had been reported in Zurich by the bank there.

"Every last one, except the bank charges," said Thurlow. "Mr. Ripley, we don't know the details, but . . ."

You never will, Tom thought, and barely listened to what fol-

lowed from Thurlow. Reluctantly, Tom sat down on a beige upholstered sofa, and lit a Gauloise. Johnny and Frank were talking fast
and quietly by the window. Frank looked angry and tense. Had
Johnny said the name Teresa? Tom thought so. He saw Johnny
shrug.

"You said there were no police," said Thurlow. "You went to
their apartment— How did you do it?" Now Thurlow fairly
laughed, maybe in what he thought was a tough guy to tough guy
manner. "It's fantastic!"

Tom felt one hundred percent turned off in regard to Mr.
Thurlow. "Professional secret," said Tom. How long could he
endure this? Tom stood up. "Got to be pushing on, Mr. Thurlow."

"Pushing on?" Thurlow had not yet sat down. "Mr. Ripley,
besides meeting you—thanking you— We don't even know your
exact address!"

In order to send him a fee, Tom wondered? "I am in the book.
Villeperce, seventy-seven, Seine et Marne.— Frank?"

"Yes, sir!"

Suddenly the boy's anxious expression looked like the one
Tom remembered from mid-August at Belle Ombre. "May we go
in here for a minute?" Tom asked, indicating what he supposed was
Johnny's room, whose door was still open.

They could, Johnny said, so Tom and Frank went in, and Tom
closed the door.

"Don't tell them all the details of that night—in Berlin," Tom
said. "Above all, don't tell them about the dead man—will you?"
Tom glanced around, but saw no tape recorder in this room. There
was a *Playboy* on the floor by the bed, and a few big bottles of
orange soda pop on a tray.

"Of course I *won't*," said Frank.

The boy's eyes seemed older than his brother's. "You can say—
all right—that I failed to keep the date with the money. That's how
I still had the money. All right?"

"All right."

"And that I followed one of the kidnappers after I made a second date, so I knew where you were being held.— But don't mention that crazy *Hump!*" Now Tom burst out laughing, and bent over.

They both laughed, with nearly hysterical mirth.

"I gotcha," Frank whispered.

Tom caught the boy suddenly by the front of his jacket, then released him, embarrassed by his gesture. "Never anything about that dead man! You promise?"

Frank nodded. "I know, I know what you mean."

Tom started to walk back to the other room, then turned. "I mean," he whispered, "so far and no farther—with everything. If you mention Hamburg, don't give Reeves's name. Say you forgot it."

The boy was silent, but he looked steadily at Tom, then nodded. They went into the other room.

Now Thurlow sat on a beige chair. "Mr. Ripley—please sit down again, if you've got just a couple of minutes."

Tom did so to be polite, and Frank at once joined him on the beige sofa. Johnny was still standing by the window.

"I must apologize for my brusqueness several times on the telephone," Thurlow said. "I couldn't know, you know—" Thurlow paused.

"I'd like to ask you," Tom said, "what the situation is now in regard to Frank's being missing or looked for. You told the police here—what?"

"Well—I first told Mrs. Pierson that the boy was safe in Berlin—with you. Then with her agreement I informed the police here. Of course I didn't need her agreement to do it."

Tom bit his underlip. "I hope you and Mrs. Pierson didn't mention my name to the police anywhere. That wouldn't've been necessary at all."

"Not here, I know," Thurlow assured Tom. "Mrs. Pierson—I— yes, I told her your name, of course, but I certainly asked her not

to mention your name to the police in the States. There were no
police in the States. This was a private detective situation. I told her
to say to any journalists—whom she hates, by the way—that the
boy had been found taking a holiday in Germany. Didn't even say
where in Germany, because that could've led to another kidnapping!" Ralph Thurlow chuckled, leaning back in his chair, and
adjusting his brass-buckled belt with a thumb.

He was smiling as if another kidnapping might have landed
him in some other comfortable spot, such as Palma de Majorca,
Tom thought.

"I wish you'd tell me what happened in Berlin," Thurlow said.
"At least a description of the kidnappers. It might—"

"You're not intending to *look* for them," Tom said in a tone of
surprise, and smiled. "Hopeless." Tom stood up.

So did Thurlow, looking unsatisfied. "I've recorded my telephone conversations with them.— Well, maybe Frank can tell me
a little more.— What made you go to Berlin, Mr. Ripley?"

"Oh—Frank and I wanted a change of scene from Villeperce,"
Tom said, feeling like a travelogue or brochure, "and I thought
Berlin was off the tourist trail. Frank wanted to be incognito for a
while . . . By the way, have you got Frank's passport here?" Tom
asked before Thurlow might ask why he had sheltered the boy.

"Yep, my mother sent it by registered post," Johnny said.

Tom said to Frank, "You'd better get rid of the Andrews one,
you know? I can take it if you go downstairs with me." Tom was
thinking of returning it to Hamburg, where it could certainly be
made use of again.

"*What* passport?" asked Thurlow.

Tom edged toward the door.

Thurlow seemed to give up the passport matter, and walked
toward Tom. "Maybe I'm not a typical detective. Maybe there aren't
any such animals. We're all different, not all of us capable of a physical fight, if it came to it."

But wasn't he the usual, Tom thought, glancing at Thurlow's
well-fed body, at his heavy hands with a school ring on one little

finger. Tom thought of asking him if he had ever been on the police force, but really Tom didn't care.

"You've had some experience with the underworld before, haven't you, Mr. Ripley?" Thurlow asked this in a genial way.

"Haven't we all," Tom said, "anyone who's ever bought an oriental rug.— Well, Frank, with your passport, you seem all set."

"I'm not going to stay here tonight," Frank said, getting up.

Thurlow looked at the boy. "What do you mean, Frank?— Where's your suitcase? You have no suitcase?"

"Downstairs with Tom's," Frank replied. "I want to go home with Tom now. And tonight. We're not leaving for the States today, are we? I'm not." Frank looked determined.

Tom gave a twitch of a smile and waited. He had expected something like this.

"I thought we'd leave tomorrow." With equal determination and a little puzzlement, Thurlow folded his arms. "Do you want to phone your mother now, Frank? She's expecting a call from you."

Frank shook his head quickly. "Just tell her I'm okay if she calls up."

Thurlow said, "I wish you'd stay here, Frank. It's just one night here, and I want you in sight."

"Come on, Franky," Johnny said. "Stay with *us*! Natch!"

Frank gave his brother a look, as if he objected to being called Franky, made a kicking movement with his right foot, though there was nothing to kick. He walked nearer to Tom. "I want to leave."

"Now look," said Thurlow. "One night—"

"*Can* I go to Belle Ombre with you?" Frank asked Tom. "I can, can't I?"

In the next seconds, everyone but Tom talked at the same time. Tom wrote his telephone number on a pad by the telephone, and added his name below.

"If we just tell my mother, it's all *right*," Johnny was saying to Thurlow. "I *know* Frank."

Did he, Tom wondered. Evidently Johnny trusted his brother usually.

"—cause a delay," Thurlow was saying with irritation. "Use your influence, Johnny."

"I haven't any!" said Johnny.

"I'm leaving." Frank stood as tall as Tom or anyone else could have wished. "Tom wrote his phone number. I just saw it. Goodbye, Mr. Thurlow. See you soon, Johnny."

"Tomorrow morning, yes?" asked Johnny, following Tom and Frank out of the room. "Mr. Ripley—"

"You can call me Tom." They were now in the hall, walking toward the elevators.

"Not much of a meeting," Johnny said with a serious air to Tom. "This has been a crazy time. I know you've taken care of my brother, really saved him."

"Well—" Tom could see freckles on Johnny's nose, eyes that were shaped like Frank's, yet looked so much happier.

"Ralph's rather abrupt—the way he speaks," Johnny went on.

Now Thurlow was joining them. "We want to leave tomorrow, Mr. Ripley. Can I phone you tomorrow morning around nine? I'll have our reservations by then."

Tom nodded calmly. Frank had pushed the elevator button. "Yes, Mr. Thurlow."

Johnny extended his hand. "Thank you, Mr. R— Tom. My mother kept thinking—"

Thurlow made a gesture as if he preferred that Johnny keep silent.

Johnny went on. "She didn't know what to think about you, I know."

"Oh, can it!" said Frank, squirming with embarrassment.

The elevator doors slid open like a pair of arms saying, "Welcome!" and Tom was delighted to step in. Frank followed at once, Tom pressed the button, and down they went.

"Whew!" said Frank, hitting himself in the forehead with his palm.

Tom laughed, and leaned against the Wagnerian interior. Two floors down, a man and woman got on, the woman with a perfume that made Tom cringe, though perhaps it was expensive. Her yellow-and-blue striped dress certainly looked expensive, and her black patent leather pumps reminded Tom of the one, or maybe two, that he had left in the kidnappers' flat in Berlin. A surprising find for the neighbors or the police, Tom supposed. In the lobby, Tom reclaimed their suitcases, but felt that he didn't breathe until he was standing on the pavement, waiting for the doorman to get a taxi. One came almost at once, letting off two women, and Tom and Frank took it, bound for the Gare de Lyon. They could make the 14:18 with a few minutes to spare, which was nice, as it avoided the awful wait for the next train at 5 p.m. or so. Frank was gazing out the window with eyes at once intense and dreaming, his body stiff as a statue. In fact, Tom thought of a statue of an angel, one of the dazed but supportive figures at the sides of church doors. At the station, Tom bought first-class tickets, and a copy of *Le Monde* from the newsstand by the trains.

Once the train started moving, Frank pulled out a paperback that he had bought at a bookshop in Hamburg, Tom remembered. *The Country Diary of an Edwardian Lady*, of all things. Tom glanced at *Le Monde*, read a column about *gauchistes* which seemed to have nothing new in it, put *Le Monde* on the seat beside Frank, and stuck his feet up on it. Frank did not look at him. Was Frank pretending his absorption?

"Is there any reason why . . ." Frank said.

Tom leaned forward, not having heard the rest in the train's roar. "Reason why what?"

Frank asked earnestly, "Is there any simple reason why Communism doesn't *work*?"

Tom thought the train was just then roaring toward its next stop, hadn't begun to put on the brakes, which would be even louder. Across the aisle, a small child had begun to wail, and his father smacked him gently. "What made you think of that? That book?"

"No, no. *Berlin,*" said Frank, frowning.

Tom took a breath, hating talking over the train's noise. "It does work. Socialism works. It's individual initiative that's lacking—they say. The Russian form just now doesn't allow enough initiative—so everyone becomes discouraged." Tom glanced around, glad to see that no one was listening to his unprepared lecture. "There's a difference—"

"A year ago I thought I was a Communist. You know, Moscow even. Depends on what you read. If you read the *right* things . . ."

What did Frank mean by the right things? "If you read—"

"Why do the Russians need the *Wall?*" Frank asked with frowning brows.

"Well, that's it. If it comes to freedom of choice— Even now people can ask for citizenship in Communist countries and probably get it. But if you're in a Communist country, try and get *out!*"

"That's what's so—uh—unfair!"

Tom shook his head. The train roared on, as if they had passed Melun even, but that was impossible. He was glad the boy was asking naïve questions. How else could a boy learn anything? Tom leaned forward again. "You saw the Wall. The barriers are on *their* side, yet they claim they built it to keep capitalists *out.*— But it could've been marvelous, sure. Russia became more and more a police state. They seem to think they need all that control over people." How to finish, Tom wondered. Jesus Christ was an early Communist. "But of course the idea is *great!*" Tom yelled. Was this the way to instruct the young? By screaming platitudes?

Melun. The boy returned to his book, and minutes later pointed out a sentence to Tom. "We've got these in our garden in Maine. My father ordered them from England."

Tom read a sentence about an English wildflower he had never heard of: yellow, sometimes purple, blooming in early spring. Tom nodded. He was worried, thinking of a lot of things, therefore of nothing, he realized, nothing that was profitable or conclusive, anyway.

At Moret, they got off, and Tom engaged one of the two waiting taxis. Then he began to feel better. This was home, familiar
houses, familiar trees even, the towered bridge over the Loing. He
remembered the first time he had brought the boy back to Mme.
Boutin's here, remembered his suspicion of the boy's story, his
wondering why the boy had looked him up. The taxi rolled
through the open gates of Belle Ombre onto the gravel, and
stopped near the front steps. Tom smiled at the sight of the red
Mercedes in the garage, and since the door of the second garage
was closed, Tom supposed the Renault was there too, and Heloise
was home. Tom paid the driver.

"*Bonjour, Monsieur Tome!*" Mme. Annette called from the front
steps. "And Monsieur Billy! Welcome!"

She seemed not much surprised by Billy, Tom saw. "And how
goes everything?" He gave Mme. Annette a peck on the cheek.

"All very well, but Madame Heloise was so worried—for a day
or so. Come in."

Heloise walked toward him in the living room, and then she
was in his arms. "Finally, Tome!"

"Was I gone so long?— And Billy's here."

"Hello, Heloise. I am intruding on you again," the boy said in
French. "But just for the night—if I may."

"*Not* intruding. Hello." She blinked her eyes and extended a
hand.

In that blink of her eyes, Tom realized that she knew who the
boy was. "Lots to talk about," Tom said cheerfully, "but I want to
get our suitcases up first. S-so—" He motioned to Frank, not
knowing for the moment what to call him, and they both went
upstairs with their luggage.

Mme. Annette was in process of baking something, Tom judged
from the aroma of orange and vanilla, otherwise she would have
seized upon the suitcases and have been relieved of them by Tom,
because he still disliked seeing women carrying men's suitcases.

"Christ, is it good to get home!" Tom said in the upstairs hall.

"Take the spare room, Frank, unless—" A peek into the room assured Tom that no one else was using the guest room at the moment. "But use my john. I'd like to speak with you, so come in in a minute." Tom went to his room, and took some things out of his suitcase to hang up or to be washed.

The boy came in with a troubled face, and Tom knew that he had noticed Heloise's manner.

"Well, Heloise knows," Tom said, "but what's there to worry about?"

"As long as she doesn't think I'm a hundred percent phony."

"I wouldn't worry about that either.— I wonder if that delicious-smelling cake or whatever is for tea or dinner?"

"And what about Madame Annette?" Frank asked.

Tom laughed. "She seems to want to call you Billy. But she probably knew who you were before Heloise did. Madame Annette reads gossip sheets. It'll be out in the open tomorrow anyway, when you show your passport.— What's the matter? Are you ashamed of *yourself*?— Let's go down. Throw your stuff to be washed here on the floor. I'll tell Madame Annette, and everything will be ready by tomorrow morning."

Frank went back to his room, and Tom down to the living room. The day was lovely, and the French windows stood open on the garden.

"I knew, of course, from the photographs. I saw two," Heloise said. "Madame Annette showed me the first.— Why did he run away?"

Mme. Annette just then came in with a tea tray.

"He wanted to get away from home for a while. He took his older brother's passport when he left America. But he's going back home tomorrow, back to the States."

"Oh?" said Heloise, surprised. "Is he?"

"I just met his brother Johnny—and the detective his family hired. They're at the Hôtel Lutetia in Paris. I've been in touch with them from Berlin."

"Berlin? I thought you were in Hamburg—mostly."

The boy was coming down the stairs.

Heloise poured tea. Mme. Annette had gone back to the kitchen.

"Eric lives in Berlin, you know," Tom went on. "Eric Lanz who was here last week. Sit down, Frank."

"What were you doing in Berlin?" Heloise asked, as if it were a military outpost, or a place anyone on vacation would never dream of visiting.

"Oh—just looking around."

"You will be happy to get home, Frank?" Heloise asked as she served him orange cake.

The boy was going through a bad moment, and Tom pretended not to notice. Tom got up from the sofa and went to look at the letters stacked where Mme. Annette often put them, by the telephone. There were only six or eight, and a couple looked like bills. One was from Jeff Constant, and Tom was curious about that, but he did not open it.

"Did you speak with your mother when you were in Berlin?" Heloise was asking Frank.

"No," said Frank, swallowing cake as if it were dry as dust.

"How was Berlin?" Heloise looked at Tom now.

"Nothing in the world like it. As they say of Venice," Tom said. "Everyone can do his own thing. Isn't that right, Frank?"

Frank rubbed a knuckle into his left eye, and writhed.

Tom gave up. "Hey—Frank. Go up and take a nap. I insist." He said to Heloise, "Reeves kept us up late last night in Hamburg.— I'll call you at dinnertime, Frank."

Frank got up and bowed slightly to Heloise, evidently with his throat too tight for him to get a word out.

"Something the matter?" Heloise whispered. "Hambourg— last night?"

The boy had by now gone up the stairs.

"Well—never mind Hamburg. Frank was kidnapped last Sunday in Berlin. I couldn't get to him till early Tuesday morning. They gave him—"

"Kidnapped?"

"I know it wasn't in the papers. The kidnappers gave him a lot of sedatives, and I know he's still feeling the effect."

Heloise was wide-eyed, blinking again but in a different manner, her eyes so wide that Tom could see the little dark blue lines that radiated from the pupils and crossed the blue irises. "No, I didn't hear a thing about a kidnapping. His family paid a ransom?"

"No. Well, yes, but it wasn't paid. I'll tell you some time when we're alone. You suddenly remind me of the Druckfisch in the Berlin aquarium. Most amazing little fish! I bought some postcards of it, I'll show you! *Eyelashes*—as if someone had drawn them around its eyes. Long black ones!"

"*I* haven't got long black eyelashes!— Tom, this kidnapping. You could not get to him, what do you mean?"

"Some other time, the details. We're not hurt, you can see that."

"And his mother, she knows about this?"

"She had to, because the money had to be put up. I only— began telling you this to explain why the boy seems a bit strange tonight. He's—"

"He's very strange. Why should he run away from home in the first place? Do you know?"

"No. Not really." Tom knew he never would tell Heloise what the boy had told him. There was a limit to what Heloise should know, and Tom knew it as if it were a mark on a scale.

19

Tom read Jeff Constant's letter, and was reassured because Jeff promised firmly to see that the half-finished or downright unsuccessful sketches done by the successor to Bernard Tufts in imitation of Derwatt were "torn up." These efforts, by some hack,

seemed inexhaustible. Tom had checked his greenhouse, plucked a
ripe tomato that must have escaped Mme. Annette's attention, had
taken a shower and put on clean blue jeans. He had also helped
Heloise polish a clothes tree she had just bought somewhere. From
the top of the clothes tree curved wooden hooks sprang out, tipped
with brass, reminding Tom of western American cowhorns. To
Tom's surprise the thing really had come from America, Heloise
told him, and this must have added to its price, which Tom did not
ask. Heloise liked it because it was comical in their house, being
style rustique of the America variety.

Around eight, Tom called Frank down for dinner, and
opened two beers for them. Frank had not been asleep, but Tom
hoped he had had a nap. Tom caught up on Heloise's family
news: her mother was quite all right now, no operation necessary, but the doctor had put her on a regime of no salt and no
fats, the time-honored French prescription, Tom thought, when
the doctor didn't know what else to say or do. Heloise said she had
rung up her family that afternoon to say she would not have her
usual date with them tonight, because Tom had just come back.

They had coffee in the living room.

"I'll play the record you like," said Heloise to Frank, and she
started the Lou Reed *Transformer*. "Makeup" was the first song on
the second side.

> Your face when sleeping is sublime,
> And then you open up your eyes . . .
> Then comes pancake Factor Number One,
> Eyeliner, rose lips, oh, it's such fun!
> You're a slick little girl . . .

Frank ducked his head over his coffee.

Tom looked for a box of cigars on the telephone table, and it
wasn't there. Maybe that box was finished. And the new ones he
had bought were up in his room. Tom didn't want one badly

enough to go up. Tom was sorry Heloise had put the record on,
because he knew it reminded the boy of Teresa. Frank seemed to
be suffering inwardly, and Tom wondered if he wanted to be
"excused," or did he prefer their company in spite of the music?
Maybe the second song was easier on him.

> Sa—tel—lite . . .
> Gone way up to Mars . . .
> I've been told that you've been bold
> With Harry, Mark, and John . . .
> Things like that drive me out of my mind . . .
> I watched it for a little while . . .
> I love to watch things on TV . . .

The easy American voice went on, the words light and simple,
yet—if one chose to take them that way—the words could be
about an individual's crisis. Tom made a sign to Heloise, meaning,
"Please turn it off," and Tom got up from an armchair. "I like it
but— How about a bit of the classics? Maybe the Albeniz? I'd like
that." They had a new recording of *Iberia* played on the piano by
Michel Block, whose performance topped all contemporaries in
this work, according to the most respected reviewers. Heloise put
it on. This was better! This was musical poetry by comparison,
unfettered by human words with a message. Frank's eyes met Tom's
for an instant, and Tom saw a flicker of gratitude.

"I shall be going upstairs," said Heloise. "Good night, Frank. I
shall see you tomorrow morning, I hope."

Frank stood up. "Yes. Good night, Heloise."

She went up the stairs.

Tom sensed that Heloise's early departure was a hint for him
to come upstairs early too. She wanted to ask him some more
questions, of course.

The telephone rang, and Tom turned the music down and
answered. It was Ralph Thurlow in Paris, wanting to know if Tom

and the boy had got to Tom's house, and Tom assured him that they had.

"I have reservations for a twelve forty-five takeoff from Roissy tomorrow," Thurlow said. "Can you see that Frank makes that? Is he there? I'd like to speak with him."

Tom looked at Frank who made a vigorously negative gesture. "He's upstairs and I think he's gone to bed, but I can see that he gets to Paris, certainly. What airline?"

"TWA, flight number five six two. I think it would be simplest if Frank came to the Lutetia between ten and ten-thirty tomorrow morning, and we'll take a taxi from here."

"Okay, that can be done."

"I didn't mention it this afternoon, Mr. Ripley, but I'm sure you've had some expenses. Just inform me and I'll see that the matter is taken care of. Write me care of Mrs. Pierson. Frank can give you her address."

"Thank you."

"Will I see you tomorrow morning too? I'd rather you—uh—brought Frank here," said Thurlow.

"All right, Mr. Thurlow." Tom was smiling when he hung up. He said to Frank, "Thurlow has tickets reserved for tomorrow noonish. You're supposed to be at their hotel around ten. That's easy. Lots of trains in the morning. Or I could drive you up."

"Oh, no," said Frank politely.

"But you'll be there?"

"I'll be there."

Tom felt a relief that he tried to hide.

"I was thinking of asking you to come with me—but that would be the bottom, I suppose." Frank's hands were clenched in the pockets of his trousers, and his jaw seemed to shake.

Come with him where, Tom wondered. "Sit down, Frank."

The boy didn't care to sit down. "I've got to face everything, I know that."

"What do you mean by everything?"

"Tell them what I did—about my father," Frank replied, as if it were a sentence of death for himself.

"I told you not to," Tom said softly, though he knew that Heloise was upstairs in her room or in her bathroom at the back of the house. "You don't have to, and you know that, so why do you bring it up again?"

"If I had Teresa, I wouldn't, I swear. But I haven't even got her."

Here was the impasse again, Tom thought. Teresa.

"Maybe I'll kill myself. What else? I'm not saying this to you as a threat, some stupid threat." He looked Tom in the eyes. "I'm just being reasonable. I thought my life out upstairs this afternoon."

At sixteen. Tom nodded, then said what he didn't believe. "Teresa may not be lost. Maybe for a couple of weeks she's interested in someone else, or thinks she is. Girls like to play, you know. But surely she knows you're serious."

Frank smiled a little. "Where does that get me? This other fellow is *older*."

"Now look, Frank—" Would it do any good to keep the boy another day at Belle Ombre and try to talk some sense into him? Tom at once doubted the success of that. "The one thing you don't have to do—is tell anyone."

"I think I have to decide that for myself," Frank said with surprising coolness.

Tom wondered if he should go to America with Frank, see him over the first day or so with his mother, make sure the boy was not going to blurt anything out? "Suppose I go with you tomorrow?"

"To Paris?"

"I meant to the States." Tom had expected a relaxation of the boy's tension, a visible lift of some kind, but Frank merely shrugged.

"Yes, but after all what good—"

"Frank, you're not going to collapse.— Have you any objection to my coming with you?"

"No. You're really the only friend I have."

Tom shook his head. "I'm not your only friend, just the only person you've talked to. All right, I'll come with you, and I want to tell Heloise now.— Come upstairs and get some sleep. Will you?"

The boy came upstairs with Tom, and Tom said, "Good night, see you tomorrow," then went to Heloise's door and knocked. She was in bed, propped against pillows and on one elbow, reading a paperback. Tom noticed that it was their well-worn copy of Auden's *Selected Poems*. She liked Auden's poems because they were "clear," she said. A funny time to be reading poetry, Tom thought, but maybe it wasn't. He watched her eyes swim back to the present, to him and to Frank.

"I'm going to the States with Frank tomorrow," Tom said, "probably just for two or three days."

"Why?— Tom, you haven't told me very much. Hardly anything." She tossed the paperback aside, but not angrily.

Tom suddenly realized there was something he could tell Heloise. "He's in love with a girl in America, and the girl's recently found somebody else, so the boy's very depressed about that."

"Is that a reason why you have to go to America with him?— What really happened in Berlin? You are still protecting him from—a gang?"

"No! A kidnapping happened in Berlin. When Frank and I were taking a walk in some woods there. Frank and I were separated for a minute or two—and they snatched him. I made a date with the kidnappers—" Tom paused. "Anyway I was able to get Frank from their apartment. He was very sleepy from sedatives— still is, a little."

Heloise looked incredulous. "All this in Berlin—the city?"

"Yes, West Berlin. It's bigger than you may think." Tom had sat down at the foot of Heloise's bed, but now he stood up. "And you're not to worry about tomorrow, because I'll be back very soon and—when is it exactly that you go on this Adventure Cruise? Not till late September, isn't it?" Today was September first.

"The twenty-eighth.— Tom, what is really worrying you? You think they are going to try to kidnap this boy again? The same people?"

274 PATRICIA HIGHSMITH

Tom laughed. "No, certainly not! They were like a bunch of juveniles in Berlin! Just four of them.— And I'm sure they're scared now, lying low."

"You are not telling me everything." Heloise was not angry, not taunting, but something between the two.

"Maybe not, but I will tell you later."

"That's what you said about—" Heloise stopped and looked down at her hands.

Murchison? His disappearance, still not accounted for? The American whom Tom had killed in the cellar of Belle Ombre by hitting him with a wine bottle. A bottle of good Margaux, Tom remembered. No, he had never told Heloise about dragging Murchison's corpse out, or told the truth about the big dark-red splotch that still refused to come out of the cement floor of their cellar, and which was not entirely due to wine. Tom had scrubbed at that spot. "Anyway—" Tom edged toward the door.

Heloise lifted her eyes to him.

Tom knelt by the bed, put his arms around her as much as he could, and pressed his face against the sheet that covered her.

She brushed her fingers against his hair. "What kind of danger is this? Can't you tell me that?"

Tom realized that he didn't know. "No danger at all." He stood up. "Good night, darling."

When Tom went into the hall, he saw that the boy's room light was still on. Tom was walking past, when the guest-room door opened slightly. Frank beckoned to him. Tom went in, and the boy closed the door. Frank was in pajamas, his bed was turned down, but he had not been in it.

"I think I was a coward downstairs," Frank said. "I think it's the *way* I said things. With the wrong words. And nearly shedding tears, good Christ!"

"So what? Never mind."

The boy walked across the carpet, looking down at his bare feet. "I feel like losing myself. It's not so much killing myself as losing myself. That's because of Teresa—I think. If I could just vaporize like steam—you know?"

"You mean lose your identity? Lose what?"

"Everything.— Once with Teresa I thought I'd lost my billfold." Frank smiled suddenly. "We were having lunch at a restaurant in New York, and I wanted to pay the check and couldn't find my billfold. I had the feeling I'd pulled it out a couple of minutes ahead of time, and maybe it had dropped on the floor. I looked under the table—we were on a sort of bench—and I couldn't find it, then I thought, maybe I'd left it at home! I'm always in a daze, I think, when I'm with Teresa. That's how it is—I want to faint. When I first see her—every time—I feel I can hardly breathe."

Tom closed his eyes for a second in sympathy. "You mustn't ever look nervous with a girl, Frank, even if you feel nervous."

"Yes, sir.— Anyway, that day, Teresa said, 'I'm sure you haven't lost it, look again,' and by this time even the waiter was helping me, and Teresa said she could pay the bill, and when she started to, she found I'd stuck my billfold in *her* handbag, because I'd had it out ahead of time and I was nervous. That's the way things always went with Teresa. I'd think things were awful—then things were rather lucky."

Tom understood. So could Freud have understood. Was this girl really lucky for Frank? Tom doubted that.

"I could tell you another story like that, but I don't want to bore you."

What was he getting at? Or did he just want to talk about Teresa?

"I really want to lose everything, Tom. Even my life, yes. It's hard for me to say in words. Maybe I could explain it to Teresa or at least say something, but now she doesn't even care. She's bored with me."

Tom pulled his cigarettes out and lit one. The boy was in a dream world and needed a jolt of reality. "While I'm thinking of it,

Frank, your Andrews passport. May I?" Tom gestured toward a
straight chair where Frank had hung his jacket.

"Go ahead, it's there," the boy said.

Tom got it from the inside pocket. "This goes back to Reeves."
Tom cleared his throat and continued. "Shall I tell you that I once
murdered a man in this house? Awful, isn't it? Under this roof.— I
could tell you the reason. That picture downstairs over the fireplace, 'Man in Chair'—" Tom suddenly realized that he couldn't
tell Frank that it was a forgery, and that a lot of Derwatts were forgeries now. When might Frank tell it to someone else months or
years from now?

"Yes, I like it," Frank said. "The man was stealing it?"

"No!" Tom put his head back and laughed. "I don't want to say
anymore. We are alike in a way, don't you think, Frank?" Did he see
the least relief in the boy's eyes or not? "Good night, Frank. I'll
wake you around eight."

In his room, Tom found that Mme. Annette had unpacked his
suitcase, so he would have to start over again with shaving kit and
so on. Heloise's present, the blue handbag, was on his desk now, still
in its white plastic bag. It was in a box, and Tom decided to smuggle the box to her room some time tomorrow morning, so that she
would find it after he had gone. Five past eleven now. Tom went
downstairs to ring Thurlow, even though there was a telephone in
his room.

Johnny answered, and said that Thurlow was taking a shower.

"Your brother wants me to come with him tomorrow, so I
will," Tom said. "I mean to America."

"Oh. Really? Well!" Johnny sounded pleased. "Here's Ralph.
It's Tom Ripley," Johnny said, and passed the telephone to Thurlow.

Tom explained again. "Can you get a place for me on the same
plane, do you think, or shall I try it tonight?"

"No, I'll handle it. I'm sure I can do it," Thurlow said. "This is
Frank's idea?"

"His wishes, yes."

"Okay, Tom. I'll see you tomorrow around ten then."

Tom took another warm shower, and looked forward to sleep-ing. Just that morning he had been in Hamburg, and what was dear old Reeves doing at this moment? Making another deal with someone over cool white wine in his apartment? Tom decided to leave all his packing until the morning.

In bed and with the light out, Tom found himself pondering the generation gap, or trying to. Didn't it turn up in every gener-ation? And didn't generations overlap, so that one could never point out a definite twenty-five year period of change? Tom tried to imagine what it was like for Frank to have been born when the Beatles were getting started in London (after Hamburg), then mak-ing their American tour, and changing the face of pop songs, to have been about seven when a man landed on the moon, when the United Nations as a peacekeeping organization was beginning to be laughed at and to be used. And before that, the League of Nations, hadn't it been? Ancient history, the League of Nations, which had failed to stop Franco and Hitler. Every generation seemed to have to turn loose of something, and then try desper-ately to find something new to hang onto. Now for the young it was gurus sometimes, or Hare Krishna, or the cult called the Moonies, and pop music all the time—social protesters sang to their souls sometimes. Falling in love, however, was out of date, Tom had heard or read somewhere, but he had not heard it from Frank. Frank was perhaps exceptional in even admitting that he was in love. "Play it cool, no strong emotions" was the tenet of youth. A lot of young people didn't believe in marriage, just in liv-ing together and having children sometimes.

Now where was he? Frank had said he wanted to lose himself. Did he mean turning loose of the Pierson family responsibilities? Suicide? Changing his name? What did Frank want to hang on to? Tom's sleepiness put an end to his efforts. Beyond his window an owl was calling "Chou-*ette*! Chou-*ette*!" In early September, Belle Ombre was sliding into autumn and winter.

20

Heloise drove Tom and Frank to the Moret railway station, and had offered to drive them to Paris. But she was going to Chantilly tonight to see her parents, so Tom persuaded her not to make the Paris drive besides. She sent them both off with well wishes and an extra kiss for Frank, Tom noticed.

Tom could not buy a *France-Dimanche*, the gossip sheet, at the Moret station, but it was the first thing he did when they arrived at the Gare de Lyon. It was only a little after nine, and Tom paused in the station to give the paper a look. He found Frank Pierson on page two, with the familiar old passport picture in one column instead of spread over two or more. MISSING AMERICAN HEIR WAS ON HOLIDAY IN GERMANY said the headline. Tom looked through the column, worried about finding his own name, but it was not there. Had Ralph Thurlow finally done a commendable piece of work? Tom felt relieved.

"Nothing alarming," Tom said to Frank. "Want to see it?"

"No, I don't, thanks." Frank lifted his head with what looked like a deliberate effort. He was again in a head-hanging mood.

They joined the taxi queue and rode to the Lutetia. Thurlow was in the lobby at the desk, paying his bill, in the act of writing a check.

"Good morning, Tom.— Hello, Frank! Johnny's upstairs making sure the luggage gets down."

Tom and Frank waited. Johnny emerged from an elevator, carrying a couple of airline bags. He smiled at his brother. "You see the *Trib* this morning?"

They had left Tom's house too early to see the *Trib*, and Tom hadn't thought of buying it. Johnny informed his brother that the *Trib* said he had been found in Germany, taking a vacation. And where was Frank supposed to be now, Tom wondered, though he did not put the question.

Frank said, "I know," and looked uncomfortable.

They needed two taxis. Frank wanted to ride with Tom, but Tom suggested that he go with his brother. Tom wanted a few minutes with Ralph Thurlow, for what they might be worth.

"You've known the Piersons for quite a while?" Tom began in a pleasant tone to Thurlow.

"Yes. I knew John for six or seven years. I was a partner of Jack Diamond. Private detective. Jack went back to San Francisco, where I'm from, but I stayed on in New York."

"I'm glad the papers didn't make much of Frank's reappearance. Is that due to your efforts?" Tom asked, eager to pay Thurlow a compliment, if he could.

"I hope so." Thurlow showed satisfaction. "I did my best to cool it. I'm hoping there're no journalists at the airport.— Frank hates all that, I know."

Thurlow smelled of some presumably masculine scent, and Tom inched back into the corner of his seat. "What kind of man was John Pierson?"

"Oh—" Thurlow slowly lit a cigarette. "A genius, I'm sure. Maybe I can't figure people like that out. He lived for his work— or money, which was like a score to him. Maybe it gave him emotional security, even more than his family. But he certainly *knew* his business. Self-made man, too, no rich father to get him started. John started out by buying a grocery store in Connecticut that was going broke, and then he went on from there, always in the food product line."

Another source of emotional security, Tom had always heard. Food. Tom waited.

"His first marriage.— He married a well-to-do Connecticut girl. I think she bored him. Fortunately no children. Then she met another man, maybe with a little more time to give her. So they got a divorce. Quietly." Thurlow glanced at Tom. "I didn't know John in those days, but I heard about all this. John was always a hard worker, wanted the best for himself *and* his family." Thurlow spoke with some respect.

"Was he a happy man?"

Thurlow looked out the window and wagged his head. "Who can be happy trying to manage so much money? It's like an empire.— A nice wife, Lily, nice sons, nice houses everywhere— but maybe incidental to a man like that. I don't know. He certainly was a lot happier than Howard Hughes." Thurlow laughed. "That man lost his mind!"

"Why do you think John Pierson killed himself?"

"I'm not sure he *did*." Now Thurlow looked at Tom. "What do you mean? Frank said that?" Thurlow's tone was easy.

Was Thurlow sounding him out? Trying to sound Frank out? Tom also wagged his head with deliberate slowness, even though the taxi was making a heavy swerve just then to pass a truck on the *périphérique* as they sped on northward. "No, Frank said nothing. Or he said what the papers said, that it could've been an accident or a suicide.— What's your opinion?'

Thurlow seemed to ponder, but his thinnish lips had a smile, a safe smile, Tom saw at a glance. "I do think suicide rather than an accident.— I don't *know*," Thurlow assured Tom, "it's only my guess. He was already in his sixties. How could a man be happy in a wheelchair—for a decade—half-paralyzed? John always tried to be cheerful—but maybe he'd had enough? I don't know. But I know he'd been to that cliff hundreds of times. There wasn't any wind to blow him over that day."

Tom was pleased. Thurlow didn't seem to suspect Frank. "And Lily? What's she like?"

"She's another world. She was an actress when John met her.— Why're you asking?"

"Because I suppose I'll meet her," Tom said, smiling. "Has she a favorite between the two boys?"

Thurlow smiled, relieved at an easy question. "You must think I know the family pretty well. I don't know them that well."

There Tom let the matter rest. They had exited at Porte de la Chapelle from the *périphérique* and entered the boring stretch of fifteen kilometers toward the horror called Charles de Gaulle Airport, nearly as offensive to Tom's eye as Beaubourg, but at least inside Beaubourg there were beautiful things to look at.

"How do you spend your time, Mr. Ripley?" Thurlow asked. "Someone told me you haven't a usual job. You know, an office—"

That was an easy question for Tom, because he had answered it many a time. There was gardening, he was studying the harpsichord, Tom said, he liked reading French and German, and he was always trying to improve himself in those languages. He could feel Thurlow regarding him as if he were a man from Mars, possibly also regarding him with distaste. Tom didn't mind at all. He had weathered worse than Thurlow. He knew Thurlow thought he was a borderline crook, with the luck to have married a well-to-do Frenchwoman. A gigolo, perhaps, a sponger, loafer, and parasite. Tom kept a bland expression on his face, since he might need Thurlow's help in the days ahead, even Thurlow's allegiance. Had Thurlow ever fought as hard for anything, Tom wondered, as he had to protect the Derwatt name—the Derwatt forgeries, really, but of course the earlier half of the paintings were *not* forgeries. Had Thurlow slain one or two Mafiosi, as had Tom? Or was it more correct now to call them "organized criminals," those sadistic pimps and blackmailers?

"And Susie?" Tom began again pleasantly. "I suppose you've met her?"

"Susie? Oh, Susie the housekeeper. Sure. She's been there for ages. Getting on in years, but they don't want to—to retire her."

At the airport, they could not find any luggage carts, so they hauled everything by hand to the check-in at TWA. Suddenly two or three photographers crouched with cameras on both sides of the queue. Tom lowered his head, and saw Frank cover his face calmly with one hand. Thurlow shook his head sympathetically at Tom. One journalist addressed Frank in French-accented English:

"You enjoy your holiday in Germany, Monsieur Pierson?— Have you something to say about France?— Why—why did you try to hide?"

His camera hung big and black in front of him from a cord around his neck, and Tom had an impulse to seize it and break it over his head, but the man swung it up and snapped Frank, just as Frank turned his back on him.

After the check-in, Thurlow sprang to the fore in a manner that Tom admired, shouldering aside the press—four or five by now—like a football linesman as they made directly for Satellite Number Five escalator and the passport control that would give them a barrier.

"I am going to sit next to my friend," Frank said firmly to the stewardess when they were all aboard the plane. Frank meant Tom.

Tom let Frank handle it, and one man was willing to change his seat, so Tom and Frank were side by side in a row that held six. Tom had the aisle seat. It was not Concorde, and Tom did not relish the thought of the next seven hours. A bit strange Thurlow had not bought first class, Tom thought.

"What did you and Thurlow talk about?" Frank asked.

"Nothing important. He was asking how I spent my time." Tom chuckled. "And you and Johnny?"

"Also nothing important," Frank replied rather curtly, but Tom knew the boy by now and didn't mind.

Tom hoped that Frank and Johnny had not talked about Teresa, because Johnny seemed to have no sympathy for the department of lost loves. Tom had brought three books to read, which he had in a plaid carryall. There were the inevitable, indefatigable small children—all three of them American—who started running up and down the aisle, though Tom had thought he and Frank might escape their racket, being seated at least eighteen rows away from the kids' presumable base. Tom tried reading, snoozing, thinking—though it was not always good to try to think. Inspiration, good or productive ideas seldom came that way. Tom woke up from a semi-doze with the word "*Showmanship!*" strongly in his ears or in his brain, and sat up, blinked at the technicolor Western now in progress on the screen in the middle of the plane, silent to him, because he had declined earphones. Showmanship how? What was he supposed to do at the Piersons'?

Tom picked up a book again. When one of the odious four-year-olds ran for the umpteenth time up the aisle toward him, babbling nonsense, Tom stretched back and put a foot out slightly into the aisle. The little monster fell on its belly with, seconds afterward, a wail like that of a wronged banshee. Tom feigned sleep. A bored stewardess came from somewhere to set the little thing upright. Tom saw a satisfied smirk from a man seated across the aisle from him. Tom was not alone. The child was steered back to its place forward, no doubt to recover *pour mieux sauter*, as the French said, in which case Tom thought he might leave the pleasure of tripping it to another passenger.

When they got to New York, it was early afternoon. Tom craned to look out the window, thrilled as always by the Manhattan skyscrapers made hazy as an Impressionist painting now by fluffy white and yellow clouds. Beautiful and admirable! Nowhere in the world did so many buildings stretch so high in such a tiny area! Then they were down with a dull thud, moving like cogs again, passports, luggage, frisking. And then the rosy-cheeked man whom Frank identified to Tom as Eugene, the chauffeur. Eugene, rather short and balding, looked happy to see Frank.

"Frank! How *are* you?" Eugene seemed friendly and at the same time polite and correct. He had an English accent, and wore ordinary clothes with shirt and tie. "And Mr. Thurlow. Greetings!— And Johnny!"

"Hello, Eugene," Thurlow said. "And this is Tom Ripley."

Tom and Eugene exchanged a "How do you do?" then Eugene continued, "Mrs. Pierson had to go to Kennebunkport early this morning. Susie wasn't feeling well. Mrs. Pierson said either to come to the apartment and stay the night, or we can take a copter from the heliport."

They were all standing in bright sunshine, luggage on the pavement, hand luggage still in hand, at least Tom's was.

"Who's at the apartment?" Johnny asked.

"No one just now, sir. Flora's on vacation," said Eugene. "We've rather closed the apartment, in fact. Mrs. Pierson said she *might* come down midweek, if Susie—"

"Let's go to the apartment," Thurlow interrupted. "It's on the way, anyway. All right with you, Johnny? I'd like to phone the office. I might have to drop in there today."

"Sure, it's okay. I also want to look at my mail," said Johnny. "What's the matter with Susie, Eugene?"

"Not quite sure, sir. Sounded as if she might've had a slight heart attack. I know they sent for the doctor. This was at noon today. Your mother telephoned. I drove down yesterday with her and we stayed the night at the apartment. She wanted to meet you in New York." Eugene smiled. "I'll just go get the car. Back in two minutes."

Tom wondered if it was Susie's first heart attack. Flora, Tom supposed, was one of the servants. Eugene returned, driving a large black Daimler-Benz, and they all got in. There was even room for their luggage. Frank sat in front with Eugene.

"Everything's okay, Eugene?" Johnny asked. "My mother?"

"Oh, yes, sir, I think so. She's been worried about Frank—of course." Eugene drove stiffly and efficiently, reminding Tom of a Rolls-Royce brochure he had once read, informing drivers that they should never rest an elbow on the windowsill, because it looked sloppy.

Johnny lit a cigarette and pushed something in the beige leather upholstery which caused an ashtray to appear. Frank was silent.

Third Avenue now. Lexington. Manhattan looked like a honeycomb compared to Paris, little cells everywhere, buzzing with activity, human insects crawling in and out, carrying things, loading, walking, bumping into one another. In front of an apartment house with an awning that extended to the curb, the car came to a quiet stop, and a smiling doorman in a gray uniform opened the door of the car, after a touch of his fingers to his cap.

"*Good* afternoon, Mr. Pierson," the doorman said.

Johnny greeted him by name. Glass doors, and then they rode up in an elevator, while the suitcases went up in another elevator.

"Anybody got the key?" asked Thurlow.

"I have," Johnny said with an air of pride, and pulled a key ring from his pocket.

Eugene was putting the car away somewhere.

The apartment was marked 12A. They went into a spacious foyer. Some of the chairs in the big living room bore white protective covers, the ones nearest the windows, though the windows now had their venetian blinds down and closed, so that one needed electric light to see properly. Johnny took care of both—smiling as if he were happy to be home, if this were home—slid the blind cords so that more light came in, then turned on a standing lamp. Tom saw Frank lingering in the hall, looking through a stack of some dozen letters. The boy's face remained tense, a bit frowning. Nothing from Teresa, Tom thought. But the boy's step into the living room was almost a saunter. He looked at Tom and said:

"Well, well, Tom—this is it. Or part of it. Our home."

Tom gave a polite smile, because Frank wanted that. Tom strolled toward a mediocre oil above the fireplace—did the fireplace work?—of a woman Tom supposed was Frank's mother: blonde, pretty, made-up, posed with hands not in lap but stretched out, as were the arms, along the back of a pale green sofa. She wore a black sleeveless dress with an orange-red flower in her belt. The mouth was gently smiling, but so worked over by the painter, Tom did not look for reality or character in it. What had John Pierson had to pay for this mess? Thurlow was on the telephone in the foyer, speaking perhaps to his office. Tom was not interested in what he might have to say. Now Tom saw Johnny in the hall looking at the letters, pocketing two, opening a third. Johnny looked cheerful.

In the living room two large brown leather sofas—Tom could just see the bottom part of the side of one under the white sheet—made a right angle, and there was a grand piano with a music score propped up. Tom moved closer to see what the music was, but two photographs atop the piano distracted him. One was of a dark-haired man holding a baby of perhaps two, the baby laughing and blond: Johnny, Tom supposed, and the man was John Pierson, looking hardly forty, smiling with friendly dark eyes in which Tom thought he saw a resemblance to Frank's. The second picture of John looked equally attractive, John in white shirt with no tie, wearing no glasses, in the act of taking a pipe from his smiling mouth as a wraith of smoke drifted up. It was difficult to imagine John the elder a tyrant or even a tough businessman from these pictures. The sheet music on the piano had "Sweet Lorraine" written in scrolly letters on its cover. Did Lily play? Tom had always liked "Sweet Lorraine."

Eugene arrived, and Thurlow came in just then from another room, carrying what looked like a scotch and soda. Eugene at once asked Tom if he would like some refreshment, tea or a drink, and Tom declined. Then Thurlow and Eugene discussed the next move. Thurlow was for taking a helicopter, and Eugene said of course that could be done, and were they all going? Tom looked at Frank, and would not have been surprised if Frank had said he preferred to stay in New York and with Tom, but Frank said:

"All right, yes. We'll all go."

Then Eugene made a telephone call.

Frank beckoned Tom into a hall. "Would you like to see my room?" The boy opened the second door on the right in the hall. Again venetian blinds had been drawn, but Frank pulled a cord so that they admitted light.

Tom saw a long trestle-based table, books neatly set in a row at the back against the wall, stacked spiral-backed school notebooks, and two pictures of the girl he recognized as Teresa. In one picture she was by herself with a tiara, a lei of flowers, white dress, pink lips smiling a mischievous smile, eyes bright. The belle of the ball that night, Tom supposed. The other picture, also in color, was smaller: Frank and Teresa standing in what looked like Washington Square, Frank holding her hand, Teresa in bell-bottomed beige jeans and blue denim shirt, with a little sack of something—peanuts maybe—in one hand. Frank looked handsome and happy, like a boy who was sure of his girl.

"My favorite picture," said Frank. "Makes me look older. That was just—maybe two weeks before I went to Europe."

Meaning about a week before he killed his father. Tom again had the disturbing, very strange doubt: *had* Frank killed his father? Or was it a fantasy? Adolescents did have fantasies and hung on to them. And might Frank? Frank had an intensity of a kind that Johnny showed not at all. It was going to take ages for Frank to recover from Teresa, for instance, and by ages Tom thought of perhaps two years. On the other hand, to fantasize about killing his father, and to have told Tom about it, would have been a way of calling attention to himself, and Frank was not the type to do that.

"What're you thinking about?" Frank asked. "Teresa?"

"Are you telling me the truth about your father?" Tom asked softly.

Frank's mouth became suddenly firm in a way that Tom knew well. "Why would I ever lie to you?" Then he shrugged as if ashamed of being so serious. "Let's go out."

He just might lie, Tom thought, because he believed more in fantasy than in reality. "Your brother doesn't suspect at all?"

"My brother—he asked me and I said I didn't—push—" Frank broke off. "Johnny believed me. I think he wouldn't even want to believe the truth if I told him."

Tom nodded, and also nodded toward the door of the room. Before he went out, Tom glanced at the hi-fi and the handsome three-tiered case of records near the door. Then Tom went back and pulled the venetian blinds' cord the way it had been. The rug was dark purple, as was the cover of the bed. Tom found the color pleasing.

They all went down and got two taxis, and headed for the Midtown Heliport on West Thirtieth Street. Tom had heard of the heliport, but never been here. The Piersons had their own helicopter, with room for a dozen people, it seemed, though Tom didn't count the seats. There was leg room, a bar, an electronic kitchen.

"I don't know these people," Frank said to Tom, referring to the pilot and the steward who was taking drink and food orders. "They're employed by the heliport."

Tom ordered a beer and a cheese sandwich on rye. It was now just after five, and the trip was going to take about three hours, someone had said. Thurlow sat beside Eugene in seats nearer the pilot. Tom looked out of his window and watched New York drop below them.

Chop-chop-chop, as the comic strips said. Mountains of buildings sank below, as if being sucked downward, reminding Tom of a film being turned in reverse. Frank sat across the aisle from Tom. There was no one behind them. Now the steward and the pilot up front were telling jokes, or so it seemed from their laughter. On their left, an orange sun hung above the horizon.

Frank sank himself in another book, one he had taken from his room. Tom tried to snooze. It seemed the best thing to do, in view of the fact they all might be up late tonight. For Tom, Frank, and Thurlow, also Johnny, it was about two in the morning. Thurlow was already asleep, Tom saw.

A different pitch of the motor's buzz awakened Tom. They were descending.

"We're landing on the back lawn," Frank said to Tom.

It was almost dark. Now Tom saw a big white house, impressive yet somehow friendly with its yellowish lights glowing under two porch roofs on two sides. And maybe mother would be standing on one porch, Tom thought, as if welcoming a son who came trudging home with a handkerchief of possessions on a stick over his shoulder. Tom realized that he was curious about the Pierson establishment here, not their only house, of course, but an important one. The sea lay on their right, and Tom could see a couple of lights out there, of buoys or of small craft. And there, suddenly, *was* Lily Pierson—Mama—on the porch, waving! She appeared to be wearing black slacks and blouse, in the semi-darkness Tom couldn't tell, but her fair hair showed in the porch's light. Beside her stood a thicker figure, a woman wearing mostly white.

The helicopter touched ground. They descended steps that had been flipped out.

"*Franky!* Welcome *home!*" called his mother.

The woman beside her was a black, smiling also, coming forward to help with the luggage which Eugene and the steward were taking from a side hatch.

"Hello, Mom," said Frank. He put his arm nervously or a bit tensely around his mother's shoulder, and did not quite kiss her cheek.

Tom watched from a distance, as he was still on the lawn. The boy was shy, but he did not dislike his mother, Tom thought.

"This is Evangelina," Lily Pierson was saying to Frank, indicating the black woman walking toward them with somebody's suitcase now. "My son Frank—and Johnny," she said to Evangelina. "And how are you, Ralph?"

"Very fine, thank you. This is—"

Frank interrupted Thurlow. "Mom, this is Tom Ripley."

"I'm so happy to meet you, Mr. Ripley!" Lily Pierson's made-up eyes gave Tom a searching inspection, though her smile looked friendly enough.

They were ushered into the house, assured by Lily that they could leave their jackets and raincoats in the hall or anywhere. And had they had anything to eat, or were they exhausted? Evangelina had prepared a cold supper, if anyone wished to partake. Lily's voice did not sound nervous, only hospitable. Her accent combined New York and California, Tom thought.

Then they all sat down in the large living room. Eugene disappeared in the same direction as Evangelina, perhaps to the kitchen where the helicopter crew probably was. And there was the painting, the Derwatt that Frank had mentioned on his second visit to Belle Ombre. This was "The Rainbow," a Bernard Tufts forgery.

Tom had never seen the painting, simply remembered its title from
a Buckmaster Gallery report to him on sales maybe four years ago.
Tom recalled also Frank's description of it: beige below, being the
tops of a city's buildings, and a mostly dark-reddish rainbow above
with a little pale green in it. *All fuzzy and jagged*, Frank had said.
You can't tell what city it is, Mexico or New York. And so it was, and
well pulled off by Bernard, with dash and assurance in that rainbow, and Tom took his eyes away with reluctance, not wanting to
be asked by Mrs. Pierson if he was especially fond of Derwatts.
Thurlow and Lily Pierson were talking now, Thurlow telling the
Paris events (telephone calls), and about Frank and Mr. Ripley
spending a couple of nights in Hamburg after Berlin, which of
course Lily Pierson must already have known. It was strange, Tom
thought, to be sitting on a sofa much bigger than his own, in front
of a fireplace also bigger than his own, over which hung a phony
Derwatt, just as "Man in Chair" at his own house was phony.

"Mr. Ripley, I've heard through Ralph about your fantastic
help to us," said Lily, blinking her eyelids. She sat on an oversized
green hassock between Tom and the fireplace.

To Tom "fantastic" was an adolescent's word. He realized that
he used the word "fantastic" in his thoughts, but not in his speech.
"A little realistic help, maybe," Tom said modestly. Frank had left
the living room, and so had Johnny.

"I do want to thank you. I can't put it into words because—I
know for one thing you risked your life. That's what Ralph said."
She had the clear diction of an actress.

Had Ralph Thurlow been so kind?

"Ralph says you didn't even use the *police* in Berlin."

"I thought it best to do without the police, if I could," said
Tom. "Sometimes kidnappers panic.— As I said to Thurlow, I think
the kidnappers were amateurs in Berlin. Rather young and not
well organized."

Lily Pierson was observing him closely. She looked hardly
forty, but was probably a bit more, slender and fit, with the blue
eyes that Tom had seen in the oil painting in New York, suggesting

that her blonde hair was real. "And Frank was not hurt at all," she said, as if she marveled at the fact.

"No," said Tom.

Lily sighed, glanced at Ralph Thurlow, then back at Tom. "How did you and Frank meet?"

Frank came back into the living room just then. The corners of his mouth looked tighter. Tom supposed that he had looked for a letter or a message here from Teresa, and again found none. The boy had changed his clothes, and now wore blue jeans, sneakers, and a yellowish Viyella shirt. He had heard the last question, and said to his mother, "I looked Tom up in the town where he lives. I had a part-time job in a town nearby—gardening."

"Really? Well—you always wanted to be that—do that." His mother looked a bit stunned, and blinked her eyes again. "And where are these towns?"

"Moret," Frank said. "That's where I was working. Tom lives about five miles away. His town is called Villeperce."

"Villeperce," his mother repeated.

Her accent made Tom smile, and he stared at "The Rainbow," loving it.

"Not far south of Paris," said Frank, standing straight, and speaking with what Tom thought was unusual preciseness. "I knew Tom's name, because Dad mentioned Tom Ripley a couple of times—in connection with our Derwatt painting. Remember, Mom?"

"No, I frankly don't," said Lily.

"Tom knows the people at the gallery in London. Isn't that true, Tom?"

"Yes, I do," said Tom, calmly. Frank was in a way boasting about him as an important friend and—maybe, Tom thought—deliberately creating an opening for either his mother or Thurlow to bring up the matter of the authenticity of some pictures signed Derwatt. Was Frank going to defend Derwatt and all the Derwatts, even the possible phonies? They didn't get that far.

Evangelina slowly and surely brought platters and wine to a

long table in a room behind Tom, and she was aided by Eugene. While this was going on, Lily proposed showing Tom his room.

"I'm so pleased you can stay at least a night with us," said Lily, leading Tom up some stairs.

Tom was taken into a large square room with two windows, which Lily said looked onto the sea, though the sea was not visible now, only blackness. The furniture was white and gold, and there was a bathroom adjoining, also in white and gold, and even the towels were yellow, and some of the fixtures including a small chest of drawers were adorned with gold scrolls in imitation of the room's furniture, which was Louis Quinze *véritable*.

"How is Frank really?" asked Lily with a frown that put three anxious lines across her forehead.

Tom took his time. "I think he's in love with a girl called Teresa. Do you know anything about Teresa?"

"Oh—*Teresa*—" The room door was ajar, and Lily glanced at it. "Well, she's the third or fourth girl that *I've* heard of. Not that Frank talks to me at all about his girlfriends—or even much else—but *Johnny* finds out somehow.—What do you mean about Teresa? Frank's been talking a lot about her?"

"Oh, no, not a lot. But it seems he's in love with her now. She's been to the house here, hasn't she? You've met her?"

"Yes, sure. *Very* nice girl. But she's only sixteen. So is Frank." Lily Pierson looked at Tom as if to say, of what importance can this be?

"Johnny told me in Paris that Teresa has another interest. An older man, shall we say. I think that upset Frank."

"Oh, probably. Teresa's so pretty, she's awfully *popular*. A girl sixteen—she'll prefer somebody twenty or even older." Lily smiled, as if the subject were finished.

Tom had been hoping to draw from Lily some remark on Frank's character.

"Frank'll get over *Teresa*," Lily added cheerfully, but in a soft voice, as if Frank might be in the hall and able to listen.

"One more question, Mrs. Pierson, while I have the chance. I think Frank ran away from home because he was upset about his father's death.— Isn't that the main reason? More than because of Teresa, I mean, because at that time from what Frank told me, Teresa hadn't cooled off."

Lily seemed to be choosing her words before she spoke. "Frank was upset about John's death, more than Johnny was, I know. Johnny's sometimes in the clouds with his photography and *his* girls."

Tom looked at Lily's twisted face, and wondered if he dared ask her if she thought her husband had killed himself? "Your husband's death was called an accident, I read in the newspapers. His wheel-chair went over that cliff."

Lily gave a shrug, like a twitch. "I really don't *know*."

The room door was still ajar, and Tom thought of closing it, of suggesting that Lily sit down, but would that interrupt the flow of truth, if she knew it? "But you think it was an accident rather than a suicide?"

"I don't know. The ground slopes up a little there, and John never sat at the very edge. That would've been stupid. And his chair had a brake, of course. Frank said he just zoomed over suddenly— and why should he have put the power on unless he wanted to?" Again the troubled frown, and she glanced at Tom. "Frank came running toward the house—" She did not go on.

"Frank told me your husband was disappointed because nei-ther of the boys wanted to— They didn't take much interest in his work. The Pierson business, I mean."

"Oh, *that*, true. I think the boys are terrified of the *business*. They consider it too complicated or they just don't like it." Lily glanced toward the windows as if the *business* might have been a big black storm coming up outside. "It was a disappointment to John, certainly. You know how a father wants *one* of his sons any-way to take over. But there're other people in John's family—he always called his office people his family too—who *can* take over.

Nicholas Burgess, for instance, John's right-hand man and only forty now. It's hard for me to believe a disappointment in the boys could've made John want to kill himself, but I think he could've done it because he really felt—ashamed of being in a chair. Tired of it, I know that. And then at sunset— He always got emotional about sunsets. Not emotional, but *affected*. Happy and sad, like the end of something. Not even the sun there, but dusk falling over the water in front of him."

So Frank had come running toward the house. Lily had spoken as if she had seen him. "Frank often went out with his father? On the cliff?"

"No." Lily smiled. "Bored Frank. He said John wanted him to go with him that afternoon. John often *did* ask Frank. John was always counting on Frank more than on Johnny—between you and me." She laughed a little, mischievously. "John said, "There's something more solid in Frank, if I can just bring it out. Shows in his face." He meant compared to Johnny, who's more of a—I don't know—a dreamer type."

"I was reminded of George Wallace's case, when I read about your husband. John perhaps had periods of depression."

"Oh-h, not really," said Lily with a smile now. "He could be serious and grim about his work, pull a long face one day if something went wrong, but that's not the same as being depressed. Pierson Incorporated, business, whatever he called it, was like a big chess game to John. That's what a lot of people said. You win a little one day and lose a little the next, and the game is never over— not even now that John's gone. No, I think John was an optimist by nature. He could always smile—nearly always. Even in the years when he was in his chair. We always called it his chair, not a wheelchair. But it was sad for the boys, so far as having a father went, because that's all the boys have known of him for such a long time in their lives—a businessman in a chair, talking about markets and money and people—everything invisible somehow. Not able to go out for walks or teach the boys judo or whatever fathers usually do."

Tom smiled. "Judo?"

"John used to do judo in this very room! It wasn't always a guest room, this room."

They were moving toward the door. Tom glanced at the high ceiling, the wide floor that would have provided space for mats and somersaults. Downstairs the others were in the living room buffeting themselves, as Tom always thought when he encountered the word "buffet," but in this case there was plenty of room and no elbowing crowd. Frank was drinking a Coca-Cola from the bottle. Thurlow stood by the table with Johnny, holding a scotch highball and a plate of food.

"Let's go out," Tom said to Frank.

Frank set his bottle down at once. "Out where?"

"Out on the lawn." Lily had joined Johnny and Thurlow, Tom saw. "Did you ask about Susie? How is she?"

"Oh, conked out asleep," said Frank. "I asked Evangelina. What a name! She belongs to some nutty soul group. Been here just a week, she says."

"Susie's here?"

"Yes, she has a room in the back wing upstairs. We can go out this way."

Frank was opening a large French window in what must be their main dining room, Tom thought. There was a long table with chairs around it, and smaller tables with chairs near the walls, sideboards, and some bookcases also. There were platters and a cake on the table now. Frank had put on an outside light, so they could see their way across a terrace and down four or five steps to the lawn. To the left of the steps sloped the ramp that Frank had told him about. After that, it was dark, but Frank said he knew the way. A stone path was palely visible, extending across the lawn, then curving to the right. As Tom's eyes became more adjusted to the darkness, he could see tall trees, pine or poplar, ahead.

"This is where your father used to walk?" Tom asked.

"Yes, well—not walk. He had his chair." Frank slowed and stuck his hands into his pockets. "No moon tonight."

The boy had stopped and was ready to go back to the house, Tom saw. Tom took a couple of deep breaths and looked back at the two-story white house with its yellowish lights. The house had a peaked roof, the porches' roofs projected to left and right. Tom didn't like the house. It looked newish, and of no definable style. It was not like an American southern house or a New England colonial house. John Pierson had probably had it built to order, but at any rate Tom didn't care for the architect. "I wanted to see the cliff," Tom said. Didn't Frank know that?

"All right, it's this way," Frank said, and they walked on along the flagstone path into deeper darkness.

The flagstones were still visible, and Frank walked as if he were sure of every inch of it. The poplars closed in, then parted, and they were on the cliff, and Tom could see its edge, defined by light colored stones or pebbles.

"The sea's out there," said Frank, gesturing. He hung back from the edge.

"I assumed that." Tom could hear waves below, gentle, not pounding and not rhythmic, but rather lapping. And far out in the blackness, Tom saw a boat prow's white light, and imagined he saw a pinkish port light. Something like a bat whizzed by overhead, but Frank seemed not to have noticed it. *So here is where it happened*, Tom thought, then he saw Frank walking past him, hands in the back pockets of his jeans, to the edge of the cliff, and he saw the boy look down. Tom had an instant's fear for Frank, because it was so dark, and the boy seemed so near the edge, even though the edge did slope up a little, Tom could now see. Frank turned back suddenly and said:

"You were talking with Mom tonight?"

"Oh, yes, a bit. I asked her about Teresa. I know Teresa's been here.— I suppose she didn't write you?" Tom thought it better to ask him outright than not to say anything about a letter.

"No," Frank said.

Tom went closer to him, until they were only four or five feet apart. The boy stood straight. "I'm sorry," Tom said. He was thinking that the girl had troubled to telephone Thurlow in Paris, once, days ago, and now that Frank was found, and safe, she was simply dropping out, with no explanation.

"Is that all you talked about? Teresa?" Frank asked in a light tone that might have implied that that was not very much to talk about.

"No, I asked her if she thought your father's death was a suicide or an accident."

"And what did she say?"

"That she didn't know. You know, Frank—" Now Tom spoke softly. "She doesn't suspect you *at* all—and you'd better let this thing blow over. Just that. Maybe it has. It's done. Your mother said, 'Suicide or accident, it's done.' Something like that. So you must pick yourself up, Frank, and get rid of—I wish you wouldn't stand so near the edge." The boy was facing the sea, raising and lowering himself on his toes, whether aggressively or absentmindedly, Tom couldn't tell.

Then Frank turned and walked toward Tom, and passed Tom on the left. The boy turned again and said, "But you know I did send that chair over. I know you were talking to my Mom about what she might think or believe, but I *told* you.— I mean, I said to my mother my father did it himself, and she believed me, but that's not true."

"All right, all right," Tom said gently.

"When I sent my father's chair over, I even thought I was with Teresa—that she—liked me, I mean."

"All right, I understand," Tom said.

"I thought, I'll get my father out of my life, out of our lives, for me and Teresa. I felt my father was spoiling—life. It's funny that Teresa gave me courage then. And now she's gone. Now there's nothing but silence—nothing!" His voice cracked.

Odd, Tom thought, that some girls meant sadness and death. Some girls looked like sunlight, creativity, joy, but they really meant death, and not even because the girls were enticing their victims, in fact one might blame the boys for being deceived by—nothing at all, simply imagination. Tom laughed suddenly. "Frank, you *have*

to realize that there are other girls in the world! You must see it by
now that Teresa— She's turned loose of you. So you must turn
loose of her."

"I have. I did that in Berlin, I think. The real crisis was there,
when I heard what Johnny said." Frank gave a shrug, but was not
looking at Tom. "Sure, I looked for a letter from her, I admit that."

"So you go on from here. Things look rotten now, but there
are a lot of weeks and years ahead for you. Come on!" Tom
slapped the boy on the shoulder. "We'll go back to the house in a
minute. Wait."

Tom wanted to see the edge, and moved forward toward the
lighter colored rocks. He could feel pebbles and a bit of grass under
his shoes. He could feel also the emptiness below, now black, but
giving out something like a sound of hollow space. And there,
unable to be seen now, were the jagged rocks that Frank's father
had fallen onto. Tom turned at the sound of the boy's steps toward
him, and at once moved away from the edge. Tom had had a sudden feeling that the boy might rush him and push him over. Was
that insane on his part, Tom wondered. The boy adored him, Tom
knew that. But love was strange too.

"Ready to go back?" Frank asked.

"Sure." Tom felt the coolness of sweat on his forehead. He
knew he was more tired than he thought, and that he had lost track
of time because of the airplane trip.

21

Tom fell asleep almost before he got into bed. Some time later,
he awakened with a violent twitch of his entire body. A bad
dream? If so, he didn't remember a dream. How long had he been
asleep? An hour?

"*No!*" That had been a whisper or a soft voice outside his room
in the hall.

Tom got out of bed. The voices outside went on, a cooing, pigeon-like female voice mingling with Frank's. Tom knew Frank's room was next to his on the right. Only a few words came through, said by the woman: ". . . so *impatient* . . . I *know* . . . what, *what* will you do . . . not matter to *me!*"

That had to be Susie, and she sounded angry. Tom could detect her German accent. And in fact he could have put his ear to the door and heard more, but Tom had an aversion to eavesdropping. He turned his back to the door, groped forward toward his bed, and found his night table, on which lay cigarettes and matches. Tom struck a match, put on his reading lamp, lit a cigarette, and sat down on his bed. That was better.

Had Susie knocked on Frank's door? More likely than that Frank had knocked on hers! Tom laughed, and lay back on his bed. He heard a door close, gently nearby, and that would be Frank's door. Tom stood up, put his cigarette out, and stepped into his loafers, which were serving again as house-slippers as they had in Berlin. He went into the hall, and saw a light under Frank's closed door. Tom rapped with his fingertips.

"Tom," he said, when he heard a soft, quick tread coming toward the door.

Frank opened the door, hollow-eyed with fatigue, but smiling. "Come *in!*" he whispered.

Tom did. "That was Susie?"

Frank nodded. "Got a smoke for me? Mine are downstairs."

Tom had his in the pocket of his pajamas. "Well, what's she on about?" He lit the boy's cigarette.

Frank said, "Fwoop!" and blew out smoke, nearly laughing. "She still says she saw me on the cliff."

Tom shook his head. "She's going to have another heart attack. Want me to talk with her tomorrow?— I'm curious to meet her." He looked behind him at the closed door, because Frank had looked at it. "Does she wander around at night? I thought she was ill."

"Strength of an ox, maybe." Frank was weaving with tiredness, and fell back on his bed with his bare feet in the air for an instant.

Tom glanced around the room, saw an antique brown table on which stood a radio, a typewriter, books, a tablet of writing paper. On the floor near half-open closet doors he saw ski boots and a pair of riding boots. Pop singer posters were tacked to a vast green pinup board above the brown table, the Ramones slouching in blue jeans, and below all this were cartoons, a couple of photographs, maybe of Teresa, but since Tom did not want to bring that subject up, he did not look closely. "Damn her ass," Tom said, meaning Susie, "she *didn't* see you. You don't expect another visit from her tonight, do you?"

"Old witch," Frank said, with his eyes half closed.

Tom waved a hand, and went out and back into his room. He noticed that his own room door had a key in the lock on the inside. Tom did not lock it.

The next morning, after the breakfast ritual, Tom asked Mrs. Pierson's permission to cut a few flowers from the garden to bring to Susie. Lily Pierson said of course he could. As Tom had supposed, Frank knew more about the garden than his mother, and assured Tom that his mother wouldn't care what they cut. They amassed a bouquet of white roses. Tom preferred to make his visit to Susie without preparation, as it were, but Tom asked Evangelina—appropriate name—to herald his advent. The black maid did so, then asked him to wait, please, for two minutes in the hall.

"Susie likes to comb her hay," said Evangelina with a happy smile.

After a couple of minutes, Tom was summoned by a guttural or sleepy "Come in," and he knocked first, then entered.

Susie was propped against pillows in a whitish room now made whiter by sunlight. Susie's hair looked yellowish and grayish also, her face round and seamed, eyes tired and wise. She reminded Tom of some German postage stamps of famous women whom, usually, Tom had never heard of. Her left arm, in a long white nightdress sleeve, lay outside the covers.

"Good morning. Tom Ripley," Tom said. Friend of Frank's, he

thought of saying, but stopped himself. Maybe she had heard of him already, via Lily. "How are you feeling this morning?"

"Reasonably well, thank you."

A television set was facing her bed, reminding Tom of some hospital rooms he had visited, but the rest of the room was personal enough, with old family pictures, crocheted doilies, a bookcase full of knickknacks, souvenirs, even an old top-hatted minstrel doll that might have been a relic of Johnny's childhood. "I'm glad to hear that. Mrs. Pierson told me that you had a heart attack.— I'm sure that's frightening."

"Yes, when it is the first," she replied in a grumbling voice. She was keeping a sharp, pale blue eye on Tom.

"I was just—Frank was with me for several days in Europe. Maybe Mrs. Pierson told you." Tom got no response to this, and looked for a vase to put the flowers in, and didn't see one. "I brought these to brighten your room a little." Tom advanced with a smile, with his bouquet.

"Thank you very much," said Susie, taking the bouquet with one hand—Frank had put a napkin around it—and pressing a bell at her bedside with the other.

In no time, there was a knock, Evangelina entered, and was handed the bouquet and requested by Susie to find a vase, please.

Tom was not offered a chair, but he took a straight chair anyway. "I suppose you know—" Tom wished he had ascertained Susie's last name. "—that Frank was very upset by his father's death. Frank looked me up in France, where I live. That's how I met him."

She looked at him, still sharply, and said, "Frank is not a good boy."

Tom stifled a sigh, and tried to look pleasant and polite. "He seems quite a nice boy to me—stayed in my house several days."

"*Why* did he run away?"

"I think he was upset. Well, all he did—" Did Susie know about Frank taking his brother's passport? "Lots of young people run away. And then come back."

"I think Frank killed his father," said Susie tremulously, wagging the forefinger of the hand that lay outside the covers. "And that is a terrible thing."

Tom inhaled slowly. "Why do you think that?"

"You are not surprised? Has he confessed it to you?"

"He certainly has not. No. I'm asking you why you think he did." Tom frowned with seriousness, and he was affecting some surprise too.

"Because I saw him—almost."

Tom paused. "You mean on the cliff there."

"*Yes.*"

"You saw him—You were out on the lawn?"

"No, I was upstairs. But I saw Frank go out with his father. He *never* went out with his father. They had just finished a game of croquet. Mrs. Pierson—"

"Mr. Pierson played croquet?"

"Yes, sure! He could move his chair just where he wanted it. Mrs. Pierson always wanted him to play a little—to take his mind off—you know, business worries."

"Frank was playing that day too?"

"Yes, and Johnny too. I remember Johnny had a date—went off. But they all played."

Tom crossed his legs, wanted a cigarette and thought it best not to light one. "You told Mrs. Pierson," Tom began with an earnest frown, "that you thought Frank pushed his father over?"

"Yes," said Susie firmly.

"Mrs. Pierson doesn't seem to think that."

"Did you ask her?"

"Yes," said Tom with equal firmness. "She thinks it was either an accident or a suicide."

Susie sniffed, and looked toward her TV, as if she wished it were on.

"Did you say the same thing to the police—about Frank?"

"Yes."

"And what did they say?"

"Ah, they said I couldn't have seen it, because I was upstairs. But there are some things a human being *knows*. You know, Mr.—"

"Ripley. Tom. I am sorry I don't know your last name."

"Schuhmacher," she replied, just as Evangelina entered with the roses in a pink vase. "Thank you, Evangelina."

Evangelina set the vase on the night table between Tom and Susie, and left the room.

"Unless you did see Frank do it—which must be impossible if the police said so—you should not say it. It has troubled Frank very much."

"Frank was with his father." Again the plump but slightly wrinkled hand lifted and fell on the bedcover. "If it was an accident, even a suicide, Frank could have stopped him, no?"

Tom at first thought Susie was right, then he thought of the speed the chair controls must have been capable of. But he didn't want to go into this with Susie. "Couldn't Mr. Pierson have sent his chair over by himself, before Frank knew what was happening? That's what *I* thought."

She shook her head. "Frank came back running, they said. I didn't see him till I went downstairs. Everyone was talking then. Frank said his father drove his chair over, I know." The pale blue eyes were fixed on Tom.

"That's what Frank told me too." The moment of lying must have been like a second crime for Frank. If the boy had only come back calmly, let half an hour pass, as if he had left his father on the cliff! That, Tom realized, was what he would have done—nervous though he might have been, he would have done a little bit of *planning*. "What you think or believe—can certainly never be proven," Tom said.

"Frank denies it, I know."

"Do you want the boy to have a breakdown because of your—accusation?" At least Susie seemed to pause at this, and Tom pushed his advantage, if he had any, and he wanted to imagine that he had for the moment. "Unless there's a witness or some real evidence, an act such as you describe can never be proven—or even believed in this case." And when was the old lady going to die, Tom wondered, and let Frank off the hook? Susie Schuhmacher looked capable of another few years, and Frank could hardly separate himself from her, because she was installed in the Kennebunkport house, where the family evidently stayed quite often, and she probably went to their New York apartment also, when the family was there.

"Why should I care what Frank makes of his life? He—"

"You don't like Frank?" Tom asked, as if amazed.

"He is—not friendly. He is rebellious—unhappy. You never know what he is thinking. He gets ideas and hangs on to them. Attitudes."

Tom frowned. "But would you call him dishonest?"

"No," Susie replied, "he is too polite. It goes beyond dishonesty, what I mean. More important even—" She seemed to be getting tired. "But what should I care what he does with his life? He has everything. He does not appreciate what he has, never did. He gave his mother worries, running off the way he did. He doesn't even care about that. He is not a good boy."

It was not a time, Tom thought, to launch into Frank's fear or dislike of his father's business empire, or even to ask what she might know of the influence of Teresa. Now Tom heard a telephone ringing remotely from somewhere. "But Mr. Pierson liked Frank very much, I think."

"Maybe too much. Did the boy deserve it? Look!"

Tom uncrossed his legs and squirmed. "I think I've taken enough of your time, Mrs. Schuhmacher—"

"That's all right."

"I'll be leaving tomorrow, maybe even this afternoon, so I'll say good-bye now and give you my good wishes for your health. In fact, I think you look very well," he added, meaning it. He had stood up.

"You live in France."

"Yes."

"I think I remember Mr. Pierson mentioning your name. You know the art people in London."

"Yes, indeed," Tom replied.

She lifted her left hand again, and let it fall, and looked toward the window.

"Bye-bye, Susie." Tom made a bow, but Susie didn't see it. Tom left the room.

In the hall, Tom ran into Johnny, lanky and smiling.

"I was just coming to rescue you! Would you like to see my dark room?"

"Sure," Tom said.

Johnny turned and led Tom to a room on the left side of the hall. Johnny switched on red lights, which gave the effect of a black cavern with pink air in it, something like a stage set. The walls looked black, even the lump of a sofa black, and in a far corner Tom barely detected the paleness of what looked like a long sink. Johnny switched off the red and put on ordinary light. A couple of cameras stood on tripods. The black sheets now seemed minimal. It was not a big room. Tom was not knowledgeable about cameras. He didn't know what to say when Johnny pointed to a camera that he had just acquired, except, "Really impressive."

"I could show you some of my work. Nearly all of it's in port-folios here, except one downstairs in the dining room which I call 'White Sunday,' but it's not snow. But—I think just now Mom wants to talk with you."

"Now? Does she?"

"Yes, because Ralph's leaving, and Mom said she wanted to see you after he left.— How was Susie?" There was amusement, or anticipation of it, in the boy's smile.

"Pleasant enough. Looking pretty strong, I thought. Of course I don't know how she usually looks."

"She's a bit cracked. Don't pay too much attention to anything she says." Johnny stood straight, still smiling a little, but his words sounded like a warning.

Johnny was protecting his brother, Tom felt. Johnny knew what

Susie was saying, and Frank had told Tom that Johnny didn't believe it. Tom went downstairs with Johnny, and found Mrs. Pierson and Ralph Thurlow with his raincoat over his arm. Thurlow must have slept late today, because Tom had not seen him until now.

"Tom—" Ralph Thurlow extended a hand. "If you ever need a job—along the same lines—" He fished for something in his billfold, and extended a card. "Ring my office, would you? My home address is there too."

Tom smiled. "I'll remember."

"I really mean, let's have an evening in New York sometime. I'm off to New York now. Bye-bye, Tom."

"Bon voyage," Tom said.

Tom had thought that Thurlow was going to depart in the black car in the driveway, but Mrs. Pierson and Thurlow went out onto the porch and walked to the left. Tom saw that a helicopter had landed or been rolled out onto the cement circle on the back lawn. The property was so vast, Tom supposed that the Piersons might have their own hangar somewhere at the end of the cement runway, which disappeared among trees. This helicopter looked smaller than the one they had taken from New York, but perhaps he was simply getting used to the scale on which the Piersons lived. Tom looked at the black Daimler-Benz whose exhaust pipe gave out faintly visible fumes, and saw that Frank was at the wheel, alone. The car moved forward two yards or so, then reversed, smoothly.

"What're you doing?" Tom asked.

Frank smiled. He was in shirtsleeves—the same yellowish Viyella shirt—and sat very straight as if he were a chauffeur in livery. "Nothing."

"You've got a driving license?"

"Not yet, but I know how to drive. Do you like this car? I like it. Conservative."

It was similar to the car Eugene had driven in New York, but the upholstery of this one had brown leather instead of beige.

"Don't take off anywhere without a license," Tom said. The boy looked in a mood to take off, though he was working the gears very slowly and meticulously. "See you later. I'm supposed to speak with your mother."

"Oh?" Frank switched off the ignition and looked at Tom through the open window. "And what did you think of Susie?"

"She was—the same as always, I suppose." Susie was giving the same old story, Tom meant. Frank looked both amused and thoughtful, and at that moment he looked very handsome, perhaps a few years older than he was. It crossed Tom's mind that Frank might have had a telephone call from Teresa that morning, but Tom was afraid to ask. Tom went back to the house.

Lily Pierson, wearing pale blue slacks this morning, was giving Evangelina instructions about lunch. Part of Tom's mind was on his own departure. Should he try to get to New York this evening? Stay a night in New York? He should give Heloise a ring today.

Lily turned to him, smiling. "Sit down, Tom. Oh no, let's go in here—more cheerful." She led him toward a sunny room off the living room.

It was a library, full of economics books in bright new jackets, Tom saw at a glance, with a big square desk on which sat a pipe rack with five or six pipes in it. The dark-green leather swivel chair behind the desk looked both old and unused, and it occurred to Tom that John Pierson might not have found it worth the trouble to move himself from wheelchair to the leather chair, when he was in this room.

"And what did you think of Susie?" Lily asked in the same tone as her sons, smiling with her lips pressed together, as were her hands. She looked eager to be amused.

Tom nodded with an air of thought. "Just what Frank told me. A bit stubborn—perhaps."

"And she still thinks Frank pushed his father over the cliff?" Lily asked in a tone that implied that the idea was absurd.

"So she thinks, yes," Tom said.

"No one believes her. There's nothing to believe. She didn't *see* anything. I really can't keep on worrying about Susie. She could make anyone as eccentric as *she* is.— I wanted to say to you, Tom, that I realize you've had a lot of expenses due to Frank, and so without any more words about it, would you please accept this check from me, from the family." She had pulled a folded check from the pocket of her blouse.

Tom looked at it. Twenty thousand dollars. "My expenses were nothing like this. Anyway, it was a pleasure to meet your son." Tom laughed.

"It would give *me* pleasure."

"My expenses weren't half this." But in an instant, in the way she brushed her hair back from her forehead unnecessarily, Tom knew that it would please her if he accepted the check. "All right, then." Tom put the check into his trousers pocket, and kept his hand there. "With my thanks also."

"Ralph told me about Berlin. You risked your life."

Tom was not interested in that now. "Did Frank possibly get a telephone call from Teresa this morning, do you know?"

"I don't think so. Why?"

"I thought he looked more cheerful just now. But I don't know." Tom really didn't know. He knew only that Frank was in a different mood, one that he had not seen before.

"You can never tell about Frank," said Lily. "From the way he acts, I mean."

Meaning that Frank could act the opposite from the way he felt? Lily was so relieved to have Frank back home, that factors like Teresa just didn't count for much, Tom supposed.

"My friend Tal Stevens is coming this afternoon, and I'd like you to meet him," Lily said as they walked out of the library. "One of John's best lawyers, though he never was employed by the company, he was just a freelance counsel."

This was the friend Lily liked, according to Frank. Lily was saying that Tal had work this afternoon, so probably couldn't arrive until six. "And I have to see about taking off," Tom said. "I thought of staying a day or so in New York."

"But you're not leaving *today*, I hope. Phone your wife in France and tell her. That's the thing to do!— Frank says you have such a pretty house there. He was telling me about your greenhouse and—the two Derwatts you have in your living room and also about your harpsichord."

"Was he?" His and Heloise's French harpsichord amid helicopters, Maine lobsters, and an American black named Evangelina! It struck a surrealist note to Tom. "With your permission," Tom said, "I will make a phone call or two."

"Make yourself at home here, Tom!"

From his room Tom telephoned the Hotel Chelsea in Manhattan, and asked if they had a single room for that night. A friendly voice said they could probably manage it with a little bit of Irish luck. That was good enough. Tom thought he should take his leave after lunch. Some neighbors called the Hunters were coming at four, Lily had said, because they were very fond of Frank and wanted to see him. Tom supposed that the Pierson household could get him some kind of transportation to Bangor, whence he could take a plane to New York.

Maine lobster was exactly what they had for lunch, as if Tom had received a premonition. Before lunch, he and Frank had driven to the town of Kennebunkport with Eugene at the wheel of a station wagon, and picked up the commanded lobsters. The town had sent a wave of nostalgia over Tom that had almost brought tears to his eyes: white house fronts and store fronts, a freshness in the sea air, sunlight, and American sparrows in trees still heavy with summer foliage—all of which had made Tom think he had made a mistake in leaving America. But this he had put out of his head at once, since it was a depressing and baffling feeling, and he had reminded himself that he was going to bring Heloise to America in late October, or whenever she got back and recovered from her Adventure Cruise, which as Tom recollected was to the Antarctic.

Though Frank had looked surprised and disappointed when Tom said he was leaving that afternoon, the boy appeared cheerful at lunch. Was Frank pretending good humor, Tom wondered?

Frank had put on a handsome pale-blue linen jacket, though he
still wore his blue jeans. "The same wine we drank at Tom's," he
said to his mother, lifting his stemmed glass with a flourish.
"Sancerre. I asked Eugene to find it. In fact I went to the cellar
with him to get it."

"It is *delicious*," said Lily, smiling at Tom, as if it were Tom's wine
and not hers.

"Heloise is very pretty, Mom," Frank said, and dipped a fork
with lobster into his melted butter.

"You think so? I'll tell her," said Tom.

Frank placed a hand over his stomach and pretended to belch,
a silent performance that was also half a bow, for Tom's benefit.

Johnny devoted himself to his food, and said only something
to his mother about a girl called Christine possibly coming at
seven, and he didn't know whether they would go somewhere for
dinner or stay in.

"Girls, girls, girls," Frank said contemptuously.

"Shuddup, you little twit," murmured Johnny. "Are you jealous
maybe?"

"Now stop it, both of you," said Lily.

It sounded like a usual family lunch.

By three, Tom had made his arrangements, reserved a place on
an early evening flight from Bangor to Kennedy Airport, and
Eugene would drive him to Bangor. Tom packed his suitcase but
did not close it. He went into the hall and tapped on Frank's
slightly open door. There was no answer. Tom pushed the door
wider and went in. The room was empty and tidy, the bed probably having been made by Evangelina. On Frank's desk sat the
Berlin bear, some twelve inches high, its beady brown eyes ringed
with yellow, its mouth jolly though closed. Tom remembered
Frank's amusement at the handwritten sign: 3 WÜRFE 1 MARK.
Frank had thought *Würfe* a funny word for throws, because it
sounded like something to eat, or maybe a dog's bark. How had the
little bear survived a kidnapping, a murder, a couple of airplane

trips, and come out looking as fluffy and cheerful as ever? Tom had wanted to ask Frank to join him for another walk to the cliff. Tom had the feeling that if he could get the boy used to the cliff, though "used" wasn't quite the right word for it, Frank's guilt might be diminished.

"I think Frank went off with Johnny to get his bicycle tires pumped up," Lily said to Tom downstairs.

"I thought he might come for a little walk, since I've got about an hour," Tom said.

"They should be back any minute, and I'm sure Frank *would*. He thinks you hung the *moon*, Tom."

Tom hadn't heard this complimentary term since he had been a teenager in Boston. He went out onto the lawn, onto the flagstone path. He wanted to see the cliff by daylight. Somehow the path seemed longer, then suddenly he was beyond the trees, with the beautiful view of blue water before him, perhaps not as blue as the Pacific, but still very blue and clean now. Seagulls let themselves be borne on the wind, and three or four little boats, one a sailboat, moved slowly on the wide surface. And then the cliff. It was a sudden ugliness to Tom. He walked closer to its edge, looking down at the grass that merged with stones then rock, and finally stopped with his feet eight or ten inches from the drop. Below, just as he had imagined, boulder-sized beige and white rocks lay tumbled as if by some landfall or rockfall in the not too distant past. Down where the water began, he could see little white waves lapping against the smaller rocks. He looked, stupidly, for some sign of the John Pierson catastrophe, such as a piece of chrome from the chair. He saw nothing manmade down there. John Pierson, if he had merely toppled his chair over at not much speed, would have hit jagged rocks thirty feet below, and would possibly have tumbled another couple of yards downward. Not even any bloodstains on the rocks now, Tom saw, and shuddered. He backed from the edge and turned.

He glanced toward the house, which was hardly visible

through the trees, just its dark gray roof ridge showing, and then he saw Frank on the path coming toward him, still in his blue jacket. Was the boy looking for him? Without thinking, Tom stepped to his right into a cluster of trees and behind some bushes. Would the boy look around? Call his name, if Frank thought he might have walked here? Tom realized that he was curious—maybe just to see the expression on the boy's face as he approached the cliff. Now Frank was so close, Tom could see his straight brown hair bobbing a little with his steps.

Frank's eyes looked to left and right, at the trees, but Tom was well hidden.

And also, Tom thought, probably his mother hadn't told Frank that he had gone to the cliff, because Tom hadn't said that. At any rate, Frank did not call Tom's name, and did not look around again. Frank had his thumbs hooked in the front pockets of his Levi's, and he strode slowly toward the cliff's edge, a little arrogantly, swinging his feet. Now the boy's whole figure was silhouetted against the beautiful blue sky, just perhaps twenty feet from Tom. The boy looked down. But mostly he looked at the sea, and he seemed, to Tom, to take a deep breath and to relax. Then he stepped backward, as Tom had done, looking down at his sneakered feet. He kicked his right foot backward, scattering a few pebbles, and took his thumbs from his pockets. He bent forward and at once ran.

"Hey!" Tom shouted, and drove forward himself. Somehow he tripped, or perhaps had merely launched himself horizontally, but his hands had been extended, and he had Frank by one ankle.

Frank was flat down, gasping, and his right arm hung over the cliff's edge.

"God's *sake!*" Tom said, and gave Frank's ankle a nervous tug toward him. Tom got to his feet, and hauled Frank up by one arm.

The breath was knocked out of the boy, and his eyes looked glazed and unfocused.

"What the hell were you doing?" Tom realized that his voice had gone hoarse suddenly. "Wake up!" Tom steadied Frank, felt in

THE BOY WHO FOLLOWED RIPLEY

a state of shock himself, and pulled the boy by his arm toward the woods, the path. A bird cried just then, an odd squeak, as if the bird also was shocked. Tom stood up straighter and said, "All right, Frank. You almost did it. Same as doing it, isn't it?— Quick reflex from hearing my voice? You flopped down like a football player!" Or had he? Had Tom stopped him by catching one ankle? Tom slapped the boy nervously on the back. "You've done it once now, okay. All right?"

"Yep," said Frank.

"You mean it," Tom said, as if asking him. "Don't just say 'Yep' to me. You proved what you wanted to prove. Okay?"

"Yes, sir."

They were walking back toward the house. The wobbliness slowly left Tom's legs, and he deliberately breathed deeply. "I won't mention this. Let's not mention this to anybody. All right, Frank?" He glanced at the boy who seemed as tall as himself suddenly.

Frank was looking straight ahead, not at the house but beyond. "Right, Tom, sure."

22

When Tom and Frank got back to the house, the Hunters had arrived. Tom would not have known this, if Frank had not pointed out a green car in the driveway. Tom would have thought it one of the Piersons' cars.

"I'm sure they're up in the *ocean view* room," Frank said, as if putting "ocean view" in quotes. "Mom always serves tea up there." He looked at Tom's suitcase, which someone had taken down and set near the front door.

"Let's have a drink of something. I could use one," Tom said, and went to the sideboard or bar table which was nearly three yards long. "Any Drambuie, I wonder?"

"Drambuie? I'm sure there is."

Tom watched him bend over the double row of bottles, index finger extended to the left, then the right, and he found it and hauled it up, smiling.

"I remember this from your house." Frank poured some into two brandy glasses.

Frank's hand was steady, Tom saw, but his face looked still pale as he lifted his glass. Tom joined him, and touched the boy's glass. "This will do you good."

They drank. Tom noticed that the bottom button of his jacket front was hanging by a couple of threads, so he pulled it off and pocketed it, and brushed some dust away. The boy's jacket had a rent about an inch long on the right breast.

Frank swung on one heel of his sneaker, made a complete turn, and asked, "What time do you have to leave?"

"Around five." Tom saw by his wristwatch that it was a quarter past four. "I don't feel like saying good-bye to Susie," Tom said.

"Oh, let it go!"

"But your mom—"

They went upstairs. Some color had returned to Frank's cheeks, and his step was springy. Frank rapped on a white, half-open door, and he and Tom went in. This was a large room with wall-to-wall carpeting and three broad windows which took up the whole opposite wall and gave a view on the sea. Lily Pierson sat near a round low table, and a middle-aged couple who Tom supposed were the Hunters sat in armchairs. Johnny was standing up with a handful of photographs.

"Where have you *been*?" asked Lily. "Come in, both of you. Betsy, this is Tom Ripley—who I've been *talking* so much about. Wally—finally *Frank* is back."

"Frank!" said the Hunters almost simultaneously, as the boy strolled forward, bowed a little, and shook Wally's hand. "Are you boring these people with your junk again?" Frank asked his brother.

THE BOY WHO FOLLOWED RIPLEY

"Finally I've met you," said Wally Hunter, shaking Tom's hand and looking into Tom's eyes as if he, Tom, might be a miracle worker—or someone who might not really have existed—but Tom's hand hurt.

The Hunters, he in a tan cotton suit and his wife in a mauve cotton dress, looked the picture of Maine summer chic.

"Tea, Frank?" asked his mother.

"Yes, please." Frank had not yet sat down.

Tom declined tea. "I should be taking off, Lily." She had asked him to call her Lily. "Eugene said he could drive me to Bangor."

Both Johnny and his mother spoke at once. Of course Eugene would drive him to Bangor. "Or I can," Johnny said. They informed Tom that there were at least ten minutes to spare before he had to leave. Tom did not want to talk about the events in Europe, and Lily managed to steer Wally Hunter off, promising to tell him about France and Berlin at some other time. Betsy Hunter kept rather cool gray eyes on Tom, but Tom felt indifferent to what she might be thinking about him. Tom also felt indifferent to the arrival of Talmadge Stevens, earlier than expected. The Hunters seemed to know him and like him, judging from their greetings.

Lily introduced him to Tom. He was a bit taller than Tom, looked in his mid-forties, and was the rugged type who perhaps jogged. Tom at once sensed that Lily and Tal had an affair going. And so what? Where was Frank? He had slipped out of the room. Tom slipped out too. Tom thought he had heard music—maybe one of Frank's records—a minute ago.

Frank's room was across the hall and more toward the back of the house. His door was closed. Tom knocked and got no answer. He opened the door a little. "Frank?"

Frank was not in the room. The gramophone cover was off, with a record on it, but the machine was not turning. Tom saw that it was the Lou Reed *Transformer*, the second side, which Heloise had put on at Belle Ombre. Tom glanced at his watch: nearly five, and he and Eugene were supposed to leave at five. Probably

Eugene was downstairs at the back of the house where the servants' quarters seemed to be.

Tom went downstairs to the empty living room, and just
then heard a clap of laughter from upstairs in the ocean view
room. Tom made his way across another central living room with
windows on the garden, found the hall again, and continued
toward the back of the house, where he thought the kitchen was.
The kitchen doors stood open, and the walls glowed with
copper-bottomed pans and skillets. Eugene stood drinking a cup
of something, rosy-cheeked, talking with Evengelina, and
jumped to attention at the sight of Tom. Tom had somehow
expected to see Frank here.

"Excuse me," Tom said. "Have you—"

"I'm watching the time, sir, for five o'clock. I have seven to.
May I help you with your luggage?" Eugene had set his cup and
saucer down.

"Thanks, no, it's down. Where's Frank? Do you know?"

"I think he's upstairs, sir, having tea," Eugene said.

No, he's not, Tom started to say, and didn't. Tom felt suddenly
alarmed. "Thanks," he said to Eugene, and hurried through the
house to the nearest exit, which was what Tom thought of as the
front door, onto a porch, then around to the right to the lawn.
Maybe Frank was upstairs, again, in the room where people were
having tea, but Tom wanted to go to the cliff first. He imagined
seeing the boy standing at the edge again, contemplating—what?
Tom ran all the way. Frank was not there. Tom slowed, gasping, not
from lack of breath but from relief. As he walked closer to the edge,
he became again afraid. He kept going.

There below was the blue jacket, the darker blue of the Levi's,
the dark head of hair with an outline of red—flower-like, unreal,
yet real against nearly white rocks. Tom opened his mouth, as if he
were about to yell something, but he did not. He did not even
breathe for several seconds, until he realized that he was shaking,
and in danger of falling over the edge himself. The boy was dead,

and there was no use of anything, of trying anything by way of saving him.

Tell his mother, Tom thought, as he started back toward the house. Good Christ, all the people up there!

When Tom entered the house, he encountered Eugene, pink and alert. "Something the matter, sir? It's just two to five now, so we—"

"I think we have to call the police now—an ambulance or something."

Eugene looked Tom up and down as if for injuries.

"It's *Frank*! He's on the cliff there," Tom said.

Eugene suddenly understood. "He's *fallen*?" He was ready to run out.

"I'm sure he's dead. Can you telephone the hospital or whatever you're supposed to do? I'll tell Mrs. Pierson.— Hospital first!" Tom said, when Eugene showed a sign of wanting to dash out of the French windows.

Tom braced himself for the upstairs, and went on. He knocked on the tea party door, and entered. They all looked comfortable now, Tal leaning on the end of the sofa near Lily, Johnny still standing, talking to Mrs. Hunter. "Can I speak with you for a minute?" Tom said to Lily.

She got up. "Something the matter, Tom?" she asked, as if she thought he might only have changed his travel plans, which would not have inconvenienced anyone.

Tom spoke with her in the hall, after he had closed the door. "Frank just jumped off the cliff there."

"Wha-at? Oh, *no*!"

"I went to look for him. And I saw him below. Eugene's phoning the hospital—but I think he's dead."

Tal suddenly opened the door, and his expression at once changed. "What's up?"

Lily Pierson could not speak, so Tom said, "Frank just jumped off the cliff."

"That *cliff*?" Tal was about to run down the hall, but Tom made a gesture, as if to say *it's done*.

"What's the trouble?" Johnny came through the door, and behind him the two Hunters.

Tom heard Eugene pounding up the stairs, and went down the hall to meet him.

"Ambulance *and* the police should be here in a few minutes, sir," Eugene said quickly, and went past Tom.

Tom looked farther up the hall, and saw a white figure—no, pale blue, paler than Frank's jacket—Susie. Eugene, who had passed the others, said a word to Susie. Susie nodded, and gave even a faint smile, Tom thought. Johnny just then ran past Tom, on his way to the stairs.

Two ambulances came, one bearing reviving apparatus, from what Tom could see as two white-clad men hurried across the lawn, guided by Eugene. Then came a folding ladder. Had Eugene instructed them, or did they remember the cliff from John Pierson's mishap? Tom hung back near the house. He emphatically did not want to see the boy's smashed face, wanted to leave at once, in fact, though knew that he couldn't. He would have to wait until the boy was up to the lawn level, until he had said a few more words to Lily. Tom went back into the house, glanced at his suitcase, which was still by the front door, then he went up the stairs. He had an impulse to go into Frank's room again, for the last time.

In the upstairs hall, he saw Susie Schuhmacher standing at the far end of the hall, her hands spread behind her and touching the wall. She looked at him and nodded, or Tom thought she did. He walked on to Frank's door and a little past it. Susie was nodding. What did she want? Tom looked at her as if fixated, but he also frowned at her.

"You see?" Susie said.

"No," Tom said firmly. Was she trying to cow him, convince him? Tom felt an animal-like hostility toward her, a sense of self-preservation that would see him through. He continued to walk toward her. He stopped about eight feet from her. "What are you talking about?"

"Frank—of course. He was a bad boy and at least he *knew* it." Now she was moving with just a little feebleness toward Tom and to her right, to go back to her room. "And you are maybe the same," she added.

Tom retreated one step back, mainly to keep a certain distance from her. He turned and went back to Frank's door, and into the room. He closed the door, feeling angry, but the anger ebbed a little. That terribly neat bed! Where Frank would never sleep again. And the Berlin bear. Tom moved toward it slowly, wanting it. Who would ever know, or care, if he took it? Tom picked it up gently by its furry sides. A square of paper on the table caught Tom's eye. It lay to the left of where the bear had sat. "Teresa, I love you forever," Frank had written. Tom let his held breath out. Absurd! But of course it was true, because Frank had died in the last half hour. Tom didn't touch the note, though it crossed his mind to take the note away and destroy it, as one might do a service for a dead friend. But Tom went out only with the bear, and closed the door.

Downstairs, he stuck the bear into a corner of his suitcase, turning its nose inward so it would not be mashed. The living room was empty. They were all on the lawn, Tom saw, and one ambulance was departing. Tom did not want to look out again onto the lawn. He wandered around in the living room, and lit a cigarette.

Eugene appeared, and said that he had telephoned the airport at Bangor. There was another plane Tom might get, if he should wish, if they left in fifteen minutes. Eugene was the servant again, though a lot paler in the face.

"That's fine," Tom said. "Thank you for seeing about that." Tom went out onto the lawn to speak with Frank's mother, just at the moment when a stretcher covered in white was being slid into the back of the one remaining ambulance.

Lily sank her face onto Tom's shoulder. There were words, from everybody, but Lily's tight grip on Tom's shoulders had more meaning. Then Tom was in the backseat of one of the big cars, being driven by Eugene toward Bangor.

He arrived at the Hotel Chelsea by midnight. People were singing in the lobby, which had a square fireplace and black-and-white plastic sofas, chained to the floor against theft. The lyric was a limerick, Tom recognized, and amid much laughter the Levi's-clad boys and a few girls were trying to fit it to guitar music. Yes, there was a room for Mr. Ripley, said the tweedy man behind the desk. Tom glanced at the oil paintings on the walls, some donated by clients who couldn't pay their bills, Tom knew. He had a general impression of tomato red. Then he went up in an old-fashioned elevator.

Tom took a shower, put on his least-good trousers, and lay on his bed for a few minutes, trying to relax. It was hopeless. The best thing to do was to eat something, though he wasn't hungry, walk around a bit, and then try to sleep. At Kennedy Airport he had made a reservation for tomorrow evening to go to Paris.

So Tom went out and walked up Seventh Avenue, passed the closed and still-open delicatessen shops, snack shops. The pavement dully glistened with discarded metal beer-top rings. Taxis lurched drunkenly into potholes and rumbled out and onward, reminding Tom somehow of Citroëns in France, big, lumbering, and aggressive. Ahead and on both sides of the avenue rose tall black buildings, some office buildings, some residences, like solid hunks of land up there in the sky. Lots of windows were lighted. New York never slept.

Tom had said to Lily, "There is no reason for me to stay now." Tom had meant stay for the funeral, but he had also meant that he couldn't do anything more for Frank. Tom had not told her about the boy's first attempt to kill himself hardly an hour earlier. Lily just might have said, "Why didn't you keep an eye on him afterward?" Well, Tom had thought, wrongly, that Frank's crisis had passed.

He went into a corner snack shop which had stools at a

counter, and ordered a hamburger and a coffee. He did not want
to sit down, and standing up was certainly permitted. Two black
customers were having an argument over a bet they had made, over
the possible crookedness of the bookie they had both used. It
sounded fantastically complicated, and Tom stopped listening. He
could ring up a couple of friends in New York tomorrow, he
thought, just to say hello. The idea, however, did not attract him.
He felt lost and purposeless, awful. He ate half the hamburger,
drank half of the weak coffee, paid, and went out, and walked up
to Forty-second Street. Now it was nearly two in the morning.

This was more cheerful, like a crazy circus or a stage-set
through which he was permitted to wander. Huge cops in blue
short-sleeved shirts swung their wooden nightsticks and joshed
with the prostitutes whom they were supposed to round up, Tom
had read lately. Had the cops rounded up the same ones so often,
that they'd got tired of it? Or were they in process of rounding
these up? Teenaged boys with makeup and very wise eyes sized up
the older men, some with money already in their hands, who were
ready to buy them.

"No," Tom said softly, ducking his head at the approach of a
blonde girl whose thighs bulged horribly under shiny black plastic. Tom read with amazement the blunt and banal film titles on the
cinema marquees. Such a lack of talent in the porn department!
But this clientele didn't want subtlety or wit. And all the blown-up
color photos of men and women, men and men, women and
women, naked and presumably making it, and Frank had not made
it with Teresa the one time he had tried! Tom laughed a little, with
a bizarre amusement. Suddenly he had had enough, and went trotting through the shuffling blacks, the pasty-faced whites toward the
darkish blob of the big public library on Fifth Avenue. He didn't
go as far as Fifth, but turned southward on Sixth Avenue.

A sailor hurtled out of a bar on Tom's right and collided with
Tom. The sailor fell on the ground, and Tom hauled him up, steadied him with one hand, and reached for his white cap, which had

fallen off. The boy looked in his teens and was swaying like a mast in a storm.

"Where're your chums?" Tom asked. "Haven't you got chums in there?"

"I wanna taxi and I wanna girl," said the boy, smiling.

He looked healthy, and probably a couple of scotches and six beers had put him into this state. "Come on." Tom took his arm and pushed the bar door open, looking for other sailor uniforms. Tom saw two at the bar, but a barman came round toward Tom and said:

"We don't want him in here and we're not serving him!"

"Aren't these his friends?" Tom asked, pointing to the two sailors.

"We do' *want* him!" said one of the two sailors, also a bit drunk. "He can get the fuck *out!*"

Tom's charge was now leaning against the doorjamb, resisting the efforts of the barman to wrestle him out.

Tom went up to the two at the bar, not caring a damn if he got a sock in the jaw for his trouble. Tom said with as tough a New York accent as he could put on, "Take care of your pal! That's a hell of a way to treat a guy in the same uniform, no?" Tom looked at the second sailor, who was not quite so under the influence, and saw that he had got through to him, because he shoved himself from the bar. Tom walked toward the door and looked back.

The soberer sailor was approaching his drunken pal, reluctantly.

Well, that was something, Tom thought as he went out, though very little. He walked back to the Chelsea. Here people were a bit pissed, or gay, or merry in the lobby, but the scene was sedate compared to Times Square. The Chelsea was famous for its eccentric patrons, but usually they kept themselves within a certain bound.

Tom thought of ringing Heloise, since it would be around nine in the morning there, and didn't. He realized that he was shattered. *Shattered.* And how had he escaped a punch in the ribs from the sailors in that bar? Tom realized that he had been lucky once again. He fell into bed, not caring when he woke up.

Should he telephone Lily tomorrow? Or would it even disturb her, upset her? Was she taking care of such things as deciding what kind of coffin would be appropriate? Would Johnny suddenly grow up and take charge? Would Tal take charge? Would Teresa be told, and would she come to the funeral, the cremation, or whatever it would be? Did he have to think about this tonight, Tom asked himself as he tossed in his bed.

Only by 9 p.m. the next evening did Tom regain some kind of composure, a sense of returning to himself. The engines had started on the airplane, and he seemed suddenly to wake up, as if he were home already. He felt happy, or happier, and he was escaping from—what? He had acquired another suitcase, at Mark Cross this time, as Gucci had become so ultra snob, Tom was inclined to boy-cott it, and the new suitcase was full of things he had bought: a sweater for Heloise, an art book from Doubleday's, a blue-and-white striped apron for Mme. Annette with a red pocket on which was printed OUT TO LUNCH, plus a small gold pin, also for Mme. Annette because her birthday was soon, the pin in the shape of a flying goose with little spiked reeds of gold below, a good-looking passport case for Eric Lanz. Tom had not forgotten Peter in Berlin. He would look for something special for him in Paris. Tom watched Manhattan's fairyland of lights gently rising and falling with the plane's movement, and he thought of Frank being buried soon in the same body of land. When the American coast was out of sight, Tom closed his eyes and tried to fall asleep. But he kept thinking of Frank, and finding it hard to believe that the boy was dead. It was a fact, and yet that fact was something that Tom could not make real as yet. He had thought sleep would be a help, but he had awakened this morning with the same sense of fantasy about Frank's death—as if he might look now across the plane's aisle and see Frank sitting there, smiling at him, surprising him. Tom had to remember the white sheet over the stretcher. No intern would pull a sheet all the way over someone's head, unless the person beneath was dead.

He would have to write to Lily Pierson, a proper letter in longhand, and Tom knew he could do it, politely and tenderly and all that, but what could Lily ever know about the little garden house in Moret where Frank had slept, or about Berlin, or even about Teresa's power over her son? Tom wondered what had been Frank's last thought as he fell downward onto the rocks? Teresa? A memory of his father falling fatally downward onto the same rocks? Had the boy possibly thought of him? Tom shifted in his seat and opened his eyes. The stewardesses had begun to circulate. Tom sighed, not caring what he ordered, beer, a scotch, food, or nothing.

What a joke, Tom thought, how useless now were the rather carefully considered lectures he had given Frank on the subject of "money" or "money and power"! Use it a little, even enjoy it a little, Tom had said, and stop feeling guilty. Give some to charity, to art projects, to whatever you like, and to whomever needs it. Yes, and he had also said, as had Lily, that there were others who could take over the administration of Pierson, at least until Frank finished school and even after that. But Frank would have had to poke his nose a little bit into Pierson, have his name (maybe along with his brother's) at the head of the directors' list, and Frank hadn't wanted even that.

At some point, miles high and in a black sky, Tom went to sleep under a blanket provided by a redheaded stewardess. When he woke up, the sun was rising and blazing—as out of step with time, it seemed, as anything else, and the airplane was over France, according to the announcement which had awakened Tom.

Roissy again, and the Satellites' shiny escalators, one of which Tom rode down with his hand luggage. He could have run into trouble with his new suitcase and its contents, but Tom put on a glassy unconcern, and made it through the Nothing to Declare barrier. He checked the timetable in his wallet, decided on a train, then rang Belle Ombre.

"Tome!" Heloise said. "You are *where*?"

She couldn't believe that he was at Charles de Gaulle Airport, and he couldn't believe that she was so close. "I can be in Moret at twelve-thirty easily. I just looked it up." Tom was suddenly smiling. "Everything okay?"

Everything was, except that Mme. Annette had a sprained knee from a fall or slip on the stairway. But even that did not sound serious, as she was getting about as usual, Heloise said. "Why didn't you write me—or telephone?"

"I was there such a short time!" Tom replied. "Just two days! I'll tell you about it when I see you. Twelve thirty-one."

"A bientôt, chéri!" She was going to fetch him.

Tom taxied to the Gare de Lyon with his luggage—which had still not been overweight—and boarded the train for Moret with *Le Monde* and *Le Figaro*. He was nearly finished scanning the papers, before he realized that he had not looked for anything about Frank, and realized also that there would barely have been time for a report of his death in these papers. Was it going to be, again, a possible "accident"? What was his mother going to say? He thought that Lily was going to say that her son was a suicide. And let history or gossip make what they wished of the two deaths there within the same summer.

Heloise awaited him beside the red Mercedes. The breeze blew her hair about. She saw him and waved, though he couldn't wave back with two suitcases plus a plastic bag of Dutch cigars, newspapers, and paperbacks. He kissed Heloise on both cheeks and on her neck.

"How are you?" Heloise asked.

"Ah-h," said Tom, loading his suitcases into the trunk.

"I thought you might be back again with Frank," she said, smiling.

It was amazing to Tom how happy she looked. When, he thought as they drove away from the station, should he tell her about Frank? Now Heloise—who had said she wanted to drive—was in the clear of traffic and light signals and heading for

Villeperce. "I may as well tell you now, Frank died the day before yesterday." Tom glanced at the steering wheel as he spoke, but Heloise's hands only tightened on it for a second.

"What do you mean *died*?" she asked in French.

"He jumped over that same cliff where his father died. I'll explain better at the house, but I somehow didn't want to say it in front of Madame Annette, even in English."

"What cliff do you mean?" Heloise asked, still in French.

"The cliff on their land in Maine. It overlooks the sea."

"Ah, yes!" Heloise suddenly remembered, perhaps from the newspaper stories. "You were there? You *saw* him?"

"I was at the house. I didn't see him, no, because the cliff's some distance away. I'll—" Tom was finding it difficult to speak. "Really there isn't much to tell. I spent one night at the house. I was intending to leave the next day—which I did. His mother and a couple of her friends were having tea. I went out to look for the boy."

"And you saw he had jumped?" Heloise said in English now.

"Yes."

"How awful, Tome!— That is why you look so—absent."

"Do I? Absent?" They were now approaching Villeperce, and Tom gazed at a house he knew and liked, and then the post office, then the bakery, before Heloise made the turn to the left. She had taken the route quite through the village, maybe by accident, maybe because she was nervous and wanted to go by a slower way. Tom went on, "Maybe I found him ten minutes after he'd jumped. I don't know. I had to go back and tell the family. It's quite a steep cliff—rocks down there. I will tell you more later maybe, darling." But what more would there be to tell? Tom glanced at Heloise, who was driving through the gates of Belle Ombre now.

"Yes, you *must* tell me," she said as she got out of the car.

Tom could see that this was a story she expected to hear in full, because Tom had not done anything wrong, and was not going to conceal anything from her.

"I liked Frank, you know?" Heloise said to Tom, and her lavender-blue eyes met his for a second. "Finally, I mean. I didn't like him at first."

Tom knew.

"This is a new suitcase?"

Tom smiled. "And a few new things in it."

"Oh!— Thank you for the German handbag, Tome!"

"Bonjour, Monsieur Tome!" Mme. Annette stood on the sun-lit doorstep, and Tom could just see a pale elastic band below her skirt hem, under her beige stockings or maybe tights, around one knee.

"How are you, dear Madame Annette?" Tom said, putting an arm half around her, and she replied that she was very well, and gave him a token kiss, but paused hardly at all before crossing the gravel to take the suitcase Heloise was carrying.

Mme. Annette insisted upon carrying both suitcases up, one at a time, despite her sprained knee, so Tom let her do it, because it gave her pleasure.

"It's so good to be *home!*" Tom said, looking around at the living room, the table set for lunch, the harpsichord, the phony Derwatt over the fireplace. "You know, the Piersons have 'The Rainbow'? Did I mention that or not? You know, one of the—a very good Derwatt."

"Rea-ally?" said Heloise, rather mockingly, as if she had or maybe had not heard of this particular Derwatt, or maybe because she suspected it was a fake.

Tom simply couldn't tell. But he laughed with relief, with happiness. Mme. Annette was coming down the stairs, carefully now, with one hand on the banister. At least he had dissuaded Mme. Annette years ago from polishing the stair steps.

"How can you look so cheerful, when the boy is dead?" Heloise had asked that in English, and Mme. Annette, reaching now for the second suitcase, paid no attention.

Heloise was right. Tom didn't know why he could feel so

cheerful. "Maybe it hasn't sunk in as yet. It was so sudden—a shock to everyone at the house. Frank's older brother was there, Johnny. Frank was very unhappy because of a girl. I told you that. Teresa. Plus his father's death—" That was as far as Tom wanted to go. John Pierson Senior's death would always be a suicide or an accident, whenever he spoke to Heloise about it.

"But that is terrible—to kill oneself at sixteen! More and more young people are killing themselves, you know? I am always reading about it in the newspapers.— Would you like some? Or anything?" Heloise extended the wineglass full of Perrier which she had just poured for herself, Tom knew.

Tom shook his head. "I want to wash up." He went toward the downstairs WC and basin, and en route glanced at the little stack of four letters on the telephone table, yesterday's and today's post. That could wait.

During lunch, Tom told Heloise about the Kennebunkport house of the Piersons, about the odd old servant called Susie Schuhmacher, who had been housekeeper and in a way governess of the boys years ago, and who was now laid low with a heart attack. He succeeded in making the house a mixture of luxury and gloom, which was the truth, Tom thought, or anyway the way he had felt about it. From Heloise's slight frown, Tom knew that she knew he was not telling the whole truth.

"And you went away the same evening—just after the boy died?" she asked.

"Yes. I didn't see what good I could do by staying longer. The funeral—it might have been two days away." Might be today, Tuesday, Tom thought.

"I don't think you could face the funeral," Heloise said. "You were very fond of the boy—weren't you? I know."

"Yes," said Tom. He could look at Heloise steadily now. It had been strange to try to steer a young life like that, as he had tried—and to have failed. Maybe one day he could admit that to Heloise. But on the other hand, he couldn't, because he was never going to

tell her that the boy pushed his father over the cliff, and that was
the whole explanation of the boy's suicide, or at least it was more
important than Teresa, Tom felt.

"Did you meet Teresa?" Heloise asked. She had already asked
for a full description of Lily Pierson, the former actress who had
married such wealth and Tom had done his best there, including a
description of the attentive Tal Stevens, whom Tom suspected she
would marry.

"No, no, I didn't meet Teresa. I think she was in New York."
And Tom doubted that Teresa would even come to Frank's funeral,
and did that matter, either? Teresa to Frank had been an idea,
intangible almost, and so she would remain, as Frank had written,
"forever."

Tom went upstairs after lunch to look at his post, and to
unpack. Another letter from Jeff Constant of the Buckmaster
Gallery, London, and at a glance Tom saw that all was well. The
news was that the Derwatt Accademia in Perugia had had a change
of managership to two artistically inclined young men from London (Jeff supplied their names), and they had the idea of acquiring
a nearby palazzo which could be converted into a hotel for the art
students. Did Tom like the idea? Did he possibly know the palazzo
to southwest of the art school? The new London boys were going
to send a photo next post. Jeff wrote:

> This means expansion, which sounds all to the good, don't
> you think, Tom? Unless you have some inside information
> about Italian internal conditions that might make the pur-
> chase inadvisable just now.

Tom had no inside information. Did Jeff think him a genius?
Yes. Tom knew he would agree to the purchase idea. Expansion,
yes, as to hotels. The art school made most of its money from the
hotel. The real Derwatt would cringe with shame.

He pulled off his sweater, strolled into his blue and white bathroom, and threw the sweater behind him onto a chair. He fancied he heard the carpenter ants shut up at his step, or had he heard the ants in the first place? He put his ear to the wooden shelf side. No! He had heard them, and they hadn't shut up. There was the faintest whir, which augmented even as he listened. At it still, the little zealots! On a folded pajama top on one shelf, Tom saw a miniature pyramid of fine reddish-tan dust which had fallen from excavations above. What were they building in there? Beds for themselves, egg repositories? Had these little carpenters put their wits together and constructed maybe a tiny bookcase in there, composed of spit and sawdust, a little monument to their know-how, their will to live? Tom had to laugh out loud. Was he going mad himself?

From the corner of his suitcase, Tom took the Berlin bear, fluffed its fur out gently, and set it at the back of his desk against a couple of dictionaries. The little bear was made to sit, its legs didn't bend for it to stand up. Its bright eyes looked at Tom with the same innocent gaiety as in Berlin, and Tom smiled back at it, thinking of the "3 Würfe 1 Mark" which had won it. "You will have a good home for the rest of your life," Tom said to the bear.

He would take a shower, flop on the bed, and look at the rest of his letters, he thought. Try to get back to normal in time, twenty to three now, French time. Frank would be lowered into a grave today, Tom felt sure, and he didn't care to figure out just when it might be, because for Frank time had ceased to matter.

If you enjoyed this novel, you'll enjoy the other Ripley novels. To entice you, here is the first chapter of *Ripley Under Water*.

1

Tom stood in Georges and Marie's bar-tabac with a nearly full cup of café express in his hand. He had paid, and Heloise's two packs of Marlboros bulged his jacket pocket. Tom was watching a slot-machine game that someone else was playing.

The screen showed a cartoon motorcyclist hurtling into the background, the illusion of speed given by a forward-moving picket fence on either side of the road. The player manipulated a half-wheel, making the cyclist swerve to pass a slower car, or leap like a horse to hurdle a fence that had suddenly appeared across the road. If the motorcyclist (game-player) didn't hurdle in time, there was a silent impact, a black and gold star appeared to indicate a crash, the motorcyclist was finished and so was the game.

Tom had watched the game many a time (it was the most popular he had ever known Georges and Marie to acquire), but he had never played it. He somehow didn't want to.

"Non-*non*!" From behind the bar Marie's voice sang out over the usual din as she contested some customer's opinion, probably political. She and her husband were left-wing no matter what. "Ecoutez, *Mitterrand* . . ."

It crossed Tom's mind that Georges and Marie didn't like the influx of people from North Africa, however.

"Eh, *Marie*! Deux *pastis*!" That was fat Georges with a somewhat soiled white apron over shirt and trousers, serving the few tables, where people drank and occasionally ate potato chips and hard-boiled eggs.

The jukebox played an old cha-cha-cha.

A silent black and gold star! Spectators groaned sympathetically. Dead. All was over. The screen flashed its silent, obsessed message, INSERT COINS INSERT COINS INSERT COINS, and the workman in blue jeans groped obediently in a pocket, inserted more coins, and the game began again, motorcyclist in tip-top shape, zooming into the background, ready for anything, neatly dodging a barrel that appeared in his lane, smoothly jumping the first barrier. The man at the controls was intent, determined to make his man come through.

Tom was thinking now about Heloise, about her trip to Morocco. She wanted to see Tangier, Casablanca, maybe Marrakesh. And Tom had agreed to go with her. After all, it wasn't one of her adventure cruises requiring hospital visits for vaccines before departure, and it behooved him as her husband to accompany her on some of her jaunts. Heloise had two or three inspirations a year, not all of which she acted on. Tom wasn't in the mood for a holiday now. It was early August, Morocco would be at its hottest, and Tom loved his own peonies and dahlias at this time of year, loved cutting a fresh two or three for the living room almost daily. Tom was fond of his garden, and he rather liked Henri, the handyman who helped him with big jobs, a giant when it came to strength, though not the man for some tasks.

Then there was the Odd Pair, as Tom had begun calling them to himself. He wasn't sure they were married, and of course that didn't matter. He felt they were lurking in the area and had their eye on him. Maybe they were harmless, but who knew? Tom had first noticed them a month or so ago in Fontainebleau, when he and Heloise had been shopping one afternoon: a man and woman who looked American and in their mid-thirties, walking toward them, eyeing them with that look Tom knew well, as if they knew who he was, perhaps knew his name, Tom Ripley. Tom had seen the same look a few times at airports, though rarely, and not lately. It could come after one's picture had been in the newspapers, he supposed, but Tom's hadn't been in any newspapers for years, he was sure of that. Not since the Murchison business, and that had been about five years ago—Murchison, whose blood still stained Tom's cellar floor, and which Tom said was a wine stain, if anyone remarked on it.

In truth, it was a mixture of wine and blood, Tom reminded himself, because Murchison had been hit over the head with a wine bottle. A bottle of Margaux wielded by Tom.

Well, the Odd Pair. *Crash* went the motorcyclist. Tom made himself turn away and took his empty cup over to the bar counter.

The male of the Odd Pair had dark straight hair, black round-rimmed glasses, and the woman light brown hair, a slender face and gray or hazel eyes. It was the man who stared, with a vague and empty smile. Tom felt that he might have seen the man before, at Heathrow or Charles de Gaulle Airport, giving him that I-know-your-face look. Nothing hostile, but Tom didn't like it.

And then Tom had seen them once cruising slowly in their car down the main street of Villeperce at midday when he was coming out of the bakery with a *flûte* (must have been Mme. Annette's day off or she'd been busy with a lunch), and again Tom had seen them looking at him. Villeperce was a tiny town, several kilometers from Fontainebleau. Why should the Odd Pair have come here?

Both Marie with her big red smile and balding Georges happened to be behind the bar just as Tom pushed his cup and saucer away. "Merci et bonne nuit, Marie—Georges!" Tom called and gave a smile.

"Bon soir, M'sieur Reepley!" cried Georges, one hand waving, the other pouring Calvados.

"Merci, m'sieur, à bientôt!" Marie threw at him.

Tom was almost at the door when the male of the Odd Pair walked in, round glasses and all, and seemingly alone.

"Mr. Ripley?" His pinkish lips again wore a smile. "Good evening."

"Evening," said Tom, still on his way out.

"We've—my wife and I—may I invite you for a drink?"

"Thanks, I'm just leaving."

"Another time, maybe. We've rented a house in Villeperce. This direction." He gestured vaguely north, and his smile widened to reveal squarish teeth. "Looks like we'll be neighbors."

Tom was confronted by two people entering, and had to step back into the bar.

"My name's Pritchard. David. I'm taking courses at the Fontainebleau business school—INSEAD. I'm sure you know of it. Anyway, my house here is a two-story white one with garden and a little pool. We fell in love with it *because* of the pool, reflections on the ceiling—the water." He chuckled.

"I see," Tom said, trying to sound reasonably pleasant. He was now out of the door.

"I'll telephone you. My wife's name is Janice."

Tom managed a nod and forced a smile. "Yes—fine. Do that. Good night."

"Not too many Americans around here!" the determined David Pritchard called after him.

Mr. Pritchard would have a hard time finding his number, Tom was thinking, because he and Heloise had managed to keep it out of the telephone book. The outwardly dull David Pritchard—nearly as tall as Tom and a bit heavier—looked like trouble, Tom was thinking as he walked homeward. A police officer of some kind? Digging up old records? Private detective for—for whom, really? Tom couldn't think of any active enemies. "Phony" was the word Tom thought of in regard to David Pritchard: phony smile, phony goodwill, maybe phony story about studying at INSEAD. That educational institution at Fontainebleau could be a cover, in fact such an obvious one that Tom thought it might be true that Pritchard was studying something there. Or maybe they weren't man and wife but a CIA pair. What would the USA be after him for, Tom wondered. Not income tax, that was in order. Murchison? No, that was settled. Or case abandoned. Murchison and his corpse had disappeared. Dickie Greenleaf? Hardly. Even Christopher Greenleaf, Dickie's cousin, wrote Tom a friendly postcard now and then, from Alice Springs last year, for instance. Christopher was now a civil engineer, married, working in Rochester, New York, as Tom recalled. Tom was even on good terms with Dickie's father, Herbert. At least, they exchanged Christmas cards.

As Tom approached the big tree opposite Belle Ombre, a tree whose branches leaned a little over the road, his spirits rose. What was there to worry about? Tom pushed open one big gate just enough to slip through, then closed it with as gentle a clang as he could manage and slid the padlock home, then the long bolt.

Reeves Minot. Tom stopped short and his shoes slid on the gravel of the forecourt. Another fence job for Reeves was in the offing. Reeves had telephoned a few days ago. Tom often vowed he would not do another, then found himself accepting. Was it because he enjoyed meeting new people? Tom gave a laugh, short and barely audible, then continued walking toward his front door with his usual light tread that hardly disturbed the gravel.

The light was on in the living room, and the front door was unlocked, as Tom had left it forty-five minutes ago. Tom went in, then locked the front door behind him. Heloise sat on the sofa, poring over a magazine—probably an article on North Africa, Tom thought.

"'Ello, chéri—*Reeves* telephoned," Heloise said, looking up, tossing her blonde hair back with a swing of her head. "Tome, did you—"

"Yes. Catch!" Smiling, Tom tossed the first red and white packet to her, then the second. She caught the first, the second hit her blue shirtfront. "Anything pressing concerning Reeves? *Repassant*—ironing—*bügelnd*?"

"Oh, Tome, stop it!" said Heloise, and used her lighter. She inwardly enjoyed his puns, Tom thought, though she would never say so, would hardly permit herself to smile. "He will telephone back but maybe not tonight."

"Somebody—well—" Tom stopped, because Reeves didn't go into detail with Heloise, ever, and Heloise professed to be uninterested, even bored, with Tom's and Reeves's doings. It was safer: the less she knew, the better, Tom supposed Heloise thought. And who could say that wasn't true?

"Tome, tomorrow we go and buy the tickets—to Maroc. All right?" She had tucked her bare feet up on the yellow silk sofa like a comfortable kitten, and now she looked at him calmly with her pale lavender eyes.

"Y-yes. All right." He had promised, he reminded himself. "We fly first to Tangier."

"Oui, chéri, and then we go on from there. Casablanca—of course."

"Of course," Tom echoed. "Right, dear, we'll buy the tickets tomorrow—Fontainebleau." They always went to the same travel agency there, where they knew the staff. Tom hesitated, then decided to say it now, "Darling, do you remember the pair—the American-looking couple we saw in Fontainebleau one day—on the pavement? Walking toward us, and I said later I thought he was staring at us? Dark-haired man with glasses?"

"I think—yes. Why?"

Tom could tell that she did remember. "Because he just spoke to me in the bar-tabac." Tom unbuttoned his jacket and shoved his hands in his trouser pockets. He had not sat down. "I don't care for him."

"I remember the woman with him, with lighter hair. Americans, no?"

"He is, anyway. Well—they've rented a house here in Villeperce. Remember the house where the—"

"*Vraiment?* Villeperce?"

"Oui, ma chère! The house where the pond water is reflected on the ceiling—in the living room?" He and Heloise had marveled at the oval moving like water itself on the white ceiling.

"Yes. I remember the house. Two-story white, not such a pretty fireplace. Not very far from the Grais', is it not? Someone with us thought about buying it."

"Yes. Right." An American acquaintance of an acquaintance, looking for a country house not too far from Paris, had asked Tom and Heloise to accompany him while he inspected a couple of houses in the vicinity. He had bought nothing, at least nothing near Villeperce. That had been more than a year ago. "Well—to the point, the dark-haired man with glasses intends to be neighborly with me or us, and I'm not having it. Just because we speak English or American, ho-*ho*! Seems he's connected with INSEAD— that big school near Fontainebleau." Tom added, "How does he know my name in the first place, and why is he interested?" Lest he seem too concerned, he calmly sat down. Now he faced Heloise from his straight chair with the coffee table between them. "David and Janice Pritchard, they're called. If they manage to telephone, we're—polite, but we're busy. All right, dear?"

"Of course, Tome."

"And if they have the nerve to ring the bell, they're not to be let in. I'll warn Madame Annette, you can be sure."

Heloise's usually clear blonde brow became thoughtful. "What is the matter with them?"

The simplicity of the question made Tom smile. "I have a feeling—"Tom hesitated. He did not usually talk to Heloise about his intuitions, but in this case he might be protecting her if he did. "They don't look normal to me." Tom glanced down at the carpet. What was normal? Tom couldn't have answered that question. "I have the feeling they're not married."

"And—so what?"

Tom laughed, and reached for the blue pack of Gitanes on the coffee table, lit one with Heloise's Dunhill lighter. "True, my dear. But why are they eyeing me? Didn't I tell you, I think I recall the same man, and maybe the pair, staring at me at some airport not long ago?"

"No, you didn't," said Heloise.

He smiled. "There've been people before this we didn't like. No great problem." Tom got up, walked around the coffee table, and pulled Heloise up by the hand that she extended. He embraced her, closed his eyes, and enjoyed the fragrance of her hair, her skin. "I love you. I want to keep you safe."

She laughed. They loosened their embrace. "Belle Ombre looks *very* safe."

"They won't set foot here."

About the Author

Born in Fort Worth, Texas, in 1921, Patricia Highsmith spent much of her adult life in Switzerland and France. She was educated at Barnard College, where she studied English, Latin, and Greek. Her first novel, *Strangers on a Train*, published initially in 1950, proved to be a major commercial success, and was filmed by Alfred Hitchcock. Despite this early recognition, Highsmith was unappreciated in the United States for the entire length of her career.

Writing under the pseudonym of Claire Morgan, she then published *The Price of Salt* in 1953, which had been turned down by her previous American publisher because of its frank exploration of homosexual themes. Her most popular literary creation was Tom Ripley, the dapper sociopath who first debuted in her 1955 novel, *The Talented Mr. Ripley*. She followed with four other Ripley novels. Posthumously made into a major motion picture, *The Talented Mr. Ripley* has helped bring about a renewed appreciation of Highsmith's work in the United States, as has the posthumous publication of *The Selected Stories* and *Nothing That Meets the Eye: The Uncollected Stories*, both of which received widespread acclaim when they were published by W. W. Norton & Company.

The author of more than twenty books, Highsmith has won the O. Henry Memorial Award, the Edgar Allan Poe Award, Le Grand Prix de Littérature Policière, and the Award of the Crime Writers' Association of Great Britain. She died in Switzerland on February 4, 1995, and her literary archives are maintained in Berne.